A Bit Of Me

Kent Lowe is a writer and artist whose works delve into humour, love and friendship. He was born and raised in East London and now lives in Essex.

A Bit Of Me

Kent Lowe

For Jeeves.

Chapter One

Wiping the sweat from his top lip, he tried to breathe in something other than stranger's body heat. It was thick. Solid. Like the air had been stuck in the carriage for years. And he knew as the doors beeped shut behind him, the five-fifty-two to London was going to be one bastard of a journey.

'Close one, Georgie boy.'

'I know.' Wheezing, George slipped into the seat next to Alfie and sucked in mouthfuls of the staleness. 'Got held up at work.'

Truth was, it had nothing to do with his job. Being late wasn't something George Taylor was good at. He was the fucking champion. Tell him where and when to meet and he'd be there. Twenty minutes after everybody else.

Dripping with sweat, he dragged the back of his wrist over his brow then yanked the neck of his T-shirt in an attempt to cool his clammy skin.

Sitting on the chav wagon for an hour was hell for him. The thought of being sat amongst thirty-odd strangers, most of whom had no idea of personal space, gave him full on anxiety. Actually doing it, made him want to vomit. But it was worth it. Nothing could bring him down. Not even a soap dodger with an allergy to antiperspirant. He was on his way to see Ellie. And that was all that mattered.

'Babes, please tell me you're not wearing that tonight.' Aimee momentarily glanced away from her phone and winced at his muddy top. 'Ells will actually kill you if you turn up in that.'

'Course not. I've got my going out gear in here.' George unzipped his torn rucksack to prove he'd packed a fresh set of clothes that morning. He hadn't needed the reminder that Ellie would disapprove of his work gear. 'I didn't have time to change.'

'Or wash by the smell of you.' Aimee turned her nose away. 'You look like you're covered in-'

'Shit!' Alfie jabbed his elbow into George's side. He was gawping at a blonde who had just boarded the train in a tight figure-hugging blue dress. 'Look at the bounce on those things.'

Never one to encourage Alfie's ogling of anyone with breasts, George made a point of rolling his eyes. He couldn't help but notice the impressive chest on the blonde himself though.

'She is *hot*.' Alfie whistled, manspreading into George's space.

Aimee peered up from her phone to give the woman the once-over. Possibly the twice-over by her look of disdain. She was one of the nicest, sweetest girls on the planet but other attractive girls brought out the monster in her. 'What? No way. She's so basic.'

'I don't care if she's basic, I'd motorboat the fuck out of those things,' Alfie beamed, following it up with a wink George's way.

'The way you objectify women is gross.' Aimee huffed, pulling at her neckline to show off her own bronzed and perky assets. 'Besides, you can tell she's a total bitch, just look at her eyebrows.'

George and Alfie shrugged in unison as Aimee continued to glare at the woman. Like she was sizing her up for a coffin. George had no idea what the woman's eyebrows had to do with her being a bitch, but by the grimace plastered on her face, Aimee seemed adamant about it. She always insisted that she had a way of knowing those sorts of things, but George had yet to see any proof.

Aimee seemed to live her life under thick layers of make-up. It was kind of her trademark. Even first thing in the morning or in thirty degree heat, the girl plastered on foundation and fake tan like it gave her life. In a way it did. Most people assumed she was plastic, or just self-obsessed. But George knew differently. That under the orange tan on her arms, were scars she'd given herself with a pair of kitchen scissors.

George chewed the inside of his cheek and gazed at the next horde of passengers stepping onto the train. He'd never understand why the majority of commuters were wrapped in thick coats even though it'd been the warmest April on record. Like some awful fashion domino effect, one person in a puffer jacket came down the stairs at the station and by the time the train pulled in, every bastard on the platform was wearing one. Creating more heat in the carriage. More body odour too.

Whilst his friends still focused on the busty blonde, clearly for different reasons, George scanned over the other passengers. All individual – separate from each other, but they all seemed to act in the same way. Headphones plugged into their ears and eyes glued to a smartphone. Being disconnected from real life seemed to be a rite of passage for commuters. It most probably helped them to forget the mundane of nine-to-five.

'Oh my actual God, look at him.' Aimee whispered, slyly pointing with a green painted fingernail. All eyes switched to a middle aged man sat by the doors, brief case perched on his lap, his navy suit complimented by the flecks of silver in his hair. 'Now that's a daddy complex I could get on board with.'

'Gross. He's ancient. He might look all smart but I bet he scratches his balls then sniffs his fingers.' Alfie cracked up at his own joke that nobody else found funny. No one ever did. Not that it ever stopped Alfie from laughing his tits off.

'Like you, you mean?' she retorted.

'I don't do that.'

'I've seen you.'

'You don't see anything because your too busy chasing dick on that thing,' Alfie moaned, then snatched the phone from her hand.

In the eternal love/hate friendship that was Aimee and Alfie, she proceeded to thump him and he pretended that her "girlie" punches didn't actually hurt. But they all knew how much they did. The whole charade went on long enough for George to check his own phone. There were no texts. Not even from Ellie. Then with a brutal twisting of Alfie's nipple, Alfie squealed and Aimee managed to grab her phone back from his hand.

'Why don't you two just get it on?' George huffed, exasperated at watching them pretend to dislike each other. It was an act he'd watched since secondary school. It was cute when they were eleven but at nineteen, it was plain weird. 'Seriously, you pretend to hate each other but everyone knows you blatantly want to fuck.'

'Excuse me, Georgie. I most certainly do not.' Aimee wiped the screen of her phone along her dress and instantly cooed over a new man's profile. 'You seen the man candy on here? Why would I settle for that?'

'Alfie's not bad looking. In the dark. If you squint.' George smirked.

'Piss off. And me and her together? Not a chance, mate.' Alfie contended, rubbing his nipple through his white polo shirt. 'She's been around so much, she's got a bench dedicated to her down the STI clinic.'

George laughed aloud. Alfie winked to Aimee and slapped a hand onto her leg. She turned away, but George could tell she was attempting to hide her own laughter. And failing. Big time.

10

George had known these two for most of his life. If they weren't with him, they would either be Face-timing or texting him. Having met at nursery, they'd all attended the same primary school, secondary school and even college. He'd lost count how many times he had been confused for Aimee's boyfriend or Alfie's brother. They'd been a foursome since secondary school actually; two sets of best friends - him and Alfie, Aimee and Ellie.

Coming from a small market town in Essex, where the street lights turned off at nine p.m., where the word "something" was liberally swapped for the word "sank," and everyone's names ended with a perfectly Essex 'e' sound. Ellie, Alfie, Aimee, and Ollie. Ronnie, Lennie, Jaime and even his sister, Darcie. His name, oddly, was George, but that didn't stop everyone, right from his chain-smoking Nan to the man behind the counter at his local corner shop, referring to him as the forever fucking annoying, "Georgie." It wasn't a name he cared for – it suited a toddler or a pet budgie. Not a grown man of almost twenty.

'Where we meeting Ellie, Georgie boy?' Alfie asked.

George huffed. 'Not sure, mate. I haven't spoken to her since yesterday. She said she would text me this morning and let me know, but not heard anything yet.'

George dug out the daily dose of mud from under his nails. Covering up the lingering smell of cow pat with deodorant and aftershave was easy but if there was one thing that Ellie hated, it was him having, what she disapprovingly called, "shit shovels" for hands

'Everything all right with you two, mate?' Alfie's brow creased but George knew it was more out of amusement than concern.

'Yeah, course. We're just both busy.' George snapped. He wasn't sure why. It seemed like he always had to defend their relationship these days. 'We've just got a lot on, mate. The apprenticeship takes up most of my time and, well, Ellie's nearly finishing the first year of her degree. Some of us actually have things to do in life.'

'Aw, my babies are growing up.' Aimee flapped a hand to her heart.

'Besides, it's only been a day, Alf. You need to calm your tits.'

'Sounds like the rocky road to singledom, if you ask me.' Alfie teased, being immediately reprimanded by Aimee's scowl.

'Mate, the only relationship you've ever had is with your hand. Me and Ells are good, thanks. She's been at uni for seven months now and we try to see each other as much as possible.' George fumbled his words, knowing the last time he actually saw his girlfriend was over a month before. 'We knew it was going to be hard, that's why we took the year out after college to go travelling together.'

The train shunted into another station and more passengers clambered on, steadily filling the empty seats and sucking up the tiny bit of fresh air that remained in the cabin. The heat they brought with them was unbearable.

Trying to ignore the feeling of impending combustion, George set his attention onto a woman with a sky-high afro, probably in her early thirties, talking loudly into her phone. Holding the thing in front of her mouth rather than next to her ear, she glimpsed at the seat opposite George but for some reason decided not to sit there. Instead she stood in the gangway and received the "bitch eye" from another woman in a hijab, reading the free evening paper - clearly annoyed that her daily dose of celebrity bullshit was being disturbed.

'You two still planning to go travelling again this summer?' Aimee looked up from her phone for a moment. 'Ells mentioned it, but you know me, babes, I've got a memory like a calendar.'

'It's colander.' Alfie stuck his tongue in front of his bottom teeth in mockery.

'Actually, it's sieve, you pair of dicks.' George corrected them both, wondering how the hell he ended up with those two. 'I don't know. It's our fourth anniversary this summer so we're deffo going to do something. Maybe do Africa.'

'Shit, you two been together for four years already? That can't be right.' Alfie asked.

'Will be in July, mate. We got together in the six weeks' holiday before year eleven. That day in the park. You were there. You'd just fingered your imaginary girlfriend behind the cricket shed, remember?' George scoffed – his joke clearly going straight over Alfie's head.

'Ah, man. I miss the six weeks' holidays. We need them at work too.'

'You don't work.' Aimee interrupted, her eyes locked once more onto her phone.

'Yeah I do. With my dad. When he's got jobs on.'

She sniggered then pouted to snap a selfie.

The train bolted past countryside and the spring-green trees outside the windows were soon replaced by steel and concrete. George counted down the minutes until he could get off the fucking train and see his girlfriend. He had never gone that long without seeing her before and had a serious case of blue balls going on. Not to mention he wanted to unload Aimee and Alfie off on Ellie's new mates. Her uni lot were okay – he'd never had a problem with any of them, but they were the kind of people that thought they were extremely interesting yet he'd not an ounce of interest in them. The kind of girls that, after a few drinks, blended into one annoying human being. The sort that overused millennial slang words like "low key" and "bae" and moped at how the new Ed Sheeran song could have been written about their lives. He just knew that Alfie and Aimee would love them.

A baby, a tiny thing being clutched in its mother's arms, started to cry a few seats away from them. George hadn't noticed it before, but the cry pierced through his ears like glass – a scream that only a new-born could muster. He offered the mother a sympathetic grin then turned his head to find Aimee gushing over the scene.

She slapped a hand to her heart again. How her chest wasn't bruised, he didn't know. She tilted her head. 'Is there anything more wonderful than childbirth?'

'A tight vagina?' Alfie's howling drew attention from the people around them.

'Did you seriously just say that?' Shaking her head, Aimee folded her arms.

Trying to conceal his laughter, George rammed a fist into Alfie's arm. 'Mate. That's really fucked up.'

'Behave. It's funny.' Alfie moaned.

The train stopped a few stations away from London, where the red brick walls were decorated in multi-coloured graffiti and the diversity that he didn't get to see at home was waiting on the platform. The doors beeped open and the next collection of safari animals boarded.

A few men dressed in hi-vis vests and hard hats clambered on, all looking exhausted, and a couple of college girls who caught Alfie's attention squeezed into the aisle. Just as George thought there was no more possible space on board, a man, possibly his age strolled on and took it.

With headphones blasting music into his ears, he casually manoeuvred his way through the middle of a group of tourists like he didn't give a shit. Sporting a dark floppy quiff and grayscale tattoos up his arms and neck, he had, what Aimee liked to call, a "resting bitch face" and an air of careless confidence that instantly made George uncomfortable. He looked like a hybrid of the urban ink trend and something from the fifties. Like if Elvis had a flip knife.

'O M G, look at him!' Aimee purred. She bolted upright and crossed her newly spray tanned legs, like she was preparing herself for a photo shoot. 'He is *so* effing hot I think I just got pregnant.'

'He looks like a dick,' Alfie retorted and slouched into his chair. His open legs clearly asserting his manliness. 'Don't you think, Georgie?

George shrugged, his gaze fixed on the man's septum piercing.

'Whatever you two.' Aimee gushed. George was shocked to witness the moment she actually clicked shut her phone and tucked it away into her bag. 'He's a total vitamin.'

'A what?' George asked, uncertain if he'd heard her right.

'A vitamin, babes. You know, something I need inside me.'

The laughter that followed was raucous, making the whole carriage turn their way with multiple frowns, and the three of them quickly composed themselves, trying not to make it obvious that they were talking about him. Even Alfie dropped his macho act to join in, just long enough to snort.

The newcomer indifferently weaved his way in between the people content on standing, and much to Aimee's delight, parked his arse on the bizarrely patterned seat opposite the three of them. George sat up straight away and, for some reason, attempted to conceal his mud-covered work clothes with his rucksack.

Aimee stroked her long hair over one shoulder and drifted her fingers through it; a brazen attempt to get the bloke's focus onto her cleavage.

The fella wore black lace up boots, black jeans that were just a little too skinny in certain areas and a black T-shirt with rolled up sleeves – everything about the fella was dark and George found himself silently humming the

Addams Family theme tune. The only visible thing that wasn't covered in ink was his face, which was only tarnished by a silver ring pierced through his septum. Feeling slightly uneasy at the man's presence, George gazed down to the fella's hands and noted the words 'live' and 'free' written in black ink across his knuckles.

George didn't know why he couldn't look away, maybe it was to see what all the fuss was about from Aimee. She was practically salivating. If it wasn't his moody exterior or his dark stubble and solid eyebrows, it could possibly have had something to do with his hazel, almost caramel-coloured, eyes.

'I'm about to slide off this seat.' Aimee whispered.

'Filth.' George sniggered.

'He looks like a bit of a cocksucker if you ask me. A proper homo.' Alfie replied, knees wide and clearly not caring if the man heard him or not.

'Shh!' Aimee frowned. 'Every good-looking man is gay to you. You're just jealous.'

'Just saying that he looks like a dick so I bet he sucks dick too.'

George leant back, blocking his mouth by Aimee's head. 'To be fair, Alf, you're the only one here who's obsessed with dick.'

'Come on, Georgie. What do you honestly think? He looks gay, don't he?'

'Who gives a shit if he is?' George retaliated, turning his gaze back to the man.

The train slowed and entered the terminal and the three of them stood in unison. With the only subtlety she knew, Aimee fell into the lap of the man with the caramel eyes. As he laughed it off, she apologised with a girlish flash of white teeth, flicked her fake eyelashes as the three of them made their way to the doors.

Pushing his way forward, George was over the moon to be getting off the fucking thing. But he couldn't help and glance back at the tattooed man who was still sitting in the seat even though the train had stopped. It was only when George's phone buzzed in his pocket that he finally ripped his gaze away from him and unlocked the screen with his thumb.

It was a text from Ellie.

'Hey Georgie. Meet us at the cloud bar.'

No kiss.

Chapter Two

Waiting for everyone to get off the train, Jack finally rose from his seat and slowly made his way to the doors. Wrestling his way through the crowds as they bottlenecked the barriers wasn't something he got involved in.

He pressed his oyster onto the scanner and welcomed the brightness of Liverpool Street station. No matter the weather outside, the brightness of white floor and glass roof always lifted his mood. Pulling his knock-off sunglasses from his collar, he stepped onto the escalator and greeted the sun.

Emerging at street level, he yanked his buds from his ears to catch the noises around him. He inhaled the fresh air, well as 'fresh' as the air is in the city, and took in the smells of London. Weaving through the pub's overspill of office bods and labourers, he declined a free evening paper before stepping into the busy road. Cars beeped their horns and he couldn't help but smile. London was his scene.

'Big Issue? Big Issue?' A man called out to people who appeared to causally ignore him. Jack nodded to him with respect.

Patting his pockets, feeling for any form of coins, he already knew that he didn't have a penny on him. Pay day was a week away and knowing that all he had in his fridge was a jar of mayonnaise and a questionable lettuce, he resigned himself to living on empty until then.

'Hey, long time no see, buddy. Big Issue?'

'I'm sorry, man,' Jack replied sincerely to the man in a ripped tracksuit. 'No money on me. Promise I'll hit you up next week though, yeah?'

'Hey, it's all good...you watch how you go.' The seller said as the pair bumped fists.

Pulling a box of cigarettes from his bag, Jack caught his reflection in one of the huge window panes of the tower bank on the corner and grimaced. His hair, his skinny jeans, even the tattoo sleeves; all he needed was a full-on beard and bow tie and he'd be the hipster he'd always tried not to be.

Four cigarettes left. Shit.

Sparking up, he passed a line of bars and envy grew inside him as their customers relished in the happy hour cocktails. His mood lifted instantly as he spotted the bright, white goat sculpture in the middle of the modern square. He had no idea why it was there, maybe it had something to do with the history of Spitalfields Market. Whatever it was, the goat was the nuts.

He took the scenic route past the vintage shops, the ones that sold old crap as upgraded furniture and six hundred pound cameras and cut a left into the Truman Breweries. There he was confronted by a mass of colourful and loud people. Art exhibitions must have been going on inside the old buildings as there were crowds standing in large groups and talking with perfectly affected accents. They nodded and shrugged enthusiastically through conversations, the way that artists do whilst drinking their white wine from plastic cups and licking their roll ups shut.

'How fascinating that bureaucracy deems the Arts unworthy for funding.' A girl with pink hair moaned, taking a drag on a brown-papered cigarette. It was crazy how some moan about not having money to paint when others can barely eat.

He laughed that thought off. He wouldn't even go there. There were three things in this world that Jack had very little interest in. Religion, politics and the Kardashians.

The street food venders undoubtedly knew about the exhibitions and had come out in force to sell halloumi fries, sweet pulled pork burgers, soggy dim sum, gin teas and all the things that his fellow millennials lived for. He'd never even heard of these things before he'd started working in Brick Lane.

But those people — the fast food sellers, the artists, the bartenders — they were like his family. He didn't know their names or where they were from, he didn't really care. But he saw them a hell of a lot more than the people he shared blood with.

Finally through the crowds, he spied a familiar fast food van that he hadn't seen in a while. Recognising the bright paint job and the a-board promoting "Good old fashioned burger and chips" — even if it had gone a little Gastro — Jack beamed and the man behind the counter stared back at him.

'Jack? Bloody hell, boy. Where you been?' His ex-uncle shouted out to him and, for a split second, Jack's chest warmed as Dave waved him over to the van.

'Hey, Dave. How are you, man?'

Clambering out of the door, Dave pulled him in for a strong embrace. Just a moment, and long enough for Jack, before the man held him at arm's length to give him the once over. Jack squirmed as magnified eyes through thick lenses scanned all of him.

'Where you been? You good?'

'Yeah I'm good, Dave. Jumping between jobs, zero hours don't pay the bills. How's you? How's Marie?' Jack nodded to Dave's wife serving behind the counter. She was in the middle of handing out a burger but gave a huge beaming smile in return.

'I wish I could help you out on here, but it's hot enough behind there with just me and Marie.' Dave winked.

'Too much information.' Jack dropped his cigarette to the ground and crushed it with the rubber heel of his boot.

'I do wish I could help you a bit more though. Honestly. I know it ain't easy for you.'

'Hey, don't be silly, man. I'm not you're problem. Besides, I'm a big boy now.'

'Speaking of which, here, take this?' Dave said, fishing a wad of folded notes from his stained apron pocket.

'What's this?'

'You know what it is. I might not be married to your aunty Shell any more, but you're still my nephew.'

Jack choked as he was handed fifty quid in tenners. Dave's kindness hit him in the chest – right under the ribcage. He'd struggled for money every day of his life, not knowing where his next meal was coming from since he left his foster home. And lord knows he could have done with the cash. But taking someone else's money left a bad taste in his mouth. He wasn't a charity case.

'I can't take this, Dave.' he finally said, pushing the notes back.

'You're only twenty-one once, Jack. I'm just gutted I didn't see you on your birthday. Been looking out for you for months. I wanted to take you for a drink or even a meal. I tried calling you a hundred times. And every time I knocked at your flat, you weren't there.'

'Sorry, man. I had to sell.....I lost my phone. I've got a new number now.'

'Well type it in here, son.' Dave slipped out his own phone and watched Jack punch in the eleven digits. 'So anyways, last time we spoke, you were saving to start your own tattoo business. How's that going? You any closer?'

'Seems like the more I save, the less I have.' Jack grimaced. 'But at least I've got a roof over my head, right?'

Dave took his phone back and typed in a name to save the number. His face beamed then dropped slightly. 'You still tattooing those dolly birds for free?'

'I need the practice, Dave.'

'And they pay you in kind, I bet.'

'I'm not like that.' Jack smiled awkwardly and pulled a cigarette out of the box and rested it on his ear. Three left.

'You've gotta look after yourself. Or let me and Marie look after you, at least.' Dave pushed his hairy hand onto Jack's shoulder. That vender was definitely his family.

'How's that *mate* of yours?'

'Not so much a mate, anymore.'

'Good. You don't need that kind of wrong'un in your life, Jack.' Dave furrowed his brow. 'Marie, pass me one of those burgers, please. The Double Whammy ones.'

Handing over a golden bun with a juicy Gastro burger inside, Dave patted Jack's elbow in a show of manly affection. Jack's belly grumbled at the very smell of it. It would likely be the only thing he'd eat that day.

The two men observed each other in mutual respect, just long enough for neither of them to feel embarrassed.

'I gotta get going, Dave. I start work in twenty.'

Being late wasn't his thing. It'd never been an option.

'Okie dokie, son. But you're taking this....I mean it.' He forced the money back into Jack's empty hand, holding his palm over it until Jack gave in. 'And eat that burger. You look like a fucking sparrow.'

Jack nodded, the returning words of gratitude stuck in his throat. He wanted to say something, anything. Instead, he watched the fella make his way back to the van with nothing less than upmost respect.

'And give up those fags too.' Dave called out.

Stuffing the notes into his jeans, warmth rushed over him with the relief that he could buy food. Fuck, he could even buy gas and electricity again.

Turning on his heel, he lifted the perfectly seasoned burger, covered in melted cheese and smoky barbecue sauce to his mouth and inhaled the delicious aromas. But before he could take a bite, the homeless man sitting underneath the railway bridge with his little scruffy dog, Bruno, caught his eye.

'Hey, how's things?' Jack asked, crouching down to the man's level. He'd never asked the bloke his name but their friendship had gone on way to long to do so. Jack scratched behind the dog's ears. 'Hello boy.'

'Hi, Jack. You're looking good.' The man stretched out a dirty hand for Jack to shake, nails blackened from years of living on the streets and his skin was as rough as the old cobbles beneath his makeshift bed.

'You too,' Jack lied, taking the man's hand without hesitation. His face drained with tiredness and his arms shook. He was visibly starving.

'Want a burger?' Offering the man the thick ground beef that had his mouth salivating seconds before, Jack smiled. 'Bruno could definitely do with some grub.'

'No, I couldn't do that, Jack. It's yours.'

'I'm not hungry, man.' Jack hoped the fella couldn't hear his stomach growling. 'My uncle gave it to me...wouldn't take no for an answer.'

'If you're sure?' The man took the burger from him.

Jack couldn't help but smile as the man split it with his hands and passed one half to Bruno who chomped at the meat in fast, desperate gulps.

'I can't thank you enough, Jack.' Bits of food fell from the man's mouth and he quickly wiped them up.

'You know what, I'm doing pretty good lately. Been working all hours.' It was another lie. Pulling out the notes that Dave had given him moments before, he unfolded them in his palm and slid out a ten pound note. 'Take this, but promise me, *no* booze. This little dude here needs a proper dinner. And so do you.'

'Ah, Jack. I couldn't….I can't….You sure?'

'Course, man. What are friends for?'

The man seemed reluctant to take the tenner at first but Jack screwed it into the fella's hand. He wasn't sure if he'd spend it on alcohol or not — he hoped he wouldn't — but at the same time, Jack didn't know how the fuck he'd cope living on the streets himself without getting wasted.

Chucking another left, Jack blocked out his own hunger and sparked up a cigarette before meeting the true hustle and bustle of Brick Lane. The variety of cultures, colours and ages all living in harmony. From the old woman with the bright red glasses and giant beaded necklace, the young Indian woman in her bejewelled orange sari and the hipster in tartan braces who puffed on a pipe. A group of school girls in navy blue uniforms were standing outside a fried chicken shop, laughing loudly as they compared filtered selfies.

But it was the streets themselves that Jack loved most. The buildings, the history, the art, the Beigel shops and the rich aromas of curry. The small world of eccentricity made by people, not seeking fame, but just living their lives. It was raw. And it was *his*. He loved the murals painted on the side of buildings, in their doorways and on their roofs. The painted women with colourful flowers for hair, giant elephants with tentacles instead of trunks and even tiny mice climbing up a drain pipe. He took them all in at once and had to smile at the new Amy Winehouse painting, nodding to her in appreciation.

This was *his* town.

Taking a final lug of his cigarette, he dropped it to the floor and stubbed it out with the heel of his boot. Walking through the gates to the beer garden, he noticed that the club's sign had been replaced. It had been changed from chunky 3D letters to a pretentious outline of a cloud in neon blue lights.

'Jackie!' The bouncer called out as Jack climbed the steps to the entrance.

'All right, man?'

'Long time, Jackie. Got anything for me?'

'Payday's not until Monday.' Jack replied, licking his lips to get rid of the instant dryness.

'That's not my problem, Jackie. You needed something and I got it for you.'

'You know full well that shit weren't for me, man. I don't touch it.'

'Jackie, Jackie, Jackie.' The bouncer closed in on him.

'It's Jack!'

The bouncer squared up to him. His nose pressed against Jack's. But Jack didn't flinch. He daren't.

'I don't give a fuck what your name is. I just want my money. Now, how much you got for me?' Jack cringed at the gross mixture of kebab meat and sugary energy drinks on the man's breath.

'Nothing,' Jack swallowed hard, keeping his stance.

'Come on now, don't make me turn you upside down and shake you. Because you know I will, don't you?'

'Fine!' Jack scowled. He knew all too well that the threat wasn't an empty one and tugged out the remaining tenners from his pocket. 'All I can give you is twenty quid.'

'Not my problem.' The bouncer snatched all of the cash out of his hand and tutted to himself whilst counting out the four ten pound notes. 'You come see me on payday, for the rest of it. Got it? Or I'll be making a little visit to your flat again.'

Jack didn't answer and walked through the newly painted entrance to the bar. His only response was his middle finger.

Chapter Three

After spending fifty pence for the privilege of using the toilets inside the station, George appeared much more presentable than the mud-stained farmer boy he'd arrived as. He hated himself for caring. He loved his job. But Ellie would have gone bat shit if he'd turned up in the muddy fleece, torn jeans and steel cap boots. It was hard enough telling her that he'd decided not to take the university's offer of the business course and go for the apprenticeship at the farm instead – so he knew she wouldn't want it paraded in front of her friends. After dousing himself in deodorant and the aftershave that she'd bought him for his birthday, he rammed his work clothes into his bag to hide them from sight.

Running slick putty through his short, blond hair and arranging it to the side the way Ellie liked, he couldn't help but feel out of place in London. In a polo shirt – white of course, mid-wash skinny jeans and tan loafers, he hated how exceptionally unremarkable he looked.

In Coggletree, there were only two styles of fashion for blokes. Essex boy daywear and Essex boy nightwear. Which usually just meant a change from shorts to trousers to accompany a muscle-fit polo. He never gave it any thought at home, but in London, surrounded by all the trends that Instagram shit out, he felt beige.

Hopping onto the escalator, his friends were on a metal bench next to the flower stall where he'd left them. Aimee, with her phone in hand, had her head rested on Alfie's shoulder whilst he curled his arm around her shoulder. That was new.

'O M G, about time, babes.' Aimee shifted away from Alfie. 'We've been sat here for ages. We were meant to meet Ells at seven. It's almost quarter past.'

'I know.' He shrugged. 'But at least one of us fellas have to make an effort. Look at Alf, all he needs is a paper cup and he can finally start earning some money.'

'Piss off, mate.' Alfie rose to his feet and playfully jabbed his fist into George's stomach.

George wheezed. 'Fucks sake, Alf.'

The play-fighting used to be okay when they were kids, when they were the same size as each other and spent hours re-enacting their favourite action movies. But they were no longer kids and Alfie had grown into a brick shithouse.

Aimee stood and twisted the thin belt on her green dress. 'Anyways, I was looking up the Cloud Bar. It's just round the corner so we can get a taxi.'

The thought of getting stuck in rush hour traffic in central London made George want to vomit. 'A taxi for something that's just round the corner?' He furrowed his brow. 'Let's walk, it's nice outside.'

'Oh please.' Aimee pouted. 'I love the big black ones.'

'That your Tinder profile?' Alfie scoffed.

'Can you even spell, Tinder?'

George watched them "argue" for a moment before losing interest and fished out his phone from his pocket to search for the bar himself. He was counting down the minutes – no seconds - until he'd be seeing his girlfriend. It'd been a good four or five weeks since they'd last seen each other. He missed her skin, her beautiful long blonde hair and that body of hers. She was so fucking perfect to him. He couldn't wait to kiss those amazing lips of hers.

It wasn't that they hadn't spoken much since she'd gone to university - quite the opposite. Having spent all their time together when they'd travelled around Asia, it had been unbearable for them to be apart when she left for her course. They'd chatted and FaceTimed on the phone pretty much all day, every day when she first moved out of Coggletree and into her uni halls, and had sent a thousand texts in between. But his work had become more exhausting with each week and she'd got overloaded with coursework. No surprise it all fizzled to just quick texts and missed calls until they both had time to sit down and chat.

Out of the station, the noises of the city took George's attention away from his phone. The street was busy. Too fucking busy. He never could understand why so many people were in such a rush. Waiting for the green man at the traffic lights, George showed the others the map on his screen.

'It's literally through that marketplace over there?'

'Would love to see you walk miles in heels, Georgie.' Aimee's protest was the norm. But her objections quickly vanished when she saw the many icons for bars on the route. 'Oooh, let's stop and have cocktails. We went in there the last time we were up here.'

George sighed. 'I swear you was just moaning about being late.'

'Yeah, we better get moving.' Alfie cleared his throat. 'Plus, that cocktail place looks packed.'

The bar was pretty busy. That was a fact. But George knew the real reason why Alfie didn't want to go inside. There was always an excuse not to go somewhere when the fella didn't have much money. Which proved more often than not. Alfie's family didn't have much money – his dad never at work and his mother spending most of her adult life pushing out babies, the benefits didn't go far with five kids. Known for their constant arguments with the neighbours, they lived in one of the handful of council houses in Coggletree. Not that any of that shit mattered to George. He loved the bloke like a brother.

'But it's happy hour. Please.' Aimee's whining sounded like fly buzzing in his ear.

'Come on, Alf. You claustrophobic or something' Smiling, George slapped his palm between the fella's shoulder blades. 'I'll buy these. It's happy hour after all.

After queuing at the three-deep bar, George coughed as the coldness of his cocktail hit the back of his throat. Well that was his excuse. It didn't help that they were free-pour and as much as he liked to think otherwise, he was one hell of a lightweight. Never one to be adventurous with alcohol, George had only bought cocktails with bourbon in. That was his go-to since he outgrew drinking cheap vodka in the park during the summer holidays. Aimee chose the overly-sweet and colourful ones with innuendo-sounding names. Something that had become a trademark of hers. In true fashion, Alfie picked two of the same - double shots of whisky, no rainbows, no straws. No fuss.

Checking the time on his phone, George threw back his drinks and urged his friends to do the same. For the first time in his life, it bothered him that he was late. Ellie was only a couple of streets away and he was desperate to get to her. He tapped his foot, fidgeting until Aimee finished giving him and Alfie tips on manscaping and drank her syrupy drinks.

'I can't believe you're actually moaning because we're late? Like seriously? You?' Alfie knocked back his drink with a belch and led the way out of the bar.

Guided by the blue line of the map app on George's phone, the three of them walked through the old market that was closing shop for the night and as the JD began to work its magic on George, they followed the directions towards the Truman Breweries which showcased the oddities of East End's latest art fads. Engulfed in crowds of people and food vendors, the smell of pulled pork caused his belly to rumble.

'I should have been an artist. My mum always says I'm the creative type.' Alfie smirked, clearly eyeing up a group of girls standing outside one of the exhibitions.

George sniffed. 'Well, you talk enough shit to be one, mate.'

'Babes, the only sculptures you make are the piles of jizz tissues on your bedroom floor.' Aimee added.

'Says you.' Alfie creased his brow with another belch. 'You've had so many men in your bed that your sheet folds like cardboard.'

'Do you even know what a bed sheet is? Last time I was round your house, you slept on a bare mattress.' She screwed up her face.

'Whatever. All I'm saying is if I did art, I could be getting it on with all these pink haired fitties.'

'They dye their hair, babes, they're not blind.'

As they made their way under a brick railway bridge, George jiggled the change around in his pocket, his fingers feeling for the thicker coins to give to the homeless man and his scruffy dog. The pooch looked in good health, but could've done with a bath. By the look of the congealed sewage on the bloke's skin, so could the owner.

'Please tell me you're not gonna give that tramp money?' Alfie growled. 'Look at him, he's a smack head. All tramps are.'

'What the fuck, Alf? People don't chose to be homeless.' George pulled out a couple of pound coins.

'Then why they living on the fucking streets then?'

George clenched his teeth and handed the homeless man some change regardless. The man beamed, thanking him, but George didn't want to get too close to stop and talk. The man stank of piss and his hands were crusted with dirt. A lot worse than just a case of "shit shovels."

'I love the paintings on the walls. They're so pretty.' Aimee beamed from building to building. 'We so should have these in Coggletree. Could you imagine one of these ladies with flowers for hair on the side of The Swan?'

'There's enough big girls with flowers in their hair in The Swan, we don't need them painted on the walls too.' Alfie laughed as Aimee shook her head.

With the smell of sweet, fresh curry floating in the air, George's belly purred. He'd only had cereal for breakfast and a soggy sandwich for lunch. He'd planned on grabbing a bite on his way to the station but running late at the farm had hampered any ambition of lining his stomach. The hipsters walking past munching their freshly made bagels, didn't help matters much.

Strolling through the green iron gates, the blue neon sign shone brightly above the doorway. No words, just the outline of a cloud. All three climbed the steps and held out their ID's in unison to the stocky bouncer before he even had the chance to ask.

Through the darkness, George scanned the large room for Ellie. She was usually easy to spot - her waist length blonde hair was always a giveaway. But before he could find her, Aimee squeaked and ran over to four girls and a bloke sitting on the sofas.

George's eyes widened when one of the girls with a short, dark, choppy hairstyle jumped from her seat and threw her hands around Aimee. His heart pounding in his chest, he almost sprung a stiffy when he realised the girl was Ellie. And fuck, he had a thing for brunettes.

'Wow,' George whistled, gripping her hips and pulling her in for a kiss. The warmth of her body and the softness of her lips made him instantly hungry for more. 'You look amazing.'

'You like it, Georgie?'

Nodding, he ran his fingers through her hair, also feeling the soft skin of her cheeks. 'When did you do this?'

'I forgot to tell you. The girls took me to the salon last week. The blonde looked so cheap, didn't it?'

'I loved you blonde. I love you like this too.' He squeezed her closer.

'Aww. Thanks, Georgie.' She pressed her lips onto his. Her kisses drove him wild. 'So it gets your approval?'

'Ah ha' George confirmed, moving his mouth to her neck, inhaling her scent.

'Georgie,' she urged, pulling away from him. 'Not in front of everyone.'

'You two are so cute.' Aimee cooed, making George reluctantly release Ellie's hips.

'All right, Ell, what you done to your hair? You look like a right banker.' Alfie laughed to himself before being whacked in the arm by George. 'What? I said banker.'

'I know what you meant, you dick.' George grimaced.

'Hey, Alf. Been on the beer? Or just the pies?' Ellie rolled her eyes and turned her attention onto Aimee. 'Aims, your eyebrows are so on point! Where'd you get them done? You're going to have to take me there when I'm back.' Not waiting for an answer, Ellie waved Alfie and Aimee over to the table. 'Anyways, you two, come and meet the girls, you're gonna love 'em.'

George snorted, knowing full well they would.

'This is Olivia, Katherine and Grace.' She nodded towards the three girls – the ones George couldn't tell apart.

'And this is Grace's boyfriend, Luke. He's doing his Masters.' Ellie continued, indicating a man that looked like he was only there because he had nothing better to do. 'Everyone this is Aimee, the one I've been telling you about since forever. She's an amazing beautician-in-training and my number one Essex BFF.' The girls all nodded and smiled robotically. 'And this is Alfie. Georgie's mate.'

'All right, girls?' Alfie winked, playing his ladies' man routine to a tee.

'Oh and you obvs know, Georgie.' Ellie weaved her fingers through his and kissed his cheek. 'Let's get the drinks, yeah?'

At the bar, away from the twelve eyes around the table, George's hands couldn't help but find Ellie's body again, tiptoeing his fingers up her spine and inhaling the sweet perfume on her skin.

'I'm gagging for it.' He nuzzled her neck. 'Wish we could have met on our own.'

'I know, but the girls really wanted to meet Aims. We'll meet on our own soon. I break up in a few weeks.'

'A couple of weeks? When?'

'I don't know yet, babes. I break up in May.'

'May? That's a whole month away.'

'Well uni is more important.'

The kick to George's chest reverberated through his rib cage. His face couldn't hide the upset.

'Sorry, that sounded so shitty, Georgie. I didn't mean it like that. It's just, well, I've got a lot of coursework to wrap up before summer break.'

Shrugging, he pulled her closer to him again. 'Well, maybe you can make it up to me tonight.' His lips found her ear lobe.

'Tonight?'

'Yeah, at your place.'

'Oh, I didn't realise you wanted to stay, Georgie.' She bit her lip, clearly surprised.

'Course I do. You're my girlfriend—'

'Hey Ellie, what can I get you?' A barman interrupted.

Scowling, George turned to face the bastard but caught his breath when he laid eyes on the man from the train. The modern-day Elvis. The moody fucker with the septum piercing was standing in front of them. He fitted in perfectly with the club, as though the interior was chosen around him. Or vice versa. Either way, his edginess was magnified and his jaw seemed to be even more chiselled than before. George sniffed, unable to lock away his apparent inferior complex.

'Oh hi, Jack. I didn't know you was working tonight.' Ellie fidgeted away from George and scraped the hair from her face with her little finger. 'This is Georgie. My...boyfriend. Georgie, this is Jack.'

'Hey man, how's it going?' The fella offered a perfect customer service smile but his gaze wasn't on George.

'All right?' George made his voice deeper than usual and immediately knew he sounded like a dick.

Jack nodded, his gaze still focused onto Ellie. 'Want the usual?'

'Please, Jack. You know us girls love the Pinot Gee.' Ellie giggled. A little too much for George's liking yet he didn't show it. He wouldn't. Never.

George wanted to stop them talking. He didn't know why, he just felt like the spare wheel to a new couple. Like the crazy relative that won't leave the newlyweds alone. Swallowing down the crippling thoughts, he held out his hand to shake the man's - to see if it would be strong or weak. Why that mattered, he didn't know. Not getting a response, he cleared his throat and reeled off the list of drinks. Two bottles of pinot for Ellie and her uni lot, the pint of wife-beater for Alfie and a spritzer for Aimee.

'He go to your uni?' George nudged his head towards the bartender who had gone out back to fetch wine glasses.

'Who? Jack?' She brushed the brown hair out of her eye. 'No. He's just a *friend*. He's so funny. He's had me screaming before. And he's such a lovely guy.'

George grumbled.

'Honestly, he just makes us laugh so much.'

Jealously tore through George. His hand shook and he couldn't work out why. They were known for having male and female mates, they were a foursome, for fucks sake. But that bloke. That caramel-eyed hipster twat was way too close to his girlfriend for comfort.

'What's wrong with you? You're acting weird, Georgie.' Ellie placed a hand on her hip and tilted her head.

Biting the inside of his cheek, he silently willed himself not to show his jealousy, but the green eyed monster clawed its way inside him regardless. 'Me acting weird? Well maybe it's because you was just all over that bloke.'

'Excuse me? No I wasn't, thank you.'

'Oh come on, Ells. Any closer and it would have been *his* Pinot Gee down your throat.'

'I can't believe you just said that.' The whites of Ellie's eyes took over her face.

'What am I to think? You are gorgeous and he is…..well look at him.'

George instantly hated himself. For so many reasons.

'What are you saying, Georgie?' She folded her arms. He quickly held onto her.

'Nothing. Nothing at all. I just got stupid. Maybe I'm jealous because I haven't seen you for so long.' George slid his hands under her arms. 'That's why I want to stay with you tonight. To be with you. *Just* you.'

Her stance softened, yet she refused to be pulled into George's embrace. 'Georgie, let's just have a good night. I don't want to argue.'

'I don't either. I love you.' George stepped in closer, filling the gap, then planted a kiss on her soft cheek.

Jack returned with handfuls of drinks. Ellie scooped up the bottles of wine without making eye contact to either of them then disappeared back to the table.

'That's my girlfriend.' George glared up at Jack who simply nodded in return. His indifference made George's piss boil.

35

Chapter Four

'Yes, mum. I'm with her now. Yes, she's good. No, I'm not drunk.'

The blond fella looked fucked. Being outside on his break, Jack tried not to listen to Ellie's boyfriend's conversation but, apparently, Jack's auto-pilot, which usually allowed him to ignore all the bullshit around him, refused to switch itself on. The bloke had been giving him the death stare all night – something he was sadly used to getting from the drunken dickheads.

The yard was rammed. April's warm evenings had brought hordes of people desperate to reunite with the beer gardens. A British pastime. Yet annoying as they were, their drunken antics whilst he was stone cold sober kept him going at work. The wide-eyed first year uni students discovering Brick Lane, the middle-classed polo players suddenly indie because they'd ordered a pint of cider and black and the never-ending hipsters apparently seeing who can wear the most tweed; a contest of who can dress up as the biggest wanker.

Taking a long drag on his cigarette, he clutched his smoking arm and watched the drunken, blond geezer squirm on the phone.

'Anyway I'm staying at hers. Yes it's safe. I'll be home sometime tomorrow. No, mum. I'm not drunk.' The bloke hung up and faced Jack with unfocused, red eyes.

Jack knew what was coming. Another drunkard wanting to make small talk. He quickly averted his gaze to the crowds, hoping that the fella would take the hint.

'It's Jack, right?'

Jack lowered his head, slyly looking to either side - wishing there was someone else called Jack standing beside him. As luck would have it, there wasn't.

'Since birth.' Jack sucked in another lungful of smoke.

The man tilted his head, a resemblance to a lost puppy. He was young and by his desperate tone during the call, clearly a mama's boy. But his shoulders were broad and he clearly took care of his body. Jack's gaze fell onto the curves of his toned muscles beneath his polo shirt and took another drag to recoup.

'You know Ellie, don't you?'

'Yep.' Jack knew where it was going. He'd had jealous boyfriends in his face countless times.

'How well you know her?'

'Not too well, man.' Jack tried to avoid eye contact. Fighting wasn't his scene.

'Because I'm George. George....her boyfriend.' He hiccupped through his words.

'Cool, man.' Jack had never wanted a cigarette to finish so quickly.

'You, like friends?' George's eyes seemed to wander. 'Or, like, you into her?'

'I've hung around with her and her mates once or twice. They come to the bar a lot. They're good as gold.'

'You know Ellie has a boyfriend, right? Me. I'm George.'

Blowing through rounded lips, Jack straightened his back. 'Listen, man. I serve drinks. She buys them. That's what happens in a bar.' Jack mocked, hoping he'd offend the bloke enough for him to piss off but not enough for him to whack him one.

Instead, the fella folded his arms and stood there, albeit slightly swaying, staring at him.

Jack slid out his phone from his pocket and silently prayed his break was over. Five minutes left. Still, he'd rather spend it being moaned at by some arsehole than be working. His time wasn't free. Just as he resigned himself to listening to Ellie's boyfriend whinge at him some more, the busty girl from the train sashayed over.

'O M actual G, Georgie. Where you been?' She slid her phone from her bag and posed whilst taking a selfie of them. Jack wasn't sure if George was even aware he'd taken part in the photo. 'Alfie is in there all over poor Katherine like a dirty rash. I feel so sorry for her. But did you see her nails? Says it all.'

George hiccupped into his hand. 'My mum kept bloody ringing me, she's worried because I'm staying in London tonight.'

Jack stifled a laugh.

'Oh bless her. You're her baby Georgie. Well, looks like I'll be going back to Essex on my own. Alf is blatantly going back with what's her name tonight. Shit, I've only got a hundred left on me…..you think that'll be enough to get home?' She continued to take pictures of herself and the drunken George.

Jack snorted. Their trivial problems were laughable. She had a sweetness about her though. Something soft. Harmless. He could see those two together though, rather than George and Ellie.

The girl noticed Jack and immediately shut off her phone screen. 'You're the barman, ain't you? Ells was telling us all about you.' She edged closer. 'Don't know if anyone's ever told you, babes, but you have that dark and mysterious look *on point.*'

'Erm, cheers.' Jack took one last long pull of his cigarette then crushed it onto the silver grate mounted onto the wall.

'Oh, you don't have a spare ciggie, do you?'

Jack slid the cigarette pack out of his back pocket and opened it up without looking inside. He hadn't need to. One left.

'You don't smoke.' George whined.

'Oh, shut up. I've just had a massive shock, Georgie. I need a fag.'

'What shock?' His eyes were glazing over.

Leaning against the wall, Jack folded his arms and watched the two of them. When did he become so interested in their bullshit?

'Err, the shock that I'll be getting a taxi home…..alone. Anyway.' She turned her attention back to Jack, smiling as though he was holding a camera. 'Ignore my mate, Georgie here….oh, sorry what's your name again?'

'Jack.' The two men said in unison and Jack raised his brow at the blond.

'Hello Jackie, my name's Aimee, with a double e, not a why. And this is Georgie.'

Jack let himself smile, wondering how many more times he was going to be introduced to bloody George. 'All right?' Jack kept his eyes on Aimee.

'You got a spare ciggie at all? Only I don't have a clue where the nearest shop is around here and I'm a bit in shock.'

George rolled his eyes and headed back inside. He was clearly pissed but the bouncer didn't care. He was too busy pocketing from his side business.

'Sure.' Jack lifted out his last cigarette.

Aimee licked her red lips and placed the cigarette between them, her green eyes stuck on him. She moved closer, close enough for Jack to smell the perfume on her skin. He knew what she wanted. He reached into his pocket and pulled out his yellow plastic lighter and spun the flint. She stepped even closer, grasping his arm, pulling it towards her until it was touching her perfectly pert breasts. Watching the girl light his last cigarette should have felt like a punch to Jack's nads. That was his journey home. But the show was worth it.

Jack cleared his throat.

'I know it's terrible. I don't really smoke.' Aimee said, grey smoke floating from her glossy lips. 'Just, when I've had a drink, I always get the urge to put something in my mouth.'

Jack froze. Holy fuck.

Chapter Five

Incessant chatter from the bedroom next to Ellie's woke George but it took a few moments for him to remember where he was. His brain pulsating in his skull, he searched the small uni bedroom for any means of a drink. Trying to sit up, his stomach whirled with the movement. Ellie groaned awake and clearly seeing him struggle, quickly passed him a pint glass of squash from the bedside table. The lukewarm drink didn't help much but he gulped it down nonetheless, sloshing the liquid around his furry teeth. It tasted gross but it was better than nothing. Handing the empty glass back, he soon perked up upon noticing that they'd both slept naked.

He couldn't remember how he had gotten back to Ellie's room last night. Or even leaving the bar for that matter. He had vague recollections of being moaned at by his mother over the phone, but nothing else. Yet he counted his lucky stars that he'd remembered to get stark bollock naked before passing out.

He was hanging - cnough to sleep for a few more hours at least - but the outline of Ellie's body under the blanket started to perk him up. Literally. He slid an arm under her neck and pressed his belly against her back to fit in the same position as hers. Then pushed his hard dick against her arse. He needed it.

George had fancied Ellie from the moment they had met in Year Seven. She was blonde and bubbly and always knew how to have a laugh. Without a doubt, she had been the hottest girl in their year, and he couldn't believe his luck when *she* had asked *him* out four years

41

later. He'd thought she had just seen him as Aimee and Alfie's mate – the spare wheel to their fucked up frenemies routine. He kind of was, but of course Alfie and Aimee didn't realise that. They didn't like each other, remember? But Ellie was pretty much George's world from the day they had gotten together and had fallen even deeper in love with her whilst travelling together. He admired other women's bodies, of course - he was only human. But his girlfriend was the only one for him. He'd spend the rest of his life with her. He planned to marry her once she'd finished uni and give her everything she could ever want.

This new look of hers was also a massive turn on for him. It made her appear older and more sophisticated somehow. She'd always insisted that she would stay blonde because she didn't want to be dark like Aimee's auburn. "Everyone needs a blonde BFF" she would say, but as the girls didn't see that much of each other since Ellie had moved into London, George guessed that kind of crap went out the window. George sure wasn't complaining.

He ran a hand over the curves of her hip and instinctively pushed his groin against her again. He had been aching for her body for weeks. Kissing her neck, the smell of her skin made his heart race. He glided his lips slowly up to her ear then nibbled her lobe. She didn't say anything but thanked him quietly with the noises that always drove him wild. His hands moved to her stomach and tugged her even closer.

He was rock hard. Harder than he'd been in months and groaned as she rubbed her arse cheeks on his cock. Biting her lip, she rolled onto her back and ran soft fingertips along his spine, up to the nape of his neck. Electricity shot through his skin and his body jolted.

'You know how much I want you?'

'How much?' She teased.

'It's been twenty-seven days since we last....you know?'

'Since what?'

'Since we last fucked.'

'Fucked? Charming Georgie. You know how to get a girl in the mood.'

He nibbled her neck. 'Well you know what I mean. Had sex. Cum together.'

'The hell is wrong with you?' She pulled away from him and sat up in the bed. 'That's all you see isn't it? Just sex. And you've been counting the days too. Makes me feel good. Thanks.'

What?

'I didn't mean it like that. I was just saying it to be....I don't know. To turn you on.'

Ellie slipped out of the bed. 'You think that counting down the days since I last made you cum is a turn on?' She clasped her head with her hands. 'See, Georgie, this is the problem. This is why I am so messed up right now. In here.'

George slid to the edge of the bed, trying to ignore the Goliath of a hangover stomping on his own head. 'What's going on? Talk to me.'

'I don't know Georgie, I really don't. I'm just....I'm not happy.'

'Is it uni? Don't you like it?' His hand reached for her hand but she shrugged it off.

'I love it. I love it *here*. That's the problem.'

'What do you mean?' George forced himself out of the bed, his feet wobbling beneath him. He flung his arms around her and rested his lips onto her neck 'I love you so much.'

She didn't respond.

What the fuck is going on?

Holding her, he hoped it'd be enough to get her to talk. But she didn't. He changed tactics. 'What do you fancy doing today? We could go sightseeing in London. Maybe walk up the river.' His hands fell to her buttocks. 'Or we could spend the day in bed.'

Ellie sighed then turned away from him. The disconnection between them like a wall in the middle of their bodies. But he clung onto her regardless.

'I can't, Georgie. I'm meeting Olivia for brunch.'

'I thought we were spending the day together. I'm not working today.'

'I can't.' She slipped from his embrace. Yanking a dressing gown from the foldable chair next to her chest of drawers, she then wrapped it around herself. Closing her body off from him.

George reached out for her, grabbing hold of the tie to her robe and playfully pulled it away. 'Why don't we stay in bed for a bit longer? Let me make it up to you?'

'So we can fuck?'

'I'm sorry for saying it like that. Honestly.'

Ellie huffed. 'I've got to get ready, Georgie. I've got better things to do.'

Her words caught him off guard. Nearly fucking floored him actually. But he tried not to show it. He had used to be the reason she'd stay in bed. Even if it was to binge watch trashy shows and eat cookie dough ice cream until they couldn't move. The distance between them had been steadily growing before last night. She hadn't wanted to talk about their relationship or Coggletree. She'd acted as though she was ashamed of the place. Ashamed of him. Alfie had told him to "man up" and Aimee had assured him it was all in his head. He never did know how to act in those situations, so he got hammered in order to not have to deal with it.

George fell back onto the edge of the bed, searching for his clothes. He had clearly flung them around the small student room the night before as his coins and keys scattered the carpet. Flashbacks of his drunken antics came back to him on noticing the food stains on his shirt but he shook the memories off. No doubt he would get a full run down on everything from Aimee or Alfie.

'Do you want to grab some breakfast at least?' George knew he sounded desperate. 'I haven't eaten since lunchtime yesterday.'

Ellie rolled her eyes. 'Don't you remember anything from last night? You bought a kebab. Ate half of it, dropped the rest down yourself and threw it up in an alley?'

George's face burned. 'Okay, but can we spend a little time together at least, right?'

Ellie bit her lip and tilted her head, softening slightly. 'I just gotta get ready. I need a shower and then I gotta get going. You can stay here if you want.'

'I'll come with you.'

'We're going shopping then having brunch. You hate both of those things.'

'Yeah, but I love you.'

Ellie didn't reply, she just smiled, her face immediately lighting up the room. The sunlight through the gap in the blind shone onto her perfect cleavage that was escaping her robe. His dick twitched again.

'Okay, Georgie. Ten minutes and I've seriously got to get ready.' She turned and began lowering the robe off her shoulder. She knew exactly what drove him crazy. With a smirk, she let the robe fall to the ground.

'What the fuck is that?' George exclaimed, his voice coming out a lot higher than he meant.

'What?' Ellie screamed, jumping back, frantically flapping. 'Is it a spider?'

'No....that under your arse cheek!' George pointed, waving a frantic hand.

'Oh, that?' She ran her fingers across a tattoo under her right buttock. The words 'live' and 'free' written in black italic ink.

'Yes, that! You've got a tattoo on your fucking arse. Why didn't you tell me?'

Her face sizzling red. 'Excuse me? It's not on my arse. Besides, it's my body, George.' The missing "e" sound off his name shocked him. 'I'll do what I fucking want with it.'

'I'm not saying that. I'm just surprised. That's all.' He tried to get another look. 'You can do what you want…. it's just…. You don't like tattoos…..why didn't you say anything?'

'Bloody hell! Do I have to tell you everything? I bought tampons a couple of weeks ago, should I have told you that too?'

'Don't be stupid.' George let out a nervous laugh. 'But a tattoo is something you tell your boyfriend about.'

'You know what, I don't care if you don't like it. The girls think it looks good and so do I.'

'Those fucking girls.' George flustered. He didn't know why, but he felt threatened by the three uni bitches.

'Oh what? Can't have friends now? Have to stick with the lot from Coggletree forever?'

'I'm not saying that, Ells. Have whatever friends you want. Just, well….you've changed. Without me. Fuck, I didn't even know you'd cut your hair.'

'You know what? I don't care if you don't like that either.' Ellie huffed, avoiding eye contact. George had never seen her so furious before.

Silence fell between them, solid enough to make even breathing seem unreasonable. His awkwardness wasn't helped by the fact that they were both butt naked, ten feet apart, refusing to look at one another.

'I do like it, I really do.' George crept forward. 'It looks hot.'

'Really?' She raised her brow then crossed her arms.

'Yes, *smoking* hot. The tattoo too. I love the new look.' He kissed her shoulder. 'How comes you chose those words?'

George thought he'd seen them before. He didn't know many people with tattoos. It must have been someone in Brick Lane. Must have seen it when he was drunk, and could barely stand without spilling Alfie's pint.

'Because I like them. And that's what I'm doing now. Living free.'

'Didn't you before?'

'Yes, of course,' Ellie curled her arms around his neck. 'I love my life and everyone in it. Just, I'm just *free* now.'

George bit hard into his lip. Free from who? Confusion swam in his already sore head. Wanting to forget it, he grabbed her arse cheek and pressed his rising semi against her. 'Whatever makes you happy.'

She kissed the side of his face as her hand wandered down his back.

'Where did you get it done?'

'Jack did it.'

'Jack who?'

She pulled away. 'How can you not remember? You weren't even drunk at that point.'

'That fella from the bar? The one with the ring through his nose?

'Yes. Him. He's trying to start out as a tattooist so I let him do me.'

'DO YOU?'

'Georgie, you know what I mean?' She huffed. 'He needed the practice and I wanted a tattoo.'

'But it's on your arse. You let another man see your arse?' George clenched his jaw.

'Don't be so silly. It's nothing sordid. It's just a tattoo.' She folded her arms, clearly pissed off. 'Why are you being so jealous? First last night and now this. I don't like it, Georgie.'

'I'm not jealous. I'm not!' Even he didn't believe his lies. 'I just think it's fucking weird that you let a stranger see your arse like that. Was it only the two of you? Alone?'

She shoved him away. 'Seriously, what is this? Twenty-fucking-questions.'

'I'm just asking.'

'You're not, George. You're accusing.'

'I'm just a bit shocked, that's all.' He furrowed his brow. 'Just ignore me.'

Ellie grabbed the robe and towel from the floor and pushed open the bathroom door.

'I really don't have time for all this. I've gotta jump in the shower. I'm meeting Livs in half hour.'

'Want some company? This is ready to go.' He nodded to his dick which was twitching in salute.

Ellie rolled her eyes then, without another word, slammed the bathroom door behind her and turned the lock.

Fuck.

Chapter Six

'Well, darlin?' George's mother, stood at the bottom of the stairs several hours later with a cup of tea in one hand, the other on her hip.

George had been in such a rush to get to the toilet that he'd ignored her and ran up the stairs as though his life had depended on it. He couldn't waste time answering his mother's thousands of questions after a night's worth of cocktails, spirits, shots and the kebab, he'd evidently forgot about all, curdling in his gut.

'Well what?' He yanked out his phone to see if Ellie had text.

'What you doing home from London so early? We weren't expecting you until this evening. Was we mum?' She called through to the living room.

George's Nan was in there. He could smell the cloud of cigarette smoke as he had turned the corner into the cul-de-sac. Most people remember their grandmothers smelling of old lady rose water or lavender talc, but George would always remember his Nan's aroma as a box of twenty menthols. Super-king. Brushing past his mother, he found his Nan sitting in her usual seat by the window and greeted her with a kiss to her cheek. His Nan was a tiny woman, with bleached blonde hair that she backcombed to make up for her short stature. Not one to age gracefully, she had a thing about wearing at least one item of leopard print clothing every day. It was her trademark. Apart from Ellie, his Grandmother was George's favourite person on the planet. Her greatest quality was saying exactly what she thought. Truthfully, her words usually stung. And mostly when unprovoked. It's why his dad called her "The Wasp."

'You wanna cup of tea, Nan?'

'No ta, love. Your mum just made me a coffee...well if that's what you want to call it.'

George smirked, observing the paleness of the coffee. Half a cup of milk to any hot drink was Maxine Taylor's speciality. Looking around the living room, he was certain that mocha, or "mo-shar," as his mother called it, was her favourite colour. Pretty much everything in the house was a shade between cream and brown. Yet throwing in the odd teal sofa cushion and rug to match, she'd always assumed she was something of an interior decorator. Essex housewife, through and through.

'Thought you would want to spend the day with Ells.' Maxine plonked herself on the reclining armchair.

'I did, mum. But Ellie had some stuff on. Fuck knows what.'

'Georgie.' His mother squealed. 'Don't say "eff" in front of your Nan.'

'Sorry, Nan.'

George's grandmother rolled her eyes then slid a white cigarette from its packet. 'Oh love, I don't give a fuck.'

Maxine shot them both a look – one that accused them of being a bad influence on each other. They both shrugged it off. They were used to the disapproval.

'Anyways, how is Ells? I miss her.'

'She's loving it up there, mum.' George bit his cheek, wishing he could forget their argument that morning. Wishing that he hadn't fucked everything up.

'We're so happy for her. Aren't we, mum?' Maxine beamed.

His Nan hummed, clearly uninterested, and took a lug on her fag; blowing the smoke in between George and his mother.

'You seen her hair?' George flicked through the photos on his phone and showed a picture of him and Ellie from the night before. It was one of the rare occasions he had gotten her all to himself and managed to get her to sit with him long enough to take a selfie together.

'Is that Ellie? With a pixie cut? And she's dyed it brown. Oh my god, she looks lovely? Show your Nan.'

George's grandmother barely looked at the screen before taking another drag. 'She looks like a lesbian.'

'Mum! You can't say that.' Maxine slapped the arm of the chair. 'Hair has got nothing to do with sexuality.'

George laughed at them both, - The Wasp's words always hurt his mother the most. 'She actually looks good, Nan.'

His mother jumped up and stood in front of the huge mirror above the fireplace and pulled back half of her beige-blonde hair to give herself a bob. She turned her face from side to side as she watched her reflection and frowned – not that the Botox would let you notice. 'I wonder what I'd look like with shorter hair.'

'Don't do it, Maxine.' His grandmother shook her head. 'You've got shoulders like a quarterback.'

Maxine's jaw dropped.

'Well Ellie looks lovely. I wonder why she didn't put anything on "Myface" though.'

'It's Facebook, Mum. And she doesn't go on it anymore. She says it's all about Insta stories now.'

'Who's going to send me lives on my game now?' Maxine visibly deflated. Her fallen shoulders showed just how heartbroken she was at not being able to reach level fifty.

'I don't know.' He huffed. His mother's worries were often somewhat self-centred.

'Everything all right with you two, darlin?'

'How can it be all right, Maxine? His girlfriend's into women now. Not that I'm surprised.' His Nan exhaled another white cloud.

George chuckled, coughing at the same time.

'Yeah, we're all good.' George stared down at his hands. Anything not to make eye contact. The fact was, he didn't know the honest answer to the question. 'It's just…..I don't know. She's changed a bit. A lot actually. And she's got a tattoo too.'

'Has she?' Maxine's eyes were as wide as saucers. 'Don't you go getting any ideas, Georgie. I can't stand all those tattoos on people. They look like the bloody Berlin Wall. You know who have tattoos don't you? Criminals and pirates….criminal pirates. They have tattoos on their knuckles too.'

George froze, remembering the words on that barman's knuckles. The same as the ones *he* tattooed onto Ellie's arse. Why the fuck did she want the same words?

'You all right, darlin?'

'Erm, yeah, I'm fine.' Clearing his throat, he avoided eye contact. 'I think I just need a shower.'

His mum leaned in and planted a kiss on his cheek, staining it with her lipstick. 'Okay, mummy's baby. Me and your Nan are going into town for lunch and then hit the shops. You want to come?'

George shot a look at his Nan who was rolling her eyes so hard he could only see the whites of them.

'No thanks.' He stifled a laugh. 'I'm going to see if Alf and Aims are about.'

George needed to speak to someone about what had happened that morning. How Ellie had turned so quickly on him. Was it his fault? He needed Alfie's brutal honesty mostly. He knew he'd never get that from his mother.

'You sure, darlin?'

Sighing, his Nan twisted her cigarette out into the glass ashtray. 'Leave the boy alone, Maxine, for fuck sakes. What kind of moron wants to be with their mother all the bloody time?'

'Well, I like being with you.' She smiled.

'Exactly.' His Nan slid another cigarette from the packet.

George left the room whilst he could still breathe.

Chapter Seven

Later that day, Jack pulled the light cord in his bathroom and huffed as nothing happened. Yet again, the electricity meter was empty and thanks to that dickhead bouncer, he had no way of topping it up until payday. It would also mean that the gas had probably gone too and the shower he was desperate for was going to be painful. Twisting the red-circled tap and holding his hand under the running water, Jack's suspicions were confirmed. Yep, a cold shower it was.

He was grateful for the council flat – one hundred percent – but it hadn't exactly turned out to be the godsend he'd hoped for when the social set him up with it. Being raised in care for most of his life, moving from house to house, care home to care home, he'd never really had anyone to teach him about money. And the social hadn't exactly prepared him for handling his own cash when chucking him out the system. He never understood why school's taught children about fucking leaf cells but not how to live as an adult.

Jack returned to his bedroom, a journey much more difficult when he knew he didn't have the choice of a light in the hallway. Even at four in the afternoon and with the sun shining outside, his flat emulated a black hole. Due to him working into the early hours Jack had painted every window black to help throw out his body clock. Some days he'd stack up eighteen hour shifts, and even though he was pretty much running on empty, he couldn't afford not to jump at the chance of overtime.

Grabbing his phone from the bed, he grumbled on noticing the battery was only at fifteen percent. There were a few texts; one from Aimee and two from Cole. That bastard could wait. Unlocking it, he couldn't help but smile from Aimee's message.

'Had a great time last night, babes. Let's deffo do it again sometime. Aims xxx.'

Jack could still smell her in his room. Her overly-sweet perfume that she'd sprayed on her perfect cleavage every half hour lingered in the air - mingling with the darkness and dust. Jack snorted, remembering her standing in the doorway wearing nothing but knickers and one of his T-shirts. She should have been his dream girl. She was amazing. But like the others before her, she wasn't for him.

Aimee had been a good laugh, a gorgeous girl that had everything going for her. And a heart of gold, once you peeled away the artificial bullshit she hid behind. He discovered, when she'd stayed at the bar even though her friends had gone, that she was sensitive and kind. Fragile even. Even though she'd pounced on him. The girl wasn't shy, that's for sure. And Jack could swear her breasts grew bigger as the night went on. She had pissed all her money away on the Prosecco Cocktails and Jack being Jack, offered her a place to crash.

Unable to find the words, he couldn't reply to her text and purposely ignored the two from Cole. Instead, he scrolled through his old messages then stopped on the last one that Ellie had sent to him. It was only a pink heart, but it had said more to him than any words could ever have done. He knew what she wanted – she'd told him as much when she'd stayed late at the bar and kissed him. She'd been drunk and slightly jaded with life – Jack was used to those girls. But he didn't kiss back, and if he'd been up for the job, he'd never allow himself to be a home-wrecker. He'd grown up with enough of those in his mother's life to know he never wanted to be that kind of man.

Jack hadn't known her long, a couple of month's maybe, but he'd never had her down as someone who would date such a kid. Sure, George was a good-looking guy and beneath all his macho bollocks, he seemed like a good egg. The perfectly groomed blond hair and golden skin. Fuck, the fella had the kind of eyes that you'd see on aftershave adverts. Maybe it had been the drink, but the fella came across vacant. As though there was nothing there between his temples.

Leaning against the doorframe, Jack tapped his fingers onto his phone whilst deciding whether to text Ellie or not. The words on his knuckles made him think about the tattoo he did on her. How she blushed as she had picked the same words as him and how he was so conscious of scratching the needle into the back of her naked upper thigh. Being that up-close to a girl that was into him, one as gorgeous as Ellie, should have made his pulse race. Had him salivating. Made him feel something. Yet, just as with Aimee, there was no feeling there. Nothing.

A loud rap on the front door jolted him back to reality and he recognised the pattern of the knock at once. He'd spent years remembering the different taps on his door, usually avoiding his foster parents banging on his bedroom and then, later in life, the bailiffs. He knew who it was and was in no rush to see him. He didn't move from the spot and, not knowing why, even held his breath. But the person there clearly wasn't going anywhere and continued to pound louder with each thud. The last thing Jack needed was for the neighbours to intervene. Again. Manning the fuck up, he marched over to the front door and yanked it open with a fake confidence.

'What the fuck are you doing here?' Jack looked through the man standing in the hallway, hoping his face would back up the conviction in his voice.

'Is that a way to greet your brother?' Cole shoved him to the side, pushing his way into the flat.

'You're not my brother.' Jack tried to show that the jab to the ribs hadn't hurt.

'Why you being a dick?'

'Seriously?' Jack bit his lip. He wanted to fly at him. 'Are you being serious right now?'

'Whoa, change your tampon, bruv.'

Cole coughed into his fist then slumped onto the sofa, lifting his dirty shoes onto the fabric. Jack scowled at the sight of Cole lying on his couch, making it filthy. Contaminating everything like he always did. His clothes were encrusted with dirt and he stank of stale sweat. Clearly, he'd just come down from another week-long hit. But the two holdalls that he'd brought in with him pissed Jack off the most.

'You're not welcome here, Cole. And neither are those.' Jack couldn't take his eyes off the bags.

'Why you acting like a bitch?'

'After last time? Really? I'm in so much shit because of you.'

'With that bouncer?' Cole laughed. 'Fuck him.'

'If we don't pay him back, he's gonna beat the living crap out of us.'

'Hey, take it easy, bruv. Why's he gonna beat me? You're the one that asked him to get the shit. Not me.'

'What? You begged me to help you. Turned up at my door in the middle of the night, begging me to help. You told me you was dying.'

'I was coming down like a whore's knickers. I ain't got a Scooby what I was saying. Not my fault you shit yourself and ran off to that dickhead. It's your problem, bruv.'

Jack balled his hands into fists. He needed to punch a wall. Or Cole.

'I'm *not* your brother. Not by blood or otherwise. I don't even want you in my flat.'

Cole sprang from the sofa and charged across the room. Grabbing Jack by the shoulders, he pinned him against the wall and grimaced with rage. It was his go-to whenever he didn't get his own way. Jack had seen that look of demented fury on Cole's face many times. The penetrating stare that had used to petrify him - once even making him wet himself when Cole held a knife to his throat. Jack had only been twelve-years-old at the time. Too young and stupid to realise the fella was bad news. But Cole's expression didn't incite that horror in Jack like it once did. In fact, the opposite. All it brought was revulsion.

Jack could've easily pushed him away. The fella must have weighed no more than seven stone, but he was frozen, in shock of how much Cole had deteriorated. His face was so gaunt, the skin sagging from his cheeks, and like the hands pressed onto Jack's shoulders were covered in scabs where he had continually picked at them. Jack winced as Cole let out a growl, the breath and the blackened teeth enough to make him gag. He was only four years older than Jack, twenty-five, but he looked like he was knocking fifty.

'I pretty much raised you, you piece of shit, and you don't want me in your flat? Who was the one that had your back at the care home, eh? Who was the one that stopped you from getting the shit kicked out of you every day for being a whiny little poof?'

'Fuck you, Cole.' Jack croaked.

'Who?' Say it!' His foul breath filled the tiny gap between.

'Get off me!' Jack huffed, waiting for the bullshit act to end.

'Without me, your life would have been shit.'

Cole released Jack and backed away, the deranged look slowly fading. He'd seen it all before.

'Shit?' Jack coughed, rubbing his throat. 'My life would be shit? Have you looked around here?'

'You've got it a lot better than me, you little bitch. Social took me at birth. Those fuckers didn't even give me a chance with my own mum.'

'Social took you for a reason, Cole. They took all of us for a reason.'

'My dad left my mum. That's all.'

'Your dad moved back to Glasgow and left his pregnant wife with six other kids.'

'So what? My dad is a prick. I hope he's rotting in a grave somewhere. Your mum was a whore. That bag of shit slept her way around Newham.'

'Fuck off, Cole!' Jack's fists were in balls again.

'You don't like it do you? Your mum is a hoe. Do you even know your dad, Jack? Even know what country he is from? You don't have that tan for nothing, bruv.'

'The fuck you bringing race into it for?'

'You've had a fucking sweet life and you're still ungrateful.'

'Everyone has had it sweet compared to you....*poor* little Cole. Had such a hard life. You had the same life as the rest of us and we didn't all turn to drugs, did we?'

'You talking about addictions like you haven't got one, bruv.' Cole's gaze rolled over Jack's tattooed arms.

Jack cleared his throat. The bastard's words had struck his insecurities. Like always. 'Better than a smack head.'

Cole laughed. It was his only redeeming feature. 'Maybe I wouldn't have had to do that if I got everything you did. I never got a council flat did I?'

Jack slammed his fists onto the light switch besides the door. Plaster from the wall flaked down onto his arm. 'No council flat? Look, no electric. Or gas. I work every hour that I can and I can't afford to have a proper shower. But you wouldn't know anything about that because you haven't been near water in years.'

'Social don't give a fuck about me!'

'Because you're a junkie.'

'It's because of you that I'm on that shit and you know it.'

Jack swallowed hard. He knew too well what Cole meant. Cole always blamed Jack for his addiction to drugs, but Jack hadn't made him do it. Jack hated drugs more than anything – especially as his own mother's life had been ruined by them. But it was to pay for Jack why Cole had started working for the first dealer. Dealers who play with the big boys always end up being junkies themselves. It's the only way to keep them loyal.

'Cole.'

'Forget it, bruv. It is what it is. You're my brother and I know we've always got each other's backs. Even if you are being a dick.'

Jack couldn't find the words to reply. He didn't want anything to do with him, but he couldn't abandon him. Not like everybody else had.

Instead, he shrugged off the argument then went to the kitchen to grab a drink from the fridge. But unless he could blend lettuce without a blender, or drink a half jar of out-of-date mayonnaise, there was no point in even looking. He grabbed a couple of glasses from the cupboard, wiped the water marks off with his T-shirt and filled them with good old tap water.

Back in the front room, he grimaced as Cole was sprinkling tobacco into a cigarette paper.

'Don't tell me that's what I think it is.'

'Na, plain old tobacco. No bud at all.' His smile was sincere.

Jack laughed to himself. The man was covered in syringe marks. Why would he even bother with a joint?

Cole passed the fag to Jack, and with a distrusting sniff of the white paper, he accepted it. He sucked the smoke in and let the release take over him. He was just as much an addict than Cole but his vice was somehow legal.

'Thanks, bruv.' Jack said after taking another gulp of smoke. He'd forced the word 'bruv'. He hadn't used it in such a long time. It connected him to the people and the life he wanted to get away from. But watching Cole's lips curl upwards, Jack was glad he'd said it.

'Cole, I'm sorry, but you can't stay here. If my landlord finds out, he'll cut my nuts off.'

'I don't wanna stay here. You don't even have electricity.' The man laughed. 'I've got my own place now. Thanks to my new boss.'

Jack's chest tightened.

'Listen, let me help you out of your little problem with the bouncer.' Cole reached deep into the pocket of his ripped coat and with a smirk full of venom, pulled out a wad of notes. 'You can thank my boss for this.'

'No way, Cole. I don't want anything to do with that money. I don't even want to know where it's from.'

'Money is money. Take it.'

Jack couldn't help but stare at the rolled up cash. There was easily a thousand there. He knew it could've sorted him out for a while. Yet coming from Cole's pocket, he assumed it hadn't come legally. It was clearly from a deal or some dodgy goods run.

Temptation swam in Jack's stomach. Taking the cash would get him out of that place. Away from Cole. It'd give him enough money to pay off the bouncer for good and get away from London. He knew where he'd go too.

'I can't.' Jack finally spoke. 'It's dirty. It's more trouble than it's worth.'

'You moan that you've got no funds and when I offer to help you out, you spit in my face. Just like all those times I set you up with a girl.'

Jack's cheeks reddened. It was a subject he hated to talk about. 'What you going on about?'

'You've always been the same. Whinge, whinge, whinge but won't let people help you. You wanted a bird so I got you one. But then you didn't like her. Or the other five I found you. There was always a problem.'

'They were all crack heads.'

Taking a drag of the roll-up, Cole's eyes narrowed. 'I think the problem was that they didn't have dicks.'

'Fuck off!'

It was something Jack had to deal with for most of his life. Of course, the rumours had started when he was young. The shy ten year old who didn't like football and cried over the smallest of things. Him being gay was clearly the only reasonable explanation. Not that it bothered Jack what those wankers at the care home thought about him.

'Face it, mate. You're a homo.'

'And you know that, how?'

'When was the last time you fucked a girl?'

'You need to go.' Sniffing loudly, Jack stood. 'I've got work soon.'

'Hit a nerve?' Cole rose slowly. Throwing the wad of notes onto the sofa his smile dissolved – a snarl now in its place. 'Tell you what. I'll leave this cash here and if you take it, good on you. If you don't, I'll just come back for it. Eh?'

'Why though? What's the catch? You wouldn't just offer that amount of money to someone.'

Cole's lips exposed rotting teeth. 'Like I said. You're my brother.'

Chapter Eight

Sucking in a lungful of fresh countryside air, George heaved a straw bale from the lorry. Being spring, there was shit loads to do on the farm. Lambing season proving especially exhausting. The rooster was having the time of his life with the hens and honey bees had not long woken from hibernation. Who even knew bees hibernated? The horses and alpacas were loving the sunshine in the fields, causing him no end of grief at close-down and the bloody goats were proving to complete bastards in the warmer weather.

George loved every moment of it.

He was happy at work. He knew that shouldn't be right, that he shouldn't love his job so much. But it was the bollocks. Ellie, along with his mother had wanted him to go to study a business course at university - to get a proper education before settling on a job. His dad, of course, wanted him to join "Taylors Properties" after his degree. But whilst filling out his uni application, he knew he wouldn't go. All his life, he had wanted to work with animals. The classroom wasn't for him. And an office was worse. He'd worked a summer at his Dad's firm and witnessed true hell. It wasn't eternal infernos or rivers of blood; it was a desk and a phone that kept fucking ringing all day. Getting hands on was what it was all about for him. Mud and rain, and the sun shining on his back. That was what it was all about. Even the eternal heaps of cow shit were all right.

Being outdoors meant he got to spend time with nature. The rabbits hopping over the fields first thing in the morning, the deer in the meadows coming to steal any dropped feed during the day and the foxes trying their luck around the hen coops at sunset. But it was the birds that George enjoyed the most. His all-day friends that kept him busy whistling to their song. Robins were rife in the spring and the blackbirds were everywhere too. Even the crows, who were the noisiest bastards on the planet, kept him company. But, no doubt about it, George had something for the magpies. Bold as brass and surprisingly colourful, those were his favourite. Hands down.

The work had been good for his body too. George had developed a bit of belly before working there, too many cheeky Nando's and drinking round Alfie's outhouse, which frankly was nothing more than a shed with a Bluetooth speaker. But since the daily manual labour started, he'd lost quite a bit of excess weight. Well, not as toned as he wanted, but well on his way.

As George lifted the straw into the pig's pen, a car pulled up to the gate. George dropped the bale with a thud, recognising the car immediately. The navy-blue BMW estate belonged to his supervisor Robert. Or as George called him, "Knobert."

'Rough night, kiddo?' Knobert asked through the lowering electric window.

George cringed hard. He fucking hated being patronised by someone he had little, maybe, no respect for.

His supervisor peered at George through his sunglasses. They were the kind that curved around the face and shone green in the light - the colour of a fly's arse. He was an all right bloke, but totally full of himself. The first time George had met him, Knobert had taken pleasure in telling him what kind of car he drove. Like George gave a fuck. He'd banged on and on about the BMW so much that George had wondered if the bloke had fucking shares in the company.

'Nah, had an early one.'

It was the truth. His head had been too busy thinking about the argument between him and Ellie. Either way, he couldn't face going out. Not that he had the offer to. Alfie had been knackered from his night and day with Katherine. And Aimee wasn't about. Obviously too busy with that wanker, Jack.

'You can't fool me, Georgie boy. I was your age once. I know what it's like.'

George fought the urge to roll his eyes.

Knobert was about six years older than him, and could often be seen steering his remote controlled car around the park. A BMW probably. The bloke had an air of creepiness about him, like the kind that goes out on his own and stands in the corner of the club. Wearing those sunglasses, probably.

'Honestly, I stayed at home.'

George's phone vibrated twice in his pocket, indicating a text. Finally. He went to get it out of his overalls but stopped when he realised that Knobert would have something to say about it. Reminding the younger staff that there was a "no phones on the job" policy was one of Knobert all-time favourites to enforce.

'A nineteen year old spending a Saturday night with his mum and dad? Sure.'

Knobert gave George that look that instantly pissed him off. The look of a smug prefect.

'Anyway, just thought I'd stop by to see if you remembered that you're working tomorrow. There's a school coming in to see the lambs in the morning and the horses need brushing. All of them.'

'Yeah, I remember. No problem.'

'Good to hear, kiddo. There's another lorry coming in tomorrow morning as well and it'll need unloading soon as. I'd like to help but I'm buying a seventy-five inch telly tonight and I wanna set it up. You ever watched sport on a seventy-five incher?'

'Erm, no. I don't' think so.' George shrugged.

'If you carry on working hard, then one day you might be able to. Got to have that dream though, kiddo.'

George's phone vibrated against his leg again.

'Anyway, I'm off. You carry on here. Clock off at five, no point you staying until half past. Don't look like you're getting much done anyway.'

George furrowed his brow. *Prick.*

As soon as Knobert's car was out of sight, George fished for his phone and swiped the screen. It was a text from Ellie.

'George, can you call me when you finish work tonight. We really need to talk.'

No kiss. Again.

Chapter Nine

'So, that's it? You two are over?' Alfie blew the foam on his pint.

George slouched in the scuffed leather-backed chair, barely moving the glass of Jack and coke away from his lips long enough to answer. 'I dunno.'

It'd been three whole days since he'd met Ellie at her uni halls and she'd told him that she needed some time out from their relationship. Three days that had felt like an eternity since his heart had been shattered by the love of his life.

'She says her head is messed up and that she needs a break. From us.' Wincing, he almost choked on the solid lump that'd formed in his throat.

Not wanting to admit what'd happened at first, George had kept their "break" to himself. It had made sense not to get everyone involved whilst the wound was still fresh – well, pissing of blood actually. But by bottling it all up, he caused himself nothing but a total headfuck. And so, seventy two hours later, he was desperate for a shoulder to ugly cry on. Not that he would ever cry in front of Alfie – the fella would likely rinse the shit out of him for the rest of his life if he did. Nonetheless, he asked his best mates to meet for him in their local, The Swan.

'So why's she dumped you?' Alfie scooped up the three stained beer mats in front of them - his tongue poking from the corner of his mouth whilst he lined them up at the table's edge.

'She hasn't dumped me. We're taking a *break*. It's different to breaking up.' George pressed his glass to his

67

lips. 'But she said we both want different things at the moment and time apart would do us good. He cleared his throat. 'But I don't want anything different, mate. I want her.

Alfie stopped flipping the mats just long enough to meet George's gaze. For the briefest of moments, George thought his friend was going to say something consoling. Something to help him. But this was Alfie, after all. 'Mate, I fucking knew it. What did I say? I said this exact thing was going to happen, didn't I?'

'No!' George furrowed his brow. 'When?'

'All the time, mate. I've said it to everyone.' The fella beamed like a child. 'Mind you, everyone knew it was gonna happen, didn't they?'

'What? Who the fuck knew? You've been slagging me off to people?'

'No, course not, Georgie. I wouldn't do that. I haven't said shit about you. Just about, you know, you and Ellie.

'Same fucking thing, *mate.*'

Scrubbing his hand over his face, George pressed his fingers into his eyelids. He needed a distraction from the ache in his chest since the moment he left Ellie's place those three nights before. It was an ache that made him feel hungry and full at the same time. Not that he could eat anyway. Contrary to what he needed, Alfie wasn't helping at all.

'It's not, mate. I've only been talking about that bitch. She's been weird for months, like she thinks she's too good for you. For all of us, actually. It pisses me off.'

'No, she don't. And don't call her a bitch. She's still my girlfriend.'

'Wake the fuck up, Georgie boy. That girl has treated you like shit since you said you wanted to do the farm apprenticeship instead of going to uni.'

'No, she hasn't.'

Alfie huffed, clearly unimpressed by George. 'Stop defending her. You know as well as I do that she's been acting like a tampon for ages.'

'What?' George raised his brow. 'What does that even mean?'

'You know. A tampon. A stuck up cun-'

'Mate!' George slammed his fist onto the tables. 'Don't ever call her that!'

He'd only ever lost it with Alfie a couple of times in his entire life but he could feel it coming. He wanted to rip the douche's head off for talking like that, he wanted to hurt him. To hurt someone to alleviate his own pain. But he knew, deep down, that his anger wasn't directed at his mate. Alfie was only looking out for him, the same way George would do for him. He knew his anger was displaced.

'All right. Sorry. I'm just looking out for you, aren't I?' Alfie leant forward and patted George's shoulder. 'But, by the sounds of it, what with the tattoo and all, she's been sleeping with some barman behind your back.'

'She promised me she wasn't sleeping with him. They're just mates.' George tried to clear the lump from his throat. 'And I believe her.' He was almost certain he did.

'Come on, Georgie. There must be something going on there. I told you he was a dick, didn't I? The moment I saw him on the chav wagon.'

'You said he was gay.'

'Ok I was wrong there because he is clearly slipping your missus one' Alfie gulped down the last mouthful of his pint then slammed the glass on the table. It was as though he had struck his gavel and the case was closed. To Alfie, Ellie was a bitch. He'd decided and that was that. George placed his glass on the table and steadied his arms as his temper rose once more.

'She promised me that she's not cheating.'

69

'Oh, come on, mate. It's clear as a gin drinker's piss.'

Is it? In front of Alfie, George shrugged it off. But in reality, it was all he had thought about. Over and over again how he'd lost his girlfriend to someone like Jack. The bloke that had everyone gawping at him on the train. Including George. The ultimate bad boy – he knew he had no chance against someone like him. George had thought so much about the bloke that he was aware it bordered on obsessive.

'It's pretty obvious from where I'm sitting that she's been playing about. Why else would she have the same tattoo as him on her fucking vadge?'

George huffed. His friend's stupidity was doing his head in. 'It's not on her…*vadge*, Alf.'

'Arse cheek then. Exactly the same thing.'

'It really isn't. And it isn't on her arse cheek either.'

'Could be on her big toe for all I care, mate, it still means the same thing. Your missus has got the same tattoo as the bloke she's fucking.'

'I don't even know if it's the same as his. Fuck sakes, I don't fucking know anything. It's a blur. My head is so messed up right now. It actually hurts to think. Fuck, Alf! Say something to take my mind off of her. Please, anything.' He gulped down his drink.

Alfie scratched the mousey fuzz on his top lip. 'Why don't you see white dog shit anymore?'

George burst into laughter, way harder than he should have. He did all he could to stop the mouthful of alcohol shooting from his nostrils.

'All right, mate. Calm down, people are looking at us.' Alfie squirmed. 'It's not even funny, I'm being serious.'

'Sorry, Alf, I just haven't laughed for so long. I think I forgot how to.'

'It's been three days, you tart. Jesus. Its only Wednesday.'

George coughed out the last of his giggles, and found the motivation to sit up to empty his glass in one mouthful. Without needing to be told, Alfie slid out from the booth and headed for the bar. Alfie could be a little too shy when it came to getting a round in - his dole money only stretched so far. But Alfie always had his mates' backs and would never think twice about buying a friend in need a drink.

The pub was pretty empty, and the usual background music that poured through the wall speakers hadn't been turned on. Midweek drinking was clearly designated for the local alcoholics and women with sale bags. And the heartbroken. George stared at a bloke at the bar, dressed in tatty jeans and a jumper which had seen better days. The man was fifty at the most, but had about three teeth in his head and bloated skin from the booze. Was that his future?

Shifting his eyes to a couple of women sat at a small table, their shopping bags took up most of the floor space around them. They drank white wine and laughed every time the other spoke. Their happiness was sickening and George wondered if either of them had ever had a bad day in their lives.

'A couple of doubles for your troubles.' Alfie sang, handing George two glasses on his return.

'Cheers, Alf.' George sipped greedily. 'Ah, mate, I just wish I knew what I can do to change her mind. She said that she's been thinking about this since we got back from Thailand. That she's had proper anxiety about it all.'

Alfie rolled his eyes. 'Girls always have anxiety. Honestly, they think way too much about everything. It's why they have periods, you know– to let out some of the pressure from their brain.'

George stared wide-eyed at his friend in disbelief. Okay, Alfie wasn't the sharpest tool in the shed but that was a shocker, even for him. Swigging from his drink,

71

George shook the fuckery from his head 'What can I do to get her back?'

'You need to find out if she's cheating first. You don't want to pump in another man's dump.'

'Honestly, what the fuck is wrong with you today? You've had two pints and turned into a really shit philosopher. Seriously.'

'Sorry mate, but I say it how I see it. And I think she's cheated on you.'

Lifting the glass to his mouth, George hid his trembling lip. He needed to cry. He could feel it coming. But he'd be damned if he cried in The Swan.

'How am I gonna find out if it's him?' George managed to speak. 'I can't exactly storm down to the Cloud Bar and confront him, can I?

'Why the fuck not? The bloke might have looked the part of a bad boy but you can tell he's a pussy. Most probably a right mummy's boy. You could take him.'

'I don't want to fight him.'

'What you wanna do then? Ask him if he'll tattoo you too? Get your arse out for him like she did?'

'Fuck off, Alf.'

'I don't even know why you're bothered. Fuck her. She's not worth your time. Or your tears.'

'I'm not crying.'

'I bet you have been though.' Alfie leant forward and rested his hand on George's arm. It was an act of kindness he'd seldom received from Alfie and it made the emotions bubble up once more. 'Don't cry over her, mate. You're better than that.'

George took a long gulp of his drink. The warming sensation it gave didn't help the fact that he was already hot. Even though it was only April, the weather was warming up nicely and, in spite of that, the pub seemed to have every radiator on full blast. It was T-shirt weather most days but the landlord was convinced it was subarctic outside. George plucked an ice cube from the glass then rolled it around his tongue for a moment.

'I just want to talk to her. I want her to see that we're good together.' George pinched the bridge of his nose.

'You know I don't like being rude about girls, mate, but she's a dick.'

'Oi!' George clenched his jaw.

'Talking of dicks, here comes their number one fan.'

George didn't need to turn around to know that Aimee had just walked in. Alfie constantly accused her of being a slut. It was his go to insult. Yet, as far as George knew, she'd only been with two guys. One of which was her ex long-term boyfriend. Oh, and probably that bastard, Jack.

He needed to see a friendly face and Aimee had a way of cheering him up. She cheered everyone up. But George choked on his breath when she arrived at the table. Instead of her usually overly made-up face, Aimee didn't have a lick of make-up on and her pulled-back hair and shapeless tracksuit added to her miserable demeanour.

'What the fuck has happened to you? You look like shit.' Alfie shouted loudly enough for the two ladies with the shopping bags to glare their way.

'Thanks, Alf,' she answered coolly then embraced George. 'Babes, what the hell has happened?'

'Like you don't know,' Alfie barked. 'And why don't you have any make-up on? You look terrible.'

'Says you?' Aimee huffed. 'You're supposed to have two eyebrows, Alf.'

'I'm a bloke. I'm meant to be hairy.' He shrugged. 'Besides, you've normally got more make-up on than Ronald Mcfucking Donald.'

Aimee ignored Alfie and squeezed an arm around George's shoulder. 'What's happened babes?'

'Me and Ell.' George jutted his chin. 'We're on a break.'

She squeezed him even tighter. 'Oh, babes, I know. It's awful. I am so sorry.'

'Told you she knew.' Alfie cut in, his forehead lined with anger. 'I knew it. Hoes before bros and all that.'

'Do you ever stop?' Aimee moaned before facing George once more. 'Babes, she literally just told me over the phone. She said it had happened on Sunday. Why didn't you tell me?

George shrugged. 'Thought you knew already.' He stared at his drink rather than make eye contact with Aimee. He couldn't deal with the sympathetic looks. 'I thought Ellie would have told you.'

'Ells hasn't said anything to me before today. She's been ignoring my texts all week. I finally got hold of her and she told me you two had finished.'

'We're not finished!' George sat up straight. 'It's only a break! Until she sorts her head out.'

'Until she's finished fuckin that slum scum.' Alfie grimaced.

'Slum scum?' Aimee raised her unshaded eyebrows.

'The one that you took home on Friday night? Or don't you even remember who you sleep with these days?'

'Jack? What's he got to do with Ellie?' Her confused look gave Aimee some colour back on her face.

'He's been dicking her, hasn't he? Even tattooed his name on her arse.

'It's not his name.' George and Aimee replied in unison.

'Oh, come on. She's fucking him, and so has this one.' Alfie nodded to Aimee. 'That's what girls do, they fuck wrong'uns and mind-fuck the good guys.'

Aimee slammed her bag onto the table. 'I'm not *fucking* anyone. Mind or otherwise, thanks. Her face had turned the same shade of red as the beer mat. 'I'm sure Ells isn't either. And I didn't take him home.'

'He took you home then. Whatever. Just another girl who's dicknotised by a bad boy.'

'How do you know I went home with him? Not that it's any of your business. Besides, didn't you go home with that Katherine?'

'That's not the point. Besides, I'm a bloke.'

'So you're not a slag because you're a man, but I am?'

Alfie nodded.

'You know he don't actually mean that, Aims.' George interjected. He couldn't take the pair of them arguing when he needed it to be about him. 'But you can't blame us for being pissed off that you slept with Jack too. He's clearly an arsehole. He could be the reason me and Ells are on a break.'

'I'm going to say this one last time. I didn't sleep with him. And as far as I know, Ellie hasn't either. Jack isn't like that.'

Alfie clucked his tongue. 'Come on. You was damper than a council house every time he spoke to you.'

Aimee slapped Alfie's arm 'You're disgusting, you know that? Yes, I went back to his flat. He's a nice guy. But between you and me, I don't think I am his type. I doubt Ellie is either.'

'What does that mean?' George chucked back his drink.

'I don't know. I actually don't know anything more to tell you. But I'm not going to sit here and get slagged off for something I haven't done. And I'm not letting Ellie get ripped apart either. You hear me?'

Alfie was clearly taken aback by her seriousness. So was George for that matter. Aimee usually gave as good as she got from Alfie and even then some. That's what they did. That was their thing.

'All I'm saying, Aims, is that he has fucked two best friends and this idiot here won't do anything about it?'

'What's George meant to do? Go and beat the man up, like you would? And then get arrested and thrown in prison for GBH?'

'Damn right. And I'd be smiling on my mugshot.'

'You idiot. George isn't like that. He's not a total dickhead like you.'

'Well at this rate, all George has gotta do is bend over for the bloke.'

'Piss off, Alf.' George growled. 'You're not the one that has been cheated on, you're not the one whose girlfriend has just broke up with him.'

'Ah, so you admit it. You have broken up with her?'

'God sakes, I don't know! I really don't. I can't even think about it. I just wanna get drunk with my mates.'

George lifted his glass and emptied the contents down his throat, closing his eyes to savour the effects of its magic. Alfie and Aimee shot each other a look, one that George recognised as being apologetic, but Alfie's body language remained taught. He clearly had more to say but George prayed that he wouldn't. He had no fight left in him.

'Sorry babes.'

'Yeah sorry, mate. I was outers. Just don't like seeing my mate like this.'

'Alf, it's cool.'

They sat there in silence for a moment or two, George didn't know what to say and sure as hell didn't want Alfie to rant anymore. He hoped Aimee would step in with something stupid, something that would make them all laugh and take the drama away. She didn't. Instead, she sat in silence, studying her bare fingernails.

'Right, let's get princess George pissed.' Alfie finally ended the silence. 'Aims, what you drinking?'

'Na, I'm good, thanks.'

'What?' George and Alfie asked in unison.

'Oh shut up. I've got some stuff going on at home.'

'You're not pregnant, are you?' Alfie didn't blink.

Aimee huffed then ran her tongue over her teeth. A tear ran down her cheek. 'Get me a lemonade. I really can't drink tonight. I have too much on my mind.'

Clutching her handbag, Aimee slid out of the booth then rushed towards the ladies toilet at the other side of the pub. It had been so long since George had seen her cry that he didn't know how to react to it. Not that he had the energy to. He was more interested in Ellie, and why she hadn't answered his last four texts. Images of her and, Jack together filled his brain and he necked more of his drink to blank them out.

'What is up with her?' Alfie asked. Clearly worried about her, his face drained of all colour. 'You don't think she is pregnant, do you? Fucking hell, what if that Jack geezer is the father?'

Hasn't that wanker Jack caused enough trouble already?

'I dunno.' George slid his phone from his pocket and opened his text messages. Still nothing more from Ellie. Nothing from anyone. Was he that unloved? Sighing, he downed his other drink in one and slouched further into the seat. 'She's most probably just being dramatic.'

Chapter Ten

Hunched over, at the desk he'd made from a couple of old wooden pallets, Jack pressed the tattoo needle into his skin - his left arm being his canvas of choice. There were only a few bare patches left on his tattoo sleeve and one on his chest. For some fucked up reason, he'd saved them for something truly meaningful. Like, maybe once he'd reconciled with his mum, he'd think of something. A piece that connected them both as Mother and son. But the needle had already pierced into his shaven wrist and one of those fucking patches was being contaminated with black ink.

Or maybe even for the *girl* that would eventually steal his heart. The one he'd fall head over heels for, like how everyone had always promised. Like those lobotomy inducing nineties rom-coms that they had to watch in the care homes when he was a teenager. That shit scarred him more than any tattoo.

The wad of cash that Cole had given him still lay on the arm of the sofa where he'd left it. It called Jack's name at least every five minutes. Like a beacon, it shone all the possibilities that he could do with it. Set himself up with a better, less noisy tattoo machine – a brand spanking new one from the shop in Bethnal Green. Maybe finally buy another set of bedding or even bloody lampshades. Jack didn't even know how much was in it. All he knew is that he wouldn't spend a penny of it. He couldn't. Even if the cash was Cole's to give away, it was dodgy. No doubt earned from someone else's pain.

But what pissed him off the most was the fella's words. Cole wasn't right about many things, but Jack not being able to make a go of it with his past "girlfriends" was bang on. Every girl that had ever shown an interest—the ones from school, college, the bars he'd worked at, even Aimee—no matter how hard he tried to feel something back, there was nothing there. Not for anyone. Not even friends.

Sighing, Jack lifted his head away for a moment to observe his life. Well, his living room. Actually, just a room. There was no living that went on there. Just him, in the dark.

The place was a minimalist's dream. Curtesy of hand-me-down furniture and a charity shop rug. The only things of any importance was his tattoo gun and the pile of records. Those were the things he'd worked his arse off to buy. Ten, twelve, eighteen hour shifts every day, just to have something to cherish. Music and tattoos went hand in hand for him. Both held more meaning than any relationship ever could.

Romance wasn't a thing he went looking for. In all honesty, he didn't even understand it. The idea of two people committing their entire lives to each other, forever, baffled him. Surely one of them would only end up getting hurt.

It's not like he didn't get the attention from girls. Far from it. The messages on his phone were proof of that. In fact, he didn't know why he kept giving out his fucking number. It wasn't like he was ever going to text them back. Ask them on a date. He'd react how he'd always had; hiding in his shell whenever anyone showed the slightest interest. Like Ellie had. He knew full well that Ellie didn't really want him. He knew she was confused. He knew she was struggling with growing up. She'd become discontent with her small-town life and wanted something bigger. London. Excitement. The beautiful girl, with a heart of gold, had discovered a new existence away from everything and everyone she knew. But what Jack didn't' know is why he'd become so preoccupied with Ellie's boyfriend, George.

Flashbacks of when he'd met him at the garden of the Cloud Bar had somehow expanded into full-blown memories. Ones he wasn't sure were reality. Yet, regardless, he'd recall whenever the world was quiet enough for him to think. The fella's blue eyes usually came to mind. Actually, they were his main thought. Jack had realised too, that what he'd first deemed as a vagueness in the bloke was actually just someone way out of his depth. The fella had traipsed all the way to London to see his girlfriend and ended up being surrounded by hundreds of strangers and peaking way too early.

Guilt gripped Jack's insides. It wasn't because of Ellie – he'd never kissed the girl back. Hadn't even led her on. But he had been a dick to George. Practically ignoring him and showing nothing but disdain whenever the fella spoke to him. He wondered how many people he'd done the same to over the years.

Huffing, he scooted over to his stack of records and let his index finger run over the covers, confident that it would stop once it found the right one. Eleven records down and there it was. His finger had found the perfect song to alleviate his mood. Ziggy Stardust would do it, all right.

He sparked a cigarette and let the smoke settle in his lungs as Bowie's voice pacified him. He didn't know what tattoo he'd started to etch into his own skin, he just knew that it had to be something that reflected his mood. And at that very moment, it hadn't been a good one. The walking cliché of the fella dressed in eternal black and actually being a miserable bastard too. He'd always wished his choice of colour would have been for something dark, brooding, different from the rest. But it wasn't. It was purely to hide the dirt. He couldn't afford to wash his clothes every day and black helped that. A lot.

Once his monthly rent and bills hand been settled, his pay packet allowed him to put a few quid on the electric meter as well as buying a basketful of cheap frozen pizzas, a can of deodorant and a packet of fags. But that was it. The rest of his wages went to the dickhead bouncer. He thanked his lucky stars that the shit storm was over and done with. Two days after payday and he was back to being broke.

He took a long drag of his cigarette as the metal machine scraped through his skin and took comfort in the vibrations that niggled into his wrist bone. It was a soothing pain, a scratching sensation more than anything, and it was the distraction he needed from being inside his own head.

Sinking the needle deeper into his wrist, not caring about the burning sensation that snaked up his arm, an outline of a small Jack-o-lantern had formed without him even realising. Halloween everyday can't be a bad thing, right? Sniffing, Jack had no idea what it meant. Only that it was shit. One of the worst things he'd ever drawn on himself. Drawn full stop. But it was him in a nutshell. Hollow.

As he dipped the needle in the tiny plastic pot of black ink, ready to sharpen the curves, all he knew was that he didn't want to be that person anymore. He couldn't be the bloke with a tenner on the electricity meter and just enough frozen meals to last him a fortnight. The bloke that lived half his life in the dark with huge black butterflies in his stomach every time someone knocked at the front door.

He couldn't be the bloke he'd so desperately tried to avoid. He couldn't be him. He needed to change, just like Ellie had.

But unlike her, he didn't want the hustle and bustle anymore. The endless late nights and wasted days. He wanted the quiet life. Family and Friends.

Real ones.

Chapter Eleven

Flicking through the playlists stored in his phone, George didn't care if the music woke the girl next to him. He was too interested in finding the most depressing song to care about her. He'd woken at the crack of dawn with a hangover pulsating in his skull and began his daily ritual of self-pity earlier than usual. He needed a melody to match his mood. Something that could keep him grounded to the emotion that he'd been living in. It'd been almost eight weeks since he had seen Ellie - eight weeks since she had told him she wanted a break from their relationship and his world had fallen apart. Well, fifty four days and eleven hours, in fact. Not that he was counting or anything.

He hated how he'd been feeling. He did. The chest pains, the nausea that came with not eating, the complete and utter darkness that shrouded his very existence. But he needed those things to keep Ellie fresh in his mind.

They'd only spoken a handful of times - over text when they did and George was fully aware that he'd become a needy bastard. Thinking up any reason to contact her, from the breezy "hey" to stupidly feigning illness, George had well and truly scraped the bottom of the cringe barrel.

George pined for Ellie. Simple as that. He missed everything about her. From that beautiful white smile, the way she'd pull her long blonde hair over her shoulder, even the tiny freckle on her little toe.

Everyone he'd spoken to, who'd obviously never suffered as much as George had, offered their two pennies worth. The lie that "time was a great healer" came up every time he had the audacity to shrug. Yet the more days that passed, the more it hurt. He couldn't hear her name without choking and the ache in his chest had become a sledge hammer to the ribs. The thought of dying alone at the ripe old age of nineteen stopped George from smiling. From being happy. There wasn't a thing on the planet that actually made him happy anymore. Alcohol helped. Wine, vodka, bourbon, gin and anything he could pour down his neck before the last bell triggered a panic attack. Getting drunk as quickly and cheaply as possible had become a pastime. Being at home was far too lonely. Unbearable, in fact. His family didn't understand. How could they? But the pub was always loud, always stocked and there to numb him.

Without Ellie in his life, he'd grown obsessed with her social media profiles, almost to the point of stalking. Those double-edged swords allowed him to see a new selfie of her beautiful face every day yet forced him to bear witness, usually blinking through tears, to seeing random guys posing next to her on nights out – some with their arms around her. Some with hands *on* her. Alfie and Aimee had begged him to deactivate his accounts, for his own mental health. But something compelled him. He needed evidence. Proof. That she'd been stolen from him and didn't leave by her own free will. That she'd left him for Jack. He needed to see the bastard holding her or something. Anything. A tattooed arm wrapped around her shoulder would have been enough. But there was no sign of him. Nothing. The fella's absence had caused such a pain in his gut that George wasn't sure if his obsession was for Ellie or Jack.

Despite having his family and Alfie and Aimee, of course, George couldn't shake the sadness that haunted him. Like a merciless fist squeezing his heart every time he was alone. The evenings were the worst, for sure.

Nightfall brought a bleakness he couldn't escape. When others found contentment, loneliness attacked him as the world went silent. He needed someone to be close with. To feel. Someone who could plug the void until Ellie came to her senses. And the girl sleeping in his bed next to him was exactly that.

George had no feelings for Jodie. *None*. He didn't know much about her - to be honest, he wasn't confident of her last name. But she seemed sweet enough and was a bloody good distraction from his shitty life whenever he'd get pissed and needed someone. Something. Anything, in fact. So it wasn't long before George gave into Alfie's instructions and found a rebound.

Jodie moaned under the duvet – the kind of half-asleep stage where every song change on his phone caused her to fidget. He wanted her to wake up and leave. To not make it awkward, or worsen his hangover and to just slip out of his life until the next time he needed to feel.

He'd met her on a night out with Alfie. To shut the fella up, he'd took her number and promised to call. Which he did. Every night since. Intoxicated on house wine and desperate to be wanted, he'd told her everything she needed to hear – convinced her she wasn't a rebound. He had to. Otherwise he'd have to admit to himself that he was just pathetic.

Alfie had been blinding. The fella was always up for a drink. Dole permitting. But George's wages had proven to stretch to anyone who was willing to help him get drunk. Aimee hadn't been as supportive. She was a blubbering mess every time he'd seen her, she seemed distant. Even though she'd explained that she wasn't pregnant with Jack's baby, not pregnant at all, actually, she wasn't herself. He suspected that his and Ellie's break had hit Aimee hard too. But, upset or not, he couldn't be around her whilst she was being a grief-thief of his heartache.

Quite easily, George let their threesome diminish into just him and Alfie getting pissed on the regular.

He observed Jodie sleeping for a moment, his eyes scanning the shape of her. Laying down, she appeared the same height as Ellie, and the same size frame too. But he knew that wasn't really the case. Jodie was more petite, fragile even, and her breasts were smaller. Not flat or even that small, just nowhere near as perfect as Ellie's. Jodie was pretty, no doubt about it. With blue eyes and long blonde hair – sun kissed skin from a recent trip to Greece. She reminded him of *her*. Not the new-fangled brunette Ellie that hopped around the London scene with her new hipster friends and went for brunch after a messy night out. But the sweet girl from the countryside who loved him. The one-day mother of his children. But Jodie wasn't her. He knew that.

'Morning, cutie.' Jodie rolled over to face him and tucked the duvet down under her chin. She beamed. Even first thing in the morning she seemed happy to see him.

'Its seven a.m.' Keeping his eyes on his phone, George flinched as she stretched her arm over his chest. He couldn't handle a cuddle from her. That was too much. 'I need a shower.'

'How long have you been awake?' Yawning, she cosied into his side and rested her head onto his shoulder. 'I hope you weren't watching me sleep.'

George tensed, trying to pull himself away. But she had hold of him. 'About half an hour. And no.' 'I wasn't watching you.' His cheeks reddened at his lie, but he knew she wanted him to watch her for different reasons.

She squeezed him tighter, seemingly unaware of his discomfort. 'That's a shame. I've heard that's something people do when they're starting out.'

Did she really think they were starting out? 'I've got to have a shower.' He cleared his throat, hoping she'd take the hint.

'Can't we just snuggle like this for a bit?'

George wriggled away, forcing Jodie from his shoulder. Guilt gripped his guts as she slumped to the pillow pouting. He just couldn't be doing with that lovey dovey shit. He wanted Ellie, not someone *needier* than himself. 'Sorry, I've got to get ready for work. I start at eight.' He lowered his eyes to avoid the awkwardness of his next words. 'Oh, and my parents are downstairs so please don't make too much noise on your way out otherwise they'll want to chat.'

Jodie sat up next to him, her hand trying to grab hold of his. 'That's ok, your mum seems lovely. But I thought you weren't working today. When you rang me last night, you said we could spend the day together.'

George cringed. 'Listen, Jodie, I'm sorry but I was drunk. I don't know what I said.' He hated how he sounded. Like the Grade A prick who lied to get girls into bed. But he just couldn't have her there, feeding his guilt that he was betraying Ellie. He knew he wasn't even cheating on his girlfriend. Ex-girlfriend. Whatever she was.

'Georgie.' Jodie finally seemed to take the hint and pulled her hand away from his, clutching the duvet to cover her breasts instead. 'If we are going to get together properly, then you can't keep treating me like this.'

George slipped out of the bed, still managing to keep all eye contact on anything but her. Instead, he kicked around the "floordrobe" that his room had become in search of his lounge pants. 'Wait, who said anything about getting together?'

Her jaw fell open. 'You did. Last night. Or don't you remember that either?' Her tone let him know she was pissed off.

Finding the jersey material bottoms with his big toe, he kicked the pants in the air and caught them before finally facing her. 'I don't know what I say when I phone you up.

I'm sorry, like I said, I was drunk. I'm really sorry but I need a shower. And you need to leave. Please.'

'Are you serious? After everything you said last night?' Her cheeks reddened and her eyes narrowed – like he didn't already know she was angry.

'Honestly, Jodie. I'm sorry. By the time I call you, I've normally spent forty quid on booze and I'm off my nut. I don't remember what I say, just that I need......well.....I dunno.' To feel. Something. Anything.

'Just need what?' She raised a brow then her face turned pillar box red. 'Sex? You just need sex? O M G, after you swore to me that you wasn't using me? You arsehole.'

Guilt flooded him. Half for betraying Ellie, half for how he'd treated Jodie. She deserved a lot better than him. They both did. He knew he needed to do the right thing and end it there and then. He never once used her for sex. He couldn't even remember doing it. He just wanted someone to sleep next to.

'Yes.' He lied. 'I used you for sex. Every time.'

She crawled out of the bottom of the bed, cursing to herself as she gathered her clothes. Pulling on her bra, he spun on his heel - he'd already been enough of a wanker to the poor girl without leering over her.

'You know what, Georgie?' She hoiked up her skirt then lowered a top over her head. 'I'm not doing this anymore. I'm through with you. You're hot one minute, cold the next. You're like the fucking menopause. You don't give a damn about me. Or anyone for that matter. All you care about is yourself.' She slammed a hand on her hip, clearly frustrated he had his back to her. 'Can you hear me?''

'Everyone can hear you, Jodie.' He grumbled, cringing to death under the mess he'd caused.

'What gives you the right to treat me like this? To be so cruel to me? You phone me up being so sweet, crying that you miss me. Telling me that you want us to be together. And then you act like this.'

Shrugging, George bit his lip. He wanted to shout aloud how fucking lonely he was. To shake everyone and tell them he wasn't coping. At all. Instead, he grabbed a dirty T-shirt from the floor then cleared his throat. He couldn't make eye contact again - the confrontation clawed way too deep into his dehydrated brain.

'Well, I'm done. I'm not some hoe you can call up whenever you want a fuck.'

'Then I don't need you.' He lied again.

'You're disgusting.' Anger shot from her pretty blue eyes.

In a split second he saw something in Jodie that reminded him of Ellie. A passion. That glint of instant rage that made her even more beautiful to him. The look that drove him crazy with lust. But in an instant, the look on Jodie's face softened and everything was wrong again. She wasn't Ellie.

'Just go. I can't be late for work.' That part was true. Too many late mornings, most being hungover, sometimes still drunk, had landed him in the shit with Knobert.

'Don't call or message me. I don't ever want to hear from you again. And I def don't want to see your pathetic face again.'

He clenched his jaw. Guilt, anger and self-pity flooded him all at once. 'Fuck off then.' He met her gaze once more, not giving a flying fuck if she hated him or not. 'Don't come back. Block me. I don't give a shit. Don't ever speak to me again if you don't want. I'M USED TO IT!'

Lingering at the door, it was obvious she wanted him to say something more. Her eyes were watery and her brow lined. Maybe she wanted him to persuade her to stay. Or apologise for acting like a complete dickmunch.

He couldn't do either.

Without another word, she grabbed her denim jacket from the coat hook and stormed from his room with her flip flops clutched to her chest.

He heard her footsteps down the stairs, then into the hall and out of the front door. He swallowed down the pain of being abandoned.

And there he was, alone. Again.

After his attempt to shower away his shame, George scrubbed the furry taste of last night's alcohol from his teeth and tongue then threw on his dressing gown. His hangover had kicked in big time, and with it, a bad mood – worse than before, had settled in.

Downstairs in the kitchen, his mother stood by the window, staring idly at the ornate bird's table on the patio. She was petrified of anything with wings – once even calling the RSPCA because a pair of wood pigeons "refused" to leave the garden. Yet still, she insisted that the birds had fresh seeds and water every morning. His father was sat at the kitchen table, his dark blue eyes fixed firmly on the property pages of the free local newspaper. As per.

'Morning, darlin. Did I hear your *friend* leave?' Maxine's smile seemed sincere yet he could see the worry in her eyes. He hoped she'd go back to staring at the sparrows. It was the same look she'd been giving him every morning for over a month. Rubbing his arm, she then quickly poured out a cup of tea from the pot for him. 'It'd be nice to meet her properly one of these days, you know.'

'You don't have to worry about that.' George cleared his throat, desperate not to be dragged into small talk.

'Oh no, why?'

He huffed. 'Jodie won't be coming back, mum.'

'Georgie, if you've ended it with her then I hope you was a gentleman about it.'

'There was nothing to end. We weren't together or anything.' He snorted. 'I don't even know her last name.'

Maxine pursed her lips and shook her head. 'That's nothing to be proud of, darlin. I never raised you to treat women like that. It's obvious that poor girl likes you.'

'That's why I won't be seeing her anymore. It's not fair on her.'

'Well, that's good, then. But you should never have made any promises to her to begin with, though.'

George sipped the hot tea, willing it to cool down so he could knock it back and get the hell out of there. 'I didn't promise anything. It's not my fault she's a mug.'

'Georgie!' Maxine's screech clearly got his father's attention as the newspaper was laid flat onto the table. He waited for his father's words of wisdom.

George had no idea he'd even been listening. In fact, George had zero fucks left. His father wasn't the chattiest of fellas at home – there was no one to sell houses to there – and so often kept out of all discussions unless Maxine demanded. 'Your mother is right.' His dad brought his coffee cup to his lips but didn't drink – the sign that Steve Taylor was about to say something profound. It never was. 'You can't treat ladies that way. And you don't talk about them like that either. It's not how the Taylors do things, son. How do you think it'll look for the family business?'

Tea burned through George's nostrils as it came shooting from his nose. The delusion was too real for him to ignore. 'Give me a break. Like me having sex with a girl will ruin your company's reputation. No one gives a fuck about stuff like that.'

'Georgie. Don't say eff.'

Steve glared at him. 'I give a fuck about it. Your mother gives a fuck about it too.' His father smiled at her in a clear attempt to apologies for his language. 'The truth of the matter is, you can't keep on acting the way you are. Going out every night getting wasted. Picking up girls every time you get blotto. Not to mention I've had two phone calls this week from Boris at The Swan, saying you're passed out in the beer garden. I get it, son. I was your age once. But if you miss Ellie, then miss her. Don't go getting shitfaced and knocking up every girl in Coggletree until you get over her.'

George gulped down a mouthful of tea. His dad's philosophies were enough to make his piss boil at the best of times. But he was bang out of order for bringing up Ellie. No one knew what he was going through. No one.

'Whatever, dad. I'm nineteen. I can do what I want.'

Steve stood and glared his son. George knew what was coming. *Great.* 'Not under my roof, you can't.'

'Stevie, let's not do this again.' His mother's eyes seemed to plead with her husband.

George took a deep breath. Sick to death of another round of house rules, he slammed his tea cup into the counter. 'No, its fine mum. I'm clearly not welcome here. Fine, I'll move out.'

'Oh come on, how about I butter you some crumpets. I don't want my boys arguing.'

George didn't want food. All he wanted was for his parents to get out of his fucking business and leave him alone. But by the look his father gave, who had picked up the coffee cup once more, it wasn't going to be that way.

'No, fuck it. That's it.' George shouted. Anger running through his veins. He then stormed up the stairs, fighting the burning sensation in his eyelids. 'Nobody gives a shit about me, anyway.'

Chapter Twelve

A shitty grey and wet morning on the farm mellowed into a more summer-like afternoon and George welcomed the sun on his back. With the hangover pulsating in his head, he'd volunteered to spend the day mucking out the pig sties in an attempt to forget the real shit in his life.

What started as a game – of how long he could not think about Ellie for – had soon became the only thing that got him through most days. He'd jump to do the jobs the others hated as it allowed him to be on his own and not have to make small talk. Sadly, those jobs were mainly clearing up eternal mounds of animal shit and chasing the bastard goats and alpaca that had escaped into the neighbouring fields. The other workers at the farm likely saw him as a jobsworth, a brown-noser to the boss. Not that he gave a fuck what they thought. But being busy helped him function when he had to be sober. And work sure was busy. The nonstop slog that came with being Perrygate Farm's newest apprentice was a great place to find escape in the day. Even with the dickhead supervisor, it let him block out all the misery in his life until drink made him forget it entirely.

As back-breaking as the work was, he hadn't given the manual labour a second thought when he'd first applied for the apprenticeship. His main concern was how to tell Ellie that he didn't want to go to uni anymore, and instead, wanted to learn on the farm. Not to mention breaking the news to his mother. Not that she ever had her heart set on him being an academic like Ellie had, or joining the family business like his father did. She just wanted him to be happy. But being slightly overprotective, well, almost to the point of smothering, she was more worried that her little boy would freeze to death in winter or be killed by a horse stampede in the paddocks. The first time his sister, Darcie, went on holiday without the family, his mother wanted his dad to phone up Spain to tell them to look after her. For him, Maxine had insisted on his Nan knitting him matching gloves, scarf and hat for the winter. And long-johns too. He didn't even know if his Nan could knit. The only white sticks he'd ever seen in her bony fingers were menthols.

As luck would have it, the weather had been nigh on perfect all spring. Not too hot, but nowhere near cold. A spot of rain in the mornings, mild in the afternoon and a light breeze in the evenings – the kind of weather that clears the air. Makes you think. Of course, just as everything else did, it reminded him of Ellie. Spring was theirs. From the moment the weather warmed up and the daffodils spread over the hills. For the three previous years, they'd spent the season laying on picnic blankets in the fields, planning their entire lives together as they spotted shapes in the clouds above.

Now, he spent his days with the animals at the farm instead, surrounded by the birdsong and the constant cackles of *his* magpies. The animals were his favorite part of the job, even though they couldn't see a Tyrannosaurus Rex drifting in the skies or bring him jam sandwiches in a picnic basket. But they were his pals. Silent friends who didn't judge his choices, or moan that he stank of last night's booze. Above all, were always happy to see him. Especially the alpacas for which he had a very soft spot for. The fuzzy monsters that constantly wrecked the stables and annoyed the shit out of the horses on the daily.

Having just chased down the youngest alpaca of the herd – the epitome of the terrible twos on four legs - George panted as he fumbled with the harness. Already pissed off with having to run through a field in steel-cap boots, and the remnants of that morning's hangover curling in his gut, annoyance prickled his spine as he heard the crunching of the stony path – knowing exactly who was coming towards him.

'Hey Kiddo.' Knobert climbed the small slope up to the gate. Dressed in wellies, shorts, anorak and those fly's arse sunglasses, George cringed, trying to decipher which season his supervisor was going for. 'I heard you actually made it on time this morning. What happened? You shit the bed?' His chortle made him look more of a dick than he already did.

'I've been on time all week.' George raised an eyebrow, not bothering to hide his disdain.

'Well, you're late now. It's gone five and you still haven't got the alpacas in the stables. You won't get paid for staying later.'

He huffed. 'I'm getting them in for the night now.' George clipped the harness around the white alpaca's neck and scratched the animal behind the ears to calm her. 'It's not easy getting them in, Kno...Robert.'

'How many times, Kiddo? Call me Robbie. I want to be a boss you can talk to.'

George folded his arms, waiting for bullshit to spew from the fella's lips.

'Anyway, kiddo, The Sausage and Cider Fest lot are on their way. They're using the east field, both entrances, so we need to get the animals locked in A-SAP.'

George snorted to himself. There was no 'we' involved when it came to working with Knobert. He was blinding at watching though.

'What time's the vans getting here?' George grumbled, his arm yanked by the alpaca, who was obviously keen to inspect Knobert a little closer.

'About an hour. Looks like it's gonna be a good one this year. Essex's biggest one yet. Can....not...wait.' He sang.

George let the animal sniff the fellas face and hair and watched as it started to nibble the wooden toggles hanging from his anorak. George didn't say anything, he just watched, half amused, as Knobert squirmed with the alpaca so close to him. It was obvious that the fella had never worked a day with animals in his life.

'You're going then?' George coughed out his laughter then finally pulled the alpaca away from him.

'Course, got tickets weeks ago. No doubt you'll be going too. My spies tell me you like a drink these days.'

'Yeah?' George avoided eye contact. Not through shame – who was a moron like Knobert to judge him? But because he couldn't bear the fella's cringe-worthy smugness.

'My brother said he saw you in The Swan last night. He said you was off your nut.'

'I wasn't.' He shrugged it off.

'We've sorted out your lateness but I can't have my staff rocking up to work drunk, kiddo.'

'I'm not drunk. I wasn't last night either. I just had a few drinks.'

'On a work night?' He laughed, making George cringe. 'I'm not having a go. You're a good kid and you *try* really hard. But if the big boss knew you weren't taking this seriously, you can kiss your apprenticeship goodbye.'

George straightened his back. 'I am taking it seriously, Knobert...I mean Robert. I really am.'

The fella glared at him, for a little longer than George could stomach. He was judging him. He could feel it.

Even though the wanker was smiling. 'So, will I be seeing you pissed tomorrow then? At the festival?'

'I didn't get tickets. Been a bit preoccupied.'

'Ah, with the missus? Still playing away with that bloke from London? I heard you've got a new girl on the go anyway.'

Swallowing down the guilt climbing in his chest, he cleared his throat. 'No, actually, I meant with work.' George shrugged it off, hoping that his supervisor couldn't pick up on his rage. He'd hate to give the fella the satisfaction.

'Saw your mum in the butchers the other week. Told me all about it.'

'My mum doesn't know what she's talking about. Ellie isn't with anyone. He's a barman that tattooed her. And she's not even with him.'

'Sorry kiddo. Didn't mean to upset you.' Knobert smirked - George didn't know if he was being sincere or not. In truth, he didn't know why he cared. 'Anyways, all sold out now. You've gotta be on the ball with these things.'

'Yeah, I guess you do.' George mumbled, wishing that their encounter would just fucking end.

Knobert backed away from the fence, his hand searching around the hood of his anorak for the toggle. George watched, with some relish, whilst the fella's face became nothing more than a double-chinned grimace as he searched for it. He didn't bother to tell him that it was on its way to the alpaca's stomach.

****

'Hello darlin, you're home late.' George's mother half-grinned and half-yawned.

George plonked his work bag on the living room floor, waiting for his mother to yell at him for dirtying her mocha carpet, but to his surprise, she didn't seem to notice.

He was only there to get changed before going to the pub. He just hoped she wouldn't bring up the argument between him and his father that morning.

Maxine was on the reclining arm chair, legs risen with a half cup of beige tea on the table beside her. Her eyes were puffy, like she'd just woken up, although her favourite game show was on the telly. She never missed the damn show and it's presenter in yet another striped shirt. So obsessed, she'd do ninety miles per hour down the bending lanes, almost killing herself and any passenger she had in the car, just to get home to watch it.

On the three-seater was his Nan's leopard print handbag yet George couldn't smell smoke. The two usually went hand in hand. Literally.

'Not bad.' George shrugged. 'I spoke with Knobert from work today, said he saw you.'

'Yeah, in the butchers. What a lovely boy. You see the stuff he wears though? Those sunglasses.' She shook her head.

George wanted to ask her why the fuck she'd been talking about his and Ellie's relationship with Knobert, of all people, but he knew his mother wouldn't remember what she had even said.

'Is Nan here?' George asked instead.

'She's spending a penny, darlin.'

'Can't smell her fags.'

'She's on one of them thingies. You know, it's like a plug in thing.'

'A vape?'

'No, darlin, this is my programme.' She didn't take her eyes away from the Television.'

'What you talking about? You been drinking or something?' Jealousy rushed over George.

'No, I'm just exhausted. I haven't sat down all day, Georgie. Got a pedicure this morning. You will not believe the amount of hard skin I had on my heels - no wonder my bed sheets have gone all bobbly. Then I had a massage and *then* had to get my roots done in town at two. I was pooped before I met the girls for a late lunch at Ziggies. It's done me in. I'll have to order dinner in tonight, I'm too tired to cook.'

George stared at his mother in disbelief. Every muscle in his body ached from working all day on the farm and his head pounded from the heat. And dehydration most probably. – Yet his mother was flat-lined from having poxy lunch. No matter how many times he had heard them, her "busy day" stories, they never failed to shock him. A pair of Jehovah Witnesses knocked on the door once, and she was so exhausted from it that she searched through holiday brochures for two days straight to find a sunny beach far away from the stress.

'Sounds like you've been rushed off your feet, Mum.' George sniggered. He couldn't deal with someone else's bullshit as well as his own.

'I have. Had to do the food shopping off-the-line too because I couldn't face the supermarket.'

'Mum, how many times? It's called online.'

'I can't keep up with all the lingo Georgie, we didn't have the internet when I was your age.'

'I'd never have guessed.' He smirked.

'Besides, now that Darcie's deserted me, there's no point me doing any proper food shopping is there?'

'Darcie hasn't deserted you.' He huffed – bored of the drama his sister moving out had caused. 'She's twenty three years old and has moved two minutes down the road with her boyfriend. You can't be mad about that. At least one of your children are happy.'

'Oh, darlin.' She momentarily looked away from the TV. 'You'll be happy again soon. Ellie will come round. You're so good together.'

'If you say so.' He shrugged, mentally counting the hours, or rather, minutes until he could start drinking.

Taking a deep breath, he rolled his head on his shoulders to relieve the ache in his neck. 'Anyways, Mum, you have me and Dad. And Nan's always here. You moan that you can't get rid of her.'

'I do no such thing. I've asked her to stay for dinner tonight actually. I'm gonna make her something lovely.'

'You said we ordering in.'

'It's the same thing, darlin. Whether I cook it or the Chinese do. Your Nan will understand.'

'I'll understand what?' George's Nan asked as she entered the living room behind him.

She took her seat next to her handbag, the same seat she sat in every time she was there and began to root around in her bag.

'If I order a takeaway in rather than cook for you, Mum.'

'I'll prefer it to be honest, Maxine. Your cooking is atrocious.'

George stifled a laugh. He loved his mum but cooking wasn't her strong point. Just as tact wasn't his Nan's.

'What's wrong with you, love?' His grandmother asked with a wink then sucked on her bright red e-cigarette. 'You look like you've got the weight of the world on yours shoulders.'

Snorting, he shrugged. 'My life's shit, Nan.'

She raised her eyebrows, obviously uninterested in his moping. 'You still knocking round with that girl?'

'Jodie?' George shook his head, fearing his mother would join in the conversation.

'That's a shame. It'll do you good to move on.' His Nan blew out a huge cloud of strawberry-smelling smoke.

The white cloud was so large that she temporarily disappeared behind it. 'A lad your age shouldn't be moping over his ex. Go and sow your oats.'

'Don't tell him that, Mum. He loves Ellie. He misses her. Maxine replied – always ready to defend her boy, Georgie.

'Don't talk to me about missing things. The doctor's got me puffing on one of these bloody things instead of my menthols. They're nothing like proper ciggies. And I feel like a fucking genie with all this smoke.'

'It's better for you, Nan. You'll live longer.'

'Oh great. What am I gonna do? Sit here in twenty years' time watching this shit on telly whilst your mum tries to poison me with her cooking?'

George laughed, so much so that he had to turn away from her. Her waving through a huge smoke cloud made it worse.

'I'm going to get changed before I head out. You want a tea before I go upstairs?' George asked.

'Where you off to? Not the pub again, Georgie?' Maxine paused the telly. Both he and his Nan gawped in disbelief.

'Yes. I'm meeting Alfie.'

'Oh, Georgie. Stay in with us. We'll get whatever takeaway you want. I'll see what's on the movie channels, yeah?'

'I'm only going for a couple.' He lied. 'I've got things to do tomorrow' He lied again. 'You want a tea, or not?'

'Yes please, darlin.'

'Nan?'

'Oh, go on then, love. Coffee though, two sugars. Your mum keeps buying those cheap teabags. Tastes worse than her cooking.'

In the kitchen, George turned to fetch the milk, but his heart cannon-balled to the pit of his stomach when he saw the photo of him and Ellie on the front of the fridge.

Attached to the black door by a love heart shaped magnet. It was a picture of them in Thailand. The smiles on their faces giving no clue of what was to come. He guessed his mum had put it there to cheer him up, She always claimed she had the best intentions when interfering with his life.

The doorbell rang and George looked up at the clock. Five minutes past six. Either his dad was early and forgot his keys or his mum would need a couple more holiday brochures.

Fearing it was his father, and not ready for another run-in, he hurried with the milk in an attempt to get out of his way and avoid another argument. Instead, moments later, Aimee walked into the kitchen, dressed in her white beautician uniform from the salon. George hadn't see her in a while, almost three weeks, and was shocked to see the shade of fake tan she sported.

'Hey, Georgie. You all right, babes?'

He ignored the question. 'Want a cuppa?'

'No thanks, babes. Only popped in to see if you fancy doing something this weekend. I haven't seen you in, like, forever.'

He kept his gaze on the mugs. 'Aims, I'm sorry…. I….'

'Oh shut up. I know you're going through your own stuff, what with Ells and all that. It's ok. Really.'

He shrugged then tilted his head, waiting for some well-earned sympathy to come his way. 'It must have been hard on you too, Aims. Me and Ellie are a big part of your life. As a couple.'

Raising an eyebrow, she stared at him for a moment. 'Actually I'm going through some family stuff. But you've got too much going on for me to burden you with it.'

Nodding, George didn't delve any further. Knowing Aimee, her problems were nothing compared to his. 'You sure you don't want a drink?'

'Yeah. Thanks. I'm not gonna stay long, gotta get some of this tan off.' Aimee licked her thumb then began scrubbing her skin.

Back in the front room, George passed Maxine her cup and placed his own onto the cream mantelpiece. Much to his mother's disapproval. She then cooed over Aimee's nails and asked if she could do something similar for her.

'Yeah, come in tomorrow, Maxine. I'm in until noon. I'll do them for you.'

'Thanks, darlin.' His mother was instantly giddy. He wondered how exhausted she'd be after that.

'Don't you look lovely?' George's Nan said as she took the coffee mug from Aimee and invited her to take the seat beside her. 'You had your tan done?'

'Yes, Mrs Daley. It's a new range at work. Bit intense isn't it?'

'Not at all, love. I think you look smashing.' His Nan sucked in a drag of the e-cigarette. 'Not many girls can pull off bright orange, but it suits you.'

Aimee hid her hands behind her back. 'Erm, thanks, Mrs Daley.'

'Call me Pam, love. Anyways, how are you? I saw your Nan the other morning in the bakers. She told me all about your poor grandad. I do wish him better.'

'Thank you, Pam. It's just so sad.'

'What is?' George sipped his tea, instantly regretting drinking the scolding liquid in his mouth.

'What? Where you been, Georgie?' His Nan barked from behind a white cloud.

'It's okay Pam, Georgie's had other things on his mind lately.' Aimee continued to rub the back of her hand with her thumb.

'Like what? Don't tell me he's been too busy whinging about Ellie bloody Denton to not care about his friends.' His Nan's stare froze him to the spot. 'Oh son, move on. I'm sure she has.'

'Ellie isn't with anyone else, Nan. She's promised me that. Isn't that right, Aims?'

'Yeah, it's true, Pam. Honest.'

'Give me strength.' His Nan sucked another lungful of smoke. 'You two are like a pair of puppies waggling your tails for the girl. You might have a chance, Aimee love, now that she's a lesbian, but you, Georgie, would be better getting on with your life.'

Aimee's eyes widened at George, clearly not understanding what the hell she was talking about. He hadn't told her that his Nan was convinced Ellie was a lesbian because she'd cut her hair short. George just shook his head and sipped his scolding tea again, burning his lip once more.

'And that's not even the problem here.' Pam continued, smoke curling from her nostrils. 'Aimee is going through a bad time at the moment with her grandad, never mind looking like a satsuma. You should be helping her, not crying over a girl that can't see your worth.'

The words hit him like a truck. A chain smoking eighteen-wheeler. All he could think about was Ellie and Jack together again and suddenly, he couldn't breathe.

Turning to Aimee, George furrowed his brow. 'What's wrong with your grandad?'

'I'll tell you another time, Georgie.' She bit her lip again. 'I only came round to see if you fancied The Sausage and Cider festival tomorrow.'

'Wouldn't hurt you to have a weekend at home, Georgie. You're drunk every night.' His mother interrupted, shaking her head.

'No I'm not.' George protested. Knowing that no one believed him.

'So, you up for it then, babes. '

'Well I've got the weekend off because of it but don't we need tickets or something? Knobert said they'd sold out.'

'Don't listen to that weirdo, babes. He gives me the creeps. Those sunglasses though.' Everyone in the room grumbled with acknowledgment. 'It would not surprise me if he's a secret gimp or something.'

'A gimp?' Pam screeched. 'Don't get me started on them, love. I don't know how they do it.'

'What happens behind closed doors is his business, mum.' Maxine pursed her lips.

'Oh, I don't care what gets his pecker up. I mean I don't get how they do it.' She puffed a cloud into the room. 'They're parading around in full body rubber and I can barely put a swimming cap on my head.'

The entire room filled with raucous laughter, except from Pam, who clearly couldn't see the joke.

Amy grabbed hold of George's hand. 'Anyways, babes, I got some tickets today, a client gave them to me for doing such a good job on her bikini line.'

George shot her a confused look.

'So, yeah? We really wanted to go last year but you was off travelling, remember? Come on, Georgie, it'll be a laugh.'

George chewed his cheek. A whole day of drinking sounded bloody wonderful.

'Come on......I've got free tickets. I've already texted Alf.'

'Your dad's gonna be there too, you know, darlin. He's got his own marquee for networking or whatever it is.' George's mother smiled.

'More like he's gonna be on the piss, Maxine.' Pam took another lug on her e-cigarette – the disdain on her face radiated.

'Fuck it, it's not like I've got anything better to do. No one wants to be with me, so I might as well.'

Aimee squeezed his arm and jumped on the spot with excitement causing George to spill his tea on the mo-shar carpet.

His mother gasped so loudly that he almost smiled.

Almost.

Chapter Thirteen

'Beautiful round here, isn't it. All this fresh air.' Dave inhaled through his nostrils as he leant on the counter of the burger van.

He was breathing in nothing but Essex's finest, but standing behind the greasy burger grill, Jack swallowed hard to stop himself retching

'If you say so.'

'I sure do. Keep telling Marie we should move out here. Get us a nice little two-bed with a bit of land. It'd get us away from Dagenham. Be blooming lovely, wouldn't it?'

Jack stared into the green field, then to the woods beyond it. The pinks and whites of the blossom trees and bright green foliage in the distance made him smile. He'd never had himself down as a nature lover, but there was no denying it. He'd always loved the sounds of London; the cars, the people scurrying in rush hour, the various languages of Londoners. But, in that moment, he wondered how the hell he'd gotten to twenty-one without taking the time to hear the birds sing. There wasn't a tower block or red bus in sight, and that was okay. Fucking brilliant, actually.

'It sure would.' Jack's gaze stayed on the scenery.

'Maybe we could push to a three-bed, Jack. We'll need a spare room for Marie's Pomeranians, but the other one is all yours.'

'Only if it's okay with the dogs.' Jack laughed.

When Jack had first ran away from his Foster parents at eleven and refused to go back, it was Dave who'd taken him in. And when he'd done it again at fourteen and his mother called the police, Dave was there to help again. Even though Dave and Jack's Aunt Shelley had divorced, Dave still tried to negotiate with social services. And again, now, years later, after Jack had done a runner in the middle of the night from his dingy flat in Forest Gate, Dave had welcomed him into his home; arms wide open and no questions asked.

With two bags of worldly possessions, Jack had been determined to start anew. He needed family around him. No more Cole, no more bouncers wanting to break his legs and certainly no more hating himself. He'd spent far too many years sailing that ship of self-loathing. Leaving everything behind seemed to be the best idea. It was a chance for him to forget all the shit he'd gone through and look ahead; and hopefully, one day, making amends with his mother.

Ok, so crashing in his ex-uncle's spare room wasn't the new life he'd imagined when he packed his things. It was barely a new bus route. But it was a good a place, as any, to start.

'We're gonna make a mint today, Jack, me old son.' Dave rubbed his hands together like a cartoon villain. 'Me and Marie did it here last year.'

'Too much info, man.'

'Plonker!' Dave whacked Jack on the back of the head then laughed. 'I meant we did this *festival* last year. These things get rammed.'

Looking out onto the open filed once again, Jack couldn't imagine the space being filled with people. It seemed too natural. Too untouched. 'Really? This place, Dave?'

'Not half, son. This little field will be full of thousands of hungry sausage munchers in an hour or so.'

Jack scoffed. Somehow, Dave hadn't seen the humour. 'Sausage munchers, yeah?'

'Thousands of 'em. That's why you've gotta get here early to get a good pitch.'

Early wasn't even a joke. Being an eternal night owl, Jack had though he'd shit the bed when Dave had woken him at five in the morning. Five a.m. was the time Jack usually got home, not up and out. He'd barely sipped his tea before he had been marched into Dave's Range Rover and forced to listen to the smooth sounds of the seventies for an hour and a half.

But when they'd pulled off the motorway and drove through the little towns complete with the thatched pink cottages, cobbled bridges and fields of horses, Jack soon perked up. It wasn't until he had been driven down a country lane, that he'd realised he'd never seen the countryside before. He didn't know that there was still so much open space in England, and just an hour away from the over-packed London. Jack had only ever seen rabbits in hutches, not roaming free on the verges of the road and he'd gasped when he'd spotted a colourful pheasant. Jack had never seen a farm in real life, not until he'd arrived at the handwritten placard declaring 'Fresh Eggs and Honey' under the huge sign welcoming him to Perrygate Farm.

'Anyways.' Dave cleared his throat. 'I know you're an *artist* and all, but you might wanna pull your sleeves down. You're a pretty lad, but the sight of your scabby tattoo is gonna put people off my meat.'

Jack laughed, unsure if his uncle meant to be a walking innuendo then looked down at the crusty tattoos on his wrists. He'd gone over a few of them whilst staying at Dave's place, including the Jack-o-lantern he had done freehand almost eight weeks' before.

'You better put on some gloves too. Folks round here aren't your Brick Lane crowd. They won't want our dirty mitts on their grub.'

'Are they up themselves?' Jack asked.

'No, I wouldn't say that. Just that London might be an hour away on the train but it's a different world.' Dave laughed as Jack frowned. 'Come on, you must have a couple of Essex mates.'

Jack didn't bother to hide his snort. Mates? He'd only ever really had Cole, and, well, he was never really that much of one. Not a good one, anyway. And the only people he knew from Essex were Ellie and her pal Aimee. And of course George. The bloke that still haunted his thoughts all those weeks on. Fuck knows why. Jack couldn't work it out. He'd met so many drunkards at the Cloud Bar. Hundreds of friends-of-a-friend. But that brief encounter with George had, for some mind-boggling reason, had stuck. Maybe it was because he pitied the guy – Ellie had obviously wanted out of their relationship. Or maybe he envied him. George was his antithesis, after all.

Dave nodded to a box and Jack yanked out a couple of blue latex gloves then slid a hand into each. He was used to them – he needed to wear them when he tattooed people, but they never felt right. Stupid as it was, it was like his hands couldn't breathe properly with them on.

Climbing into the van through the side door, Dave made the little room that there was even smaller. It wasn't the best fit without the extra person, Jack could just about stand up straight without his quiff being flattened by the ceiling. Pulling at his collar, Jack blew out through rounded lips.

'Right, Jack, we gotta start getting the beef on.' Dave pulled white boxes from the fridges, all of them filled to the brim with patties.

'Won't the customers want sausages?'

'You're kidding aren't you? These people might like the idea of a sausage and cider festival but at the end of the day, they want my good old British beef.'

'Dave, man, stop it with the meat references, man. Especially with you so close to me.'

'You sound just like Marie.'

They both laughed, clearly comfortable enough in each other's company to not care that the joke sucked.

Dave was the kind of bloke that Jack could spend time with and not have to worry too much about life. He was the easiest bloke in the world to get on with - honest and reliable. The man wouldn't let him down no matter what and if by some chance he ever did, he'd be there the second he could be. Jack had never had a dad, never really cared for one either. His mum was all he wanted. Not that she'd ever shown much interest in him. But if he ever had to pick a father, he'd walk past all the millionaires with their mansions and private jets and walk straight up to Dave.

Chapter Fourteen

George slammed his palm against the centre of the steering wheel – his blood boiling as it sounded the horn again. It was the fourth time, yet Alfie still hadn't emerged from his house. Running late, he'd asked Aimee to text ahead, to let Alf know they were on their way. But with a fifth blaring of the horn and a no show from Alfie, it became clear that she hadn't bothered.

True to form, Aimee's phone had been glued to her palm the entire drive from her house to Alfie's, her gaze not once lifted from the screen. George couldn't see what she was staring at, but because of her silence, he was certain she was swimming through the river of cock on Tinder. Aimee's expressions could speak volumes, and by biting her lip and raising her brow, it become obvious she had more important things on her mind than George and Alfie.

Huffing, George pulled down the visor and flipped open the mirror. Tilting his head to get a better view of his face, he tried to see the small wound on his cheek closer. A couple of hours with Alfie at the pub the night before, and payday burning a hole in his pocket, George guzzled down cheap white wine and house vodka until the chest ache became mostly just acid burn. The majority of the evening was a blur – sleep had seen to that - but the flashbacks of him stumbling out of The Swan at closing kept filling him with the fear. The kind that made him think everyone was judging him. Even the silent Aimee beside him.

He didn't remember doing it, but by his smashed phone, torn jacket and the inch long purple cut on his cheek, he'd likely fell over at some point on his way home.

'Fuck sake, where is he?' George beeped the horn again with his fist. 'This shit is getting on my nerves.'

'What's up, babes?' Aimee's focus was still on her phone, seemingly oblivious to everything around her.

'Fucking Alf.' George's knuckles shone white around the steering wheel.

'Why don't you text him?'

'I have. Twice. Wouldn't have hurt you to text him when we left your house, would it?'

Aimee looked up, her forehead lined. 'You should have said, Georgie.'

'I did, for fucks sake.' He grimaced at the pain in his cheek.

'Oh, sorry, babes. My mind was someone else.'

'Let me guess, a bloke.'

'No actually. It's not.'

'Well it looks like you're on a dating site to me, Aims. I can tell by your face.' George punched the centre of the steering wheel again.

She shifted in her seat then cleared her throat. 'Actually, babes, I'm texting Ellie. She's asking about my grandad.'

George froze, his chest tightening like a vice. Although he knew she spoke to Ellie regularly, it seemed like a betrayal with him being so close. Rubbing his nose in it, in a way. He couldn't help but wonder if he'd come up in their conversation at all.

'You know, Ellie doesn't care about you. She doesn't care about anyone. Remember that. That's why she left everyone behind.' He sniffed. 'It wouldn't hurt you be there for your real friends.' Aimee straightened her back then shut her phone screen off – the sound of the click preluded the tirade he knew was coming.

She turned to face him – her head twisting as though she was possessed. He waited for the pea-green projectile vomit to come shooting from her mouth.

'Not there for my friends? Babes, that's rich.' Her eyes met his. Narrow and accusing.

'What?' George recoiled.

'How can you say I'm not there for my friends? When you're…..you're acting like…' Aimee furrowed her brow, 'What's that on your face? Georgie? Have you been in a fight?'

'Eh?' Huffing, George turned away. He knew exactly what she was talking about and wasn't in the mood to explain how he couldn't remember anything after nine p.m.

'What happened?' Aimee continued her inquest. She even tucked her phone into her handbag.

George shrugged. 'Done it at the farm yesterday.'

'You didn't have it when I saw you yesterday.' Her eyes narrowed again. 'Tell me, babes, what happened?'

'I don't know.' Shrugging, he finally faced her. 'I must have fell or something. I honestly don't remember.'

'Were you *that* drunk?' She nibbled the corner of her acrylic thumb nail. 'I knew it was a bad idea letting you two go out on your own. I've just had so much to deal with lately, Georgie. How much have you really been drinking?'

'We had, like, a few drinks. Just the usual amount.'

Aimee squeezed her hand over his and for the briefest of moments, George forgot about everything else in his life. All that haunted him was gone just by the warmth of her soft, manicured hand. George swallowed hard, unsure why her touch had affected him so much.

'That's what worries me, babes. And the fact you don't remember falling over. Or getting punched.' The concern

114

on her face was real. 'Georgie…. I'm so worried about you. You're one of the most important people in my life.'

'I'm okay, Aims.'

'Why don't I come over a couple of nights in the week? Just me and you. We can keep each other company. Snuggle up, watch trashy films and order a pizza? Like we used to.'

Furrowing his brow, he couldn't hide his confusion. Was the girl coming on to him? He'd never, not once in his entire life, looked at Aimee in that way. She was always going to be just a mate. And that was final.

'Like Netflix and chill? Aims, I'm sorry but I'm not into you like that.'

'Oh babes, no. I meant like how we used to. You know, like back in school. Duvet days. Ice cream and pizza.' She smiled weakly. The kind that said he'd just made things totally weird.

He cleared his throat. 'Yeah, I know. I was joking.' He cringed. 'I don't think I'm much company to watch films with at the moment.'

'Well we could just talk. You know I love to talk. And listen.' She smiled – sincerely that time.

George pulled his hand away from hers and slammed it into the horn. 'Not being funny, Aims, but we're talking now and it's doing my fucking head in.'

'Georgie, you're so angry lately. I really hate seeing you like this.'

'I'm not angry. I'm just sick of waiting.'

'For Ellie?'

'No! Not fucking Ellie!' His growl vibrated through the car seat. 'Fucking Alf. I'm sick of waiting for him to get out of his shitty little council house. It's got like two tiny rooms, what can he be doing?'

'Georgie, calm it, babes'

He bit his lip and fought the overwhelming desire to tell her to fuck off. Instead, he ignored her entirely and unbuckled his seatbelt, throwing it back against the door in rage. He shuddered as the metal clanked loudly against the window. His dad would kill him if he smashed it. Even more angered by his mood, he grumpily pulled at the door lever to get out but stopped when Alfie stepped out of his house with a smile.

'What the fuck, Alf?' George asked as the fella climbed into the backseat.

'Sorry, Georgie boy. Needed the toilet. Had to make room for all the pints of scrumpy I'll be guzzling today. I'm not queuing up for a portaloo for an hour.'

'How long does it take you to have a piss though, mate? We've been out here for fucking ages.'

'Ah mate, it was more than a piss. Actually that weren't a shit….that was an exorcism.'

'O M G Alf, that is so gross.' Aimee recoiled in fake horror, clearly trying her best not to laugh.

George grimaced in shock, not due to Alfie's crudeness, but because Aimee was actually beaming at the fella. She stared at Alfie with the look he hadn't seen her give him before. It wasn't the usual disgust or even the rare smile Alfie's sarcasm could muster from her. More like appreciation. Like she was grateful for him. What?

'Made you laugh though didn't it, Aims?' Alfie leant forward and rested his hand on her shoulder. 'That's all that matters.'

'Aww, thanks, babes.' She put a hand to her chest as her cheeks turned pink. Was they actually being nice to each other?

George couldn't hide his distaste. Didn't even try to. Why should he? Seeing his friends getting along so well when his life was in the shitter sent fire raging up his spine.

'Hope you washed your hands, Alf.' George sneered, delighted when Aimee shrugged Alfie's palm off of her shoulder.

'What? Sort it out, mate. Course I did.'

George sniffed hard. He knew his anger was misplaced. He knew he shouldn't have done that to Alfie. It was great to see Alfie and Aimee getting on but his foul mood controlled his mouth. He couldn't face having to endure Aimee and Alfie flirting all fucking day whilst he stood their alone. *Eternally alone.*

'Mate, that cut looks well sore on your cheek. You got proper lamped, didn't you?'

George winced as Aimee glared at him from the corner of his eye.

'What? Who lamped you?' Grabbing his chin, she pulled George's face closer to inspect the damage. 'Did somebody hit you?'

He shrugged. He couldn't exactly answer something he didn't know. He drank for a reason – to forget. Thankfully, it'd never failed him.

'Who hit him?' She barked at Alfie. 'And where the hell were you?'

'Whoa, Aims. I was dribbling for a piss. When I came out of the toilets, I saw Georgie boy chatting up a girl at the bar. He was telling her she was the second most beautiful girl in the world.'

George sank in the driver's seat. The memories now coming back to him in waves. Tsunamis even. Cringing the fuck out of his own skin, he strangely needed Alfie to finish the story.

'So? She didn't like being the second prettiest or whatever?' Aimee rolled her heavily lashed eyes. 'What were her eye brows like?'

Alfie shrugged. 'I don't think she cared. She just kept telling him to leave her alone.'

Clearing his throat, George turned the key in the ignition. The vibrations of the engine seemed to exacerbate his nerves, both purring in rhythm.

'And?' she asked.

'Well, George got on the defensive. He asked her if her dad was a builder…He said she had so much make-up on that she looked like she'd been rendered.'

Closing her eyes, Aimee slowly shook her head. 'Well good on her. I'd have hit him too.'

Alfie bellowed with laughter. 'No, she didn't hit him. Her boyfriend did.'

Aimee scowled at George, her glare seemed to drill through his retinas. Alfie, the eternal goon, howling on the back seat.

'Whatever. Let's just get a fucking move on. I need a drink.'

Pulling away from the kerb, George flicked the radio onto full blast, allowing the shitty Spanish song that no one could understand, to drown out his passengers.

Chapter Fifteen

Dave hadn't been wrong. The field was rammed. Hundreds of people – the ever-cheery Essex folk – seemed to emerge from nowhere, filling the huge green space in mere moments after the gates had opened.

Just hours earlier, he was adamant he'd stick out like some urban sore thumb in an Essex field – a bloke that'd never worn a pair of chinos in his life. A bloke that didn't belong. Not that he knew where he belonged. Truth be told, good old London Town never quite fit either. But the more that people arrived to "Essex's Sausage and Cider Festival," the more he realised he wasn't a commodity after all. There was an assortment of people, not only the stereotypes that Jack had seen on reality TV shows that looped on the digital channels - but the regular Joes with no interest in the latest fashions, the tattooed alternatives who nodded to Jack – seemingly in recognition of some sort of kinship, the bottle-bronzed beauties and men with beer filled bellies. Even the wannabe hipsters that he'd thought he'd left back in Brick Lane.

Flipping a row of burgers over on the sizzling griddle, Jack's attention floated past the crowd and onto the horizon once more. The endless blue sky from set-up that morning had dissolved into an opaque white and the bright green in the distance, had too, dulled into something slightly less majestic. Still, it was beautiful. The lack of sunshine clearly hadn't dampened the spirits of the punters.

The festival catered for all walks of life, with various stalls selling crafts, handbags, handmade furniture and

119

gourmet cupcakes. The food vans were lined around the edge of the field, most of whom provided the sausages and cider that brought the people there. Yet, none, it seemed, were as popular as Dave's "Good old fashioned burger and chips."

In the middle of the field, huge white marquees were full of long wooden tables with people sampling the local farmer's goods and chugging cider from glass tankards, sat around them. Like chimes, the sound of clinking glass echoed through Perrygate Farm. Not deterred by the threat of rain, the crowds spilled out into the open air too, with revellers dancing to the live folk band. It wasn't Jack's cup of tea– let's face it, there's not much soul in a banjo – but, surprisingly, he'd discovered the charm of the accordion.

As nice as it was, jealousy had bitten Jack a good few times throughout the day. Another customer service role where he'd got to watch people have fun and spend wads of cash whilst he worked. Same shift, different job.

But as the day went on, Jack learnt to appreciate Dave even more. He took up most of the van, purely because he rushed to serve people like his life depended on it. In a way, it did. Dave who, quite honestly, was the biggest stress-head when it came to getting food out quickly, hurried Jack along with the orders most of the day, but never raised his voice. Not once. The bloke was a diamond and Jack was annoyed at himself for forgetting so. Every time someone with a tattoo came up to the counter, Dave would recommend Jack's 'artistic skills'– always ready to drum him up some business. Even handing out Jack's phone number on the napkin. Not the classiest move, but Dave earned even more diamond-points when he suggested that, if Marie agreed of course, Jack could use their garage as a makeshift tattoo parlour. As long as Jack stopped the "mate's rates" he had been giving the girls, that is. If only he knew.

'Dave, man. You sure I can use your garage?'

'Course, son. Marie will be all right with it. She's been chewing my ear off for years to clear it out.'

'I really don't know what to say.'

'Nothing to say, Jack. We're family. All right, maybe not by blood, but what's that got to do with anything. I don't have any kids….not that I know of.' He nudged him then winked. 'And you don't have any parents….not really, eh? So it makes sense.'

Dave's words struck Jack. They were true and should have hurt. But they warmed him instead. Dave was family. That's why Jack knocked on his door.

'Dude, you really are a top bloke, you know that?' Jack bit the inside of his cheek then swung his arm round Dave's shoulder.

'All right, all right. Don't get soppy on me.' He laughed, squeezing Jack in return - the brief hug filling Jack with contentment. 'It's died down a bit. Why don't you go for a ciggie?'

'You sure, man?'

'Go on, you deserve a break.' Dave pinged open the till and pulled out a ten pound note. 'Take this and go have a walk around too. You need to enjoy yourself now and again, son.'

Jack beamed at his uncle but ignored the offer of the money. He'd already done enough. Jumping down from the burger van, he welcomed the fresh June air onto his face. Gagging for a smoke, he knew it was a shame to ruin it.

Sliding the box of cigarettes out of his back pocket, he breathed in their aroma before lighting up. The first drag was always the best. Nothing better than that intoxicating inhale – the smoke rushing to the lungs.

He ignored the other caterers with their trays of pork and apple sausages and foot-long hotdogs – there's no way he could play his uncle out like that – and strolled towards the stall at the other side of the field that sold paintings and prints. Passing the gauntlet of revellers and their kids, he took a free sample of booze from a waiter. He sipped it at first, looking back to see if Dave was looking. He knew his uncle wouldn't have minded either way, but working in bars for so long had instilled the paranoia. Shaking his stupidity off, he chucked the rest of the sample back and tapped the empty plastic cup back on the tray.

At the art stall, he flicked through a stack of sealed prints – not looking for anything in particular, just taking in all the colours and patterns that other people's talent had created. At the side of the small gazebo hung a canvas with a hand painted octopus on it. His eyes widened as the greens, browns, blacks and golds of the creature drew him in almost completely. He'd always found beauty in the grotesque. But it was the blue pigment in the painting that captivated him the most. They reminded him of someone. Those blue eyes that he'd struggled to move on from. George.

He stood there transfixed, gawping at the painting, ignoring the world around him until someone tapped him on the shoulder.

Jack's eyes widened once more. Aimee, the sweet girl he'd met a month or so ago, was stood next to him in a short dress, looking even more gorgeous than the last time he'd seen her.

'O M G! Jack, what you doing here?' Her white smile beamed.

'Hey, Aimee.' He ran his hand through his quiff. 'Look, erm, sorry I haven't been in touch.'

She was the girl he should have tried again with. She was into him back then, there was no doubt in his mind, but he just couldn't. Even at his place, when she asked if she could stay, braless and in his T-shirt, he still couldn't make it happen.

'Oh, no worries, babes. I've been a little busy lately myself. My family has had some bad news and it's just been hard, you know?'

Stretching out his hand to her arm, Jack furrowed his brow. Voicing empathy wasn't his strong point. Speaking, full stop. 'I hope, erm, you're okay. Your family and everything.'

'We'll get there. Thanks.' She flashed that pretty smile again. 'So, you're a fan of the sausage, eh?' Clamping her eyes shut, she shook her head. 'I mean, you know. This place.'

'Well I haven't tried the sausages yet.' Jack cringed – wishing the ground beneath his feet would swallow him whole.

She twisted the bangle on her arm, clearly thinking of what to say next. A moment, not even a second passed but it was fucking the most awkward moment of his life.

'Well, I didn't have you down for this kind of music, that's for sure.' She nodded to the folk band who had, it seemed, been playing the same song for the entirety of their set.

'I'm getting used to it, actually. Besides, this place is amazing. I'm here helping my uncle out.' He pointed over to Dave's van.

To his surprise, Dave was watching him. And sporting a mischievous grin at that.

Grabbing two samples of cider from another waiter, Aimee passed one to him. 'Oh no, you're working. That is so rough, babes. We could have caught up. Had a proper drink.'

'I know.' He rolled his eyes.

Embarrassment rushed over him and he hated himself for it. It was like putting his uncle down in some way. There shouldn't be anything wrong with working on a burger van to survive but it made him feel inferior. But it hurt that she was out having a good time, spending shit loads of money on booze whilst he was working. *Again.*

'There's actually someone I want you to meet. Well, you've already met him. But as you're here, I really *really* need you to do me a favour and tell him you haven't been sleeping with his girlfriend.'

'What?' Jack choked, the cider burning his throat. 'Who?'

'Remember George? Ellie's boyfriend?'

Rubbing the back of his neck, he furrowed his brow. Of course he remembered him. In a way, he was his aspiration. 'I don't think so.'

'You met him at the cloud bar a few weeks back.'

'Doesn't ring a bell.' He hoped a fake cough would conceal his lie. 'But then I met lots of people working there.'

Jack drew hard on his cigarette. It burnt close to his fingertips yet he didn't want to take his eyes off her. He wanted to see any hint from her. Anything she was going to say without opening her mouth.

'Well, my mate Georgie is proper struggling. Ellie broke up with him and he's got it in his head that's it's something to do with you.'

'Huh? What have I got to do with it?' He dropped the cigarette to the ground and twisted it into the grass with his shoe, hoping the brief break from the conversation would help him get his head around what the girl was saying.

'He thinks because you tattooed Ellie with the same words as you've got, that you had a thing going on.'

'Man, I don't know what you're talking about. I'm a tattooist. Nothing has happened between me and Ellie.'

Grabbing his hand, she squeezed it ever so slightly. 'Babes, I know. I mean, I *really* know.'

Her smile seemed genuine – as though she was offering some sort of olive branch rather than judging.

But Jack didn't like it. Shifting on his feet, he pulled his hand away.

Silence filled the gap between them. Tension was building and he knew that it was *his* doing.

'Jack, gonna need you back here in a minute, son.' Dave shouted, leaning out of the van door. The timing couldn't have been more perfect.

'I gotta get back. No rest for the wicked.'

'Listen, Jack.' Aimee grabbed hold of his wrist, her fingers pressing against the healing tattoo underneath his sleeve. 'I know you're not into Ellie. I can sense these things. Honestly, I can clock hair extensions from a five mile radius. But my mate, George, is in a bad way. I really need you to talk to him? Let me get him.'

'Erm, I gotta go.' With anxiety gripping his intestines, Jack backed away. 'I better get back. Maybe we can hang again sometime?'

'I'll text him. It'll only take a second. I promise it won't kick off.' The look on Aimee's face told Jack that she had no confidence in her statement at all.

'Aims?' A voice from the crowd called out and Jack recognised it immediately.

It was George!

Fuck.

Chapter Sixteen

George couldn't move. His body was aflame with rage. Confusion. Betrayal. His so-called best friend had been getting too close for comfort with his mortal enemy. And in Coggletree too. The bloke haunted George, like a shadow. Like Alfie's massive shit that wouldn't flush.

'Georgie. Listen…' Aimee flashed her teeth.

'What's he doing here?' George glared at Aimee and the tall, dark man beside her. It made his piss boil that the fella didn't bother to look at him.

His upset worsened because of Jack's appearance. Over the last few weeks George had built an image of a dark, brooding home-wrecker. A Casanova so fucking edgy that it twisted his guts to think how ordinary he was himself. His imagination had made him forget what the bloke really looked like and now the reality proved even more devastating.

George's navy blue chino shorts and check shirt were somehow deemed inferior to Jack's ripped black jeans and a black T-shirt with it's perfectly positioned tears. His style bit at George's ego like a fox ripping up a rabbit. He wasn't the modern-day Elvis that George first thought, but more like a 60's rocker that shagged his way through swinging London. Jack had the edge that George always wanted but could never accomplish. Never.

Jack raised his brow then hooked his thumb over his shoulder. 'I better go. Nice to see you again, Aimee.' Walking off, Jack didn't look back. A sign of just how self-absorbed he really was.

George stepped forward - the space between him and Aimee seemed like no man's land now. 'You kidding me, Aims?' He spat.

Aimee's gaze fell to the ground – obviously uncomfortable under George's scrutiny. Eventually, she lifted her head with a perfectly rehearsed smile. 'Babes, You've deffo got it wrong about him. Why don't I get him to come meet us in a bit and we can all talk it over?'

The noise around him suddenly became deafening and dizziness took over his balance - the slightest movement could've easily had him face-planting the grass. After a few moments, once he regained his control, he swiped a sample of free cider from the tray wielding man beside him. Just like the waiter's smile, the overly sweet alcohol, did nothing to settle the bile rising in his throat.

'What's there to talk about?' George scowled

Aimee squeezed his arm, the way she would usually do when worried about him, but he shrugged it away coldly. She was tainted. She'd betrayed him. And he couldn't see past it.

'Georgie. Seriously, babes. Why you angry with me? I haven't done anything wrong.'

'He split me and my girlfriend up and you're all over him.' George's stomach tightened. 'The man's a dick. But I guess that's why you like him, isn't it, Aims?'

George hated himself for that low blow. That wasn't him. That wasn't what he thought. But he had to hurt her – like she'd hurt him. He wanted to see a confession from her. He wanted her eyes to give away her guilt. He didn't even know what her and that tattooed lothario had even spoke about but the speaking itself destroyed the loyalty. Aimee wet her lips, seemingly preparing to speak, but she didn't.

'What the fuck, mate? Why'd you walk off?' Alfie came out of nowhere and nudged George in the side. The force of his elbow elevated George's rage.

He'd left Alfie in his father's tent when he'd noticed Aimee leave. She had been on her phone and George had been curious to see if it had been Ellie on the other end. Ellie had been on his mind all day. He wanted to be at the festival with his girlfriend. And the thought of Aimee speaking to her, and not him, drove George wild.

'Mate, it's boring in your dad's tent. Why's he doing a networking thing anyway? I thought he worked in property, not computers.'

George didn't answer. Alfie's stupidity would have to wait. He focused all energy, all hatred, on Aimee.

'What's up, mate? Everything all right?' Alfie planted his palm on George's back and gripped the muscle a little too tightly.

George gritted his teeth so hard he could hear them squeak. 'Ask her!'

Aimee shuffled closer but stopped when George narrowed his eyes. George hated the way he felt for her at that moment, he didn't want to hate her but that's the only emotion he could summon. He wanted to run out of that field before he said something that he would never be able to take back, but hate cemented him to the spot.

'What's going on with you two? You fighting or something?' Alfie picked up a couple of free samples, leaving the tray empty, and knocked them back before thanking the waiter with a wink.

'No, course not, babes.' Aimee's smile seemed more forced than ever. *Natural liar.* 'Just a little misunderstanding.'

'Too fucking right we're fighting. This little slag has been fucking me over the whole time.'

Aimee's gasp mirrored Alfie's dropped jaw.

'Whoa, mate. No need for that.' Alfie stepped between them, raising his eyebrows. 'Tell me, what's going on.'

'Jack. Fucking Jack. That's what's going on. He's here and she knew all along. She was talking to him, just now.

128

I saw her. No wonder she wanted to come here so badly…she planned it all.'

'Aims?' Alfie seemed hurt but it was nothing compared to what George felt.

'O M G, I didn't even know he was here. I literally just bumped into him. You've got it all wrong.'

'Bumped? With what?' Alfie balled his hands into fists. 'So you and him *are* a thing?'

'No, Alfs. Honestly, I didn't plan anything. I was only given the tickets yesterday, remember? For the bikini wax. There is nothing going on between me and Jack.' Aimee rubbed Alfie's arm, bringing him closer to her.

George's temper burned through his body. Seeing her win Alfie over so quickly was the last straw. What Aimee was saying should have made sense but the logic became lost on him. Betrayal had fogged his brain. He'd been abandoned. Rejected for a better model. First by Ellie, now Aimee. And Alfie, too, by the looks of it.

'Fucking liar!' George barked. 'She was practically kissing him, Alf.'

'WHAT?' Alfie puffed out his chest and rubbed his knuckles. The redness of his face gave George a sense of accomplishment. 'Where is he? I'll fucking have him.'

'Don't be stupid, Alfs. I wasn't kissing any one. Why would you say that, Georgie?' Shaking her head, she bit the corner of her nail. 'Nothing is going on. And it didn't with Ells either. I've spoke to her so many times about this and she says nothing happened'

The disloyalty magnified. George understood the girl's friendship but Aimee talking to everyone about his relationship felt like an attack.

'She was texting him earlier, when we was in the car waiting for you.' George looked away.

'The Fuck?' Alfie's voice boomed so loudly the stall holder in the gazebo next to them jumped.

'No I wasn't. I was texting Ellie. George, you know that. I'll show you both if you don't believe me.'

Alfie turned his back on Aimee and grabbed George by the shoulders. 'You see where he went?'

George bit the inside of his cheek. He'd seen Jack walk back to a shitty burger van and could still see the dickhead out of the corner of his eye. He wasn't even sure if Jack was looking at him but the side of George's face burned all the same. He wanted to see that dickhead get what was coming to him, but he wasn't willing for Alfie to be the one that delivered the blow. George wasn't the violent type, but he sure as hell wanted to smack the fucker one - right in that perfectly chiselled jaw of his. But if he did, he'd destroy any hope of him and Ellie ever getting back together.

George felt exposed. Observed by his enemy. It weakened him and as much as he hated himself for it, he knew he had to rise above it all. George had to take control of the situation before it got out of hand and he looked even more of a pushover.

With Alfie still gripping his shoulders, George gulped in the warm afternoon air, hoping to calm his tight nerves. George clamped his eyes shut and counted down from ten in his head, slow enough to add a 'Mississippi' in between each number. The world around him grew louder than ever, the music from the shitty band drilling into his brain, but the darkness helped all the same. He let his thoughts of Ellie and Jack, as well as Aimee, get lost in the noise.

He had two choices. He could fall apart, act the prick and ruin relationships that had taken a lifetime to build. Or, he could sort his shit out and come out on top.

Blinking, he straightened his posture and raised his head high. He calmly pulled Alfie's hands off him and lowered them to his friend's sides. If he showed that he wasn't bothered by it, Jack couldn't win. None of them could.

'Well?' Alfie clapped his hands together in front of George's face. 'Where is the fucker?'

'Let's leave it, Alf. I don't want any trouble,' George raised his head even higher. 'I'm not giving that dickhead the satisfaction.'

'You're kidding me, Georgie? The boy is in our town, on our turf, and you still don't want to get pay back.'

Alfie's mock gangster speech bellowed in the air. If Jack hadn't been looking over before, he sure as hell was now.

'Calm down, Peaky Blinders. I said, leave it.' George glared at Alfie and then to Aimee. He could see the damage his words had caused.

'You leave it. I'll happily knock the bastard out for you. Just tell me where he is.' Alfie's face grew a brighter shade of red.

'Alfs, seriously, babes.' Aimee grabbed his arm. 'Don't do this, please. Georgie doesn't want any trouble. You both really need to calm the hell down. Jack isn't and never has been with Ellie.'

George's stomach twisted at the mention of her name again. Alfie scowled, the demonic creases in his brow reminded George of that vampire TV show from the nineties.

'Alf! I told you to fucking leave it.' George snarled through gritted teeth. 'If I wanted anyone to knock him out, I would do it myself. Now back the fuck off.'

Alfie's eyes widened before his body slumped.

'I'm gonna go sort this bullshit myself. I'll show *Jack* that he's not better than me.'

'What?' Aimee asked, arms now folded. 'You honestly just need to hear his side. There is no need for all this aggression.'

George pinched the bridge of his nose and sucked in long deep breaths. The girl's voice had started to go through him - like nails on a chalkboard. Both Aimee and Alfie were getting on his nerves. His very last one, in fact.

'You two go to my Dad's tent, I'll meet you there in a minute.'

'No mate, I'm coming with you.'

'Don't make me tell you again, Alf.' George raised his brow - so high he'd sworn it reached his hairline.

After a few groans from both Alfie and Aimee, he watched his friends then walk away and waited for them to enter his father's tent before he turned to face the burger van.

He needed to show Jack that he wasn't someone to mess with.

He was ready. He had this. Just about.

Chapter Seventeen

'What can we get you, buddy?' Wiping his hands onto a chequered apron, the older man beside Jack offered a smile to his new customer.

The fire that had roared in his belly moments before reduced to nothing but embers during the twenty yard walk to the van and George froze to the spot, unable to answer. He hadn't even thought about what he was going to say when he'd got there. Or *do* for that matter. He just wanted to prove, well, something. Food hadn't even crossed his mind.

He couldn't decipher whether the man who had spoken to him was Jack's father or not. He didn't really care either way, if he was honest. He sure didn't look like Jack. He was shorter and stockier, with thick-lensed glasses magnifying his eyes. Unlike Jack - perfect fucking Jack – this man was rather featureless. An average bloke. Maybe Jack got all the looks in the family?

Coughing into a balled fist, George remained at the back of a small crowd of customers and pretended to read the menu on the wall behind Jack's head – all the while taking in every detail of the bastard that had stolen his girl.

In the sobering light of day, the fella was even more of a threat. His clothes and hair, and those fucking tattoos, were foreboding enough. Everything about him oozed confidence. Jack didn't even seem bothered that George was there scowling at him - the boyfriend of the girl he was sleeping with. Obviously, the fella didn't have a conscience. There was something about Jack that made

George angry and jealous at the same time. The bloke's demeanour alone made him feel inferior. He was too cool, too effortless. Too *easy*. George hated himself because of it.

Running a finger under his collar, George faced the older man and matched his grin. He didn't care less what he ordered, or what they sold. He had no desire to fund Jack's womanising lifestyle by handing over his hard earned cash. But he needed a delay until he worked out what the hell he'd been playing at by marching over to the van in the first place.

'Can I get the chilli and cheese burger, please?' His own smugness pinched his cheeks. Spicy food wasn't his thing. Truth was, he could barely handle a Korma. 'Extra jalapeños.' But an extra spicy burger would make him look tough. And with all conviction lost on the walk over, he needed that front.

'Course, matey. Be a couple of minutes, Jack here has just put a fresh lot on.'

Jack kept his gaze on the grill. So George tapped his foot, silently begging for the bloke to make eye contact — even for a split second — so he could show Jack that he wasn't intimidated by a fucking burger flipper.

The instance Jack raised his hazel eyes to meet George's glare, George shifted his attention to the older man. One-nil.

'Perfect.' George faked another grin. Then with all the confidence he didn't feel, he turned his attention back to the tattooed twat. 'We've met before haven't we, *Jack*?'

'Have we?' Jack didn't even raise an eyebrow. Nothing. Stone, fucking, cold.

'Yeah, but I think you served drinks instead of burgers then.' *Two-nil.*

Watching the fella move the meat patties around on the hot metal griddle, George snorted. Was there anything more boring?

'You two know each other?' The older fella gawped. 'Small, bloody world, eh? I'm Dave. Jack's uncle.'

Squaring his shoulders, George moved in closer. 'Well, he knows my girlfriend. He tattooed her. Didn't you, Jack?' The snarl from George's mouth surprised even him and he was suddenly aware that the other customers were listening in to their conversation. Let 'em all know what an arsehole this bloke really was.

'Oh....um.....Good day for it today. Good turnout.' Dave was clearly trying to change the subject. Maybe he was used to defending his nephew against scorned boyfriends? How many times had Jack fucked someone over?

Resisting the urge to roll his eyes, George hummed in agreement. He wasn't there for small talk yet there was something about the man that made it hard to be rude. 'Yeah, I've never seen this place so packed. It's usually just for horses.' George pulled his wallet from his back pocket, hoping that the sight of it would make Dave ask for the money for the burger and stop talking to him.

'You from round these parts, then?'

Huffing, George stuffed his hands into his pockets. 'Yeah, just up the road. I actually work here at Perrygate Farm. It's like my second home.' George puffed out his chest proudly, 'cause if there was something to feel proud of it was having a decent job.

'You a farmer or something?'

Jack glanced his way, intrigue peeking through his nonchalance.

'Actually, I'm an apprentice. My dad has got his own business but I'd rather work doing something I love doing. There's more important things than money.' George shrugged.

'Good for you, matey. And you're absolutely right there. People like us have to work for most of our lives so why not bloody enjoy it.'

Jack nodded, as though he was in agreement with what his uncle had said. A sudden pang of remorse struck George as he realised how ridiculous he'd been acting. Fair enough he didn't serve drinks or flip burgers for a living like Jack, but clearing out animal pens everyday didn't exactly scream tycoon either. Deflated, George glanced down at his palms. Ellie had hated him how dirty his hands would get at the farm, so much so, she'd squirm away from him. Shit shovels. That's what she called them.

'Wish Jacky boy would sort his act out and get into his art properly.' Dave patted Jack's shoulder. 'He's only doing this until he becomes a professional tattooist though. Isn't that right, son?'

Jack mumbled something in agreement from behind the counter and the very sound raised George's hackles.

'He does seem to get enough business his own way.' George glared at him. 'My *friend* is a huge fan.'

Jack's reddening face made it obvious that the bastard was bathing in the glory, regardless of his awkward fidgeting. It showed George just how vain the fella was.

'Oh yeah? Dave beamed. 'His work is bloody good. I keep asking him to tattoo me.' Dave patted his nephew's back but Jack didn't raise his head.

Regardless, pride radiated in his uncle's eyes. Clear as day. And like a kick to his gut, it reminded George how disappointed his dad was when he'd turned down family business for the apprenticeship. He'd never had that beam of pride from his own father – not like the one Dave had given Jack. That was unashamed love. And it fucking hurt.

Sliding his phone from his pocket, George longed for a distraction. There weren't any texts or notifications but it diverted his attention from Jack's perfect existence just enough to swallow the humble pie.

Dave opened his mouth, as though he was ready to ask more questions, but two blonde girls around George's age, both with hair just like Ellie used to have, approached the scene and took everyone's attention. They were dressed like they were off to a beach party, in bikini tops and unzipped denim skirts, definitely not for a muddy field. Taking a moment out from proving something to Jack, whatever that was, George roamed his gaze over them both.

Giggling loudly, the girl's presence had undoubtedly caught Jack's attention. And his eyes for that matter as they scanned exactly where George had been checking out moments before. The dirty letch was all over those poor girls.

'Jack, will you serve these ladies whilst I finish these?' Dave offered another crowd pleasing smile then hurried to give the customers their orders.

'Course, man.' Jack lifted his head fully and George instantly hated himself even more. The bloke's face beamed, like someone had turned on his light with a noticeable effect on the opposite sex. 'What can I get you?'

George didn't listen to their order, he didn't care. Instead, he focused on Jack. The way he half-smiled and tilted his head whilst listening intently to whatever the fuck it was the girls were ordering. The way he blew away a stray strand of dark brown hair that had fallen in front of his eyes. And the way the girls tottered ever closer to him. He clearly had talent way beyond George's skills. The cut on his cheek was proof of that. As Jack nodded to their every whim, biting his bottom lip, the girls were swimming in the charm of the bastard's hazel eyes.

Whistling, Jack pulled the freezer door then ripped open a bag of onion rings. Unsure why, the fact that he didn't use scissors just pissed George off even more. The bloke was blatantly showing off and it was working.

One of the girls slid a cigarette from her handbag and, placing it between her lips, she fished around in her bag. George never got why women kept so much crap in their bags, but disbelief nearly blew his head off when the burger flipping Don Juan lent over the counter and held out his lighter for her. Flame already burning.

Clearing the bile from his throat, George looked away. He couldn't stand to be a witness to Jack's effortless seduction. It was too much. *He* was too much. Images of his seduction routine on Ellie flooded George's mind. Flash after flash of Jack working his magic — his voice, his effortless charm, his inscrutable presence. George had thought he could show the fucker that he wasn't intimated. That he wasn't bothered by him. But the cold, hard, bastard truth proved that George *was* intimidated. *Was* bothered. And that stung like a bitch.

'Excuse me, don't I know you?'

That caught George's attention. 'Course they'd know Jack. How many places had he stuck his dick? He waited, breathing hard, for Jack's irritating response and charm offensive, when he realised they were talking to him.

'Sorry?' George raised his eyebrows, barely containing his disdain for every human near him.

'You're Georgie Taylor, aren't you? Ellie Denton's boyfriend?'

'Erm…' George forced a broad smile. Jack's presence had smashed any self-esteem he had left and he needed to outdo the bastard - just once. He wasn't sure why it even mattered, he just knew that it did. Checking the time on his watch – blatantly showing it off, he nodded.

'O M G, it is you. I knew it. I'd remember your smile anywhere. Me and Ellie played netball on a Saturday morning…. you used to come to our games.' The girl with the cigarette laid her hand to her chest and George couldn't drag his gaze away from it. 'You were so sweet, coming to watch her. She's so lucky to have you. Like, honestly, you're just the cutest boyfriend, ever.'

'Thanks. That's what you do when you love someone.' Shifting on his heels, he tried to hide his burning face. He could no longer fake a smile – the reality of his situation too heavy.

'Awww, you're such a babe. How is Ellie? Is she here with you?'

George didn't respond. Couldn't. Instead he huffed at the fact that he'd been a complete legend for getting boyfriend points without actually being anyone's boyfriend. He wasn't prepared to answer any questions. That wasn't the deal - he hadn't thought that far ahead. All he wanted to do was confront Jack and warn him off Ellie.

'No. She's not here today. She's just finishing her first year at uni, so I'm giving her some space. Her education is so important.'

'O M G. You are literally the nicest guy on the planet.'

Unable to cope with the compliments, or scrutiny of Jack bearing witness, regardless if he was watching or not, George backed away from the van. He needed a drink.

Awkwardness now making it hard to breathe, George hadn't even realised that the other customers had left and Dave was there, focusing on him.

'Ah, to be young again,' he said, winking.

This was too much. Too invasive. All of it. He'd wanted to make Jack feel like shit but it had rebounded and had made himself feel worse than ever. Defeated, he knew that even if the fella was sleeping with Ellie, there's nothing he could do about it. George was like an earth worm going head to head with a fucking eagle.

'Tell Ellie I said hi, yeah?' The girl curled her lips then sucked on her cigarette.

'You'd be better off saying that to him.' George nodded to Jack.

He didn't care about one-upping Jack anymore. Fuck showing him that he didn't care. He *did* care. He wanted his girlfriend back. Sucking in the smell of burger grease, a red mist engulfed him. He bit the inside of his cheek, trying to feel real pain, rather than whatever the fuck was making his gut swirl. All he'd wanted to do was drag that bastard over the counter of the van and beat him until he suffered how George had.

Tightening his fists, he stopped himself. *Leave it. Just walk away.*

'Tell me one thing, Jack.' He might have been able to stop the physical altercation, but he couldn't stop himself from asking what had been taking up his daily existence. His tone had obviously startled the fella and his uncle. The girls didn't seem too giggly anymore either. But he didn't care and just asked, 'Why the fuck did you steal my girlfriend?'

Chapter Eighteen

'Eh? What's he talking about, son?' Dave muttered through the side of his mouth.

'I don't know, man.' Jack squirmed. His face was burning, as if he was an inch away from the griddle. 'Honestly.'

George had put Jack on edge from the moment he saw him. Aimee's revelation was enough to blow his mind but the fella following him to the van and clearly begging for confrontation was way too much. Jack was no fighter. *Fact*. Violence had always been something he'd steered clear of – he couldn't even use fly killer. But George was gunning for him. And by the look of his tight fists and tensed biceps, he had the guns for the job. What the hell had been said? Trying not to antagonise him anymore, Jack couldn't ignore the fella's blue eyes that were slicing into him like a steak knife.

Jack's impression of George at the Cloud Bar, the one he often thought back on, had turned out to be a diluted version of what he actually was. Up close, in daylight, the fella was something else. Something Jack only wished he could be. George's steel-blue eyes and perfectly white-toothed smile seared through Jack like lava. Much like his stare.

Adding insult to injury, George was dressed in gear that Jack could never afford. He'd seen clothes like that in Oxford Street, in the shops where the sales assistants only smile to those that can afford their brand. His expensive silver watch alone must cost a few month's wages and Jack winced every time the silver strap caught the light.

Jack's shabby clothes made him feel like a hobo in comparison. He wasn't far from it to be fair. He'd had his jumper for so many years that it'd become more holes than fabric. Thank fuck ripped clothes were in fashion.

He could see why someone like Ellie would go out with him. George was the whole package. He was going places. He had some style. Fair hair, bright blue eyes and a whiter than white smile out of an American Teen film - what Jack had always wanted. The "boy next door" look that Jack couldn't ever achieve, even before he'd covered himself in ink. George was one good looking fella – simple as that.

Ruffling a hand through his quiff, he instantly regretted doing so. The latex glove that his uncle made him wear nearly ripped off half his scalp. And the look from Dave, the reprimand for touching his hair whilst behind the counter, was another kick in the nuts.

'Well?' George scowled.

Blowing out through rounded lips, Jack waited for another onslaught. Be it from George or Dave. Either one, his insides cringed.

Dave wiped his top lip with his wrist then huffed. 'I really hope this kid has got the wrong end of the stick, Jack. I don't like what I'm hearing.'

If only they both knew.

The disappointment in his uncle's eyes fucking hurt, much more than any tattoo needle had across his skin. Jack didn't give a fuck what the George thought of him – didn't care what anyone thought really, but disappointment from Dave was unbearable.

'He has. Believe me, man. I don't know anything about this.' Jack didn't even know if he sounded convincing, regardless that it was the truth.

'Like fuck you don't!' George's balled fist was ready to strike.

'I don't want any trouble.' Jack held up his hands, staving off anything being launched his way. 'I didn't even know there was beef until your mate Aimee told me.'

'Bollocks.' George spat.

'Seriously. I've not done anything with Ellie. And I'm not going to fight you to prove it.'

'Fight? You're not worth it, *Jack*.' The leer of contempt was enough to turn the burgers cold.

'I don't get it, man. I've told you that nothing happened, so why you being a dick to me? You don't even know me.'

'I know what you did though.' The fella's eyes were merciless and fixed on their prey. *Him*. Jack.

'Man, listen.' Jack stuffed a burger and onions into a bun then handed it to Dave. He didn't even know who the order was for, he just needed the distraction. 'I've not done anything to you. Aimee was saying some stuff earlier and I honestly had no idea there was any *trouble*.'

George huffed again. It seemed to be the natural response of the spoilt brat. 'Don't act fucking innocent with me. I know *everything* you did.'

'Man, calm it with the F-bombing. This is my uncle's business.' Jack flashed an apologetic smile to Dave and the two girls.

'I don't give a fuck about your uncle. Or you. I'm not a fucking burger flipper.'

Dave shot Jack a look. One that he'd never seen before. It was one of urgency, to sort out the mess and stop embarrassing him. Swallowing hard, Jack smiled once more to the girls then quickly climbed down from the van to meet George in front of the counter. He stood in front of the fella, regretting it at once. George was broad with arms like boulders. One punch and Jack could say farewell to his nose. Ignoring the trembles in his stomach, Jack held his hands up.

'The fuck?' George scowled, backing away.

'Just hear me out, man. I don't know what you think you know or what you've been told but *nothing* happened between me and Ellie. As far as I knew, she was with you. I haven't seen or heard from her in weeks. And to be fair, man, I don't go around sleeping with women.....' Jack cleared his throat. 'Who are taken, that is.'

'Bullshit.'

Jack observed the girls once again – their faces just as amused with the situation as he was panicked. 'I'm telling you the truth, man!'

'Don't call me man?' George snorted then gestured to Jack's knuckles. 'I've seen the tattoo you did on her....those words.....on her.......*bum.*'

'So you're pissed with me because I tattooed her. That's what I do.'

'Really? On their arses?'

'If they pay me, yes. I'm not going to stand here all day trying to make you believe me. I doubt I'll ever see you again in my life.'

'Good.' George sneered.

'Believe what you want, man. But all I'm going to say is that if you can't deal with her talking to other guys then that's your problem. Not mine.'

George stepped closer. Jack instantly backed away. 'But we both know you did more than just talk, don't we?'

'Now, now matey," Dave's voice hollered from the van. 'Let's not go get ahead of ourselves. Jack's told you it's all a big misunderstanding and we're not in the best place to be having a row.' He indicated to the field of people then froze, his eyes widening. 'Bloody hell, that isn't who I think it is, is it?'

Transfixed, Dave stared into the crowd. George tutted at the ignorance, then followed his line of sight and Jack allowed himself a peek, fully aware that a fist could fly his way any second. Through the crowd, a man waved. He was probably the same age as Dave and marched towards them with a dazzling and gobsmacked expression that matched his uncle's.

Without explanation, Dave flung his apron onto the counter and jumped down from the door like his life depended on it. A few roars of excitement sounded from them and the two men stood fixed to each other in a manly embrace, patting each other's back as though they were both choking.

Jack snorted. Two grown men acting like teenage best buds seemed ironic given the current situation.

'Davie, mate. I can't believe it. What you doing in these parts?' The bloke asked, flashing his very own set of pearly whites. Did the Essex tap water have bleach in it?

He was the kind of fella that Jack expected to see at a sausage and cider festival. Side parting, tweed jacket, pink shirt with the top buttons undone, dark blue jeans and tan loafers. The typical middle-aged Essex boy.

'Dad?!' George's eyes were wider than ever. They seemed bluer too. Almost glowing under the sun's rays.

Gobsmacked, Jack observed father and son. George's future double. Jack wanted to kick himself for not realising straight away. He was George. Just older.

'Hello, son.' He flung an arm around George's shoulder – who appeared to seize up from the impact. 'You getting yourself some grub. My mate, Davie here, is known for the best burgers in London.'

'What's it been, Davie? Fifteen years?'

'Nigh on twenty, I'd say, Stevo. How's your business going? Heard you're doing well for yourself. You're a big shot property tycoon now, aren't you?'

'Bloody hell, no one's called me Stevo in a long time.' The two fellas laughed, patting each other's backs. 'My business is going all right, not a tycoon just yet. I've heard some blinding reviews about your grub.'

145

The pair beamed at each other. It was a look that warmed Jack's chest, seeing two friends so happy for each other. That was real friendship. How people were supposed to treat each other. All he'd ever gotten from Cole was trouble.

'Talking of, Stevo, what can I get you? On the house, of course.'

'Actually, Davie, I only came over to get my boy here, then I see your mug.' The man smiled, squeezing his arm around George's shoulder. 'Small bloody world, isn't it?'

Jack had to look away. The sight of parents loving their children stinging the way it always did.

Dave shook his head. 'I should have known he was your son. He's the spit of you.'

'Handsome bleeder, isn't he? This your boy, Davie?' George's father asked. 'Who'd have thought you'd have made such a good-looking lad, eh?'

The two men chuckled and Jack couldn't resist but show his own teeth too. It wasn't because George's dad had just called Jack "good looking," he couldn't give a shit about any of that, but he liked seeing his uncle laugh. It was infectious.

'You cheeky git! I was a right lady killer in my day. More birds than sense. But no, sadly not. He's my nephew. Shell's sister's boy. You remember?'

George's dad raised his eyebrows and Jack knew why. He was used to it. If he knew Dave's past, then he would know all about Jack's mum too. It seemed like everyone knew about Jack's mum. Apart from him, that was.

The man stretched out an arm to Jack and flashed a white smile. 'Steve Taylor. Me and your uncle go way back….And your aunt, Shelly.'

Jack whipped off a glove and suffered the scorch of George's gaze on his knuckles as he shook the bloke's hand. He could guess why - the word "Live" etched in black ink over his skin.

He sniffed. 'I'm Jack.'

'Nice to meet you, mate. Hope your uncle's paying you to put up with him.' Steve's smile was as contagious as Dave's laugh. Jack couldn't help but grin back. 'You got a couple of minutes, Davie boy? I got a networking thing going on today. Got my own tent over there with a couple of big shots that'll love your grub for their functions.'

'Actually mate, I don't think now is a good time.' Dave cleared his throat. 'There seems to be a bit of bother going on. Between these two.'

Jack squirmed, biting the inside of his cheek.

'Eh?' Steve furrowed his brow. 'You're not causing trouble are you, Georgie?'

For the briefest moment, Jack had forgotten that George was there. The Dave and Steve show had been too captivating to focus on the fella with a grudge. But it was clear that George hadn't forgotten, not if his razor sharp stare on him was anything to go by.

'Too fucking right I am. This is Jack. You know, the one that slept with Ellie.' George barked, folding his arms like a stroppy teenager.

'What? Oh no, not this again, Georgie.' Steve pinched the bridge of his nose. 'You can't be doing this. These are my friends.' Shaking his head, he faced Dave and Jack. 'I'm sorry if my boy has been making a nuisance of himself. He's going through a rough time. Hope we're all still friends here.' His smile appeared weak but sincere enough for Jack to accept it as genuine.

'Friends? You've never mentioned him once. And I'm not being a *nuisance*. I'm just trying to find out why this bastard slept with *my* girlfriend.' George stuffed his hands into his pockets, giving Jack the side eye.

'Georgie, the girl has told you a hundred times that she wasn't playing away. Why can't you believe her?' Steve shook his head.

147

'I know something went on.'

'Georgie, you're acting like a dickhead.' Steve let out a deep, nervous laugh. Dave did too. 'Now you're going to apologise to these fellas and me and Dave are going to network for a bit.'

'Like fuck I will.' George jutted his chin.

Jack wanted to roll his eyes so badly. George's juvenile routine had somehow outweighed the fear he'd bought moments before. He was too ridiculous to be a threat.

'It's all right, Stevo. No need for apologies. We were young once, remember the trouble we got into?' Dave gently bashed his fist into Steve's shoulder. 'And don't worry about the networking lark, we can do another time.'

'Don't be silly. I've got people you need to meet. George will be leaving you both alone. He won't be bothering you again.' Steve faced his son. 'Isn't that right, Georgie?'

'No!'

'Did I say no when you asked for that car? Or your tablet. Or those clothes on your back? No. I didn't.' Steve's face reddened, the disappointment and anger clear in his eyes.

'But, Dad!'

'No buts, Georgie. Stop acting like a spoilt child and do as your fucking told for once.'

Silence filled the air between the four of them. Wincing, Jack's entire body cringed and he could only imagine how George was feeling. He looked wrecked, like he hadn't slept for a month. Although he'd been a dick, Jack empathised with him – the guy was so obviously suffering. And all because he wanted to be loved. The saddest part of it all was that what had started out as a happy reunion between Dave and Steve had somehow merged into an awkward display of unhappy families. Maybe George didn't have it all.

'So Davie, let's get a move on.' Steve beamed as though all had been forgotten. 'I'll do all the talking. You know me.'

'Unfortunately, I do.' Dave chortled. 'But I don't know about leaving Jack on his own. He's only just learnt how to flip burgers.'

Six eyes turned on Jack. Two from Dave, two from Steve and two narrowed daggers from George. Jack didn't blink, just shrugged. The panic was as clear on his face as the tattoos on his neck. 'I'm cool, man. You go do your thing.'

It was all the persuasion that Dave needed. There were no words from him, just a look of gratitude. Gone was the urgency or embarrassment that he'd shot at Jack. The kindness was back and Jack couldn't help but beam at his uncle.

Watching the two long-lost pals walk off to the biggest gazebo at the festival, Jack sucked in a deep breath, of disbelief mainly. He'd been certain that he was going to get a fist in his face at one point. The anger in George's blue eyes was too intense not to expect it. But even though George lingered behind, still glaring at him, he was deflated. The wind ripped from his sails.

Climbing into the van, Jack scooped up the orders for the two girls who he couldn't believe were still there, waiting for their food. For a moment, everything had been sucked into a surreal bubble. Anger, family, disappointment, happiness. All in the space of a few minutes. The fuck?

Jack nodded to the girls as they took their food and walked off, he didn't even remember if they'd paid or not. One customer was still there and he needed to deal with that before he could think of anything else. He sorted the burger, adding extra jalapenos like the fella had asked for and held it out to him. 'You still want your burger, man?'

Jack spoke softly. Keeping it safe, he only met George's gaze for a split second

'Don't talk to me.' George snorted, slamming a fiver down.

In that moment, Jack was certain that George was going to grab him and drag him over the counter. He didn't. Instead, he snatched his burger and spun on his heel with a snarl.

Exhausted, Jack watched the crazy blond kid stomp all the way to the tent his dad and Dave had disappeared into. So much shit didn't make sense. But all Jack could do was sigh a breath of relief that it was over.

Shaking the last few moments from is head, Jack observed the crowds, letting them steal his attention once more. Hundreds of people there, some dancing, some drinking, most eating. And not one of them had a single clue how close he was to just being beaten by a bloke who had it all wrong.

He laughed, to himself. He had to. It allowed him to make some sense of it all. He laughed even harder when his uncle ran over to the van – his brown eyes magnified by his thick lenses and larger than ever.

'Jacky, me old son. Get the rest of those bloody burgers on the go. We got some bloody networking to do.'

Chapter Nineteen

'Can't believe your dad invited them back to your gaff!' Alfie growled into George's face. Drunk on a day's worth of free booze, curtesy of "Taylor's Properties," his breath was a rancid mixture of cider and pickled jalapeños. George flung that fiery beast of a burger Alfie's way as soon as he was out of Jack's sight. But, regardless of the stench, George shared the same sentiment.

'I think it's lovely. Look how happy they are.' Aimee gushed at Steve and Dave. George snarled under his breath.

In true Steve Taylor style, he'd hyped up Dave's cooking skills to every business owner in Colchester, sealing catering deals and further meetings. The bloke could sell spectacles to the blind. It's what made his property business such a success.

Dave seemed all right to be fair and his food was clearly a hit. But after cooking all their burgers for the networking do, Jack had come along for a bit of promoting too and proved to be just as successful as the fucking food. Was there anything the fella wasn't good at?

'I just can't believe that Jack is coming into your house, mate. Fucking mental.' Alfie mumbled through a string of belches.

After touting him as the 'best burger chef in Essex,' Steve invited Dave, and *everyone* else, back to the house for drinks to celebrate. But with Dave giving them a lift home, George endured the most awkward car journey of his life. Even a bellyful of booze couldn't block that tension out.

With four people piled into the back of the car, Aimee had to perch on Alfie's lap whilst George and Jack were squashed together like battery hens. Way too close for comfort.

'I'm sure you'll get over it, Alf. Just stick with Aimee….like usual.' George clenched his jaw as he followed them into the house. Alfie's already flushed face turned a deeper shade of red under the warm glow of the hallway chandelier and Aimee, clearly annoyed, silently removed her jacket.

He'd needed the emotional support from both of them but he hadn't got it. Nothing. Especially not from Aimee. She's proved herself to be a snake and George found himself in the grass she slithered in.

Once he'd got to his dad's tent and chucked Alfie the shitty burger, George tried to apologise to Aimee on his own. He reminded her how she'd been a shit friend when he was going through such a bad time and that she had betrayed him. But her response was folded arms and a pout. It was usually proof that she was guilty of something.

George ran his tongue over his teeth and turned his attention to Jack – his tattooed hands were tucked into his jean pockets as he gawked at Taylor family photos on the walls. He didn't look right in the house at all. In fact, he even made the silver crushed velvet chaise longue look classy in comparison. George couldn't wait for his mother to see him, standing in her hallway with ripped clothes and "criminal pirate" tattoos all over himself.

'Show our guests in, will you, Georgie?' Steve asked as he rubbed his hands together. 'Your mum is gonna wet herself when she sees who's here.'

With an air of smugness, George avoided eye contact as he summoned them with a nod. As he entered the lounge, his mother beamed at him and his Nan winked through a cloud of smoke. The lights were off and the curtains drawn. Cream coloured candles were lit all around the room and a mixed fragrance of warm vanilla and his Nan's fruit and aniseed vape hung in the air. The TV was playing that radio station full of slow songs that everyone over forty seemed to love. If there weren't opened prosecco bottles on the table, he'd have thought they were holding another one of his mum's séances.

'Maxine!' Dave bellowed into the room with open arms. The flames of the candles reflected off his gasses.

'Davie Bretton? Oh my bloody god!' George's mother nearly threw her wine glass, and its contents, into the air as she jumped out of the arm chair. She was clearly tipsy, which made her wide-eyed expression even more hilarious. 'Come here and give me a hug. I can't believe it.'

'Bloody hell, girl. Look at you, you're still as a gorgeous as ever.' Dave wrapped his arms around her.

Aimee cooed with a long 'awwww' and George even let himself chuckle too. Just for a second.

'Mum, Mum, look who it is. It's Davie. Davie Bretton!' Maxine squealed to Pam.

'I know who it is, love. I heard you the first time.' She blew out another cloud of vapour and remaining seated, stretched out an arm and tilted her cheek towards Dave. 'Give us a kiss, Davie. It's good to see you again.'

'Pammy Daley!' Dave planted a loud kiss on the side of her face. 'Well I'll be damned. Look at you. It's been almost twenty years and you don't look any different. What's your secret?'

'Nothing. She's always looked like the crypt keeper.' Steve howled behind them. Alfie erupted into laughter too, the exaggerated kind that comes after ten pints, but was immediately hushed by Aimee.

'Shut your noise, you.' Pam scrunched up her bleached-white hair with her fingers and raised her chin. 'But sorry, Davie, love. A lady never reveals her secrets.'

'Looks like mummification to me.' Steve mumbled under his breath.

'Anyways, love, how's your mum?'

'She's good, Pam. She's passed, bless her.'

'Oh, I'm very sorry to hear that.' Pam sucked on her vape then smiled sincerely. 'Still, she was never happy after Bullseye ended. She's at peace now, love.'

'Mum!' Maxine moaned - the excitement on her face just moments before had been replaced with embarrassment. Clearing her throat, she turned to Dave. 'Well, Davie, what can we can get you?' Her smile stretched from ear to ear. 'Stevie, get our guest a drink. We need to make a toast or something. It's been donkey's years.'

'I'm on it, my dearest.' Steve squeezed her waist as he lent in to meet her lips. George recoiled at the, yet another, display of sickening affection.

'Want a beer, Dave? Or ale? I've got spirits if you like. What about you, Jack?'

'Jack?' Maxine raised an eyebrow. The excitement of seeing Dave had seemingly given her tunnel vision.

'I beg your pardon, Maxine. Let me introduce you to Jack.'

Steve, Dave and Aimee quickly moved out of the way, and Alfie followed suit once his polo shirt was tugged by Aimee. George bit his lip, the anticipation of seeing his mother's reaction to the tattooed yob in her living room was giving him life.

Maxine clamped a hand to her mouth as Jack stepped forward. George noticed how his mother scanned the bloke's clothes and saw shock in her eyes. Everything she disliked about society was standing in her front room.

His Nan sat up straight, shoulders back and chest protruding – grinning wildly, just like when she first saw the new postman. The one with the muscles. The one that was too scared to come to the house when she was around.

'I never knew you had children, Davie.' Maxine said.

Dave flushed red. 'I wish. He's Shell's sister's boy. Jack.'

'Oh?' Maxine's face dropped. 'Jackie, darlin. Come here.' Maxine threw her arms around him and squeezed him around the shoulders. She seemed like she wanted to cry. 'I haven't seen you since you was a tiny baby. Oh my god. Look at you. You're so handsome.'

Rage rushed over George. So much so, he thought he was going to set on fire. What the fuck?

'All right, Max, we've got all night for reminiscing. What you drinking, fella?' Steve patted Dave's shoulder like they were 'buds' from a cheesy eighties movie. It was nice to see his Dad happy – he'd been moody ever since George chose the apprenticeship over the family business so any break from the gloom was welcomed.

'Got lager? But only the one though. I'm driving.'

'No, you're not, matey. I haven't seen you for bloody years. We are having a good old catch up.'

'But I've got my motor here and the van....I don't fancy paying a oner for a taxi.'

'Don't worry about that, mate.' Maxine hooked her arm around Jack's elbow. 'We've got a couple of rooms here you can sleep in, Davie. My daughter has deserted me so Jack can stay in her room. You can have the spare room. Come into the kitchen and I'll get you a nice cold beer.'

After Alfie slumped onto the sofa and shouted for them to fetch a couple of beers in for him, George automatically followed the others into the kitchen. He couldn't give a shit what his parents spoke to Dave about but when his Nan had trailed behind waving an empty glass and her handbag, he didn't want to miss out on the action. He didn't trust Jack in his house either, not for a second

In the kitchen, his mum was searching the back of the cupboard for the "good glasses" as his dad came in from the garage with a six pack of lagers in one hand and George's bottle of bourbon in the other. George instantly scowled. He couldn't hide it and wasn't willing to try. That was his booze and he was not sharing it. Not with Jack. Not on his watch. 'Dad, that's *mine*.'

'Sharing's caring, son.' Steve laughed him off, handing the bottle to Jack.

George chewed his lip. He could taste blood. All he wanted to do was snatch the bottle from Jack and whack the fucker over the head with it.

'Is there anything for us ladies to drink or do we go without all night?' Pam clutched her handbag in a sulk.

'There's bottles of Prosecco in the wine cooler. I got them especially for you and Maxine.'

'Not any more, there's not. You know what she's like when she starts knocking 'em back.'

George's mother pouted. 'I've only had two glasses.'

'Honestly, that girl has always been the same. Drinks until she blacks out. I had nipples like coat hooks when breastfeeding her.'

'Ah Pam, do you have to? We're here for a good night. No one wants to know about your nipples.' George's dad grimaced. 'But if it'll shut you up, I'll go get you some more Prosecco.'

Sliding a couple of notes from her purse, Pam steadied herself against the breakfast bar. I've had enough of prosecco. Will you grab me something else?'

'Don't worry about it, Pam. I'll get it.' Steve rolled his eyes and tutted. 'What do you want?'

'No you won't.' She waved the two twenties with a frown 'Get me some gin. My rule is cheapest bottle with the highest alcohol percentage.'

'We've got gin in the garage.'

'Not any more, you haven't. She nodded to Maxine then hiccupped. 'She's like the fucking Exorcist. Clears your house of all spirits.'

'Dave, do you mind giving me a lift? It's just round the corner.'

Jack moved closer to his uncle, clearly hoping to be invited with them to the off license and George couldn't help but snort loudly.

'Course Stevo. If I'm staying then I think we need shots anyway.' Dave clapped his hands together and beamed at him at the idea. He then turned to Jack and squeezed his shoulder. 'You stay here, son. I won't be long. Honestly, it'll be all right.'

George knew that was aimed at him.

Moments later, laughter echoed through the hallway as the two fellas left the house. Jack cleared his throat before pulling the ripped black jumper over his head and George frowned as Pam's eyes widened at the fella's tattooed and flat stomach exposed by his T-shirt riding up.

'Come in the front room with me, Jack. You can tell me how low those tattoos of yours go.' Pam curled her manicured fingers around his arm and walked him and George's bourbon out of the kitchen. Aimee giggled to herself as she scooped up a couple of beers for Alfie and followed them in.

Maxine grabbed a glass off the side but before she could leave the room, George gripped her arm, keeping her behind. His entire body was hot with rage.

'Mum, is everyone ignoring the fact that that's Jack.'

'I know, darlin. He's Davie's nephew.' Her eyes were bloodshot but still able to focus. 'I remember him when he

157

was just a baby. He had all that dark hair even then, you know. He looked like a little monkey.' Her smile slipped. 'Such a shame he's covered in all those tattoos now. He looks like he works at the fairground.'

George shook his head and took a deep breath. 'No mum. That's "Jack" Jack!' His enlarged eyes drilled into hers.

'What? Jack as in Jack, Jack? Ellie and you, Jack? O M God, such a small bloody world, isn't it?'

George rolled his eyes. Why the fuck did everyone keep saying that?

'Mum!'

'Darlin, you need to get over it. Ells told me that nothing went on between her and that boy. She's sworn to me that she didn't cheat on you.'

'What? You've been speaking to her?' George asked a little too loudly. Betrayal kicked him the second time that day. He quickly craned his neck, checking the doorway of the front room. He didn't want anyone else hearing that his own mother had gone behind his back.

'Yeah of course I've been speaking to her. I love Ellie. Me and her mum have been BFFs since you two kids were eating playdoh at nursery. Remember when you wet yourself on the reading corner? Aww.'

'Mum!'

'Well, I wanted to see if Ells was all right. I miss her. So, I 'whats-upped' her. Oh, she's going through such a tough time, darlin.'

'I know…. So am I for fuck's sake! Remember me….your son? The one who's heart's been broken?'

'Darlin, don't say 'for eff sake' when your Nan's in the house.' His mum grabbed George's shoulders. More so to steady herself it seemed. 'You and Ells will work it out. I deffo got that vibe when I met her for lunch.'

'WHAT?' George's mouth fell open.

'Oh yeah, I forgot to tell you. You know how busy I've been. Well, anyways, I met Ells and her mum last week. We went to that new shopping centre in Stratford. It's so busy, Georgie, but the John Lewis is amazing.'

'Are you actually joking?'

'No, Seriously. I got a lovely bedspread, on sale too.'

'MUM! I mean about meeting Ellie. Behind my back!'

'Stop shouting, we've got guests.' She swigged the remainder of her prosecco. 'And get over yourself, darlin. Ellie is an independent woman studying whatever she's studying at university. She can talk to anyone she likes. And so can I. It's the twentieth century, I'll have you know.'

George shook his head and squeezed the bridge of his nose. 'It's the twenty-first century, Mum. And he's not just a mate, is he?'

'Darlin, she's told you nothing happened and she's told me that too. I'm sure that *graffitied* boy in there will tell you the same.'

'He has…..But, mum. I just know.'

'No more buts, Georgie. You've gotta move on from this, just like your Nan and dad say. And you know they never agree on anything. That's the Gemini in them. I know it's difficult but…..you can't keep acting like this.'

George's body slumped. His eyelids burned as he blinked the rising tears away.

'I better get in there before your Nan strips that poor boy off.'

Alone, George slid his phone out of his pocket and stared at the screen. He knew what he wanted to do, yet he knew that he shouldn't. Shaking off the logic, he unlocked the phone and pressed onto his messages app. His finger lingered over Ellie's name for moment before opening up their last conversation. The words on her last message, the ones telling him that she needed more time, sat heavily in his chest.

He began typing but his thumb froze over the keypad as Jack stepped into the kitchen. George met his gaze and the silence bounced off of the walls. The ticking from the clock boomed, annoying George with each tick. But it was the sound of Jack breathing that infuriated him most. George slammed his phone on the side, not giving a fuck if the screen had cracked. He tapped his foot to drown it all out but as Jack twisted the mouthful of his JD, he lost his shit.

'Fucking hell, what is wrong with you?'

'I've just come to speak to you. Properly.' Jack creased his brow.

'You're so fucking annoying. Why are you even here?'

'Your dad…..he told us to…'

'Just because my dad and your uncle are acting like they fucking love each other, don't mean that I have to talk to you. You got it? I think you're a prick and don't want you here.'

Jack hunched his shoulders and took swig of George's bourbon.

'Go fuck yourself, Jack.'

'Man, I don't want to be here, just as much as you don't want me here. This ain't up to me.'

Snarling, George lunged at Jack. Grabbing him by the shoulders, he pinned him against the fridge with his arm. His face was so close to Jack's that he could see the green specks in his eyes. George's stomach raged with anger and his other fist automatically tightened into a ball. The bloke might have had a trim body but he was weak as shit. And George knew could take him.

'Not your fault? All this is your fault. You broke me and my girlfriend up.' George pushed him into the wall again.

'Fuck, man. Not this again.'

'Why can't you just admit it?' George pressed his arm into Jack, making sure it hurt.

'I didn't do a thing.' Jack pushed his body off of the wall, pressing his weight against George. 'Okay, she came on to me. Tried to kiss me. That's it. She was blind drunk.'

George leant in harder, he needed to see the man in pain. 'She came onto you?'

'Yes. But I didn't do anything back, man. Honestly. Ellie is a sweet girl, but I'm not into her. If you two have split up, it's nothing to do with me.'

'We haven't split up. We're stronger than that.'

'Then what's the problem? Why you hating on me?'

George looked away, the man's focus and the realisation of what Ellie had done hit him too hard to meet his gaze. He'd been a dick. A complete and utter dick. All this time, he had blamed Jack when it was Ellie. Their relationship must have been shit for a while for her to try it on with other guys and dump him. He just didn't see it. That fact was unavoidable.

'Oh, get a room boys.' Pam stood at the doorway, hand on hip and steely faced.

'Nan….we were…..I was…..'

'What you do with your love life is none of my business, Georgie. But, if you don't mind, I'd like to steal your boyfriend for a minute. I need a proper cigarette.'

George knew he had to let go, but he couldn't. Not just yet. But it wasn't Jack that he found hard to release, he knew that. It was Ellie.

Pam laid her hand on George's arm, squeezing it lightly. 'Let go, love.'

George huffed hard as he released the fella, the breath he had somehow been holding onto, finally came out. He gulped down his guilt and wiped the frustration from his burning eyes. 'I'm sorry….I just.'

'It's cool, man.' Jack rubbed his throat.

'Why don't you go and splash your face then get yourself a drink, Georgie?' Pam stepped between them, clearly creating a barrier that George would never advance. He could feel Jack's eyes on him but that didn't bother him anymore. George had nothing to prove. There was nothing to fight anymore. 'Come on, let's put all this nonsense behind us. We'll all have a drink together, eh? Even have a bit of a sing-song. It'll do you good.'

'Nan….I…I just can't be without her.' George's shoulder began to tremble in spite of himself.

Pam rubbed her thumb softly over his cheek and pulled up his chin. 'Georgie love, you've always had your mum and your dad, and me and your sister. You're stuck to your mate's side. You don't know what you're capable of because you've never had any time on your own to think about it.'

George sniffed and swallowed the lump in his throat. His anger was still bubbling away but if he was to say anything else, he'd end up crying. His Nan nodded and the smile she gave reassured him somehow.

'Jack, love. Will you come to the garage with me? I'm sure that tight arsed son-in-law of mine has got a karaoke box in there.'

'Of course, Mrs…..erm…I'm sorry, I don't know your name.'

'Call me Pam, love.' She slid her arm through his and walked him to the back door. 'You never did tell me about those tattoos of yours.'

Chapter Twenty

A light rapping at the door awoke Jack from his drink-induced coma and pain throbbed through his head. Blinking a few times - the only movement he could handle – he tried to get his bearings. It took him a couple of moments to remember where he'd ended up the night before. In George's house.

The place seemed like a palace. Unlike any home he'd ever been in. Dave's house, always cosy and spotless, had nothing on George's gaff. It was something out of a magazine. Every room, a different shade of cream with chandeliers and real wooden floors radiated comfort and style. It even smelled expensive. Last night, there had been candles lit around the front room and not because they couldn't afford the electricity either. How the other half live.

He leant for the glass of water beside his bed and almost spat out the gulp he had taken. He remembered Pam handing it to him on his way up the stairs. But it seemed that the only clear liquid she knew was Gin and Tonic.

Another rap at the door jolted him to life and it opened, bringing in the daylight. 'Morning.' Dave peered in and the look of sympathy on his face filled Jack with dread. The fear that came after a night of drinking gurgled in his chest.

'Hey, man.' Jack ran his tongue over his furry teeth. He almost gagged at the stale taste of alcohol and cigarettes.

'Sorry if I woke you, but Maxine is cooking up a right treat down there. You don't wanna miss out on that.'

The mere mention of food filled the room with the aromas of crisping bacon and coffee. Jack swallowed down the urge to vomit.

'Here, I made you a cuppa. Thought you might need it.' Dave held the mug out to Jack.

Jack closed his eyes to sit up, his brain making a jellyfish motion in his skull. 'Dave, man. I'm dying.'

'I never knew you were such a light-weight, son.' Dave laughed, perching himself on the bed. Jack closed his eyes again.

'I've never drank that much. Ever.'

'You chucked back two shots and you was off your nut'

'Ah, man, don't tell me.' Jack cringed. 'Was I a dick?'

'Not at all, mate. Everyone was pie-eyed by the end of the night. Tell you what, I've never seen a bunch of people get so excited over karaoke.'

'Ah shit, the karaoke.'

Memories of the night before came flooding to him - his head swirled more with each flashback. Alfie had passed out on the sofa whilst Aimee and Pam had sung an ABBA song and Maxine had done her best impression of Adele. He didn't want to think anymore. He wouldn't like what he'd remember.

'Did I sing?'

'Did you? You was singing your little heart out, son. Never had you down as Whitney fan.'

Jack clamped a hand to his head, a little too hard, then rubbed his throbbing temples to soften the memories.

'You was fine until you had a couple of Gee and Tees. Boy, you like some depressing songs. You didn't even look at the screen for the words.' Dave raised his eyebrows and placed his hand on Jack's arm. 'Everything all right with you?'

'Yeah, all good, man. Just out of it, I guess. So, I made a massive twat of myself?'

'Not at all. Everyone had a sing song. Even me and Stevo gave it our all for Meatloaf. And Pam.....I think she's taken a shine to you.' Dave burst into laughter, seeming to completely ignore Jack's fragile state.

'What?'

'Bloody hell. You must have been pissed coz there's no way you would forget something like that in a hurry.'

'What did she do?'

'Let's just say that she knows all the words to "Like a virgin."

Jack snorted, instantly regretting it. Whatever size his brain had shrunk to in the night, it was rattling around his skull like a pinball machine.

'Can we go?' I've gotta get out of this place.' Jack frantically searched the room for his phone and fags.

'What's the rush? Maxine is cooking us a fry up. Stevo's got a bit of news too.'

'Dave, it's a bit awkward for me here, man. George is not my biggest fan, is he? In fact, the fella hates me.'

'I know, matey. Elsie is it? He didn't shut up about her all night. But, I'm glad you've both put it behind you, eh?'

'What you talking about?'

'Bloody hell, you was either pissed or you've got the onset of dementia. After his mates went home, who by the way are a great laugh, you and Georgie boy were like best buds.'

'Piss off, Dave.' All Jack could remember was being thrown against a wall in the kitchen and then spending the next hour or so trying to stay out of the fella's way.

'Seriously! You two belted out "Let it go" like you were a pair of Disney princesses on your way to the ball.' Dave chuckled. He stood and slowly made his way to the door. 'Anyways, come down stairs once you've sorted yourself out.'

Jack plonked the tea next to the glass of gin on the bedside table, and fell back onto the pillow, attempting to block out the embarrassment.

Most of the room, like the rest of the house, was painted cream, with one wall decorated in pink flowery paper. The bedspread that he sprawled on matched the roses and a magenta sheepskin rug on the floor. It was obviously George's sister's room, although other than a plaque with the name 'Darcie' painted with pink letters and a box of books on the floor, the room looked like it'd never been lived in. It was too immaculate.

After a few moments, he sucked in a deep breath and dragged himself off the bed and onto his feet. Focusing on his boots on the rug, he managed to steady himself and sipped the tea that Dave had made. It was far too milky for his taste and laid heavily on his tongue. He swallowed down the feeling before he could bring it back up.

He slipped on his boots and taking what seemed like a mug of full fat milk with him, he ventured from the room and instantly felt drunk again. The morning sun shining through the hallway shot a pain behind his eyes and momentarily paralysed him. The walls were clustered with matching framed photographs of the family. The staged poses with white backgrounds and them climbing over each other with overly happy faces was slightly nauseating, but Jack could still appreciate them. They showed a family that were happy in each other's company and the love they shared for each other burst through with every sparkling white smile.

Before he got to the landing, light snoring vibrated from the next bedroom. It was more like a sniffle than the full roar he was used to hearing from Dave's house. Although his uncle always blamed it on Marie.

Jack peeked through the gap in the door to another immaculate room. With just a few recently worn clothes strewn on the dark wooden floor, the room too looked unused. George was sprawled face down on a king-sized bed, the chequered covers were scrunched at the bottom of the mattress, and Jack narrowed his eyes to focus on the definition of George's back. The muscles bulged and rippled along his shoulders and the non-tattooed skin filled Jack with envy. George's cheek was squashed against the pillow but the bloke still looked every bit of the boy next door. Jack wished he was awake just to see those blue eyes.

His hangover doubled on reaching the kitchen where the noise rushed over him; Dave and Steve ranting over the sports pages of the Sunday newspaper, whilst Maxine sang along to the digital radio on the worktop. Oil sizzled in a frying pan and the kettle sounded like a rocket as it boiled. Everyone seemed fine, as though they hadn't even touched a drop of alcohol, and were way too chirpy for ten a.m. on a bloody Sunday. Jack scanned the rest of the room. Luckily, Pam was nowhere to be seen. He sighed in relief.

They all greeted him at the same time and he offered a weak smile in return. Just for a moment. Even curling his lips proved painful. He hated talking to people he barely knew. Not because he was antisocial or uninterested, he just could never find the right words.

'Morning, Jack. How you feeling, darlin?' Maxine asked. 'You look a bit peaky.' She took the mug from him and tried to give him a glass of fresh orange juice. He recoiled. He was way too close to chucking up for that.

'I'm ok, thanks, Mrs Taylor.' There was no way he was going to projectile vomit all over her pristine kitchen.

'Oh, behave yourself.' She forced the glass into his hand. 'You need some food in you too. You need looking after, darlin. That's what mothers are for.'

The room fell quiet, until Steve stood and cleared his throat, coughing it into a balled fist. Dave then turned the conversation to the rain outside. Jack was used to it.

167

Whenever anyone mentioned his mother, or even anything about mothers in general, the people aware of his situation always changed the subject.

'What about a cup of coffee while I heat up the beans?' Maxine busied herself with the dials on the cooker. 'I'll get some more toast on too.'

'Erm, I'm not a big coffee drinker.' Jack admitted. 'Can I have another tea? Strong, please.'

'Course you can, Jack.' Steve fetched a teapot from the counter and placed it on the table in front of him. 'I'm the same. Strong enough to stand your spoon in.'

'Thanks.' Jack nodded, lowering into a seat.

'Want a cuppa, Dave?' Steve asked, fetching the semi skimmed from the fridge.

'Please matey. Just a spit of milk, ta. Can't stand a milky brew.'

Jack snorted.

'It's been great to meet you, mate.' Steve patted Jack's back and took a seat opposite him. 'Davie, here, has been telling me about you all morning. You're the apple of his eye.'

Jack smiled, his chest warming.

'Well, he's a bloody good kid. Even though he does look like a hooligan with them tattoos.'

'How comes you've got so many, darlin?' Maxine asked, plonking a square plate in front of him, jam-packed with food. Bacon, sausages, hash browns, mushrooms and baked beans. Jack thanked her, trying not to breathe in the smells wafting under his nose.

'Erm, I just like body art, Mrs. Taylor.' Jack sat on his hands.

'Nothing wrong with that. I think you look good. It's all the rage these days. Besides, your uncle tells me that you're looking for your own place, Jack.' Steve kept his focus on Jack and slid a glob of marmalade over his toast.

'Erm, I actually have a flat in Forest Gate. But I'm staying at Dave's for a bit. I can go back whenever though.' He turned to his uncle. 'If you want me out, man, just say.'

'Not at all, son. My house is your house.'

'Sorry, Jack, I meant a place for your business.' Steve bit the corner of his toast, a globule of orange marmalade dripped onto the table.

'My business?'

'Yeah, tattooing.' Dave interrupted. 'You can't keep working for me forever.'

'Your uncle's right, mate. You need a place so you can earn yourself some cash. We work for most of our lives, its only right we spend it doing something we love.'

'I'd love to, Mr. Taylor. But I've, erm, literally got fifty quid to my name, I'm still paying rent at my old flat.'

Jack's stomach flipped, recalling the drugs money stashed in the airing cupboard back at his flat. He hadn't been back to the flat once. He'd relished the distance. And knowing Cole, the fella had already broken into the place already. He'd done it before. A couple of times actually. When Jack had the audacity to leave it unattended whilst working double shifts. Even the reinforced lock he'd saved up months for hadn't stopped him getting inside by force. Jack was always shocked how Cole's weakness for drugs could give him super strength. But a part of Jack hoped he had broken in and took the money. That would somehow ease his conscience for deserting him.

'Don't worry about any of that now, Jack. I remember being twenty one. Me and Maxine didn't have a pot to piss in. It's even harder for youngsters these days so that's why we're gonna help you out.'

'What do you mean?' Jack scooped up a forkful of beans but couldn't quite bring himself to eat them.

'Your uncle's grub was a hit yesterday. My phone hasn't stopped buzzing all morning about it. He's onto a blinder there.' Steve winked at Dave.

Jack raised his eye brows - his hangover overruled by his pride for his uncle.

'We've been talking and we're gonna expand Dave's business up this way, get him a regular site. I've got the perfect little cafe on the books for him, smack in the middle of the town.'

'That's amazing, Dave!' Jack shovelled the beans into his mouth before snatching a triangle of toast from the rack.

'Yeah, it feels right. Me and Stevo are going into business together. We haven't worked out all the small print yet but Steve's gonna inject a bit of cash.' Dave nodded to his friend. 'And in return he's gonna take a percentage of the income till I pay him back.'

'Holy fuckballs, that's fucking great.' Jack sloshed down a mouthful of tea and noticed Maxine staring in shock at the men around the table.

'I'm, erm, sorry for swearing, Mrs. Taylor.'

'It's ok, darlin. It's my mother that hates swearing. I'm….I'm fine with it.'

Jack licked the corner of his mouth before turning to Dave. 'That's amazing. Honestly, couldn't be happier for you, man.'

'Hold up, hold up. We haven't told you your part yet, son.'

'Eh?'

'Above the café is a flat that comes with the tenancy. A sweet little two storey number. Your uncle thinks it'll do you good to get out of London. You could easily make the top floor into a cosy studio flat and have the lower half as a fully legit tattoo parlour. Bit of cash and some business insurance needed, obviously.'

Jack's mouth dropped, along with the chunk of toast he had just bitten off. He had a thousand questions to ask but couldn't find the words. And so preoccupied with what they had just told him, he hadn't even noticed George standing in the doorway. Half yawning and dressed in a fluffy, navy blue dressing gown, the fella looked as rough as Jack felt. Taking a cup of tea from his mum, George nodded to him and Jack smiled back apprehensively.

'So, as soon as you've eaten your breakfast, Jack, me and your uncle will take you to have a butchers at the place. What do ya say?'

'Erm...' Jack answered.

Chapter Twenty One

Pushing the car door open with his foot, George groaned. Every part of him ached from the moment he'd rolled out of his pit and munched his way through a full English. The hangover had hold of his guts and flashbacks from the night before left him cringing out of his skin and wanting to vomit. Lugging himself from the backseat, he zipped up his hoodie and winced through the rain to hurry into the old café after his father, Dave and Jack.

George had little interest, if any at all, in his dad's new scheme. Although he no longer hated Jack, he had no reason to like him. Helping the fella and his uncle set up a business in his home town was not at the top of his list of things to do on a Sunday morning. Especially when he was so close to death. He'd only tagged along for the free lift — too delicate to walk back to the farm for his car. That and, well, curiosity had got the better of him.

Stepping into the old café brought pangs of nostalgia as well as a lungful of dust. It was like the place had been abandoned for decades, and not just the two years it had been closed. George had spent most of his teens in there, along with Ellie, Alfie and Aimee, of course.

The cafe had been their haunt, there go to. Each afternoon after school, they'd spent sipping milkshakes and recalling the juvenile dramas of Coggletree High.

Lunging into the booth, where they once sat as a foursome, his head spun as he nuzzled into the back of the worn red leather.

Steve and Dave were already in the kitchen, tapping their knuckles on walls and "guesstimating" measurements for how they envisaged the new Burger joint. Jack, silent and solitary, stood by the old Panini press that for some reason had been left behind. The fella seemed indifferent with the place. Or maybe, just in awe. George was way too rough to work out which.

The emptiness of the place pulled at George's already weary stomach. The café had once buzzed with teenage chatter, sizzling grills and a steaming coffee machine. All that had now gone and the prospect of yet another changed feature in his life caused his brain to spin like the Slushies once had.

'This place is a little beauty, isn't it?' Dave pushed his way through the saloon doors, his voice echoing through the empty café. 'Why'd the owner sell up?'

Steve followed him out, his gaze taking in every detail of the place, no doubt looking for ways to up-sell it. George had seen it a thousand times. His dad could sell meat to vegans – or so his mother would say. 'Health reasons, mate. Such a shame. He was a decent chap, eh, Georgie?'

George nodded, regretting it instantly. 'Yeah, old Sam had a heart attack.' The very thought of the old man sent waves of sadness through his own chest.

'There's everything you need to start here, Davey boy. The griddle could do with replacing but Bob only changed the vents, stove and counters a few years back.' Steve ran his hand over the metal heat lamps that hadn't been lit for over two years. 'Bit of a dust and this place is good to go, mate.'

'Might have to do something about the booths though. They look a bit knackered. I know a bloke in Hackney that could whack a bit of pleather on them for a few quid.'

'You're right, there.' Steve patted Dave firmly on the back. 'They could do with being ripped out, couldn't they?'

'What? You can't do that. These seats are part of this place.' George blinked in disbelief.

'He's right. I think you should keep them how they are.' Jack said, sliding into the seat opposite, knocking his knee against George's. 'They look good as they are. It's got that retro feel. That's what people want.'

George observed Jack through half opened eyes. The fella had a face that didn't give anything away. But, nonetheless, George appreciated the back-up.

'Yeah, see? You don't want to go changing everything that people loved about this place. You remember how busy it used to get?'

Dave and Steve shrugged in unison and mumbled to each other as they measured the width of the serving hatch with their arm spans, each centimetre and foot calculated by the size of their hands. If George wasn't trying his hardest to not blow chunks all over the table, he would have allowed himself to laugh. "Tweedle Dee and Tweedle Dumbass" came to mind. Jack, too, seemed to be stifling a laugh.

'Why don't you go look at the flat upstairs, Jack?' Steve slid the keys out of his back pocket. 'Us old geezers have to finish measuring up down here.'

'Sure.' Jack sprang from the booth. 'Thanks, man.'

It didn't bother George to see the fella happy but it didn't stop him snorting either though as Jack's cheeks glowed with excitement.

'Why don't you go with him, Georgie? You look bored off your nut there.' Steve disappeared beneath a counter. Seconds later the lights came on, illuminating the dusty café.

'What? I'm hanging.'

'Go on, Georgie. You'll be helping with decorating the place so you might as well pull your finger out now.' Steve emerged with cob webs stuck to his brown hair. 'You want a lift to the farm, don't you?'

George bit into his bottom lip to stop himself from swearing.

'Why? Why am I decorating it? It's your businesses. Nothing to do with me. Not like I'll be seeing a penny from it.' George huffed, yanking his hood over his head.

'I don't take any house keep off you, do I? Besides, it wouldn't hurt you to help your old man out. So that's why.' Steve hooked his thumb towards the rear exit that Jack had just vanished through. 'Now get up there.'

Huffing, George hauled himself out of the booth and dragged his feet towards the back door. 'Always fucking moaning.'

'I'm your dad, that's what I do.' Steve laughed. 'And measure the top window for me too. It needs replacing.'

'What with?' George's whine ricocheted off the walls.

'Use your bloody hands.'

The iron stairs to the flats above the shops were cold and slippery from the pelting rain. Jack flew up the fuckers like they were on fire, but George followed at a glacial pace, forcing himself up each flight with the enthusiasm that only the dying could muster.

He didn't know what to say to Jack. He didn't even know if they were on speaking terms. He couldn't remember. Flashbacks of sing-a-long Disney was all he had. And getting pissed and singing karaoke didn't mean they were mates. All George wanted to do was get his motor from the farm and piss off back to his bed to watch films on his fifty-five-inch TV until his mum called him down for his Sunday roast.

Jack was already at the door of the flat when George reached the top of the stairs. Shivering and soaked, the fella twisted the key in the stubborn lock.

'You gonna come in?' Jack bit his lip.

George scanned the outside of the place. Kids had broken into the empty flats a couple of times, but it wasn't half bad from the outside. Even with the large blue sign pinned to the wall, reminding him of what a terrible son he was. The yellow words stung at his throat. *"Taylors Properties – A Family Business."*

George shrugged, swallowing the guilt. 'Yeah, whatever.'

Following behind the eager Jack, he lowered his hood and passed through the hallway, into the kitchen. The smell did nothing for his hangover but apart from a couple of knackered worktops, the room wasn't too shabby. It had a shiny stainless-steel sink and up-cycled cabinets, a new cooker and fridge had been installed too. All it needed was a box of floor tiles and a second coat of wholesale paint. For some reason, there was an old Singer sewing machine on top of a door-less cupboard.

Ignoring the gutted bathroom, George trailed behind Jack to the front room which overlooked the street and choked on the smell of urine. The gaff was a decent size, no doubt about it, but looked like a bomb had hit it. The local kids had done a job on the place. The walls were half stripped of yellowing paper and the usual giant dicks drawn on the walls in permanent marker. A small patch of green damp creeped up one of the corners and the foam stuffing from the disembowelled sofa laid in clumps on the floor. It was common for old places like that to need a good fix-up, but seeing the threadbare carpet, flaky ceiling and filthy single paned windows made George grimace.

'Holy fuck! Look at this place.' Jack's mouth fell open, clearly taking it all in. Grey clouds wheezed from the once-burgundy carpet with each step. 'Can you believe this?'

'I'm sorry, mate.'

'This is a palace! A lick of paint and some laminate flooring and this could be a fucking beautiful tattoo shop.' He beamed. 'What's upstairs like? Is it just as good?'

George furrowed his brow. The disbelief too great for his dehydrated brain to register. 'Dare to think, mate.' Laughing, he edged out of the way to let Jack past.

The stairs were sturdy enough but a long thick crack from the ceiling to the floor did little to make George feel at ease. Jack didn't appear to notice and grinned like a toddler in a toy shop.

There were two rooms on the second level, one's door ajar, offering nothing but a dismantled bed and bare floorboards. It looked like a good size. Big enough for Jack to bring all his girls back, no doubt. A loud bang came from the other room, followed by a crash and a squeal. Both George and Jack straightened their backs, edging away from the closed door in sync.

'You heard that, right?' George whispered, backing into Jack's chest. Clearing his throat, he quickly leant forward and gripped the door handle.

'Shit, man. Don't open it. Could be squatters. Or a drug den.' Jack retreated further.

'We don't have squatters round here.' George checked the front door for a quick escape. 'And definitely not drug dens…I don't think.'

Sucking in a deep breath, George prayed he'd been right. He twisted the silver handle and shoved the door open with his fist. The room was dark and quiet - the perpetrator had stopped whatever it had been doing just moments before. George patted his hand on the wall in search of a light switch but when his fingers found it, nothing happened. Jack stepped beside him, his hands balled into fists. Quite impressed by Jack's bravery,

George slid his phone out of his jeans, pressed on the torch icon and nodded for the fella to enter with him.

'Hello?' George hated that his voice trembled.

With the flash light proving futile, Jack sped across the room and tugged a large rug from the sash window. Light flooded in from the broken pane and the sound of shuffling from the far corner made them both flinch.

Something small was frantic, banging about under a pile of empty and upturned boxes. It seemed desperate, ready to pounce. George was used to animals. He could handle them. But he usually knew what he was dealing with. Still, with fear gripping George's spine, he edged closer to Jack. Biting into his bottom lip and holding his breath, he lifted one of the boxes with the toe of his trainer.

'What the fuck is that?' Jack jumped back, face red and eyes almost bulging.

George exhaled, finally. 'A barn owl, mate.' He cleared his throat. He hadn't realised how fast his heart had been thumping.

A tiny owl had managed to get caught up in the cord from the broken blind laying under the window. Wrapped around its legs and one of its wings, the cord had cut into the small bird's flesh, seemingly from its attempt to escape.

'An owl? Shit. A real fucking owl?' Jack's jaw dropped.

'Yep. You not seen one before?'

'No, never. I don't think we have them in London. Do we?'

George shrugged. 'They must have them in the zoo though.'

'Dunno, man. Never been.' Jack's gaze focused on the bird.

'Well you've gotta have seen them on telly?'

'Don't have one. Dave's only got one in his living room but he's always watching snooker.'

George raised his brow. 'You're joking?'

'No, man. He watches it all the time.' Jack's lips curled.

'I mean about not having a telly.' George allowed himself a snort of laughter. Instantly regretting the shooting pains within his skull. Maybe the fella weren't so serious after all.

Smiling, Jack ran his hand through his dark hair. 'I know what you meant. How do you think that thing got in here?'

'Probably fell down the chimney. Happens a lot in these old places. I'm sure my dad will sort it. He'll get the builders to block off the fireplace or something.'

'Shit, its bleeding. We got to help it, man. It looks in pain.' Jack pulled his sleeves down over his hands and closed in on the bird.

'Whoa, don't fucking kill it.' George shouted.

Jacked looked stunned. 'What? Course I won't.' Turning back to the bird, he lowered his voice to a whisper. 'Come here little fella,'

The owl flapped its free wing in blind panic, desperate to get away from the two enormous strangers. George shuddered as Jack struggled to grab it, each time forcing the bird to become more tangled in the cord.

'You've gotta be quicker than that. One quick swoop.' George mimed the process he'd used a hundred times at the farm. 'If you think owls are bad, try catching ten chickens a day.'

Jack smiled again. It suited him. And George noticed a sparkle in his caramel eyes. 'But can you see the beak on this bad boy? And its toenails?' He hesitated.

'They're talons. And, yeah, they're pretty lethal. They can take chunks out of you.' George laughed as Jacked jumped back. 'Come out of the way, I'll grab it.'

In true farm apprentice fashion, George took a swift lunge at the bird and closed both of its wings onto its body, holding them tightly enough so it couldn't flap anymore. George dug his teeth into his bottom lip as the scared bird sank its beak into his thumb. With his other hand, he tried pulling at the cord, only to be hissed at by the trembling bird.

'I can't do it. We need to cut it free. You got a knife or something?' George tried holding the owl still and gained another bite to his thumb for the attempt.

'A knife? No. Why would I?'

'I dunno, you're from East London aren't you?' George grinned.

'I left my blade in my other jeans, man.' Jack flashed a smile then nodded to the bird. 'Want me to hold it whilst you get the cord off?'

'Yeah, swap with me. You might want to cover your hands though. Little bastard is eating me alive here.'

Jack moved closer, the smell of cigarettes and rain-soaked clothes attacked George's nostrils. Without taking the advice to pull his sleeves over his hands, he slid them over George's to take hold of the bird. – Jack's soft palms tingled George's skin, smooth and delicate. George sucked in a breath. So, that's why the ladies love him so much.

Jack grimaced as the owl took its revenge on the skin between his index finger and thumb and as George hurried to slink the cord over the bird's wing, he couldn't hide his cruel delight in seeing the man suffer. Just a little.

With the wing free, George focused on the owl's legs. Well, the monster talons on the end of them to be precise—razor sharp and perfectly curved to cause damage. With a fine accuracy that came with years playing Operation with his sister, his fingers plucked at the cord like he would the wishbone in the metallic man's chest. Each touch caused the bird to flinch and with sweat glazing George's brow, he noticed Jack poke his tongue out of the side of his mouth in concentration. With one quick tug, and a close miss from nearly having one of his fingers sliced off, George slipped the cord over its legs and freed the bird from its snare.

'Yes!' Jack shouted, his face beaming with achievement. His curved lips showing his pride.

George found himself smiling from ear to ear too. He'd thought Jack to be the kind of guy that would be too cool to give a fuck. A chancer, living life with not a care in the world. But seeing the man dressed in black, covered in tattoos and could easily pass for what his mum called a "criminal pirate" – it proved difficult not to be affected by the fella's elation at freeing an owl.

'You got him whilst I crack open the window?' George nodded to the glass with the large splinter running through it.

'Course, man.' Jack slowly turned on his heels, preventing any quick movement that could cause him or the bird more injury, and followed George to the window.

George lifted it with a grunt before turning to check the bird over. Moving Jack's hand slightly, feeling the softness of his skin once more and ignoring the words tattooed on his knuckles, he ran his fingers over the animal's feathers, carefully lifting them to see the damage.

'Apart from a little friction burn from the cord, he seems fine.' George sighed then laid his hand on Jack's back. He felt the fella relax slightly. 'Thanks, mate. For this.'

'Hey, I couldn't let the little guy suffer.' Jack tilted his head, exposing more of his neck tattoos. George couldn't help but stare. 'Just look at him.'

George snorted. 'We got to let him go.'

'Can they fly in the daytime, man?'

181

'Yeah of course.' George laughed. 'Although I bet he's shattered. And hungry.'

Lifting the bird to the window sill, Jack's lips curled. 'Come on little one, let's get you back out there so you can eat some worms. Or whatever owls eat.' As soon as his hands opened, the bird pounced from the ledge and flew into the grey, rainy sky.

The two of them lent against the window frame, George could no longer see the bird but something kept him looking for it anyway. It wasn't until Jack rested his elbow onto his shoulder that George came back to reality.

'Thanks for that, man.'

'No worries mate. My dad would have sorted it out before you moved in anyway.'

Jack ran his hand through his hair. 'Na, I don't care about that. I mean thanks for saving the guy. Means a lot.'

George caught Jack's gaze. His hazel eyes trapped him for the briefest moment and right there and then, George realised something he fought so hard to deny. The fella wasn't the biggest dickhead after all.

In that instance, George saw Jack for the first time. The man with the tatts, the moody exterior, the lady's man, the charming smile. The *person*. George coughed away the dust, and most probably his months of hatred. Half annoyed with himself and half even more so at Jack for being so decent. With all his faults, he was kind of all right. He knew he shouldn't have been hating on the bloke – he should've been taking notes from him.

'So, this looks like it could be a great gaff for you, don't it?' George pulled down the window and wiped the rain from the sill with the sleeve of his coat.

'I can't even tell you, man. I've never had anything this good in my entire life.'

George observed the room — the chipped paint, the scuffed flooring, the shabby fireplace that would need to come out or at least do with a fair bit of wood filler and

George had an unexpected pang of guilt. Taking a deep breath, he noted the broom propped up in the corner and knew he was going to have to help this bloke out.

'Why don't I get the old boys downstairs to grab us a couple of coffees from over the road and me and you can get started on this place?'

'Na, man. You're hanging. And besides -.'

'It's cool, mate.' George grabbed the broom and tossed it to Jack. Then, with his arms stretched out in front of him, he placed his fingertips either side of the pane of broken glass. 'Let me just measure this fucking window first.'

Jack smiled, and George returned it. Sincerely.

Chapter Twenty Two

With July being the hottest on record and temperatures stuck way into the thirties, George scorched in the sun at Perrygate Farm. Yet even with sweat running down from his hairline, his attitude was surprisingly chipper.

Spending the best part of a month helping Jack do up his gaff had helped quite a bit. A lot actually. George had been so preoccupied trying to sort out the damp stained walls and replacing the crumbling floorboards to not think about much else other than surviving in the place. He'd managed to get at least one whole day without Ellie's blue eyes filling his thoughts. With Jack there, her absence somehow became bearable, a bittersweet memory rather than a crippling ache. But what'd shocked George most in the weeks gone by, was not that Jack's flat had turned out to be a nice little place, but that he couldn't imagine his life without his new friend.

With most nights drinking at the flat and listening to the fella's records, Jack had become an addiction to him. Just as much as the alcohol had and he knew his happiness depended on both of them being in his life. Jack's ability to stay chilled in all situations was enviable. Just like his looks. George hadn't realised that he'd let himself miss the barbers and had actually started to grow a quiff himself. He liked it though, even if his mother hated it. Maybe it was all a bit ridiculous, but Jack was someone he wanted to be. A man so indifferent to all the shit around him.

Imitation is the best form of flattery. Or some shit like that.

Red hot spasms shot up George's spine with each twenty-kilo bag of livestock feed he heaved to the ground but he refused to give up. Four weeks prior, he would have wanted to throw the boss the middle finger and fuck off to the beer garden. He still wanted the booze, mind you, but he could wait until home time to pacify his urge.

Unloading the lorry had seemed like a good idea, most of the animals had refused to come out of their shady enclosures and the paddocks had been singed to nothing but yellow wastelands. Even the trusty crows and magpies had fucked off. July was known for being hot, hot for the UK that is, but he'd never known a heat like it.

Two hours spent working in the scorching heat, and with Knobert leaving him to do it all on his own, the remaining bags seemed to be just as many as when he started. He peered up to the cloudless sky and begged for rain.

Heaving what felt like the fortieth-thousand bag of feed, and thankfully the last, from the lorry, George threw it onto the ground then jumped down himself. His knees burned and his back played tribute to Quasimodo. He was done. Knackered. The aches were bone deep and his arms so numb that his hands seemed to belong to someone else. He peered at the open doors of the food barn and sighed at what was left of the job. How the hell could a couple of feet feel miles away? Admitting defeat, he whipped of his T-shirt, flattened it onto a bale of hay and laid out on top of it – letting his bare chest and stomach soak up the sun.

'You okay there, George?'

He knew that voice - it was somewhat new to his life yet he'd grown accustomed to it so quickly. And there was only one person he knew that called him "George" rather than "Georgie."

Shaking the weariness away, he lifted his head to see Jack standing at the fence, and couldn't help but grin. It was Jack's eyes that drew George in. Those hazel orbs, speckled with green were somehow intoxicating. He could swear they saw right into him.

With arms resting on the wood, his nose and ears were reddened by the sun. Dressed in his usual black jeans and black T-shirt, Jack's trademark dark quiff was curling from sweat and humidity onto his forehead.

'All right, mate?' Wincing, George sat up, straightened his back and hid his "shit shovels" under his thighs. He didn't know why. 'What you doing out here?'

'You said you were working on your own today. So I thought I'd come up and see what it is you do round here.' His gaze flitted around the farm, clearly taking in every piece of scenery before settling back onto George. Onto his reddened shoulders. 'But apparently you just lay around sunbathing.'

The pain in his lower back cut his laughter short. 'I fucking wish, mate. I've been lugging these bastards all morning.' George punted a bale with his steel toe cap boot. 'Should have only took me an hour but I'm flagging today.'

'You look it, man. No offence. But its boiling out here and you drank a lot last night.' Jack wiped away the sweat from his forehead with his wrist. 'Shit, the countryside is mad.'

'Could be worse. One year it rained the whole summer. Every damn day.' George managed a giggle at Jack's raised brow. 'But if it gets any hotter, I don't know how I'm gonna manage working out here. I'm pretty much dead.'

'Well seeing as I'm here, I'll give you a hand. We can get the job done quicker together.'

George cleared his throat. 'No, don't be silly. I've got this.' Forcing a laugh, George observed the bags of feed and hay. 'I was just getting my strength back before I lug this lot into the barn.'

'I'll help, man.' Jack wiped his brow again then climbed over the fence - his arms shaking slightly as he lifted his leg over. 'I know you've probably got a long line of friends to ask for help, but I'm here now, so, might as well.'

George snorted, realising that Jack had been the first person he'd spoken to all day. How the hell had he become so pathetic?

'Thanks for the offer, mate, but I don't think you're gonna be any help. Not with those little girl arms. Remember what happened when we were carrying the mattress up to your room? Mate, I thought I was gonna die at the bottom of those stairs.'

Jack jumped down from the fence, his cheeks flushed the same colour as his nose. 'All right, so I'm not built like a fucking tank like you, but to be fair, you pretty much used your head to knock through that partition wall.'

'You calling me thick?' George smirked.

'Hey, man, you said I've got little girl arms. Truth hurts doesn't it?'

George raised his middle finger, trying not to smile.

'Anyways, I bought you this.' Pulling a dark green flask from his backpack, Jack sloshed the contents as he shook it in front of him. 'Didn't have fizz, or juice. So I brought you some good old fashioned tap water.'

The man he'd known for a matter of weeks, the one he blamed for fucking his entire world up, seemed to care more than the people he'd known for years.

He was the thing missing in his life. There was no drama, no fake love/hate bullshit – just company. He crashed at Jack's place almost every night, once the booze had numbed him, of course. He'd never shared a bed with a fella before, well not since Alfie in year seven, but

187

having someone to sleep next to, soothed his demons. And his once, overwhelming, need for rebound girls.

Leaning forward, George took the flask from him. 'Excuse my hands, mate, they're filthy.'

'You're a farmer. What else would they be? It's a sign you're doing something you love.'

George's chest warmed. He wished Ellie had seen it like that.

'You know what, mate? I was just thinking about how I'd got you all wrong. And then you go ahead and bring me a drink to fucking prove it.' George nodded to the bale in front of him. 'Seat?'

Jack pulled the backpack off his shoulders and plonked himself opposite. Wiping the beads of sweat from his brow, he sniffed in the fresh air of the farm. 'Thinking about my little girl arms?'

'Yeah, something like that.' Blushing, George poured some of the cold water into the metal cup and leant forward for Jack to take it. Unsure why, he caught his breath as the man's fingers brushed against his own. 'How… how'd you get up here anyway? Dave in town?' He stuttered.

'No, I walked. Only took me about forty-five minutes. I got a bit lost down one of the lanes though. You hicks not heard of street signs?'

'We normally just spray paint arrows onto the sheep.' George couldn't help but snigger at the confusion on Jack's face. 'Seriously, though, you need to get yourself some lighter clothes. You must be hot as fuck in all that black.'

Jack snorted, choking on his drink. 'I need to get some money first. I'm hoping to start tattooing again soon. When I get things up and running, you know. Need to get some customers too.'

'I'll be your customer.' Swigging from the flask, George sighed as the liquid cooled his throat.

'Yeah course you will.' Jack rolled his eyes.

'I'm serious, mate. The more I look at you, the more I want one.' George's cheeks burned. 'A tattoo I mean. And those sketches you have are the bollocks. Did you draw them all yourself? Like design them, I mean?'

'I copied some from tatts I've already seen but, yeah, most are originals.'

George stretched his arm out towards him. 'You mind that I've drunk out of it?' With a nonchalant shake of the head from Jack, he refilled the fella's cup. 'You're fucking talented, you know that?'

Jack scrubbed a hand through his hair, scrunching the front with his fingers. 'They're just drawings on paper. My hand isn't as steady when it's dragging needles through someone's skin.'

'Mate, I've seen your work, remember?' George kept eye contact. It was a discussion they'd skirted on many times over the weeks, but he'd always dropped the subject before things grew too awkward.

'Man, I....'

George nodded, catching the sincerity in Jack's hazel eyes. 'I know. I'm honestly not blaming you. I'm not. I just still miss her. And I don't have anyone to talk to about how I feel. Fucking pathetic isn't it?'

'You've got shit loads of people there for you, George. Your mum and dad seem like they're supportive. Your Nan, well she's crazy, man, but you're obviously her little angel. And Aimee and Alfie, those two would walk on hot shit for you.'

Water spouted from his nose. 'Hot shit? But yeah, my parents are pretty cool.' It was true. George was getting on with them a lot better since Jack arrived. The arguments had dissolved into eye rolling strops. 'I just can't talk to them about *things*. They don't get it. Nan has got a new dog, so she's not been around for weeks. And Alf and Aims, I've been ghosting them.'

'Why?' Jack furrowed his brow.

'You know what? I don't know.' It was true. He had no idea why he'd avoided them. Maybe it was seeing them getting on too well that pissed him off. Seeing them happy. It felt like a kick in the nuts when all he needed was stability. 'I've just been ignoring them. Fuck I sound like a dick, don't I?'

'I kind of get it, man. Must be hard with things changing around you.' Jack nodded. It was like the fella had drilled into his skull and seen the thoughts dancing around inside. 'Listen, I've never been in a proper relationship. But I know they say that *time's a-*'

'Great healer? Yeah, so I've heard.'

Standing, Jack downed the rest of his cup and made his way to George. 'Well it's going to take time to adjust. And if you want, I'll listen to your shit if it's going to help you.' Jack wrapped his arm around George's shoulder.

Fire burned under George's ribcage. He wanted to pat Jack's hand, or arm. Or leg. However the fuck you pat someone to say thanks. But he couldn't. He couldn't really move to do anything.

'So you up for tattooing me?'

'You're fucking with me, right? You actually want some ink?'

'Seriously, mate. I've been thinking about getting myself a new image. Lose a little bit of Coggletree me and get a bit more.....I don't know.' George's cheeks burned. And not from the sun.

Jack ruffled George's hair. 'That's what this is about? Trying to be someone else?'

'I just think a tattoo would be good for me. Would you do it for me? Please.'

Jack nodded but creased his brow, filling George with unease.

'Man, I'd be honoured. But you've got to be sure you're doing it for the right reasons. Believe me. This shit gets out of hand.' Jack held out his arms.

'I definitely want this done. I even know what I want.'

'Yeah? You got a picture?'

'Not exactly. But I see them here every day.'

Jack sniffed then quickly looked behind him at the farm buildings. 'Not a camel?'

'They're alpacas.' George stifled a laugh, remembering the fella had never been out of East London before. He hadn't even known what an owl was. 'But no. I want a magpie?'

'The bird? The noisy black and white one? How comes?'

'I don't know.' He lied. I've always liked them. 'Besides, they have like meanings or something. There's a song I think.'

Jack's brow knitted again. 'Really? What song?'

'I'm not a hundred percent sure.' George lied again. 'Something, like, "one for sorrow, two for joy.'

Jack rolled his tongue over his lips. 'And how many magpies do you want?'

A shiny BMW roared along the lane, forcing their conversation into silence. Its alloy wheels splattering the wet mud onto its sides. George swigged at water, holding the cold liquid in his mouth hoping it'd somehow help cool the conversation he was about to have with Knobert.

The vehicle slowed to a stop just centimetres away from the bale that George was sat on. Jack sat down opposite him again. George rolled his eyes as the electric windows buzzed down and the green tinged sunglasses came into view.

'What's this? A tea party?'

The look on Jack's face said it all. Most people that met Knobert were impressed by his cars, the gadgets, the talk.

But Jack, just like George had done all those months ago, clearly saw the bloke for what he was. A dick.

'All right, Robert?' George finally swallowed and offered a grin. 'I'm just having a quick break before I get this lot into the barn.'

'I thought you'd be done by now, kiddo.'

Jack shot George a wide eyed glare. George knew exactly why. *Kiddo.*

'I've been on my own, remember. And its hard work for one. Especially in this weather.'

'You think I don't know that?' Knobert mock laughed. 'Who'd you think used to do it before the big boss took you on? Baking under the sun all day. Muggins here, that's who.' Knobert peered over his sunglasses to Jack. 'But I did all of it with my top on. Company policy, kiddo.'

Knobert's conceited chuckle sent rage through George's already painful spine.

'I know. I'm just boiling. I've been out here on my own all day. I couldn't even get into the lodge.'

'You're meant to be working, not messing about in the lodge anyway.' He laughed to himself.

Jack cleared his throat.

'I'm allowed a break.'

'Well I'm not paying you to make drinks all day. Or to catch up with your *friends*. I'm paying you to do a job?'

Clearing his throat again, Jack slid a box of cigarettes from his jeans pocket and plucked one out with his teeth. 'So, you own this place, man?'

Knobert's eyes narrowed. 'Pretty much, yeah. My dad owns Perrygate Farm and all the land associated with it.' His lips curled with arrogance. 'No smoking on the premises.'

Poised, Jack slid the cigarette back into the box, keeping an air of indifference as Knobert glared at him. 'Ah right, so it's your *dad* who's paying George then?'

Silence set amongst the three of them. Thick and solid like the knots in George's shoulders. He'd usually have cringed at the tension but he found the awkwardness amusing. Seeing his supervisor's own arrogance bite him on the arse was something he'd been waiting for.

Knobert revved up the car again. 'Get this done by the end of the day, kiddo, or *my dad* won't be paying you anymore.' The car backed out of the lane, turned and sped up the road.

'Fuck, mate. He's gonna make my life a misery for that.' George laughed, gulping the dregs of the flask.

'Man, I'm sorry. But that bloke is a wanker.' Jack tossed George his empty cup then stood. 'Right, let's get this lot in the barn. I'm boiling.'

Chapter Twenty Three

Exhausted and soaked with his own sweat, Jack sought the shade under the tree. An hour of manual labour had all but broken his back. Nevertheless, the hay, feed and god knows what else was piled into the barn. And his arms were on fire because of it. How the fuck George did it six days a week, he'd never know.

'Want some water, mate?' George sloshed the flask at him. Even though they'd kept it in the shade, Jack was sure the contents would have been just as hot as he was, but he nodded anyway; his throat too dry to produce a sound.

'Please tell me you're finished for the day.' Jack swallowed down the warm water. He was too parched not to.

He slid his phone from his cargo shorts and rolled his eyes. 'Can't shut this place until five. Got forty five minutes?'

'Even though you're done for the day?'

'Can't risk Knobert not paying me.' He laughed to himself. It was so good to see him laugh. George was the epitome of gloom at the start - if there was anything negative to be found, the fella would find it. Live it, too. He had seemed to dwell in it. But as the weeks went on, he noticed a different side to him. One that started to love life again.

George slipped off his damp work top and wiping his brow with it, shrunk to the ground under the tree's canopy. The boy deserved the break.

'Cheers for your help, mate. Means a lot.'

194

Grabbing his bag, Jack's boots squeaked with each step – the sweat between his toes making him gag. His entire body was aflame. Fuck, he'd just used muscles he didn't know he had. There wasn't a part of him that wasn't either sore or soaked.

He'd never given George the credit he deserved before. For the work he actually put in, and in the shittiest weather since Pompeii. He knew the bloke was strong – lifting box after box of all Jack's crap up to the flat without complaining. And not to mention smashing down that wall upstairs to make the two rooms into one. He wielded the sledge hammer like it was part of him.

'Man, I didn't realise you went through this on the daily. I feel bad for having you help at the flat. You should have told me to fuck off.'

George laid out onto the grass then slid his arms behind his head. The muscles in his torso glistened with sweat. 'I'm used to it now. And besides, what are mate's for?'

Jack swallowed hard. He'd never had a "mate" – not a real one at least. And he'd never spent as much time with someone as he had with George. Not even in the care homes. George had shocked him. Okay, he was still a spoilt brat at times but he'd proved that he would do anything to help. And the more Jack had been around him, the more he resented him not being there. He knew that the fella had a way of bringing out something in himself, something he'd never felt before. Like he belonged. Mattered even. He never, not once, imagined he'd grow so close to someone.

Jack observed him shade-bathing – the golden, untainted skin on his broad shoulders and chest. He was like a new age Adonis. A Greek myth in modern day Essex. One that blended so well with the natural world that being half naked suited him.

'Come sit, mate. You must be knackered There's some spray in the bag there, set of clothes too if you want them.' George nodded to a navy blue hold-all under the tractor.

'You bring spare clothes to work?' Jack averted his eyes from George's body, quickly concentrating on the field around them. The greenery went on for miles and not one sound of traffic.

'Nowadays, yeah. I never used to change my clothes, like what's the point? I'm gonna jump in the shower when I get home, anyway. But I try and make an effort. Just in case.'

'In case of what?' Jack pulled his wet T-shirt away from his stomach.

'In case *she* turns up one day, I guess.'

Jack ran his hand through his wet hair, unsure why George's answer bothered him so much.

'I don't want her thinking I'm just a farm apprentice.'

'What's wrong with being a farm apprentice?'

'Mate, look at me, George held out his arms, his biceps tensing. Blushing, Jack fixed his gaze on George's eyes. 'I'm constantly covered in mud. Who's going to want that?'

'Bet the pigs don't mind.'

'Ha. But, seriously, it takes a lot of effort to look half decent. Unlike you. I'm beige. Vanilla. I need something to make me stand out. Something that she wants.'

'If you aren't yourself, then what's the point?' Folding his arms – Jack grimaced, instantly regretted the wet fabric clinging to his chest.

'Take your top off, mate. Knobert won't be coming back today.'

'Na, it's cool, man, I'm good.' The anxiety of revealing his body next to someone like George made his throat close.

'You're not getting in my car wet.'

'I'll walk.' Jack shrugged, wringing out the hem of his T-shirt.

'I'm not letting you walk back. What sort of mate would I be?' George's smile lit up his face. 'Besides, my Nan would kill me if I let anything happen to you and that pretty face of yours. She's got a thing for you.' George threw the bottle of water for him to catch.

Dread poured over Jack as he sidestepped into the shadows of the tree. Turning his back to the fella, his desperate fingers fumbled to find the collar of his soaked top.

'Holy shit.'

Jack froze to the spot. Afraid to move. Afraid to expose his puny body any more than it already was. Biting back the panic, he slumped to the floor and laid on his side next to the fella. Facing away from him, of course.

'I knew you had tattoos, mate, but I didn't realise you were a walking piece of art. Those are amazing.'

'You taking the piss?' Stress tightening his guts, Jack peered over his shoulder to the man staring at his back. He could feel his gaze burning into his skin.

'Not at all. They are…..fuck…..wow. How many you got?'

Jack tensed even more so. 'Lost count after about forty. Pretty much the whole top half of me is inked. Few on my thighs and one my shin.'

'What's with the bare patch?' He nodded to Jack's chest.'

'Just waiting for the right tattoo. That's all.' It wasn't exactly a lie.

George pulled at his shoulder, trying to get a better look. Jack instinctively flinched. He wasn't used to anyone being that close to him, to anyone, shirtless.

'Sorry.' George moved back. 'I just wanted to see what they felt like.

'THEY DON'T FEEL LIKE ANYTHING!' His abruptness shocked himself as much as it did George. Sucking in a deep breath, he ran a hand over his arm. 'Some can be a bit bumpy if the needle goes in too deep, but they're pretty much smooth.'

George bit the side of his cheek, clearly perplexed. His eyes still scanning over his skin and Jack cringed with every moment. 'I didn't mean to…..freak you out. You not like people looking at them?' Confusion was clear in George's voice too. 'If I had them, I'd never wear clothes.'

George raised an eyebrow. His bright blue eyes seemed to search for an answer amongst the tattoos. Much to Jack's embarrassment.

Shaking his head, Jack snorted. 'If you were me, you definitely would.'

Jack cringed. He'd made shit awkward. He always did when his body was exposed. Sitting up, he ran a hand through his hair and exhaled, long and slow. Facing George, he wanted the ground to swallow him whole.

'I've not exactly got a good body.'

George raised his brows. 'What? I wish I was as slim as you. Takes so much work just to keep my gut off.'

'Man, you don't have a gut. I've tried everything to beef up. It just don't happen.'

The fella chortled then tilted his head. He could feel his gaze drifting over his skin. He could see intrigue in them, probably trying to work out what the tattoos meant. Everyone was always desperate for them to have meanings.

'What do they mean?' George asked.

Squeezing the bridge of his nose, Jack sighed. He wasn't annoyed, just out of his comfort zone.

'Some do. Most are just *moments*.'

'Eh?'

Jack showed his wrist, where the jack o'lantern tattoo had not long healed. 'Like this. The last one I did. Freehand. I needed a tattoo so just did it.'

George ran his thumb softly over the pumpkin's outline. His rough skin brushing over his. Jack hadn't realised he'd been holding his breath the entire time George was touching him. 'Mate, how can you *need* a tattoo? You have hundreds of them.'

'They're a way to help me heal. Like bandages.' Jack bit the corner of his thumb nail. 'And the more I had done, the more I needed.'

George caught his gaze – his eyes making it unable to look away. 'The stuff with your mum?'

'Kind of, man.' Jack hated the subject of his mother. Truth was, he didn't know how he felt. Was he pining? Probably. Could he explain why? Fuck no. But knew he'd have to say something to George before the poor fella's head exploded. 'Living in care, I used to get bullied pretty much every day. I missed my mum so much that I used to cry. A lot. They called me poof, a fag. Queer. All that shit. I got beat up pretty much every week. My mate, Cole, used to hit me the most. Said it was to toughen me up. Then he blamed me for getting him onto drugs and the beatings got worse.'

George raised his eyebrows.

'Man, I didn't get him on drugs. He started dealing then using. It had nothing to do with me.' Jack could feel his cheeks glowing. He hated how much he was giving away but couldn't stop himself. 'So I used to sketch things that helped me forget the bullying. The sketches soon became graffiti over the park and when I grew out of that, they became ink on me.'

George squeezed his arm. 'I didn't realise you had it so tough. I could never imagine you being bullied. You're so confident. Well, look at you.'

'This has taken a lot of years, man. And the confidence you see is mainly painted on. By these tatts.'

'But why?' George shuffled closer on the grass then leant in closer, his scent filling Jack's nostrils. That earthy aroma mixed with wet skin.

Jack blew through rounded lips. He needed out. Needed to get away before he gave more away. But George clearly wasn't going to drop it. The sincerity on his face said as much.

'Well...' Jack cleared his throat. 'I might look like I don't care. Like I'm not even listening to what's going on, but truth is, I remember every insult. Every bad thing people have said about me. Each of these tattoos are like a scar from them.'

'But why would you want to remember insults?'

'Fuck knows. But I couldn't leave the house without having all this over my body. People look at the tattoos and not me. Not the real me. It's kind of like my armour, I guess.' Jack choked on his own words. He'd never told anyone that before. He didn't even know if he'd realised it himself before that very moment. 'Fuck knows what I'll do when I run out of skin to ink.'

George laid a hand on his back, the coarse skin of his palm scratching against his shoulder. 'Mate, I would never have thought that about you. But as much as you need armour, you can't hide who you are. You moaned at me for wanting to be something different and here you are, faking it up, yourself.'

'I'm not faking anything, man.' Jack let his gaze wonder over the blades of grass. 'I just don't want people looking at me. The "care home kid." The bloke who only has one change of clothes and works shitty jobs to just about pay his rent. The bloke that has nobody to love him and is unable to get close to anyone. The bloke who....whose mother couldn't even love him.' Burning his throat, Jack struggled to swallow the lump down. 'They can't get disappointed by the real me.'

'Mate.' George's voice rumbled through him. 'There's not one thing wrong with you. Okay, if I'm completely honest, I think I actually hated you at one point. But that was because I thought you and Ellie were fucking behind my back. But I know that's not true. I know you now.'

Jack smiled to himself. 'You think so?'

'What is there to know?'

'Nothing, really. Just me. I usually close myself off from everyone. Except you.'

'That why you've never had a relationship?'

Jack chewed the inside of his cheek. He'd first told George that pathetic revelation when they were blind drunk at the flat, singing to George's playlists about lost loves.

'You'll know it when the right girl comes along.'

'That's just it.' Jack cleared his throat. 'I don't think the "right girl" ever will.'

George's hot, rough hand gripped his shoulder, squeezing the tiny muscle beneath gently. The bloke actually seemed like he cared for him.

'You will find the love of your life. Believe me.' George's gaze seemed to melt every ache in Jack's body. 'You deserve to find happiness. But just don't fuck it up like I did.'

'It weren't you, man. You're a great guy. You are. These things just happen.'

'Fuck, I really did have you wrong, didn't I? You know, I wanted to blame someone else for fucking up my life.' George's smile was genuine. Apologetic, even. 'So, what are you hiding from me? What don't I know?'

Jack snorted. The noise coming from his chest rather than his mouth. 'How messed up I am. Like I said, I've never let myself get close to anyone before. I've avoided it like the plague, man.' He met George's gaze.

'Why'd you think that is?' George's eyes narrowed slightly as though he was trying to see him clearer.

'Dunno, man. But I think it's pretty safe to say that we're both a little fucked up.'

'Lucky we've got each other then, eh?' George flashed a smile and for the briefest moment, it seemed like they were the only two people in the world. Clearing his throat, George wiped the corners of his mouth. . 'So you going to do my tattoo for me. I'll pay you.'

'I don't want your money.' Observing the fella, Jack shook his head. He didn't want the bloke to get a tattoo when he was down and regret it. 'You sure you want the magpie thing? Because of the song?'

'Hundred percent.'

'And just the one magpie?'

'Yep, just the one.'

His words winded Jack. He just wanted the fella to be happy. To see that the sorrow would fade.

'Man, listen…..'

'No need, mate. I've made up my mind.' George's lips curled softly. Half sad, half happy – it seemed to be his only state. He then laid onto his back, breathing in deeply – letting the country air flow through his lungs. 'You know what? Out here, in the breeze with the sound of the trees rustling and the birds singing, it really puts things in perspective, don't it?'

Jack sucked in the air from his nostrils – he could still smell the dampness of the hay bales. It was obvious to him that it wasn't the time to dig deeper into George's mental state. 'Like what, man?'

'Well, you've been through a lot of shit in your life and whatever scars you've got from it, you should wear with pride. They've made you the great guy you are today. I'm proud just to be your mate.'

Jack didn't reply. He couldn't speak. Instead, he just laid down on the grass, under the tree, breathing in the fresh air.

The best thing about it was that he was next to George.

Chapter Twenty Four

Looking around the flat - *his* flat, Jack couldn't refrain from beaming. Newly painted white walls and a brand new geometric print rug that Dave had bought him was the beginnings of a real home. Despite a pile of boxes full of junk from his old flat, the lack of sofa and a bare lightbulb above - the place was the bollocks. The two rooms turned into one, courtesy of George's hammer wielding brawn, made the upstairs of his place look like some high end studio apartment.

With his dirty clothes hanging over the clothes airer, Jack lounged on his bed still dressed in the gear that George lent him for the drive home. Grey jersey shorts and white tee. They weren't his thing – muscle fit clothing wasn't the look he'd usually opted for but their smell made them too good to take off.

Jack didn't know why he couldn't stop sniffing at the collar of the T-shirt. The smell was intoxicating. Something he couldn't put his finger on. Maybe it was the pleasant smell of flowery fabric soften - what clothes should smell like. What *homes* smell like. The homes where parents love their kids and wash their clothes. Fair enough, George wasn't a child anymore but Maxine seemed like the kind of mother that'd sneak into her son's house and wash his clothes even once he was married and had his own children. She was the perfect mother. The mother Jack had always wanted.

Running his hand over the front of the top, Jack clenched his eyes shut at the memory of what happened earlier that day. George had seen his body. The bloke, made of perfect, unblemished, golden skin and just the right amount of muscles also had a front row viewing of the insanity that he'd tried to hide for years. And under the unapologetic glare of the July sun, no less.

Cringing beneath the memory of George's wide-eyed stares over his body, Jack scooped up his glass of water from his bedside table and drank with the hope it would bring amnesia.

Yet with each mouthful, the memories became even harder to swallow. His rib cage seemed to tighten with thoughts of George rushing home to tell Maxine and Steve about the knobhead who uses tattoos as a coping mechanism. Because he got upset by people's words and missed the mother that gave him up. Jack didn't know how he'd ever be able to look the bloke in the eye again.

A loud bang ricocheted along the hall, up the stairs and into his new room. Jack knew the culprit. George had always knocked so hard that the walls of the hallway seemed to shake from the impact. The fella had thick hands, grafting hands, attached to perfectly toned arms that would, no doubt, smash the knocker through the door one day. Jack hadn't estimated that the mere thought of those strong arms would cause his top lip to sweat. Wiping it away with his sleeve, he leapt from the bed.

Racing down the stairs, the eagerness of seeing George seemed to have full reign of his legs. He yanked the door open and George was there, holding a bag from the local offy – he'd never turned up without booze - and his clothes pretty much matching what Jack was wearing.

'Hey, man.' Jack scrubbed his hand through his hair. He knew that the act of nonchalance he'd always used in awkward situations seemed to be wearing thin.

George's perfect lips parted, exposing pearly whites beneath. 'All right, mate? I prayed all day for rain at the farm and it pisses down as soon as I finish.' He lifted a bag for life to eye level. 'Anyway, I got us a bottle of wine.'

Jack couldn't help but laugh. Judging by the sounds of the clinking glass in George's bag, it was more like a gallon. 'Come in, come in.'

Stepping inside, George stepped out of his wet shoes and shook the rain from his hair. 'I didn't know if I'd left you enough time to draw the tattoo but I was getting too fidgety at home waiting. Least I'm not late, eh. For once.'

'No, it's cool. Finished it about half hour ago.'

'Fuck. Can I see?' George rushed past him.

'Course, man.'

Following the bloke into the downstairs room – his new tattoo parlour, a grin crept onto his face. The room was nowhere near done – the white walls were void of the photos and artworks he'd always envisioned his shop would have, but the fake zebra skin stretched over the floorboards, the floor length mirror and polished work station undoubtedly set the scene of things to come.

'Wow!' George's exclamation was followed by a long whistle. 'This place is looking good. My Nan would love that rug. When did you get the table-draws thingy?'

'Dave lent me the money. I have a shitty desk at the flat in Forest Gate but I'm pretty behind on my rent there so didn't want to go back and face the bastards waiting to be paid.' He hadn't told George the full story about Cole. The drugs. The bouncers and the money. He wasn't withholding the information, there had just never been a time to tell it. 'I'll need to face my problems sometime soon though.'

'Just say, mate, and I'll drive you.'

Jack smiled awkwardly, unable to tell the fella that he dreaded going back to that place. He knew Cole was waiting for him - probably chewing his fucking gums off in anticipation.

'I'm, erm, going to get a second hand chesterfield to go over there and I want to buy some prints for those walls. When I get some cash.' Jack grabbed the black moleskin sketchbook from the station then held it out to George. He took pleasure in watching as his white smile spread even wider.

'I'm nervous. Not because I think you've done a shit job, I know you haven't. Just……I'm getting a tattoo.' He stuttered.

Handing over the pad, Jack held his breath.

'HOLY FUCK!' George's voice filled the room. 'Jesus. I mean, fucking hell, this is amazing.'

Air rushed out of Jack – he had no idea he'd kept it in so long.

'MATE.' The fella grabbed him, pulling him into a bear hug. 'This. Is. Fuck.'

Grinning, Jack peered down at the black and white magpie that George had wanted, the one he'd detailed on the drive home – its wings spread with glints of bright blue and green prominent throughout it's feathers.

'Yeah?' Jack cringed.

'Mate, it's…..' George's jaw paused mid-sentence.

'And you definitely want a magpie? This can't be a rash decision. This shit is for life.' Spotting the jack o' lantern on his wrist, Jack realised the irony in his statement.

Although he appreciated the symbolism, Jack didn't like the idea behind the magpie. The fella had a lot more going for him to think like that. He had *everything* going for him.

'Hundred percent sure. It's something I need right now. You know? "One for sorrow" sums my life up at the moment. I know I'll laugh about it in a few years. And if me and Ella get back together, I'll just get another one. Two for joy.'

Jack sniffed hard. It was the second time that day that George's words had pained him. 'Okay, man, but remember I said this; a tattoo is for life, not just for a break up.'

'Dickhead.' George laughed. 'I know it's permanent. But if she doesn't take me back then I'm going to live with this sorrow for the rest of my life.'

'Man, you've got to stop thinking like this.' Certain his words would fall on deaf ears, Jack placed his hand on George's arm instead. The muscle twitched beneath.

'I know. I'm just being a fucking cliché. But haven't you ever been in love? Even a tiny bit?'

Biting the corner of his lip, Jack shook his head.

'Not ever? Like, you've never fallen for one of your *girlfriends*?'

'You know I've never had one.' He shrugged, wishing that the subject would change back to George's life instead.

'So you just play about?'

Jack ran his hand through his hair. It'd always been a tool to show nonchalance. Indifference. But George asked too many questions and he knew he couldn't avoid them all. It wasn't that he wasn't overly nosey or anything, more so that he was genuinely interested in Jack's life.

'I've been on dates with a *couple* of girls. Nothing serious. When I was younger, my mate Cole would set me up.'

'The prick that used to beat you?'

Jack nodded. 'I think, in his head, he thought he was helping.'

'By beating you up?' George shot a judging look. One that cut.

'It was different back then. We weren't *normal* kids.'

'I don't give a shit, mate. It's fucked up. Friends have each other's back. They care for you. Because of that dickhead, and no offence, your mum, you can't open up to anyone. You're like a jar of gherkins.'

Jack stared into the fella's eyes. Maybe for a little too long before he spoke. 'It's not like I don't try.'

'Don't you want to fall in love?'

Squirming, Jack stepped away and slid a cigarette from the packet. 'Let's not, man. I don't want to get into all this right before doing your tattoo. I need a clear head.' He faked a smile.

'Okay, mate. Sorry.' George sniffed. 'So, honestly, you drew this? Like, actually drew this?'

Jack nodded, unsure why his neck had started to sweat. He was usually proud of his sketches, well as proud as a self-deprecating artist could be, but this one seemed different. For some reason, this one meant more.

Grabbing one of the foldable camp chairs from the corner, Jack popped it open for his guest. His customer. 'Take a seat, man. I'm gonna have to outline this onto a stencil anyway. That's if you're definitely sure?'

'Mate, I'm fucking sure.' George fell into the stripped chair, blue eyes wide, staring at the image in his hands. 'I fucking love this. Honestly, I didn't imagine you'd be able to make it look this good. No offence.' That perfect smile was back. 'But you've gotta promise me one thing.'

Jack raised his eyebrows.

'You can't tell my mum, okay?'

'Ha! You pussy.'

George huffed. 'I just don't want my mum knowing. That's all. You know what mums are like. Fucking nightmares, aren't they? I bet yours weren't happy the first time you got a tattoo, was she?'

Jack coughed. The words had caught him off guard. 'I wish I knew.' He shrugged.

'Fuck!' George clenched his jaw. 'Mate, I don't even know why I said that.'

Jack shrugged it off – his usual response to anything related to his mother.

'When was the last time you spoke to her?' George asked.

'When I was about fourteen. I found out her address and ran away from my foster parents. My mum's refused to speak to me ever since.'

'Why? What did you do?'

'Well, I showed up uninvited and begged to live with her. I didn't want to leave. She had a boyfriend at the time and he went berserk. He actually hit me and social services got involved. I was such a dick.'

'Just by wanting to be with your mum? I don't see what you did wrong. It's not like you wanted to cause trouble?'

'I don't know. I refused to leave. I was just a bratty teenager that wanted his own way.'

George snorted. 'Mate, that's not being a brat. That's a boy desperate to be loved.'

Jack choked. The fella's words struck him more than any insult ever had.

'Do you know where she lives now?' George raised an eyebrow.

'Nope. Dave said he's trying to find out but, who knows? I don't think she wants to be found and I don't really have any right to intrude in her life.'

George's expression hurt him – like a blade into his gut. It was that sympathetic look he'd come to despise. 'Anyway, man. Your mum is sweet, she wouldn't bat an eyelid about a tattoo.'

George shifted on the seat. 'Mate, you don't even know what she's like. My sister came home from Magaluf with a henna tattoo on her wrist and my mum thought she'd joined a cult.'

Jack spat out a laugh.

'I'm serious. She called the police and everything. Even got the vicar involved. We had to go to church for five months afterwards just to keep face.'

'All right, all right. So your mum can definitely never see it. But I don't get how she won't.'

'Why would she?'

'All I'm saying is that if your mum is proper crazy about this stuff then maybe somewhere more hidden.'

'I know you've got experience of tattooing arses, but I doubt you'd wanna see mine.' George winked.

Jack turned Scarlett. The room appeared to shrink on him.

'Fuck. That weren't a guilt trip by the way, mate. Honestly.'

Jack's cheeks burned even brighter. 'Didn't think it was.' He was unsure what he'd thought, to be honest. But the image of George's arse had him sweating.

'Well I don't really take my top off anyway. Especially not in front of my mum.'

'You had your top off today, man.' Jack teased.

'Yeah, but not in public. And I don't walk round the house like it.'

'But you're a born and bred Essex boy aren't you?'

'And?'

'Isn't it in your bible that you take your top of as soon as the sun's out? And that's just the girls.'

'Dick.' George's laugh had somehow become infectious. 'My mum won't ever see it. Not until I've moved out anyway and then she won't be able to do anything. So you got to promise not to tell her. Deal?' He rested the pad onto his lap then held out his hand.

Shaking it, Jack exhaled. 'Deal. But, if she does find out, you're on your own, man.'

Applying pressure for the last strokes of the outline, the vibrations from the machine buzzed through the bones in his hand as the tip of the needle scored into George's skin. Thick, black lines were imprinted onto the fella for good. There was no going back from there. Whether that was a good or bad thing, Jack wasn't sure.

No denying it – the fella had been a champ. Not a peep out of him.

With arms hanging over the stool and head down, George had spent most of the time tapping away on his phone. It wasn't unusual for him to be fixated with his mobile, he was on it as much as the next nineteen year old, but it was obvious that he needed it then to distract him from the pain more than anything else.

The corners of his eyes creased tightly when the pain had seemingly become too much and the muscles in his back tensed under his skin.

It wasn't long into the tattoo that Jack realised why he'd been so intoxicated with the smell of his T-shirt. It wasn't a "home" it reminded him of, it was George. The aroma wasn't just flowery fabric softener, but rather, the outdoors. The freshness of countryside air. Grass. Fields. Hard work. And the closer Jack got, the more he inhaled it in.

George's skin was flawless – just as he discovered earlier that day. But up close, under the scrutiny of his artistic eye, and the glare of the LED lamp, George's body was a work of art all of its own.

The muscles on his back dipped and arced in all the right places. Even when not tensed, they bulged from the skin like golden dunes. His body was pretty much perfect and envy's green claws scratched into Jack.

'You can sit up for a bit, man.' Jack stretched out the ache from his fingers. 'How's it feeling?'

'Yeah, all cool. It's quite relaxing, isn't it?' George sat up straight, grimacing slightly.

Jack scooped up a blob of petroleum jelly and spread it over the red, angry skin on George's back. 'You're the only person I know to ever say it's 'relaxing.' First ink is normally the worst. I swear my first hurt the most out of all of them.'

'Really?' He bit the corner of his lip.

'Hell yeah, man. Hurt so much that I wanted to rip my skin off.'

'Thank fuck for that.' George scrubbed a hand over his face. 'Cause this shit fucking kills. Although it was a lot quicker than I thought. I expected it to go on for hours.'

Jack sniggered. 'Man, that's just the beginning. All I've done is the outline.'

The colour drained from George's face. 'You kidding me?'

Lifting the machine once more, Jack stretched back the elastic band and unhooked the needle. 'Want to continue?'

'I can't go through all that to not finish it. Unless you don't want to carry on. Like if you want to rest or something I totally get it.'

Raising an eyebrow, Jack ripped the sterile packaging open then pulled out the seven-pointed shading needle. Making a point of the showing it to George, He then spun the stool with his foot. 'Sit, you big girl.'

Dipping the needle into the tiny pot of black ink, Jack sucked in a deep breath and stretched George's skin with his index finger and thumb. A singular line of sweat snaked down his brow – his concentration fixed on creating the best tattoo he'd ever done. If Maxine was going to kill him, then it better be for something amazing.

The vibrations from the machine sent pulses through his arm once more yet his hand instantly steadied the moment it touched George's skin. The masterpiece well on its way, warmth seeped through the glove, settling

213

into his fingertips. Sniffing, Jack cleared the bubbling in his throat.

'Mate, this is even worse than the other needle. It feels like its cutting me to shit. Like scraping my bones or something. Is this going to fuck up my spine?'

'Relax. Go with it. If you stop tensing, it won't hurt as much.'

'You know, that sounds pretty fucked whilst you're pinning me down.'

'Hey, it's not my fault you've got a dirty mind.'

'Seriously thought mate, how the hell have you done this a thousand times to yourself? You're nuts.'

'I think it's pretty clear I'm not in my right mind. I'm doing this knowing that your mum will chop my bollocks off if she finds out. '

'Don't worry, if anything happens, I'll protect your bollocks from her.'

Choking, he was so fucking grateful George couldn't see his burning cheeks. 'Try and think of something else. Like, take your mind off it. That works with me. Especially when I had my throat done.'

'What did you think of? Like what the hell is gonna make me forget there's a needle drilling into my spine.'

'Thank fuck you're not *extra*.'

'Piss off. Anyway, aren't you supposed to ask me if I'm going anywhere nice or talk about holidays or some shit?'

'I'm not a fucking hairdresser. Although you could definitely do something with your hair.

George snorted, his back heaved. 'Yeah? And what would you have me do? Shave my sides and grow a floppy quiff to run my hand through….Just like every other bastard in London.'

'Fair point.'

'I surprised you haven't grown a beard.

'I'm no fucking hipster. And you should be careful, *Georgie boy*, remember I'm the one with a needle in your back.'

'Threaten me all you want but I know you'd never fuck up a tattoo. Especially on me.'

'Oh yeah? What makes you think that?'

'Mate, I've seen the way you look at me.'

Jack's mouth was suddenly dry. Like he'd downed a packet of cream crackers. He couldn't swallow. 'What?'

'I saw it today at the farm. Your eyes were all over me like a dirty rash.'

'Fuck off.' The burn intensified.

'It's cool. I get it. I can tell you've been dying to get your hands on me.'

Jack couldn't breathe. He could hear his heart beating louder than the clock ticking on the wall.

'What?'

'I'm a blank canvas to you.'

Jack shook his head in relief. 'Oh.... Right....Erm...Yeah.'

Blowing through rounded lips, Jack lifted his foot from the pedal to stop the machine and laid it onto the workstation. He wiped the sweat off his forehead with the back of his wrist then scrutinised the tattoo.

It was a thing of beauty. The blacks, blues and greens shone from George's golden skin. The bird seemed real, a part of George's body.

Wiping the remaining ink and spots of blood from the bloke's back, Jack finally sat upright.

'That's it, man. You're all done.'

'Really? Fuck....I'm so nervous.' Why am I so nervous? Can we open the wine yet?'

'Maybe because I just spent three and a half hours tattooing a giant cock onto your back.'

215

George's face contorted – an initial look of uncertainty followed by amusement. 'I didn't ask for a picture of you, mate.'

Smirking, Jack rose from his stool then moved out of the way to give George room. 'All yours.' He said, nodding to the mirror.

George crept from his seat slowly and stared at his reflection. Clearly unsure of what to expect, the fella turned slowly.

Jack had witnessed the anticipation many times. For him, he was just as nervous as them. Holding his breath, he waited for what seemed like an eternity for George's reaction.

His eyes were as wide as saucers and his mouth curved into an enormous grin.

'Fuck....king....hell. Look at that. It's fucking beautiful.'

'You like it, yeah?' Jack breathed properly for the first time that night.

'Mate! That's amazing. I can't believe it. I've got a tattoo. A *fucking* tattoo.' George's beautiful smile was wider than ever. 'That's....that's a bit of me.'

Jack stared at the man in front of him. The man with the perfect body and shining blue eyes. He just nodded. Unable to tell George that, right then, he was thinking exactly the same thing.

Chapter Twenty Five

Twisting the key into his front door, George nodded for Jack to follow. Stepping inside they both flinched at seeing Maxine standing in the hallway, arms folded and pouting – blatantly waiting for him.

'Where the hell have you been, Georgie?' She looked upset, more miffed really, even though the Botox kept her from frowning. 'I've been worried sick.'

'Huh? I stayed round Jack's. I though you knew that.' He kept his gaze low – his mother had a gift of reading guilt and he'd managed to keep the tattoo a secret for a whole week. The scabs were healing well but his panic at her finding out was still as fresh as ever. Not wanting to keep his back to walls for the rest of his life, he'd taken to wearing navy blue and black T-shirts to hide any sign of it. His selection of identical white polos would've given the game away in seconds. 'I brought him round to see Nan's dog before he goes to work. I haven't met her yet either.'

'Oh, you didn't come to see me? I only sat by the front door for half the night waiting for you. You said you was popping out for a couple of hours and never came home. I slaved over that oven to make your dinner too. Now the frozen pizza is in the bin.'

He bit his lip, doing his best impression of looking apologetic. 'Mum, I'm sorry that you *cooked* for me and I didn't eat it. I bet it was lovely. I just lost track of time. You know what I'm like.'

'You were drunk again, weren't you? You're going to end up in trouble, or doing something you regret. Like get

217

a piercing or something.' She shot a smile at Jack. 'No offence, darlin. They look lovely on you.'

Shaking his head, George caught Jack's outline in the corner of his eye. He couldn't look directly at him – he wouldn't be able to keep a straight face. 'We just had a few drinks. I wasn't even drunk.' It was true. Four, five drinks tops. It was almost as though he didn't need it as much. 'Tell her, Jack.'

'It's true, Mrs. Taylor. Honestly, we just had a couple of beers and listened to some Ska.'

Maxine gasped, the kind that only a mother does when she's shocked by her children's behavior. 'Ska? You don't like that music, Georgie. I thought you were a *Swiftie*.'

'Mum!' He winced. That's wasn't something he shouted about. 'I'm allowed to like different things.'

'That's what worries me, Georgie. You're changing. You've let your hair grow out, you're listening to *funny* music. And you've been wearing dark clothes for days now.' She put her hand to her mouth. 'Just tell me the truth, Georgie. I need to know. Are you a…a…goth?'

'What?' George snorted.

'Oh god. There used to be one in town when you were a kid. They said she went to university but I've always known the truth. She joined a cult. Don't you dare leave me for those lunatics, Georgie.'

Side eyeing Jack again, it was all he could do to not laugh. His mother was hilarious at the best of times, even if she didn't realise it, but her delusions had grown tenfold since Darcie had moved out. 'Mum, I'm not a *goth*. I've stayed round Jack's loads. You know where I am.' He made his way past her, careful not to scrape his back on the wall. 'And I used to stay round Ellie's all the time. You didn't worry then.'

'I worry because you're not yourself. You're drinking every night and I barely see you anymore. I miss my little

Georgie.' Maxine clamped one hand to her mouth again and the other to his arm. Trying not to laugh at her – he wriggled out from her motherly death grip. 'Mum, I'm still me. I'm just trying new things.'

'Oh my God, it's drugs isn't it? I knew it. Is it the wacky baccy? Or the……Oh no, you're on crystal meth!' She fell against the door frame, her face lost all colour. 'Don't you worry, Georgie. I'll get you into rehab.'

'Mum!' He helped her straighten up. 'I'm not taking fucking drugs. Jesus. I just like spending time round Jack's place. We chat and listen to music. He's got records, actual records. Plus, I'm helping him set up all his tattoo stuff.'

'Tattoos? Don't you go getting any ideas, Georgie.' She folded her arms, colour back in her face and redder than he'd ever seen it. 'I'd rather you lose all your teeth to crack than get a tattoo. No offense, darlin.' She smiled sweetly to Jack. He nodded in response.

'I know mum, *criminal pirates* have tattoos.' George rolled his eyes. 'Anyway, you could have texted. Or rang me. You didn't have to wait up all night.'

'I wouldn't do that, Georgie. I'm not one of those overbearing mothers.'

Snorting, he indicated for Jack to follow then made his way towards the smell of cherry menthol vape smoke wafting from the living room.

'All right, Nan?' George said, immediately parking his backside next to his grandmother and began to stroke the dog perched on her lap. 'Oh wow, look at her.'

'Isn't she just perfect? We're kindred spirits.' Pam beamed. George couldn't recall the last time he'd seen his Nan so happy. Well, maybe when the burly window cleaner had his top off the previous summer.

'Ah, Mrs. Daley, she's too cute.'

'Isn't she just. But call me Pam, love.' She pouted to Jack whilst running her fingers through the dog's curly white coat. 'Your mother chewing your ear off, Georgie?'

'Always.'

'Well, she worries. That's what mothers do, you know. All we care about is our children. And our fur babies.'

George instinctively looked at Jack. He didn't mean to. But he knew the fella recoiled every time somebody mentioned the relationship between a mother and child. In a way, George felt guilty for having a family.

Sighing, Maxine slumped into the recliner, still visibly weakened from the imaginary drugs revelation. 'Steve tells me the café is nearly done, Jackie. How's your flat coming on? I've seen some lovely towels I'm going to get you. They're a lovely "latty" colour.'

Jack smiled, whether it was the pronunciation of the word "latte" or Maxine's kindness, George couldn't decipher. He'd discovered early on that Jack's face rarely gave much away.

'It's going great, Mrs. Taylor. Me and George, well George mainly, have just finished fixing the floor boards.'

'You should get some carpet. A nice mo-shar would look lovely. Like this one.' She scrunched her toes into the pile.

George scrubbed a hand through the dog' fur, ruffling the curls on its head. He couldn't resist making a fuss of animals – it was built into him. 'She's so quiet. How old is she, Nan?'

'We think about three. She's a rescue so we don't know exactly.'

'Oh, it's so lovely you've given her a good home, Mum.' Maxine gushed. 'She's such a beautiful colour too. I've never seen a colour that pretty. What do they call it?'

George shook his head. 'It's white, Mum. The dog's white.'

'No, she looks like lovely washing up bubbles to me. Or clouds.' Maxine pressed the recliner lever, immediately raising its feet. 'What's that colour?'

He pinched the bridge of his nose. 'Also white.'

She wrinkled her nose. 'Well I think it's beautiful. What *make* is she, again, Mum?'

'She's a "bitching freeze," Maxine.'

Jack shot a look at George – it was almost impossible to contain his laughter.

'I think they pronounce it Bichon Frise, Mrs Daley.' Jack said without a hint of sarcasm.

'Call me Pam, love. Anyway, however you say it, I knew she was the one for me as soon as I saw her.' Pam brushed her fingers against the leopard print collar slinked around the little dog's neck. 'Look at this collar I bought her. We've even got the same taste.'

'Where did you get her from, Nan?'

'Oh, it's a terrible story. Makes me want to cry just thinking about it. She's one of those poor puppy farm dogs. And it's nothing to do with tractors. No. This sweet, innocent baby was used as a breeding machine – popping puppies out all year round, bless her. I don't know how she did it. One child was too much for me.'

'Charming.' Maxine tut-tutted then insisted she'd make everyone a hot drink before she was insulted further.

'I don't think she had much of a choice, Mrs Daley.'

'Pam, love.'

'Those puppy farms are evil.' Jack knelt down to the dog on Pam's lap then began to tickle its chin. She looked up at him, tail wagging, her tongue licked the air, desperate to get to him. 'You're a likkle princess, aren't you? Look at you. You're so fluffy. Yes you are. Like a likkle ball of fur.'

'I hope he's talking to the dog.' Pam winked, nodding down to her groin.

'What's her name, Mrs. Daley?'

'Pam, love.'

'He meant the dog, Nan.'

'I know what he meant. It's Pam.'

'Nan, you called your dog Pam? That's ridiculous.'

'Why is it? I like the name and don't get to use it much myself.'

The two of them erupted in laughter, confusing his mother as she came back into the room with a tray of hot drinks.

'I tell you what, Maxine. This little dog has half done wonders for my social life.'

'Really? I would've thought it'd been a tie for you. What with having to stay in all the time.'

'Stay in? I've barely put my telly on for a fortnight. Saved a fortune on electricity too. I'm always out these days and I've met so many people. Men too. Lots of them.' George cringed as his Nan smirked to Jack.

'Really, Mum? You meet some nice fellas?'

'Oh yes, love.' Pam passed Jack the little dog then crossed her legs before slipping her vape from her handbag. 'I've been introduced to the world of dogging and there's no going back.'

George's coffee erupted from his nostrils. The burn of the scorching liquid made worse by his mother's panic that it'd sprayed onto the carpet.

'What?' Maxine's face turned ghostly pale, matching the cream walls.

Pam nodded. 'I love it. There's a group of us. We all meet in the park in the morning and go at it for hours.'

'Dogging?' Maxine gasped, seemingly unable to blink. George didn't know how much more his mother could take. 'Mum, you're not serious?'

'Yes, love. I'm a huge fan of dogging. I go every morning, sometimes in the afternoon too if I can handle it. I do it until I can barely walk sometimes.'

Maxine's eyes grew wider than George had ever seen. Shock horror radiating from her face, she didn't notice that her tea had spilt from her shaking hands onto the teal cushion.

'Calm down, Mum.' Leaping from his seat, George eased the cup out of her hands. 'I don't think Nan knows what dogging is.'

'Course I know what it is. I do it every bloody day. Sometimes there's at least ten of us there at once.'

'MUM!' Maxine's shriek ricocheted around the living room.

'Maybe I should tell her?' Jack bit his lip, stifling a laugh. Leaning into Pam's ear, he whispered.

Whatever he'd said, Pam's face flashed red before she took another drag of her vape.

'Well, that's not the dogging I do. My hips wouldn't let me hang out of a hatchback.' She blew out the smoke as though she was exhaling the imagery. 'I only take little Pam out for a walk round the park and chat to a few fellas on my way round.'

'That's definitely not called dogging, Mrs Daley.'

Giggling, Jack held the dog in his arms as though she was a new born baby and George could feel his chest warming. The sight of him – Jack – the man dressed in eternal black and tattoos painted all the way to his jaw line, looked so out of place holding that fluffy white dog. But it was definitely right at the same time. Knowing Jack like he did, he knew the guy was a massive softie at heart. George couldn't stop himself from beaming.

'She might need a *wee-wee*. She hasn't been out in a while.' Pam went to stand.

'I'll take her.' Jack blurted, obviously desperate to spend more time with the dog. 'I don't mind.'

The three of them watched the fella leave the room with the dog. George had no idea why, but he was certain he'd held his breath until he heard Jack close the back door behind him.

'So gorgeous.' Pam sucked on her vape, rolling her eyes at the sound of bubbling liquid.

'Yeah, she is seriously cute, Nan.'

'Pam's lovely, but I was talking about Jack. What I wouldn't give for him to scoop me up in his arms like that.'

'Mum, you're old enough to be his grandmother.' Maxine retorted.

'Say what you like, love. But when his head was near my crotch, I nearly started ovulating.'

'Nan, you're gross.'

'Oh, come on the pair of you. That boy is a walking lubricant. Georgie, you must have seen him naked....what's he like?'

Mum!' Maxine screamed. 'I don't want you talking like that. Not in front of Georgie.'

With silence booming around the room, George couldn't help but think back to the day under the tree. Jack's amazing art on full display. The fella had kept his top on at all times since but George could remember it perfectly. So much so, he couldn't look Jack in the eye when he returned from the garden, cradling the dog in his arms.

'You two boys want dinner tonight?'

'I'm going to the pub to meet Alf and Aims tonight, Mum.'

'Oh, that's lovely. I miss seeing those two around here. I need to ask Aimee if she can fit me in for a pedi. Are you going too, Jackie?'

George kept his gaze averted - the guilt of not inviting Jack clenched his stomach. It's not that he didn't want him there, in fact it was Jack's idea for him to meet them. Jack was his mate now, he needed him in his life. It was just that he had to face the attack from Alfie, for ignoring him, on his own.

'Jack is meeting his uncle later. So he can't come, anyway.' George faked a smile.

'Yes, Dave is coming to the flat. He's got some news about my mum.'

'Oh?' Maxine's attempt at frowning said it all. It was one she'd displayed many a time, usually when Darcie had admitted to buying make up from the pound shop. 'I didn't know you were still in touch with your mum, darlin.'

'I'm not, Mrs. Taylor. Dave is trying to find an address for her…..I don't know if he'll even get it. It's been years since any of us saw her.'

Maxine pressed the button on the side of the chair to sit up straight. It was obviously a conversation that needed an upright position. The sound of the chair's electrics made the anticipation of what she was about to say even more awful.

'Well, if he does find it, it might be better to give her a call first, eh? I don't want you getting your hopes up.'

The room fell silent again. It wasn't so much an awkwardness, more a whopping great big pink elephant in the room. One that was taking a massive shit on the mo-shar carpet.

George could see the pain in Jack's eyes. Even if no one else could. He'd spent enough time alone with him to sense an unspoken change in his mood.

'Mum, leave it out.' George mocked. He needed to defuse the situation. 'You're moaning at me for not coming home enough and now you're trying to persuade Jack to *not* see his mum.'

'I'm doing no such thing. I want Jackie to see her. Every boy needs his mum. But…' she faced Jack again. 'I don't want you getting upset.'

225

'I won't, Mrs Taylor. I've got a feeling it's gonna work out this time. We've all grown up. It's gonna work.'

George's chest warmed. He couldn't help it. He was happy for his friend. He deserved some happiness. He just fucking prayed that the women wouldn't let his friend down. He meant too much to him.

Chapter Twenty Six

Observing the carnage in front of him, George froze on the doorstep of the pub. The Swan – his local, his cosy affirmation of adulthood had gone. The familiar red and gold-patterned carpet that held the hospitable aroma of stale beer and the burgundy wallpaper that flaked just the right amount to look homely rather than rundown, had vanished. There were gleaming white walls, grey laminate flooring and copper cage lampshades hanging over the newly marbled bar. The old tables that often sported the carved initials of pissed punters had been replaced with white and grey up-cycle jobs that his mother and her liquid-lunching buddies would coo over.

He'd been excited to see his friends, mainly wanting to tell them about his tattoo. Something that made him strangely proud. He wanted to show them that he was no longer the clean-cut George, and hoped that his new style would somehow get back to Ellie. There was no way that Aimee could keep it quiet. But the shock of seeing the pub's new look somewhat overshadowed his own transformation.

The Swan was the place that he had his first drink. Well, legal drink. Ellie had planned a surprise Eighteenth Party for him with all his family and friends. It was a special place. Just like springtime, it was theirs.

Navigating his way through the new layout, George realised that the place's disastrous new look had brought with it a different crowd – most of whom, George had seen before in the bars closer to Colchester, but never in *his* pub. The regulars and retired day-drinkers that

227

would've been settling in for a night of cheap drinks were nowhere to be seen – instead, girls with deep tans sipped pink gin whilst groups of gym rats clustered together in matching muscle tees. The shit-swamp that was once The Swan had somehow transformed into the place-to-go for Essex's most beautiful. For some reason, the place made him think of Jack. It was far from the fella's style, but it made him want to be with him. Cosy in his flat, listening to records on his turntable and talking about life.

'Good evening, sir. What can I get you?' A server asked in a plummy accent as he reached the modern marble-top bar. She was clearly not from Coggletree. Her pronunciation of each word proved that. She was quite pretty, her blonde hair and large eyes reminded him of Ellie. The old Ellie. But she was nowhere near as beautiful.

Drawing his eyes to the back of the bar, his stomach clenched. The old optics that once hung on the back wall had been replaced with glass shelves of free-pour bottles and the alcove that was adorned with photos of past patrons had been overlaid with a glimmering mirror. His reflection shot back at him, showing a confused five-foot-ten lad way out of his comfort zone.

'Sir?' The barmaid's pearly grin and look of genuine interest unnerved him. She was new too, and by the look of the band of aproned bar staff congregated at the state-of the-art coffee machine at the end of the bar, she was just one of many fresh recruits.

'Erm, can I get a double JD and coke, pint of Stella and a white wine spritzer…..lemonade, not soda?' Dodging the onslaught from the mirror, he attempted a smile back. 'Please.'

He slid a tenner from his jeans pocket and scanned the pub for his friends before spotting Alfie in the corner where the flashing fruit machines used to be. Instead of flipping a soggy beer mate - his usual past-time, Alf was picking his teeth with the corner of a laminated wine list. Aimee wasn't with him, but with the amount of man-sausage in the place, that was hardly surprising.

Although his thoughts were silent, George cleared his throat, reminding himself to lay off of Aimee. Jack's laid back nature and his way of seeing the best in every situation had taught him many things over the last few weeks - one being that Aimee had done nothing wrong apart from trying to be everybody's friend.

Watching the blonde pour his JD with the silver measuring cup, he rolled his eyes and tapped his fingers on the cold, soulless bar as she then pissed about collecting lime wedges and black plastic stirrers for the drink he had every intention of knocking back before even tasting.

Her smile broadened as she passed the glasses through the gaps in the chrome beer pumps - one at a fucking time – then pecked her French tipped nails onto the touch screen till to tally the drinks.

'That's twenty-three pounds, thirty, please, sir.'

'Huh?'

'Twenty-three, thirty, sir.' Her smile seemed fixed, mask-like.

Seriously. What the actual fuck had happened to the place?

With his pockets much lighter than expected, George weaved his way through the hordes of pretty prosecco drinkers and plonked the three full glasses onto the table in front of Alfie.

'All right, mate?' George slid into the seat opposite his friend. Alfie nodded but his eyes remained focused elsewhere. On the blonde barmaid.

Undoubtedly half cut, Alfie drained the remaining mouthful of lager from his glass before snatching up the new one and demolishing half its contents in one quick gulp. 'Where you been hiding, you tosser?'

'Nice to see you too, Alf.' George guzzled his own drink – the mix of the cold coke with the warming bourbon hitting just the right spot. At least that hadn't changed. 'Where's Aims?'

'She's gone for a slash.' Alfie stretched his neck, shooting the barmaid a wink. George didn't need to turn his head to see her reaction. Alfie's curled lips and wink said it all. 'I'm telling you, Georgie boy, these posh girls love a bit of Braintree beefcake.'

George choked on his drink. 'Is that what you are?'

'I was talking to her earlier and I swear I got her wet.'

'Because you spit when you talk?' Smirking, George clinked his glass with Alfie's. 'What's up with this place though? Who knew Boris was into this kind of thing. I didn't even know it was getting a re-furb.'

'It was shut for weeks. Where you been?'

George ran his fingers over the smooth painted table top and sighed. 'Not here apparently.'

Alfie waved at the girl again and within seconds she was stood at the side of the table with a shiny tablet in her hand. 'What can I get you, sir?'

'Can we get the same again, gorgeous? Looks like my boy here is thirsty.' Alfie made a show of tensing his biceps as he scratched the barely-there stubble on his jaw. 'Get one for yourself too. Whatever you like.' Watching every bounce of her buttocks, the bloke nearly fell off his chair as she returned to the bar.

George scooped up a cube of ice from his glass, sucking the remnants of bourbon, wishing she'd hurry up. 'Table service? In The Swan?'

'Fuck, yeah. You've got to admit, Georgie, this place is the tits.' Alfie finished his pint. 'And thanks to B.O. Boris selling up, a bunch of hotties have been hired instead. I'm not going to lie, I've had a semi since I got here.'

'What? You serious?'

'Mate, I've been pocket stroking for the last fifteen minutes.'

'I meant about Boris. He's sold the place?'

'Yep. Sold it to buy a villa in Benidorm. All right for some. Anyways, where you been hiding, thought I'd pissed you off or something. You haven't replied to any of my texts in weeks.'

'Not at all, mate. Just been busy helping......erm, well, you remember Jack?'

Alfie rolled his eyes. 'I thought you might have got yourself some. You know, banging a new girl or something? After you fucked over Jodie.'

The fella's words stung. That wasn't the kind of man George wanted to be known as. 'I've not even looked at another girl.' It was the truth.

'So, you've been with that wanker then?' Alfie shook his head, clearly unimpressed. 'You don't need to text back now you've got your new *friend*?'

George flipped his phone on the table – hiding the screen somehow helped his guilt. 'It's not like that mate. You know how it is. You get busy and forget to text back.'

'Text, full stop, you mean. Aims hasn't heard from you either. She thought you still had the hump with her because of what happened at the festival?'

'Really?' George bit the inside of his lip, cringing as he remembered how he treated her. 'No. I was just being a douche.'

Alfie nodded in agreement. 'Aimee was shitting it about coming here tonight. So be nice, yeah?'

'Of Course.'

'Good, 'cause here she comes and she's not been too good lately.'

'Huh?' George raised his brows but the toe of Alfie's loafer punting his shin silenced him.

Aimee laid her glittered bracelet-bag onto the table before leaning in to stain George's cheek pink with her lipstick. Her skin had lost the ultra-orange hue she sported just weeks before but the smell of biscuits suggested she'd recently doused herself in fake tan. Her auburn hair was redder than usual, almost scarlet, and with it trailing down to her hips – the majority of that was fake too.

'O M G, the ladies toilets are so much nicer now. Toilet tissue and everything. No more drip-drying in The Swan.'

'Good to know.' George laughed.

She winked and thanked him for her drink. 'You okay, babes? Feel like I haven't seen you in forever.'

'Not bad, Aims. Feeling a bit better actually. How's you? I'm liking the do.' He indicated to her hair.

'Oh thanks, babes. Fancied a bit of a change. I'm liking your hair too. You growing it out?'

Before George could answer, Alfie coughed into his fist. 'Actually, just need to get to the barbers.'

'Bet you've been too busy.' Alfie scoffed.

George stared at his friend for a moment. Alfie was blatantly annoyed. He had a right to be. George had pretty much gone AWOL on them. But he was in a better place – they needed to see that. 'Talking of change.' He cleared his throat. 'I've only gone and got myself a -'

'Sorry, sir.' The barmaid interrupted as she slid a silver tray topped with their drinks onto the table. In her usual near-glacial fashion, she placed the drinks in front of them before pulling the tablet from her apron. 'That is Twenty-three, thirty, please.'

George snatched his drink from the table and downed half of it in one go.

Biting the side of her lip, the barmaid turned to face Alfie - who had kept one hand in his pocket the whole time. 'Can I get you anything else, *sir*?'

'Your number?' He smirked.

Amy popped open her bag and pulled out her glittery purse. 'Here, let me get these, babes. I don't think that's his wallet he's got his hand on.' Aimee grimaced, tapping the screen with her bank card. 'Sorry. He thinks he's God's gift.'

Alfie thrust his groin as the barmaid giggled her way back to the bar. 'Tell you what, I'm so fucking jealous of her heart right now.'

'What?' George and Aimee asked in unison.

'It's pumping inside her and I'm not.'

'Seriously, mate.' George choked on his drink.

'You really should leave that girl alone.' Aimee popped the lid off her gloss and ran the wand over her lips.

'Why? You're all over guys.'

'Yeah babes.' She pressed her shiny lips together. 'But I don't look like Shrek.'

'No, more like Fiona with that hair.'

Bourbon shot from George's nose. Fuck, he'd missed those two. Through his laughter, he gave Aimee an apologetic nod.

'It's ok, Georgie, I just ignore him. He talks so much bollocks that his tongue's sprouting pubes.'

'That's actually gross.' Alfie belched loudly.

'Well stop hitting on the poor girl. She's obvs not from round here - did you see her French tips? It's not even the nineties.'

'It's not her nails I'm after.' Alfie kicked George again. 'Well, unless they're scratching down my back. You know what I'm on about don't you, mate?'

Clearing his throat, George knocked back a third of his glass, greedily taking in the alcohol before someone else had a chance to make him laugh. 'Listen, I've been meaning to text. I feel like shit for not getting back to you both. I've got to tell you, I've got a tattoo.

'O M G, Georgie. No way.' Aimee's face lit up. 'Where? Does your mum know? Where did you get it done?'

He smiled. He couldn't help it. 'On my back. And, no she doesn't know. She's already adamant I'm on meth.'

Alfie was scowling, like he'd just licked piss off a nettle. 'I think she's got a point. *Are* you on drugs?'

'Eh? No. Why'd you say that?' George straightened his back.

'Well, you've been hanging 'round with that druggie. I bet it's him that tattooed you, isn't it? Most probably infected you too.'

'Alf!' Aimee slapped Alfie's leg.

'Jack isn't a druggie. He's actually a really good bloke. And yes, he did my tattoo. It's fucking amazing, what he's done.' George's show of courage extended just enough to knock another mouthful of bourbon back. 'I've got some photos of it if you want to see.'

'No thanks.' Alfie barked.

Yes, please.' Aimee cooed as George passed her his phone. 'O M G. I love that. It's so realistic. Why the magpie though, Georgie?'

'No real reason.' He lied. He couldn't tell them it was because he was so caught up with his own shitty life that he needed to mark the occasion by permanently etching sorrow into his skin. He may as well have had "TWAT" tattooed on his back.

'They just remind me of work. I see them every day and am always working these days. It seemed right.'

'Tell me about it, babes. Adulting so overrated. I miss the days when our GCSE's were the most stressful thing in our lives.'

George nodded. He'd commit murder just to have those years back. When everything was going well in his life.

'The salon is like *crazy* busy at moment. Honestly, the amount of waxing I've done in the last week - I could make a fur coat out of all the hair.'

'You two moaning about work like you even do anything.' Alfie moaned. 'You wanna try being a labourer. Real work. It's been boiling. Some days I wanted to pass out. And it's not like I've got much to look forward to either. Winter is fucking freezing. I could barely see my cock for the whole of January.'

'What's new, Alfs? Aimee winked at George.

'Fuck you!'

'Not with that cashew dick, you don't.'

JD and coke spouted from George's mouth – the fizz burning his throat.

'Dickheads. The pair of you.' Alfie's narrowing eyes turned from Aimee to George. He stood from his seat then wiped the beer from his chin. 'I'm getting another drink. And that sort's number. You want one?'

'A number?' George laughed.

'A drink, you knob.' Alfie pulled a handful of scrunched up notes form his pocket. 'That's if you're not too busy, *Georgie boy*.' He sniffed then stomped off to the bar.

'What's up with him?' George furrowed his brow.

'Ignore him, babes. He's just sulking because you haven't been about and he didn't get that apprenticeship he went for.'

'What apprenticeship?' George thought back to the many texts he'd ignored from Alfie yet couldn't quite place it. Had he not told him? To be fair, George knew that even if he had, he wouldn't have paid attention. Life had thrown a spanner in the works and instead of sucking it up, George let himself become a dickhead. One that wasn't there for his friends.

Leaning over the table, Aimee pulled her red hair over one shoulder to block their conversation from Alfie. 'He went for a Mechanic thingy but he didn't make it. Failed his maths. And English. Twice.'

'Oh, shit. Really?' George swallowed his guilt.

'Yep. So he's been proper *extra* ever since. Then he found out you've been hanging round with Jack all the time and O M G.'

'Jack is a really nice bloke, Aims.'

'Oh babes, I think it's great you've got a new mate. I like Jack. I told you he was a babe, didn't I?'

'He is.' George beamed. 'Been meaning to ask you. Erm.' He cleared his throat. 'Did you two? You know?'

George ran his finger over the rim of his glass. He felt like someone had punched him in the chest. It was akin to the jealousy pains he suffered when he thought Ellie had cheated.

'Nothing happened with me and Jack. Don't get me wrong. I tried. But he weren't interested.' She rolled her eyes then giggled. 'But you keep that to yourself. I've got a bad reputation to keep.'

Confusion swirled in George's brain. 'Why weren't he interested?'

'I don't think I'm his *thing*, babes. Honestly, how hard is it to find a decent bloke? All I want is to be shown off like a hospital bracelet on Snap Chat.'

George laughed into his drink. The alcohol was just about taking over, lifting the headache that comes with overthinking and replacing it with that comforting haze he needed.

'To be honest, Aims, I thought something was happening with you and Alf. You seemed so much closer last time I saw you both.'

'No, babes. The only thing fucking me is life. It's so much lately. But I'm treating it like eyeliner and just winging it at the mo.'

'You okay, Aims?'

'My family's just going through it, what with my poor Gramps.'

'What's wrong with your grandad? You've never told me.'

'It's okay, babes. You've got enough to deal with.'

Alfie slammed a tray onto the table. Their usual drinks accompanied by two shots each. 'What you got to worry about, Georgie?'

'Nothing. I didn't say a thing.'

'Still crying over Ellie? Change your fucking tampon, mate.'

'Sambuca? Babes, you know I can't drink this stuff.' Aimee swiped one of the tiny glasses off the table and raised it up.

Alfie lifted his too, holding it out for George to join in. 'Here's to mates. Even if they do fuck your girlfriend.'

George raised a shot and tapped their glasses before throwing it back. The thick aniseed slivered down his throat.

'Mate, I've had it all out with Jack. Ellie was drunk and kissed him. He never did anything back. Aims, you can vouch for him – he's not like that is he?'

'He was lovely when I stayed over. Slept on the sofa and everything.'

'He's a dick.' Alfie gulped down his pint then wiped his mouth with his palm. 'And you've been having little picnics with him. What's going on? He sucking your dick or something?'

George's cheeks burned bright red. The heat made him squint.

'Alf, if there's one thing I've learnt from meeting Jack, it's that you've got to let go of all the shit and enjoy life. We're not here long enough, mate.'

'O M G, that is totes motes.' Aimee slapped a hand to her chest.

Alfie necked the rest of his lager, slamming the glass onto the grey table top. 'The fuck is motes?'

'Motivational, obvs. And Georgie is right.'

Turning his attention to George, Alfie's face contorted. His eyes were glazed from the beer but there was still anger behind them.

The table fell silent. The noise of alcohol-fuelled chatter resonated around them around in waves. Other people's laughter and joviality seemed to wash over them only to make it more awkward.

Aimee's phone buzzed on the table and she scooped up her bag. 'I've got to take this. It's my mum. But you two need to sort this out. We're friends remember. We've know each-other forever.'

Watching Aimee make her way through the groups of pretty people, bile rose to George's chest.

'Why you being a wanker, Alf?' George raised his eyebrows as well as his drink. The buzz of the liquor didn't seem to have the same effect anymore.

'I'm not. You are. Fucking ignoring me and Aims 'cause you've bagged yourself a boyfriend. I wouldn't even mind, but the fella *fucked* your missus.'

'For god sakes!' George spat. 'He didn't fuck her!'

Seething, the two of them sat fixed in each other's glares. Eyes unflinching – waiting for the next remark to bite back at.

Aimee returned amidst the stand-off, her painted lips trembled. 'Sorry, boys. But I gotta go. I'll make it up to you both. I promise.'

'What's up, Aims?' George tried to offer concern but was pipped to the post by Alfie's arm wrapping around her.

She shook her head. 'I can't talk. I just gotta go.' Clutching her bag, she fled from the pub before either of them could respond, bringing back the tension between them.

'What the fuck was all that about? I swear, you two are mental tonight. She's gone and you're acting like I've pissed in your pint.'

'Get your head out your arse.' Alfie's face turned red. 'While you've been crying over Ellie and hanging round with your new bestie, other people are going through some real shit. Shit that actually matters.'

'What you talking about?' George lifted his glass but couldn't bring himself to drink from it. 'Why is nobody telling me anything?'

'You haven't been around, mate. You couldn't give a shit about anyone else these days. You've been a complete wanker for ages.'

'Yes, I've been going through a shit time. But I'm getting better.'

'Your bird dumped you. Move on.'

'She didn't dump me.'

'For fuck sakes! She's been dicking around with god knows how many guys. Look at your new best mate for starters. She fucked him and now *he's* fucking you over for a bit of help decorating his flat.'

'They didn't fuck!'

'No? Face it, George.' Hearing Alfie say his name in its true form winded him. 'Ellie don't want someone like you. She wants someone like him.'

Anger had become such a wall between them that the clamour of everyone and everything around disappeared into quietness. Numbness. He needed a drink before he thumped the fella.

'I'm getting another. You want one?' George stood from his chair, his heart racing in his chest.

'You know what mate? No. I don't. Not from you.'

Alfie kicked back his chair, grabbed his jacket from the back of it and, without another word, left George in the shithole that was once The Swan.

****

Outside, in the pelting rain, Alfie nor Aimee were anywhere to be seen. The streets were empty with only the winds bringing the hissing of heavy rain onto the pavements. His proper first night out in weeks had turned into a handful of drinks and a stinking headfuck. With his friends abandoning him, he needed someone to talk to. He needed Jack.

Sliding his phone from his pocket, he swiped his thumb over the screen and searched for his name in his favourites. Tapping it once, he watched the screen shift and felt the ringing in his palm before slamming his thumb down to cancel the call.

A call wasn't going to be enough. He needed to see him.

Chucking a right, he walked across the small bridge with his chin buried into the collar of his polo shirt. The sound of rain splashing against the river soothed him slightly, just enough to take the noises in his overcrowded mind away.

His phone vibrated in his hand and, expected it to be Jack calling back, his heart sank as he saw the name of the caller.

'Georgie?' The voice on the end of the line sparked electricity up his spine. Weeks of reciting what to say, rehearsing every single word of the conversation he wanted to have just vanished. Gone. In that defining moment, a mumble of recognition was all he could muster.

Choking on nothing but oxygen, he cleared his throat. 'Ells?'

'How you doing, Georgie?'

'I'm.....I'm.....you know.' His voice cracked. '.....all good.'

'So happy to hear that, babes.'

He tried to remember his rehearsed script. The jokes. The come backs. 'Yeah. Proper loving work. I'm out pretty much every night.'

'Wow, you sound like you're living your best life, Georgie.'

'I am. Even got a tattoo now and everything.'

Winning.

'You've got a tattoo?' Her pitch rose. He didn't know if it was shock or admiration. He wanted it to be both. 'Does your mum know?'

'Probably, I haven't tried to hide it or anything.' He recoiled at his own lie. 'Anyways, how's everything with you? How's, erm, uni?' He shrugged to himself.

'So good. I know this sounds crazy but I can't wait to start my second year. You would have loved it here too. You really would have.'

He sucked in a deep breath. It was a conversation they'd had many times before – it always ended with him feeling inferior. But he wasn't going to let that happen this time. 'I couldn't be stuck in a classroom. You know that. It's soulless.' He smiled to himself. Fuck, he was on fire.

'Ha, I know. And I love that.' She cleared her throat. 'Anyways, I know you're out with Aims and Alf'

'I was.' He interrupted. 'In The Swan.'

'Oh god, you poor things. That pub is so rotten. I always hated it there.'

George straightened his back. The Swan was *theirs*. How the hell could she hate it?

'It's, erm, changed a lot, actually. It's really pretentious now and up its own arse. You'd love it.' Silence buzzed through the line and he cringed at the insult.

Slinking under the cedar tree at the bottom of the bridge, George found the driest spot and blew through rounded lips. He hadn't spoken to her in so long that he'd forgotten how to actually do so. 'Sorry, I didn't mean it like that.'

'It's ok, Georgie. It's just nice to hear your voice. I feel like I haven't spoken to you ages.'

George furrowed his brow. For his benefit, more than anything. 'It *has* been ages.' He couldn't remember how many weeks it'd been. What surprised him more was that he hadn't realised he'd stopped counting.

'So you're not with Aimee?' Ellie asked. 'She's just miss-called me. I tried Alf's phone but think he's blocked me.'

Her words winded him. She wasn't even calling to speak to him and he knew it. 'No, she ran out of the pub.'

'Oh no, it's not her grandad is it?'

'That's it! What the fuck is wrong with her grandad? Why won't anyone tell me?'

The phone went silent again and then he heard a few hushed mumbles from the background at her end.

'You don't know?'

'No. Just tell me. Please.'

'Oh, Georgie, her grandad is dying. He's riddled with cancer and….he's going to die any day now.'

'Oh shit! Why didn't she tell me?' It was like someone had kicked him in the balls. The guilt swirled in his guts. Why hadn't Aimee told him?

'I don't know, George.' Her voice sounded weak. Then the mumbles in the background returned, this time a little clearer. It was a man's voice. Deep and well-spoken too. Another kick in the nuts. Who the fuck was she talking to?

'Georgie, I got to go. I'm on my way out to meet the girls and I'm running so late. I'll try Aims again.'

'Who's that with you?' George cringed at his jealousy but if he didn't get it out, he feared he'd vomit. 'Doesn't sound like one of the girls.'

'I can't talk now, Georgie. I'm coming to see Aimee soon so maybe you and I can catch up.' Her words was rushed, she was clearly desperate to finish the conversation.

'Oh! I know you kissed Jack.' He blurted. He didn't even know he was going to say it.

'I heard you've been hanging around with him. That's so…..weird. But great. Listen, I wanted to tell you –'

'I don't care about that.' Strangely, he didn't. 'Are you seeing someone else? Is he with you now?' He had to ask.

'I don't really want to go through it right now, Georgie.' The deep voice mumbled in the background again.

'What about what I want?' He kicked his heel into the tree behind him. 'No one has ever asked me what I want in all of this.'

'What's brought this on? I thought you was good.'

'Ok, Ells, enough bullshit. Life's not good. It's fucking dire. I just really fucking miss you. So much it that it hurts.'

'I miss you too, Georgie. You was such a massive part of my life for so long.'

George fell backwards onto the tree. She hadn't winded him, more like she'd ripped his lungs from his body. His legs began to tremble, matching his chin.

The sound of the rain suddenly filled his ears, swirling in his brain. There was nothing to divert his thoughts other than the black river in front of him - the glare of the pubs garish lights reflecting how much everything had changed.

A tear ran down from his eye, washed away quickly by the falling drops from the leaves above. 'So, you have a boyfriend?'

'Georgie, I don't want to upset you.'

'I'm not upset.' Tears streamed down his cheeks. He needed to keep try and it to-fucking-gether! Just for a moment more.

'Please tell me.' His voice had grown frantic.

'He's not my boyfriend, no. But I am seeing him.'

More tears ran down his cheeks. He could taste them. ''Ells, answer me one thing? And you've gotta be a hundred percent honest. Please! I promise I will leave you alone.'

'I'll try, Georgie.' He was certain she was crying too.

'Ok.' He wiped away the water from his face. The lump in his throat had grown so thick that it almost suffocated him. 'Are we ever getting back together? Are we over?'

'Babes.'

'Please, just tell me. I can take it.' He couldn't see through his tears.

'Georgie, if I'm honest. I don't *think* we will get back together.'

'What, ever?'

'I'm sorry, Georgie. Honestly, I am so sorry.'

'It's okay.' His heart fell hard into the pit of his stomach.

'Georgie, please don't hate me.'

'Don't be silly.' He choked on each word.

'I just know I want something different from life. I just want something new. Something -'

'Something that's not me.'

'Georgie.'

Pulling the phone away from his ear, he stretched his arm backwards and flung the thing into the dark rushing water. With a splash, barely audible, the reflection of the pub at the side of the river rippled into pieces.

Panting, he spun on his heels, desperate to face away from it. His eyes shot to the streets either side of the bridge, flitting from shop to shop in search of something to remind him of better times.

Everything was dark. Coggletree the epitome of unreasonable opening hours. Then there it was – the light shining from a bare bulb in a flat above the shops. Its glow pouring through blinds that he'd help hang. In the entire row of flats, it was the only one George had ever been inside. Something moved within and he knew who the slim silhouette in the upstairs living room belonged to.

It was Ellie's something different. It was *his* something different.

It was Jack.

Chapter Twenty Seven

Creaking open his front door, a confused Jack couldn't help but smile when he saw George standing there in the rain.

'You all right, man? Didn't think I'd be seeing you tonight.' He opened the door wider, signalling for George to enter. '

'Sorry.' George grumbled as he shuffled into the hallway.

'Don't be. Aren't you supposed to be out with Alfie and Aimee?

George shrugged, his stare fixed on the ground. He was drenched, his hair flat to his scalp and his eyes were bloodshot. Jack could instantly tell that something other than the rain was troubling him He wasn't so much drunk, although the slouched shoulders suggested he'd put a few drinks away, but there was something else. Like a black cloud had followed the fella to his door.

'You been swimming? You're soaked.' Jack quickly pulled a clean towel from his washing pile at the foot of the stairs. 'Take this.'

Barely stretching for it, he then grabbed the towel and wiped his face and forearms with little enthusiasm.

'Dave still here?' The fella finally spoke. 'I can go. Just say. I don't want to bother you.' His gaze remained on the ground.

'Bother me? It's Friday night. Don't know if you've noticed but you're the only friend I have around here. Only friend full stop.'

George passed the towel back to Jack, his perfect teeth remained hidden under tightened lips.

'Want to come upstairs? Been going through my records.'

George didn't answer, he just climbed the creaking stairs with hunched shoulders. Following him, Jack couldn't help but study the fella's back muscles underneath his wet top. He'd been captivated during the tattooing and now had to stop himself from looking further down George's body. Jack knew it was getting out of hand, that he and George were just friends. But his gaze couldn't help but wander.

Jack quickly straightened out his unmade bed and kicked some dirty clothes into the corner. 'Sit, man.' He popped open a striped camping chair and plonked it in front of him.

George grumbled again, slumping into the seat. Water ran down from his hairline onto his face but he didn't bother to wipe it away. His stare remained on the floor.

'What's up?' Jack pulled his own chair to face George and fell into it with a sympathetic frown. 'Tell me.'

'Nothing.' He sniffed, finally wiping the rain from his brow. 'Just a shit night to match a shit life.

Jack inhaled, long and slow, trying his best not to laugh. He was well accustomed to George's mood swings. 'Thought you was out with your mates.'

'Mates? I don't have any!'

'Ouch.' Jack mocked.

'I didn't mean you. You're the only person that likes me at the moment. Aimee must hate me and Alfie, well, I know he does.'

Jack grabbed a new cigarette packet from the coffee table he made from pallets – his only DIY ability– then used his teeth to rip off the plastic wrappings. Peeling back the lid, he lapped up the aroma.

Jumping up, he cranked open a window and sparked up his cigarette before blowing the smoke out to the wet street. 'You had an argument? What was it? He wearing the same white polo shirt or something?'

George remained indifferent whilst Jack winced at the failure of his joke. Shaking his head, he scooped up his glass of rum and coke and silently hoped that George would buck up soon. 'Can I get you a drink? I have half a bottle of rum, lager or tap water. That's if you're staying.'

'Tell me to go if you want, mate.'

Jack didn't have the power to persuade him to snap out of his self-pity, he'd tried many a time and failed. He knew that George needed to come out of it himself. But, nonetheless, he hated to see him suffer. Yes, he was knackered - slogging an eight hour shift at the burger van with Marie was hard work when all he could do was think about the bloke sat in front of him. 'I didn't mean that. Believe me, man. I like spending time with you.' Jack sucked in a lungful of smoke. 'How about I get you a glass of water?'

'Fuck off. Water? I don't want to be sober.' He lifted his head. 'Can I have one of those?'

'You want rum?' Jack asked, knowing it wasn't the fella's thing. 'Sure, man.'

'No, I meant that.' George nodded towards the cigarette. 'I'll give you the money for it.'

Raising an eyebrow, Jack indicated to the box on the table. 'Help yourself.' He then shook his head as George fished his wallet from his wet jeans. 'Keep your money though.'

George fumbled with the box, seemingly unaware of which end opened at first, then pulled a cigarette out as though his fingertips were surgical tweezers. 'Got a lighter?' He mumbled then placed the cigarette delicately between his full lips and walked towards Jack.

Unable to keep his amusement hidden, Jack quickly put his glass on the window sill and slid his green lighter from his back pocket. Leaning forward, he held out the flame, catching his breath as George placed his hand over his to steady the flame.

George's eyes stayed fixed onto the lighter until he drew in a mouthful of smoke then finally met Jack's gaze. That's when Jack saw them properly. The two blue orbs were saddened by redness but they were still the most striking eyes he'd ever seen. Choking on his own lungful of smoke, Jack became aware that he hadn't let out his breath. He'd just stood there - unable to move - to breathe even, for what felt like hours. There were no words exchanged, Jack wasn't even sure whether he could speak anymore. As George turned away towards the open window, Jack lifted his hand to his own mouth to make sure he wasn't dribbling as George blew out a stream of white smoke. It suited him, as though he'd always smoked and Jack was half impressed that he didn't cough. The other half still expecting him too.

'So you had a falling out I take it. You and Alfie?'

'Yep. He thinks I'm a dick.'

'I doubt that, man. Alfie seems like a decent guy.'

'You wouldn't be saying this if you knew what he says about you. He fucking hates you.'

'He's your pal. Course he hates me. He probably still believes that me and Ellie…..' He cleared his throat. '….You know. What *you* thought.'

To Jack, the name 'Ellie' had become a dirty word. He liked the girl – she and the other uni girls seemed good as gold. But the poor bloke sat opposite him had his loyalty now.

'And he's probably pissed off that you've been spending all your time helping me with this place and ignoring him.' He raised his brow.

'But I like hanging around with you. You've helped me change. Not that it's done any good. Not really.' George took another lungful of smoke. 'I don't blame him for hating me.'

Jack furrowed his brow and stubbed his cigarette into the charity shop ash tray. 'Right, if you're going to talk in riddles, I'm going to need another drink. I don't think either of us are nearly drunk enough to start hating ourselves yet.'

'I already do hate myself. But, yeah, I need a fucking drink.'

'As I said, the choice is endless.' Jack smirked.

'Rum.' George creased his nose. 'Seems to do you good.'

Moments later, Jack returned, handing George a glass of cold rum on the rocks. Well, rock. He'd forgotten he was low on ice.

'So, I was going to tell you tomorrow, man, but seeing as you're here.' He beamed. 'Dave has found my mum. She's quite close to my old flat. I know the street.'

George stared at him wide-eyed. The look was similar to what Maxine had given him that morning when she heard he was looking for his mother. 'That's good, then. Right?'

'Yeah, man.' Jack shrugged it off. 'I'm going to try and get down there on Sunday. I'm working tomorrow afternoon with Dave, otherwise I would have gone then.'

'You gonna ring her first? Like my mum said?' George asked, inhaling his rum.

'Erm, I don't know. She can't hang up on me if I knock on her door.'

'But she can slam on the door on your face.'

Jack giggled nervously then sipped his drink. 'She won't. I know she won't.' He was reassuring himself more than anything. 'So, whats really up with you? It can't be that Alfie called you a dick. I never had you down as a snowflake.'

Shaking his head, George swigged more of his glass. Jack was always amazed how the fella could drink anything, as long as it was alcohol.

'Come on, man. You gotta tell me or I can't help you.'

George's gaze fell to the ground once more and Jack fought the urge to roll his. 'It's Ellie. It's over. Definitely.'

Jack's stomach tightened at her name. He knew it was ridiculous, but it hurt him to know that George still loved her so much. 'Ah.' He whispered, 'I thought you were moving on. You seem so happy lately.'

'I thought I was. But hearing it from her has floored me. I think she's got someone else.'

'You spoke to her?' Jealousy's green fingers clawed at his chest.

'Yep. She said that she can't see us ever getting back together. It's just a *shock* I knew was coming.' He blew out his last drag and awkwardly crushed it into the ash tray. 'And I threw my phone. In the fucking river.' A tear crept down George's cheek.

Jack wanted to slip out of his seat and wipe away his pain, tell him that he would be okay. But something stopped him. A feeling in his gut. He knew he was getting in too deep.

'Don't get upset mate.' Jack faked a laugh. 'You can get a new phone.'

'Dick!' Snorting, George flashed his white teeth for just a second.

'Made you smile though.'

'Why have you got to be so nice? I'm so horrible to everyone. Fuck, when we met I had you up against the fridge. I had no right to put my hands on you.'

Jack's cheeks burned so red he thought his eyes were going to melt.

'Hey, thought we'd forgotten all that.'

'See, you're a fucking top bloke. No wonder the girls love you. I tried the hair, the tattoo, even tried smoking and I still can't ever be as good as you.'

'Whoa, don't tell me all this is because of me. Don't get me wrong, you look good. But you don't need to change, man.'

George didn't answer, just sipped his drinks through the now constant streams of tears.

'Being like me isn't a good thing. You know why I have these tattoos. And I smoke because I'm a dickhead. Believe me, I only have this hairstyle to hide my weird shaped head.'

George snorted again, quickly wiping his tears with his palm. Looking up for the first time in what felt like forever, Jack got to see those eyes again. Riddled with sadness, their beauty was still there. And they still held Jack to the spot.

George coughed away the last of his tears and gripped Jack's shoulder. 'Why doesn't she like me? I mean, what can I do? I try to be someone else, someone she fancies the fucking arse off and she still doesn't want me.'

'You don't have to be anyone else, George. You're you. And you're fucking amazing.'

'I'm a dick. A generic Essex boy with twenty fucking white polo shirts.' He knocked back his drink.

'Okay, you need to get over all this shit.' Jack's hand fell onto George's knee. 'Yes, you've had it a bit shit. Your first love has dumped you. But you're doing this to yourself now.'

'You've never been in love. You don't know how it feels.' George grumbled.

'You're right. But I know how it feels to be rejected, don't I? I know that there's no pain like it.'

George nodded. It was a breakthrough. If Jack knew well enough, then the fella would be laughing any minute and demanding that Jack put his saddest records on.

'Listen, man. You are the kindest person I've ever met. You'd help anyone. And you're doing an animal apprenticeship? You love animals. That's a thousand boyfriend points right there. And you're fucking smart too. Don't let anyone ever tell you different. I hate seeing you upset. You deserve so much more.'

George didn't reply, just blinked for a moment then rushed forward, his lips pressing against Jack's. Electricity flushed along Jack's spine, sending pins and needles throughout his body. Every sensation he had been feeling took over his body and he didn't want it to end. George's kiss grabbed his stomach - fire slithered through his veins and into his hands that so badly wanted to take hold of George. But after the briefest of moments, the fella pulled away and slumped back into his chair.

Jack's mouth hung open in shock. Confusion spiralled inside. But one thing he knew is that he loved what was happening.

George licked his lips – by his look of panic, it was obvious he was just as puzzled. 'Fuck. I am so fucking sorry. I don't know why I did that. I…I….I'm just so fucked up. I've been thinking about you so much. Weird things.'

'Like what?' Jack waited with baited breath, uncertain if he was ready for an answer.

'I don't know. I…..I wanted to see what all the fuss was about. To see if all it takes is for one kiss for people to fall in love with you.'

Jack stared. Unable to tell if what just happened was reality or not. 'And?' The word was barely audible.

The fella rose from his chair, his back straight and his head high. He was confused. That was clear on his face. Yet the George he knew seemed to be returning. The George he had fallen head-over-fucking-heels for. That smile was almost back too. 'Ignore me, mate. I'm a dick.' George shook his head. 'Can I stay tonight? I promise I won't fucking kiss you again. Fuck! Can we just drink some more and forget all about it.'

'Yeah, man.' Jack scratched the back of his neck. 'We might need another bottle of rum.'

Or two.

Chapter Twenty Eight

The drive up to Forest Gate wasn't as bad as George had imagined. Being on the outskirts of London, the traffic was far from the gridlocked scenes he'd watched on the news. But the tension in the car was more solid than any traffic jam he'd ever witnessed.

That kiss - that second of spontaneity had left George too embarrassed to look the fella in the eye. He'd managed to shrug it off initially, hoping that a bellyful of rum would cause amnesia. But it didn't. And he found himself creeping out of the flat just after dawn. He'd even managed to ignore Jack for a whole day after – not that it was difficult after he'd lobbed his phone into the river. Nonetheless, it was the first time he'd not spoken to or seen him since they'd rescued the owl together in the flat and the day felt longer and lonelier than any other he'd wallowed through.

George was embarrassed more than anything, Ashamed that he'd done that to his friend. How he'd treated all his friends, to be honest. Mugging off Alfie for weeks, not even noticing Aimee was going through all that stuff with her grandad because he was too selfish and, well, kissing Jack. Thing was, he'd had suspicions that the fella wasn't straight for a while. He'd never had a girlfriend, never really had anything more than a fling with a couple of girls. He didn't kiss Ellie back, and fuck, he didn't jump at the chance to sleep with Aimee who undoubtedly offered it to him on a plate. But that just made him feel worse. If that was the case and Jack was gay, then George was even more of a dickhead for abusing that.

His actions had him doubting himself too. Doubting everything actually. He was certain the events of the evening had fucked him up; drinks with Alfie and Aimee had gone tits up and then the phone call with Ellie. Well, that pushed him over the fucking edge of sanity. He'd been expecting it for months, since she'd first declared she needed a break. But that didn't stop it from feeling like his heart had been ripped out and trampled on there under the cedar tree.

Regardless of his inner turmoil and being unable to look the fella in the eye, he'd offered to take Jack to his mother's house that night, and in an attempt to keep face and salvage their friendship, he had no choice but to deliver on his promise.

George's stomach was in knots, had been since Jack knocked on his door that morning. He'd tried to act nonchalant, fake it, but that kiss - that fucking kiss - sat between the pair of them like a boulder on the entire journey.

Turning into the estate, George's struggles extended to navigating the narrow roads. All of the houses looked the same – pebble-dashed square buildings with flat roofs. Like Lego blocks.

He pulled up in one of the marked parking bays then, with a sigh, leant back onto the headrest. He didn't know what to say. Didn't even know if he should say anything. Jack seemed like he'd gone back into his shell. The one he'd hid himself in when they'd first met. His indifference was back and it made everything so much more painful. Blowing through rounded lips, George leant forward to adjust the air-con. He needed air. Cold air. Fuck, he needed to speed off back home and wallow in the guilt he'd suffered since that night.

Neither of them had mentioned what he did – George had even managed to avoid all eye contact. He didn't know how Jack was feeling. He felt even more of a shit stain for not asking. But he couldn't do that. That would likely open up a can of worms that needed to stay sealed.

'Thanks for this, man.' Jack kept his face forward. 'You really didn't have to.'

'No worries.' George bit his lip a little harder than he meant to.

'You want to come in with me?'

George kept his gaze to the windscreen, not looking at anything in particular. 'I would mate, but I think you need to go alone. You need to speak with your mum by yourself. And I've really got to go see Aimee. I haven't been there at all for her. Her grandad. You know?'

George hated himself for deserting him. But he knew, sincerely, that Jack and his mother needed to bond, just the two of them. It had nothing to do with the *kiss*. Honestly.

'Course.' Jack's hand fell onto the handbrake. George wanted to put his on top of it. To give support. But his hands wouldn't move from his lap. 'I'm fucking bricking it, man.' His voice trembled. 'What should I do?'

It was the longest conversation they'd had all morning and George's chest warmed.

'If Aimee was here, she'd tell you that "life's like eyeliner." Or something like that.'

Jack's lips curled and it was bloody good to see. Felt blinding too. The fella was a different person when he smiled. His eyes shone. As though someone had switched on a light. 'What does that even mean?'

'No idea.' George found himself smiling.

'You about tonight?' Jack asked, finally turning to face him. 'However this goes, I think I'm going to need a drink.'

George sucked in a deep breath then met his gaze. It was the first time that he'd looked into Jack's hazel eyes since he'd kissed him. He hadn't realised he'd missed them so much. Still, he couldn't hide his embarrassment. 'I don't know, mate. I need to cut down the booze. Been a bit of a dick, haven't I?'

Jack's hand reached out to his, squeezing it slightly. George bit his cheek as electricity surged up his arm. 'It's cool, man.'

Clearing his throat, George pulled his hand away. 'Good luck in there, anyway.' He knew his tone came across as cold, uncaring and it killed him. That wasn't his intention.

'Thanks.' Jack opened the car door but didn't budge from the seat. George curled his fingers around the wheel, afraid that his hand would reach out to him if he didn't.

'You better go, mate. If I stay here any longer, the locals are going to steal the alloys off my car.'

Jack snorted. His laugh was a relief. 'Alfie's right. You are a dick.' And there it was again – that smile. 'But seriously, would be great to see you later, man.' Running his hand through his hair, Jack then climbed out the car.

Watching Jack walk off towards the row of houses, George switched on the ignition and shook his head.

He knew, as he drove out of the estate and left Jack behind, the real reason why he'd kissed him that night. It wasn't the drink, nor was it Alfie giving him a hard time. Maybe it was a little because Ellie had broken his heart. But he knew deep down that it was because he'd wanted to.

Chapter Twenty Nine

'Can I help you?' The woman standing at the front door furrowed her brow. Her green eyes seemed to drill into him. Arms folded, she was clearly annoyed that Jack had yet to mutter a word. 'Well?'

He'd watched George drive off and had a few cheeky, yet much needed, drags on a cigarette before ringing the doorbell. The anxiety inside too strong to enjoy a full one. He knew those streets; the paving slabs, the tower blocks. The smells. It was East London. A concrete jungle that he'd spent most of his life exploring. Yet under the glare of the July sun, his old world felt nothing more than a bad memory.

He wanted, actually, needed George for support. He'd spent so long in the fella's pocket that he'd grown to depend on him.

'Mum.' Lowering his eyes, Jack fidgeted on the doorstep. He wanted to step up and kiss her on the cheek but couldn't. Kisses seemed to ruin everything anyway. 'It's me. Jack.'

Her face didn't change. Not even a flinch. It was a relief that she didn't react, that she didn't recoil in horror and slam the door on him, but it also stung like a bitch that she couldn't afford him a smile.

'What you doing here, Jack?' The colour drained from her face right in front of him.

'Can I come in? Please? I won't take much of your time up.'

Expressionless, his mother turned on her heal and retreated into the house. Swallowing his nerves, Jack took the door she left open as his invitation to follow.

The house was not like he'd imagined. He didn't know why he expected it to be any different but it didn't fit his idea of her home. He hadn't seen his mother in nearly eight years, not since he was fourteen and had ran away from his foster parents and back then she was clearly going through a rough time.

Her old house had been grubby and littered with dirty ashtrays and strewn damp-smelling clothes. But this house was clean and tidy – with the scent of freshly sprayed air freshener lingering. Floral wallpaper throughout the hallway and the magnolia living room was immaculate except for a corner piled with children's colourful toys and a scooter leaning against a chalkboard.

'You have more kids?'

Glancing over to the toys, she then plonked herself onto the edge of the brown armchair and nodded. 'Two girls and a boy. They're at swimming lessons with their dad.'

Jack's gaze zoomed to her hands. There it was, a gold wedding band. 'So I have brothers and sisters?' He couldn't stop himself from beaming - he'd always wanted siblings. More so than anything. 'I'd love to meet them sometime. What's their names?'

'They've.....we've got a lot on at the moment, Jack.' She curled her dyed blonde hair around her ear. 'We don't need the upset.'

'I'm not here to upset anyone. Honestly. I'm not a teenager anymore. I just want to talk. To you.'

His mother smiled for the briefest of moments and Jack couldn't help but grin back at her. He'd always remembered her smile – it was one of the only things etched in my memory. 'Would you like a drink? Tea? Coffee?' She stood then lingered by the door.

'Tea, please, Mum.' Her shudder at that word instantly cut through his elation.

Alone in his mother's living room, Jack's gaze scanned over everything. He wanted to take it all in to get a better idea of who she was.

The room was void of trinkets and ornaments, and apart from a few scatter cushions and a couple of pictures on the walls, lacked any real character he could associate with his mother. It was clearly just maintained for the kids – his brothers and sisters – to make as little damage as possible. There were a few birthday cards on the fireplace, all celebrating a birthday, and by the images of pink flowers and glittered glasses of wine, they were for his mother. The fact that he didn't know when her birthday was, was overshadowed by cards saying "mummy," "sister," and "daughter."

He'd only met his grandparents when he was a baby. Too young to remember them. But that hadn't stopped him from spending many a sleepless night wondering why they hadn't tried to get him out of care. To take him into their home and raise him in his mother's place. Nonetheless, a comforting warmth clutched his chest and he knew he looked ridiculous smiling to himself. He couldn't wait to meet them again. To be a real family.

He heard his mother's slippers slap against the laminate flooring before he saw her, and prayed that she'd regained her smile for him.

Not wanting the disappointment, he focused on a canvas on the wall, one that was printed rather than painted, above the mantelpiece. It was an image of a horizon – green trees and open meadows – it instantly reminded him of George.

Sucking in a deep breath, he couldn't believe how things had turned icy between him and George. Just a couple of days before, they were pals. The best friend Jack had ever had. And a moment of, whatever the hell that

261

kiss was, it was all gone. George was embarrassed, that was obvious. He'd all but ignored him for a whole day. And the car ride was almost unbearable. But Jack didn't care about any of that. Not one single fuck. Did he like the fella? Hell, yes. Did he love him? Probably. But all he wanted was his friend back.

Clearing her throat, his mother passed him the mug of tea then stood by the French doors – the furthest spot away from him in the room. She sipped her tea through pursed lips and watched him with narrowed eyes.

'You've got a nice place here, mum.' Jack forced a grin, hoping his show of cheeriness could be enough for both of them.

'We've been here since Lola was born. Four years now. The council set us up with this.'

'I can't believe how close you've been this whole time. I live just over the park. A ten minute walk from here. Well, I used to. I now live in Essex. In a place called Coggletree.'

'I've never heard of it.' She moved closer slightly then perched herself on the furthest end of three-seater. It was something at least.

'Mum, are you okay?' He cleared his throat. 'You haven't looked at me properly since I got here.'

'I'm just in shock. This is all out of the blue to be honest.'

'A good shock?' He hated how desperate he sounded. Still, he needed to know.

'I'm not sure. I didn't expect to see you standing on my doorstep. How did you find me?'

'Uncle Dave, Shelly's ex. He helped me find you.'

She rolled her eyes. 'He always had a knack for sticking his nose in. What gives him the right to meddle in people's business? He did the same when you were little.'

'It's not like that.' Jack had to defend him. 'I asked him. He's been great to me. Especially recently. Helped me get a place to start my own business.'

'Doing what?'

'Tattoos.' He held out his arms. 'Kind of my thing.'

She huffed. 'Just like your father. He had all that rubbish over his skin.'

Jack bit his lip. He was used to people's comments about his ink – varying from gushing adoration to utter contempt. Yet hearing his mother's scorn for how he looked cut into him more than any strangers disapproval could.

Clearing his throat, Jack tried to make eye contact with her. 'You still see my dad?'

'God, no. I haven't seen that good-for-nothing since the night you were born.' Swigging her tea, she shook her head. 'He came down the maternity ward to see if you was his and then I never saw him again. I think he must have gone back to Turkey.'

'Did he even hold me?'

She snorted. 'He was only there a couple of minutes. Chucked me a twenty pound note and went. Parenting isn't for everyone.'

He knew what she was getting at. He'd heard it from her many times before. She'd blame his father then tell him she couldn't cope on her own. Nevertheless, the rejection always clawed at his chest.

'You know if he lives round here? You got an address for him or anything? Or just give me his name and I'll search for him myself.'

'Why do you want to go into all that? It's in the past.'

'Yeah but it's my past. I've found my mum again after all these years, it'd be good to find my father too.'

'I don't have any money to give you. If that's why you're here.' Her focus seemed to return to the French doors. 'I've got three kids under ten......I haven't got anything to give you.'

Standing, Jack placed his cup onto the coffee table and sat himself next to her. He wanted to be closer to his mother. Taking her hand into his palm, he silently begged her to look at him. 'I don't want money. I don't want anything except my family.'

Her green eyes finally met his. 'Listen, Jack. I don't want any trouble.'

'I'm just here to get to know you'

'That *is* trouble. I like things the way they are. I've finally got my life together. I've got kids, a house, and a husband. I've got my own family.'

'I'm your family too, mum.'

She rose from her seat. 'You was better off in the foster homes. I told you that when you turned up at my flat all those years ago.' She turned her head towards the hallway. Her intention was clear. 'You need to forget about me.'

'I can't. You're my mum.' He grabbed her arm, recoiling when she flinched.

'Jack, I wasn't ready for kids back then. Best thing that ever happened to both of us was them taking you away. It gave us a chance for something better in life.'

Jack choked. Her words had winded him. The pain drilled into his guts. 'My life wasn't better for it.'

'I'm sorry things didn't work out for you, I am. But I just wasn't in the right place to be a mother then.'

'But you're ready now?'

'For the three children I have, yes.'

Jack couldn't breathe.

Her shoulders loosened and she turned to him once more. Her gaze met his, although it was a loom of pity. He'd always remembered the intensity of her green eyes. They'd filled his dreams for years. Yet now they seemed faded. As though everything he'd remembered about her was a fantasy. A lie.

She patted his hand, just the once, but it vibrated through his skin. Somehow he knew it'd be the last time he'd ever feel her touch. 'I'm sure you're a great boy, Jack. I just can't do this. I can't be your mum.'

She slipped from his hand and made her way to the hallway. Jack followed. It was the only control he had over the situation.

He wanted her to look at him just one last time. Once more to see how much he loved her. But she didn't.

'I'll leave you my number and you can just give me a call when you're ready.' He pulled his phone out of his pocket and searched for his own number – his hands shook the entire time. 'Maybe I can come back and meet the kids.'

'You need to move on with your life, Jack. It's the best for all of us.' His mother cleared her throat. It was final. 'I'm sorry.'

'I need my mum.' He did. He really did.

'I'm sorry. I am. I just can't go back to the old me. I'm clean. I've got a good life now. I don't want to revisit the past.'

'What about me?' Jack hated how selfish he sounded but a lump in his throat was growing too big to swallow.

'Go and live your life, Jack. Go find someone to love, settle down and be happy.'

His mother opened the front door, the bright sunlight forced him to squint. Stepping out of the house, his eyes settled on the space where George's car had been. He knew the fella had gone – he watched him go. Yet that didn't console the pain tearing through his body.

'Mum?'

'Goodbye, Jack.'

Jack didn't respond. He didn't have the energy. The hurt that burned through him was by his own doing. He knew he needed to leave well alone – to leave his mother in peace. Like she'd always wanted.

He didn't turn to face her – there was no point. Nor did he flinch when the door closed between them. Sealing their future apart.

Patting his jeans, his trembling fingers outlined the phone in his pocket. He'd gotten used to talking to someone. The only person in his whole life apart from Dave who'd ever bothered to listen to his troubles. But George didn't even have a phone anymore. And it was clear the bloke didn't want anything to do with him anyway.

His eyelids burned, the desperation behind them eager to escape in rivers. But he wouldn't let that happen. Ever. That wasn't him. He couldn't cry. They'd seen to that in the care homes.

He slid a cigarette from his packet then rolled the flint, cursing as the slightest breeze blew it away. Closing his eyes, he huffed – almost deflating entirely right there in the street outside his mother's house.

He slumped onto the low wall and swallowed his pain. He was broken. Angry, humiliated and devastated all in one. He could see his old flat; the top half of the tower block visible above the houses. He'd been so close to his mother the entire time. A few minutes' walk away. That's all. Yet he knew none of that mattered. Not anymore.

With a trembling hand, he rolled the flint of the lighter again, and again. Each time, the wind snatched the flame away.

'Let me help, mate.' Two thick hands curved around his, blocking the flame from the breeze. He followed the arms to the shoulders, over the muscles he'd studied for weeks on end, until his gaze settled onto the man's face. Onto those blue eyes.

Gawping, Jack bit his lip. He couldn't stand, too afraid the movement would allow the bubbling in his throat to spew out. Instead, he rolled the flint once more and sucked in a mouthful of smoke, allowing the relief to rush over him. 'I thought you was going home.'

'Yeah. So did I.' George's beautiful lips curved at the sides. 'I got half way down the road and realised there are more important things in life than being embarrassed.'

'George, about that, man.'

He shook his head. 'I'm sorry for what I did. And I'm fucking sorry for acting like a douche all morning.' George's flash of white teeth warmed Jack at once, melting away the anguish just enough for him to smile himself. 'Friends?'

'Course, man.'

'So, what happened in there? Are you okay? You don't look it?'

Jack lowered his gaze, unable to take the man's kindness. He was certain he'd suffocate from the lump in his throat again. 'She…..she doesn't want me, George. She never has.'

'It's okay, mate.' George slung an arm around his shoulder. The warmth from his body doing more to pacify him than any cigarette ever could. 'I'm here for you.'

Suddenly, Jack could no longer keep in his tears. They ran down his face as years of pain flooded out. He didn't know, sitting on that wall in the middle of the street, if he'd ever stop crying. All he knew was that George had come back for him. And that's all he needed.

Chapter Thirty

'You could have waited in the car, man.' Wheezing, Jack couldn't pretend the climb to the tenth storey hadn't almost killed him. With his eyes still swollen from crying and his head pounding from overthinking, it was a wonder he made it even beyond the first flight.

He'd warned George to avoid handling the sticky banisters, yet couldn't do anything about the lingering waft of ammonia that came from human piss. He'd actually forgot about the stench, right up until he'd heaved open the heavy red door to the stairs. Still, seeing the "out of order" signs taped to both elevators again was kind of nice.

Being so close to his old flat, he'd asked George if they could stop in to grab the last few things he'd left behind. Some sketches he'd done in the early days and a box of crap he'd kept from school. None of it meant dick to him – he took all he needed in those two bags the night he'd fled to Dave's house in Dagenham. But his relationship with his mum was clearly D.O.A., and wanted to see the place one last time before finally surrendering it back to the council and flipping his old life the finger once and for all.

'You've said that five times, mate.' George wiped his top lip, clearly finding it hard to breathe himself. 'Don't you want me here or something?'

Truth was, 'course he wanted George there. When Jack was at his lowest, the fella with the blue eyes that he'd happily drown in, had come back for him. But he felt sick to the stomach with the thought of George seeing his old place. He wasn't ashamed of the gaff, it'd been his only sanctuary for years. It was run down, empty and unloved; something he used to relate to. And he knew that George wouldn't judge him for it - the bloke was the only real friend he'd ever had. Besides, they'd both ugly cried in front of each other within the last two days so embarrassment wasn't anything new to them. It was the fact that he didn't know what mess Cole had left it in.

He had no doubt the drug addict had broken into the flat. He'd done it many times before. It was a perfectly reasonably thing to do for someone like Cole. There was no real conscience. And if the bloke never bothered to change his needles, why the hell would he change his behaviour? Besides, Cole would have returned at some point for that money. No doubt about it.

With a huff, Jack pulled open the door to the landing that led to the flat, dreading what he'd find. He could count well into double figures the times he'd found Cole and his junkie pals passed out in the hallway. The stench of their piss and puddles of vomit was something he'd never forget. But to his surprise, all was fine.

Allowing himself a short sigh of relief, he turned to face George. 'Listen, man. There's something I need to tell you. About my mate, Cole –'

'That dickhead from the care home?'

Jack nodded, knowing the subject wasn't something George took lightly. He'd said as much each time Jack had mentioned him. 'Well, he's most probably turned over the place. Knowing him, he's smashed it up. That's why I didn't really want you coming with me.'

'You kidding me?'

Jack shook his head. 'He's got form. Last time, he kicked the shit out the front door and stole my new turntable and a stack of records. Classics too.'

'Did you call the police?'

Snorting, Jack turned to the fella. 'Man, this is Forest Gate. Being a grass is worse than being a thief.'

George raised his brow and Jack suddenly realised he'd memorised the lines on the bloke's forehead. Fuck knows why, he just had.

Stood at his old door, Jack straightened his back upon discovering he didn't need his key to open it. From the state of the hacked-into wood and scraped lock, a claw hammer was the likely culprit. He should've shrugged it off - how predictable Cole actually was – but his stomach dropped nonetheless. Sucking in a deep breath, one he hoped would stall the situation for just a moment more, he then pushed the door with his foot. Another stench met them.

'Fuck!' George whispered, stepping back.

'Yep.' Jack remembered the day they rescued the owl together. 'It's definitely druggies and squatters this time.'

He squinted into the flat. The black paint he'd used to cover the windows to help him sleep was clearly still doing the trick so the only light was coming through the kitchen window.

Fumbling his hand onto the wall, he snorted when the lights didn't come on with the flick of the switch – of course he never expected them to, but then he never expected himself to fall in love either.

He kicked through the pile of letters that had accumulated in his absence, mostly bills no doubt and last warning letters - not bothering to pick up any of them.

Just as he expected, it was carnage. Cole was behind it, there was no doubt in his mind. He would likely have returned for his money the day after giving it. Rubbish, empty cans and wrappers were strewn over the floor, the sofa had been disembowelled – it's stuffing in clusters around the room and drug foils everywhere. He didn't need to look in the other rooms, he could only imagine what horrors were in them. He just needed to get the hell out of the place.

Jack saw the look of discomfort on his face but didn't know what to say to reassure him. The pongs of piss, burnt drugs and human shit couldn't be sugar-coated with words.

'What should we do?' George asked nervously.

'Nothing, man.' Jack had done what he wanted to do, to see the place one last time. And to see the chaos Cole had caused. Both, he was ready to leave in his past. 'Let's go.'

'What about your stuff?'

He met George's gaze and didn't fight the urge to beam. He knew that having George was all he needed. He'd spent so many years decaying on his own that he couldn't think of one single possession that was more important than friendship. And it had taken him twenty-one years to work it out. 'I don't need any of it.'

He glanced around the grotty flat once more, ready to never see it again, but before he could say good riddance once and for all, his attention was drawn to his old bedroom. And the clambering coming from inside.

Without realising, Jack stood in front of George. Guarding him. Fuck knows why – George, by far, had the bigger muscles. But they were in Jack's manor, and some unwritten duty took over him.

'Who's there?' A gruff voice croaked from the dark hallway.

Jack stiffened, waiting for the intruder to emerge. He knew full well who it was. Even though a decade of drug abuse had rasped the fella's voice, Jack would remember it forever.

'Cole?' His chest tightened when his care home "brother" edged into the light. Sporting a black eye and busted lip, Cole was yellow with jaundice. He was thinner than ever – his cheekbones barely covered by flesh. He looked more like a zombie from a shitty sixties movie than a man of twenty five. How had he deteriorated so badly in a matter of weeks? Jack could barely look at him. The person he knew was almost completely gone.

George obviously found it harder not to look and stared open mouthed at him. The revulsion written plainly on his face.

'Fuck me. He come back.' Cole yawned, exposing a missing front tooth. His rancid breathe filled the air between.

'Cole……you look.' Jack couldn't finish his sentence.

Closer, Cole was visibly shaking. Usually the tell-tale sign he was crashing down from his latest hit. But this time was different. He was much weaker. Frail. 'Like what I've done to the place, bruv?' His laughter was interrupted by violent coughing.

Jack didn't hide his distaste. What was the point? He had nothing to prove to him anymore. Hell, he didn't even want to look at him. There wasn't pity anymore, and for the first time in his life, he didn't feel responsible for Cole's addiction. He'd done everything to himself. For himself.

'I don't care. I don't even know why I came back here.'

At first it seemed as though Cole hadn't heard him, or ignored him more so, but after picking up a squashed dog-end from the sofa, he turned to Jack with an ugly smirk. 'This is where you belong. This is all you'll ever be.' He hocked back phlegm then spat it onto the floor. 'Always killed me that you got a council flat and I didn't.'

Jack rolled his eyes hearing the same old shit. 'Change the fucking record, man. Thought you had your own place anyway. Had a new boss.'

Cole exposed his decaying teeth with a grin. 'That dickhead. Got his boys to jump me, didn't he?'

'For no reason, I bet.' Jack shook his head then turned to George. 'Man, if you want to go wait in the car-'

George clamped his hand around Jack's arm. 'No way am I leaving you with him.' He grimaced.

'Who's that?' Cole asked, observing George as though he hadn't noticed him before. His arms trembled. 'Finally got yourself a boyfriend, bruv?' Obviously there was life in the walking corpse yet.

The old Jack would have blushed. Probably protested his straightness and shouted abuse back. But this time, he ignored him. Didn't even blush. Cole's insults couldn't wound him anymore because they meant nothing to him. Words. Labels. That's all they were and Jack had lost interest in them. He didn't know what he was. He didn't really care anymore. He knew how he felt for George and that was all that mattered.

'I'm giving up this place, Cole. They'll be coming to chuck you out soon.'

'The fuck you mean? Where you going?' He spat again. 'What about me?'

Jacked snorted. 'What about you?'

'Not got time for your own brother?' Cole stepped closer and Jack felt George's hand tighten around his arm. 'Too busy with your boyfriend?'

'How many times, Cole.' Jack lolled his head back. 'We're not brothers. We don't share any blood. We don't owe anything to each other. Not anymore.'

'You what? You didn't say that when you took the drugs money from me, did you?' He snarled and for a moment, Cole looked like himself again.

'What drugs money, Jack? George asked. There wasn't so much disapproval in his voice, more concern. Jack felt worthless, nonetheless.

'You ain't told your boyfriend about the money you took from me? Made me end up like this 'cause of it.'

Cole's wheezing made Jack ball his fists. Always the fucking victim.

Turning to George, he saw the nervousness in his eyes. It was a face he made whenever he was out of his depth. Jack had seen it at the burger van all those weeks ago, when he back-chatted Robert at the farm and the moment right after he kissed him two nights previous. Each time, Jack knew he'd been responsible. 'Man, I didn't take any money from him. He left it here-'

'Liar!' Cole shouted to his back.

Jack took a deep breath and met George's gaze. 'He left it here for me. But I knew it was dodgy. Look at him. That's when I knew I had to get out of this dive. Away from him. I didn't even touch the cash. I left it in this flat knowing he'd come back for it.

Cole pulled at Jack's shoulder and barged between them, his contorted face inches away from George's. 'Your boyfriend's a fucking liar. He took my money. Got me beat up too. That's why I'm like this.'

'From what I've heard, you deserved it.' George hadn't flinched.

'Your queer boyfriend been telling you lies? Has he told you how he got me onto drugs in the first place? That dirty queer made me a fucking junkie.'

Before Jack could retort, George had Cole by the throat. His thick hands tightening around the yellowing skin. 'Listen 'ere, you prick. It's not Jack's fault you're a druggie. It's not his fault that you used to beat him either. It's you. You're a worthless piece of shit and don't deserve to even talk to him. And you ever call him a "dirty queer" again, I'll break your neck. You hear me?'

'So he is gay then?' Cole's response came out as wheezes. The man that was once so ferocious, so frightening, was now just the petrified little boy that Jack had once been in the care homes. Cole deserved it.

Deserved more even. Nevertheless, Jack would never stand by and watch anyone suffer. Not even him.

'George, man.' He pleaded. 'Let him go. He's not worth it.'

But George seemed fixed with rage. Just like the night he'd pounced on Jack. He remembered how strong he was, how easily he pinned him to fridge. He'd forgotten that side of George but knew him well enough to know that it wasn't the real him. He also knew that words rarely consoled the fella. Without saying anything, Jack placed his hand onto his shoulder and squeezed it gently.

Instantly, George's muscles loosened and he threw the panting junkie to the floor. Straightening his back, those blue eyes met Jack's. The nervousness and aggression had both gone. It was just George.

Facing Cole again, all Jack had left for him was pity. He didn't defend himself. He just smiled.

'Mate, can we go?' George whispered.

Jack nodded. It was all he needed to hear. He was ready to leave everything behind him.

'No....fucking....way.' Cole coughed out his words whilst using the gutted sofa to stand then pulled something out of his pocket.

Jack froze on the spot as the blade shimmered in Cole's hand. He remembered the knife from his days in the care home. It was the one he used to terrorise him.

'What you doing, man?' Jack furrowed his brow.

'What I should have done all those years ago.' Cole spat. 'You took my fucking life away from me. From the very first day you came into that home and cried like a queer.'

'Man, how many times you going to sing that same old tune?' Jack laughed nervously. 'I'm so fucking bored of this.'

'I'm going to slit your throat?'

The man charged at him but Jack just saw white. The anger, the desperation. Everything he'd let bubble up inside him since he was a child blinded him. Grabbing Cole's bony wrist, he slammed it against the sofa's carcass until the knife fell to the ground. Kicking it backwards with the toe of his boot, Jack made sure it was out of the bastard's reach. Cole lunged forward again but Jack pushed him away. He had the power now. He had the strength in himself.

'You're not going to do anything to me!' Jack growled. 'Never again.'

Cole shrank to the floor. His body clearly too weak to take the physical exertion. 'I'm all you have. You're nothing without me.'

Running his hand through his hair, Jack let out a laugh. 'If you said that a year ago, I would have believed that. You made me feel worthless. Made me hate myself.' Jack stood straighter than he ever had done in his life then glanced at George. 'I know who I am now, Cole. And I'm not ashamed of me. Because, you know what? I'm all right.'

'You're nothing.' The junkie wheezed.

Without another word, Jack spun on his heal to face George again. Those blue eyes shone with pride. All he could do was smile. He *was* all right. He had George.

Nodding, he made his way to the door and looked back to his old life one last time. 'I'm ready to go now, man. I'm done.'

Chapter Thirty One

Back at Jack's Coggletree flat, far from the tower blocks and that wanker, Cole, George stared at the window that once had the broken pane and wished life could be as easily fixed.

In a few months, his life had changed so much that he barely recognised himself. Everything was fucked up. And it was all on him. He and Ellie were over. Fact. He'd known that all along, he just couldn't admit it. And Jack. Who would have fucking thought? The bloke he once hated was now the person he was closest to in the world. But it was how things were between himself and his two best mates that blew his fucking mind. Never in a million years had he thought he'd treat Alfie and Aimee so badly. Through every up and down, they'd been there for him. And all it took was for him to get dumped to show his true colours.

George knew he should have been with them, telling Alfie he was sorry for being a dick and begging Aimee to forgive him for not being there for her. Yet, with all the intention of putting them first, he still found himself sitting in a camping chair in Jack's living room. Ever since he'd drove back to him that morning and found him almost broken on the brick wall, George could not stop thinking about Jack. The vulnerability, the strength, even the tears. They made him someone he couldn't live without. Even sat upstairs whilst Jack made teas in the kitchen below, George's stomach tightened at the thought of seeing him – The minutes apart somehow felt like days, and he had no idea how to stop it.

With a creak from the landing behind him, George shook the blur from his head and tried his hardest to pull his shit together before Jack entered the room.

'You working tomorrow?' Jack asked, handing him a mug of hot tea then held up his glass full of dark liquid. 'I've got rum.'

'No. I just don't fancy it.' It was true. The thought of alcohol made his head whirl even more so.

Jack chuckled, raising his eyebrows to mock. Since leaving London, the fella seemed happier. Much happier. Lighter even. Like all his troubles had been left in that piss and shit stained flat in Forest Gate. And it was great to see. 'Everything okay? You're normally demanding we get drunk.'

That was true. There hadn't been a night since they'd became friends that they hadn't drank together. Well, apart from the one when George ignored him after the kiss. It was the longest night of his life. But holding Jack earlier that day, he'd realised that his insomnia hadn't been from guilt. It had been longing.

'I'm good.' He lied as Jack snatched his cigarettes from the arm of his chair, his warm fingers touching his skin for the briefest of moments. 'Just thinking.'

'About Ellie?'

Fuck, was he that pathetic? 'No, actually, not her. That's dead in the water. Just like my phone.' George snickered. 'Just. Everything, really. Today has been full on.'

'What bit? When I wept like a new born or Cole?'

George smiled. The problem was that it was those two moments that had made him understand exactly how he felt about Jack. Seeing the bloke cry, seeing how *human* he was and then watching him throw away all the bad stuff in his life; it made him realise just how much he, well, loved the fella.

He'd only ever loved one other person. Her. But the feeling was there again, deep beneath his ribs. Aching for the fella with the hazel eyes. He'd never thought he'd feel like that about a man. And to be honest, he didn't know what the fuck to do about it.

'Shrugging, he lowered his gaze onto the cup, certain his eyes would give his secrets away.

Placing his glass onto the floor, Jack sat forward, and leant closer to George. 'Man, you okay? You haven't said much since we left London.'

'All good.' George stared harder into his cup of builder's tea.

'Have I done something?' Jack asked, running his hand through his hair.

'No.' The word was barely audible.

'Then what is it? It's like it was this morning on the way to my mums.'

George lifted his head and finally met Jack's gaze. Those fucking eyes beaming into his for answers. He was certain they would be absorbed from him. 'It's just fucked up.'

Lighting a cigarette, Jack frowned on the exhale 'What is, man? '

'Me! I am.' He stood, too troubled to sit. 'Do you know how shit I've been lately? To everyone? I moan, constantly, about my life and how I feel. How I hurt. How nobody understands. I just go on and on about myself.'

Nodding, Jack sucked in another drag. 'Yep.'

'And I'm not just fucking self-absorbed. No. I'm the most miserable bastard on the planet.'

'Well, yeah.'

'Honestly, Jack.' George huffed, more for release than anything else. 'I've rolled my eyes so much lately that people think I'm fucking possessed.'

Jack howled with laughter. A moment later, George joined him. It was too bloody ridiculous not to.

'Okay, I'm not going to lie, man. You're proper miserable.' Jack stood too. 'You need to get over it. Get over her.'

George inhaled deeply. 'I think I am.'

'Good.' Jack smirked, obviously not believing him. 'Then whats the problem?'

'Me! I ruin things. Look what I did to you. The other night.' George's skin was aflame but he didn't squirm. He wasn't embarrassed anymore.

'When you…erm…? -'

'Yes. When I kissed you?' He needed the issue resolved with Jack before his head exploded. 'We need to talk about that.'

'Forget it.' He chipped out his fag.

Without a word, George set down his drink and stepped towards him. His head seemed to have no control over his body and the next thing he knew his arm was around Jack for the second time that day.

'I still need to apologise. I should've said something this morning but I didn't want to embarrass you even more.'

'George-'

'I was a dick. But I need to be completely honest with you.'

Jack cleared his throat and George felt the fella's shoulders tense. 'Wait. There's something I have to tell you. I *need* to tell you.'

'What?'

'I've been wanting to….I just….didn't know how.' Jack combed his fingers through his hair. 'I've really been struggling. Like really bad, man.'

'What is it?' George was certain what was coming but he wouldn't allow himself to spoil it for the fella. This was Jack's time and he needed the spotlight.

'It's about me. Who *I* am. I've never really known, not totally. But, because of you I think I'm starting to.'

280

George's couldn't hide his smile.

Jack's inhale silenced the room. Even the evening birdsong from the open window seemed to cease. 'I'm gay?'

Nodding, George beamed. Pride for Jack rushed over him. It was as though it was the first time he'd ever heard the fella speak. This was the real Jack. The one George had been waiting to meet.

'You *knew*?'

'Pretty much since the first night round my house.' Georges squeezed him tighter. It was instinct to. 'You said that Ellie kissed you and you couldn't kiss her back. She's hot. So I knew it must have been something else. And then you wouldn't sleep with Aimee. I mean, come on.'

'And you're not bothered? You're okay with it?' Jack's cheeks flushed red 'George, I wanted to tell you, man. I did. I just didn't know myself. I've never known. Not for sure. Until I met you.'

'I don't care what you are. None of that matters to me. It's your life, mate. I'm just fucking happy you're happy.'

George's guts twisted. He'd not lied. He couldn't give a fuck who was gay, straight, whatever. It didn't enter his mind. Love is love. So why the fuck was he giving himself such a hard time?

'But that's why I shouldn't have kissed you.' George whispered. 'Because if your head is fucked, then I had no right to do that to you. I just want you to know that I didn't do it because I see you as something I can experiment with when I get drunk. That's not why I did it.'

'I know. You did it to see what all the fuss was about?' Jack bit the corner of his lip.

George sucked in the warm summer air. 'That's not it either. I did it....I did it....because I wanted to.'

The fella tensed even more so. With his face burning red, George pulled his arm away but Jack caught it and took his hand into his.

'Do you know how long I've wanted to kiss you?' Jack asked, his chin trembling.

'What?' Stunned, he couldn't help but step back. 'Really?'

Nodding, the fella scratched the back of his neck. 'Since that first day in this flat.'

George stared at him deeply. There was so much to say yet he knew his throat wouldn't let him. For a moment, all he could do was stare at Jack's lips. Then the words came flooding back. 'Then kiss me.'

Jack's caramel eyes seemed to shine beneath his knitted brow. 'Man, are you serious?'

He nodded.

With desire clear on his face, Jack stepped forward then both his arms curled around George's waist. He pulled him closer, enough that he could the man's heart bashing against his own chest. Then it happened. Jack kissed him.

George's body burned as Jack's soft lips caressed his. The taste of cigarettes and rum almost drove him insane. Trailing his fingers up his back to the soft skin of his nape, George relished in Jack's moans. Inhaling him, he let the pleasure of Jack's mouth take over his.

It was new. Different. Something he never thought he'd ever experience. But it was fucking amazing. Waves of heat flushed over him and he was certain his legs would give way.

Tongues met with greediness, the warmth, softness, strength all entwined. Both breathed hard through their nostrils, the sounds echoing in George's ears. Driven wild with lust, he moved in deeper to Jack, biting his bottom lip with eagerness.

'Jack, are you okay?' He whispered as their lips parted for the briefest moments.

There was no response, instead Jack leant into him, clearly wanting more. His tongue caressed George's – the taste overtaking him and for a second, George was certain his own body heat would set the pair alight.

As George gripped his shoulders, pulling him harder, Jack's hand lowered from around his waist onto his fly. The fella's fingers flipped the metal button in an instant then his hands were on the waist band of his boxers, his fingertips brushing against the hair underneath. His spine tingled as all air left his lungs. He knew what was coming. And wanted it so badly.

George was hard – he didn't know how long it'd been that way, nor did he care. But he grew stiffer still when Jack's hand curled around his dick.

George instantly searched for the fella's belt buckle, pulling at it as though life depended on it.

Jack stepped back, pulling at George's neck to make sure they didn't part, then guided them to the bed. And there was no way, not a fucking chance in hell that was George going to stop him.

With Jack on top of him, they fell onto the mattress, still wrapped in each other. Both aching for more.

His hands grabbed at Jack's body, around his stomach and onto new territory his fingers hadn't roamed before.

With his hand wrapped around another man's cock, the alien sensation drove him crazy with lust. But Jack pulled his mouth away for a moment, his gaze set on his. Those hazel eyes filled George with greed.

Jack then lowered himself to the edge of the bed and slipped George's jeans and boxer shorts from underneath his buttocks in one clean swipe, exposing him entirely.

Embarrassment was outweighed by lust instantaneously and all George could do was stare at the man that had caused such yearning.

He stretched out an arm, his fingers longing for the contents of the fella's boxers again but Jack was clearly in his own world – in his own moment. Without a word between them, Jack lowered his mouth onto George's dick, enveloping the tip with warmth.

George's fingers scrubbed through the man's dark hair, holding him in place as Jack groaned with hunger.

Warmth, pleasure, lust. They all flooded through him. Wave after wave until his lower back was sparking with electricity. Jack's moaning intensified as his tongue ran over the head of George's cock, circling it as his lips slid up and down the shaft. George curled his fingers through the man's hair, knowing what was imminent. He had never felt so intoxicated. Never. The waves intensified, spasms pulsing from the bottom of his stomach to the tip of his dick.

'Jack.....I'm. I'm gonna. Gonna....' George's voice echoed around his own brain, only muffled by Jack's longing groans. He tried to lift his head away but it was clear he wouldn't budge. Unable to fight it any longer, George's balls tightened and the release came pouring out of him.

A moment passed, even two - all George could do was pant through his euphoria. The embarrassment – that brief moment of self-doubt and uncertainness that comes with an orgasm, could wait.

'Jack?'

The fella raised his head with a wicked smile that George had never seen then he pressed his lips onto George's chest, squeezing him in tight.

It was George's turn to repay the favour.

And he was fucking ready for it.

Chapter Thirty Two

George was awoken by a cackling magpie perched on the window ledge. Squinting against the invasion of daylight, it took a moment to remember what he and Jack did the night before.

He'd spent many a night in Jack's bed, actually, he'd lost count. But that was the first time he'd woken up sober and stark bollock naked, with his arm under the fella and his hard dick pressed tightly against his back.

Jack was asleep. His breathing somehow made everything right and George beamed at the man next to him. He wanted him to wake up too, to see that face light up. But the longer he watched him sleep, the louder the regret thumped in his chest. And he hated himself for it.

Suddenly, he needed to get out of the flat before there was any awkwardness between them. Maybe he could ignore the fella a day again. Maybe a couple of days would work.

Carefully, George slid his arm from under him and crawled off the mattress. Keeping his eyes off of Jack, he searched for his underwear amidst the pile of clothes they tore off of each other, then grabbed them along with his jean shorts, T-shirt and trainers. Something kept him lingering at the door for moment – the same voice that drove him to make love to Jack just hours before. But he shook it off. He couldn't stay.

George pretty much crashed through his front door, desperate to wash his face, to wake up from the dream-like state he'd been in the entire drive home. Having sped through the town in his car, he hadn't the balls to look at anyone in the street in case they knew his secret.

He didn't know if he was embarrassed, ashamed, delighted or just head over heels in love. All of the above, probably. His heart raced just as furiously as his head pounded – and for the first time in what felt like forever, he couldn't blame it on alcohol.

Slamming the door behind him, he threw his keys on the console table in the hall and was met by the tapping paws of his Nan's little white dog, Pam.

'Hello, girl. You okay?' He knew how ridiculous it was to talk to animals, but even with full-on headfuck, he couldn't break the habit.

'Nan?' He yelled out, hoping to find her there. She was the only person that never failed to give him the awkward truths he needed. And, fuck, he needed them. 'NAN?'

With no answer, he stomped to the kitchen and switched on the kettle. Hearing it start up, he craved something stronger.

Yanking open the fridge, he instinctively pulled out an opened bottle of Pinot and twisted off the cap in an instant.

'Bit early for that, isn't it, love?' Pam surveyed from the doorway. She didn't judge, just acknowledged the situation.

'Fuck, Nan. Where did you come from?' George slid the bottle onto the side, his hand begrudgingly letting go.

'I heard you calling but I was caught in the group chat. Those bingo girls are doing my nut in. They want to do a bake sale for charity.' She stared at her phone screen with umbrage. George observed her with the same expression.

'That's a good thing right?'

'You sound just like them. Well, fuck that noise.' Switching her phone off, Pam then flung it onto the table.

George could have acted surprised or even disappointed at his Nan's indifference to the suffering, but what was the fucking point? She'd shown him nothing but disdain when he was heartbroken. She wasn't mean, not really. She'd always help her family. She's just her. At least she was consistent.

'Why don't we have a cuppa instead, Georgie?'

'Tea isn't going to solve my problems, Nan.'

'Oh, love.' Smiling softly, she stroked his arm. 'Stop being such a fucking cliché.'

'Nan.' George shrunk into the kitchen chair. 'I'm having a proper breakdown here.'

'Aren't we all? But we all don't do it as loudly as you. Honestly, love, you've been whinging for months.'

'Jesus, Nan. Don't you have sympathy for anyone?'

'I do, love. The homeless. The terminally ill. People that say "hunni."' Pam rolled her eyes before grabbing two cups from the draining board. 'But you, Georgie, you got dumped, son.'

'It still fucking hurt, Nan.'

'I know, love, but you don't need to drink away your life because of it.'

'It's the only thing that helps.'

She huffed and George awaited The Wasp's attack. 'Love, all that drink has done for you is kept you sad. If you stop for just long enough, you'll see how happy you are now.'

Wide eyed, George chewed the inside of his cheek. Pam couldn't have been more right. He hadn't drank the night he ignored Jack and it'd made him realised how happy he was with the fella.

Plonking down two cups of steaming tea, his Nan sat opposite him at the table. 'Nothing's worse than a midday hangover so you're having a cuppa and you're gonna tell me why you're acting like the world is ending.'

'Because it is.' He sighed.

'Would you listen to yourself? You've got everything anyone could want in this world. A family that loves you, friends that would kill for you. Not to mention every bloody gadget a boy could want.'

George huffed. Not because he was annoyed – more for acceptance. She was right. Well, once he made amends with Alfie and Aimee she was. He needed to sort everything out with them before they hated him forever.

Pam called little Pam in and clapped for her to jump onto her lap. 'So go on, tell me. What's wrong with you?'

'Nothing, Nan.' Shrugging, George could barely lift his shoulders from the weight he felt under. 'I don't know what to do about someone.'

'Ellie?'

George shrugged again. He wasn't sure how to answer that question. 'I dunno.'

It was true. He didn't know how he felt about her anymore. He loved her, he was certain that he always would.

'You heard from her lately?'

George nodded. He hadn't told his family about their conversation the night he threw his phone in the river. He didn't want the sympathy or the fuss his mother would make. 'Yep, the other night. It's over.'

'Well, I'm sorry, love. But thank fuck for that.'

George winced. He didn't expect for it to still hurt. 'Nan, she's not a bad person.'

'I know she's not. But you're too good for her.'

'You're the only one to think that.'

Okay.' Pam stretched out a hand to his. 'She's a pretty girl. Lovely hair before she whacked it off. And a great rack. But, to me, she always had her head looking round for better things to come along.'

'That's not true, Nan.'

'No? Remember how she acted when you got the apprenticeship? She didn't want to be with a farmer. Not that I can blame her, you stink of shit most the time. But, Georgie.' She leant over the table to take his hand. 'You were babies when you started going out. Things change. And sometimes we just grow apart.'

George lifted his cup but couldn't face drinking it. 'I know.'

'So stop crying over her, please. It's like watching a really bad TV movie.' She smiled. 'The ones they play in the afternoon and you wish all the characters would die.'

He snorted with laughter. He fucking needed it too. Inhaling for courage, he knew he had to tell her.

'Nan, I've done something so stupid.'

'Oh, you haven't gone and got another bloody tattoo have you?'

'No, it's nothing like that…..Wait, how do you know I've got a tattoo?'

'You've got a massive penguin on your back and all you wear is tight polo shirts.'

How could she see through his darker tops? George's blood ran cold. 'Does mum know?'

'Who cares? You're a grown man.' She pursed her lips. 'Besides, you know what your mother is like. She only ever sees what she wants to. And when she looks at you, all she sees is her little baby.'

His chest warmed. He was beginning to feel normal again.

'So why are you trying to get blotto at ten a.m. if it's not Ellie?'

'I thought it was her. Then I realised it hasn't been her for weeks.' He scrubbed a hand over his face. 'Have you ever done something you *think* you regret? But you don't know if you do? You just feel weird about it?'

'I did. A long time ago, yes. Thought I'd ruined my life.' She lifted little Pam and lowered her gently onto the tiled floor. 'But your mother is nearly fifty years old, I can't keep regretting that.'

'Nan!'

'Only joking, love. Your mother is my best friend. Has been since the moment she ripped me in two.'

George gagged.

'Well I think I've done something I'm going to regret.....I don't actually know.' His Nan nodded for him to continue. 'Okay, there's someone I kind of like. Like a lot actually. But I can't. I shouldn't even be *telling* you.'

Pam slid a menthol from her pack and tapped the filter onto the box. 'Well Jack is a good looking fella.'

George froze - winded by her revelation. He didn't need a mirror to know his face was glowing scarlet.

'Oh, come on, love. You're crazy about that boy.'

'What?' The dog's ears twitched from George's much higher-than-usual voice. Clearing his throat, he shook his head. 'I....I don't know...how?' He stuttered.

'You can't fool me, son. I'm not an idiot. It's obvious you like him. And by the look of your hair all messed up, I'd put money on it that you didn't get much sleep last night.'

George couldn't respond. He couldn't lie to his Nan, she'd only see through him anyway. Yet the awkwardness grew in his throat. Her nonchalance somehow made it worse.

'How did you know?'

'Well your hairs a mess and looks like you've got a bit of irritation from his stubble on you neck. Plus, I haven't seen you glow like this in months.'

He wanted to die right there. 'I meant, know about my *feelings* for Jack.'

'It's been clear as gin drinkers piss, love. I've known since you had him up against that wall right there that something was going to happen with you two.' She lit her cigarette then blew the smoke over her shoulder. 'And then I saw your face when he picked up little Pam the other day. You was gawping.'

George laughed. There was nothing else he could do. She could read people. It was her gift. And his curse.

'So whats the problem? Why the regret? He not feel the same way?'

'It's not that at all, Nan. He's totally into me. Has been for ages apparently.'

'Well what's the problem? He not any good at *it*? The pretty ones rarely are.'

George's cheeks could've burned through steel. 'No, it's not that. I just never thought I was into blokes. I had a girlfriend for three years, remember.'

'Oh for god sakes. Why does your generation have to put a label on everything? When I was younger, we just had fun. Girls, boys. The lot.'

'You? With girls?'

Nodding, Pam flicked the ash into the ash tray. 'I was tempted by the bi bus many times. Beautiful girls back then. But I never bought a return ticket, mind you. It was the seventies and full bush was all the rage.'

George raised his brow. 'I never realised you oldies did stuff like that.'

'You think millennials invented sex?'

'No.' He squirmed. 'But.'

'Oh, believe me. Everyone was into everyone back then. We didn't have the TV channels there is now, you see.' She leant over and squeezed his knee. Her smirk warmed him from head to toe. 'But you call me old again, you poof, and I'll rip this leg clean off.'

George erupted into laughter. He didn't even want the wine anymore. 'So what do I do?'

'It's pretty simple from where I'm sitting.'

'You mean….go with Jack?' He scraped his teeth over his bottom lip and could still taste him there. 'But what will people say.'

'Jesus! No one is asking you to wear arseless chaps and start waving a fucking rainbow flag. Your family won't care. And Alfie and the orange girl won't either. They love you. We all do. We just want you to be happy. And you seem it with him.'

George slouched. She was right. Again. Suddenly, his head pounder harder. 'Fuck! I didn't even wake him this morning. I couldn't look him in the eye after……erm…..I just had to get out of there.'

'We'll get back there, love. You should never leave a good man in bed alone. Especially not one as gorgeous as Jack.'

'Nan.'

'Go on, love. Go tell him how much he means to you.'

Her words rang true in his ears – echoing through his skull until all he could think about was Jack. He'd been a massive knob by sneaking out like that. Treating him like a dirty secret. Running away from his problems again. And for what? A woman who was as offensive as halitosis to read him the riot act. He knew what he needed to do. He had to get himself washed and changed then back to Jack.

'Thanks, Nan.' He sprung from his seat and planted a kiss on her forehead. 'You're the best, you know that?'

She took a drag. 'I do, love. I do.'

Splashing his face with cold water, George smiled at his reflection. It'd been months since he'd been able to tolerate the person staring back at him. And yet it wasn't the old "Georgie boy" in the mirror – that fella had long gone. He'd died somewhere in mid-May under the burden of self-inflicted depression and bourbon. The reflection showed a new man. A new George.

Dashing to his bedroom, he grabbed the after shave Ellie had bought him but stopped himself just before spraying it. That was no longer him. Instead, he rolled on some deodorant and ran for the stairs.

'Georgie!' Maxine called out, panting at the front door - her arms loaded with colourful shopping bags but her face was ashen. She didn't look her usual delighted self after spending hundreds in the shops. She looked ill. In shock. 'Why haven't you answered your bloody phone, Georgie? I've rang your Nan a hundred times too. All I'm getting is voicemail.'

'Erm.' He hadn't told her about lobbing his phone. 'What's wrong? Jehovah's?'

'It's Aimee.' Maxine threw the bags down and grabbed his wrists. 'Her mum's just called me. She's in the hospital.'

Dread filled him. Fuck! He should have gone to see Aimee first thing instead of wallowing to his Nan about Jack. 'Shit, is it her grandad?' Guilt kicked him square in the stomach. He'd go there straight after he spoke to Jack.

'No, darlin. It's not.' She began to tremble. 'It's Aimee. They found her car in the lanes. It's a wreck.'

'What? Is Aimee okay?' The hallway seemed to close in on him. Fear became heightened by the immediate claustrophobia.

Her eyes filling up with tears, Maxine shook her head. 'She's in a bad way. In a coma. Tammy is beside herself.'

He couldn't breathe. Couldn't think. He grabbed his car keys and stormed from the house.

Chapter Thirty Three

George couldn't remember the drive to the hospital, his sole focus had been on getting there, and as quickly as possible. After begging for help at the Information Desk, he'd navigated his way to the ICU with the same determination too. Pushing through the burning pain in his shins, he stormed along the windowless corridors. Panic mode well and truly switched on.

Finally, he barged through a pair of blue double doors with his shoulder and found Alfie waiting outside the ward. There were others there too; their faces matched the colour of the pale grey chairs they were sat on. He recognised an aunt and maybe a cousin from Aimee's family parties and gave them sympathetic grins as they acknowledged him. The whole thing was eerie. Just a collections of bated breath and looks of desperation.

It made him aware of how much of a prick he was for not being upset himself. But, honestly, he hadn't had time to register anything beyond anxiety. Well, that and guilt for being a bastard to Aimee for the last few months. More so, he hated that even as one of his best friends was in hospital, all he could think about was himself and how he fucking felt.

Alfie was standing alone, arms folded and head down, he looked as though he was lost. It took the fella a couple of seconds to notice George, but even once he had, the vagueness didn't shift.

'Alf, are you okay? What the fuck happened?' His voice echoed along the hall and he cringed as the others observed him with disapproval. 'Was you there? Are *you* okay?' He whispered that time.

Shaking his head, Alfie blinked. His eyes were bloodshot and face puffy. George had only seen him cry twice in all the years he'd known him – the first time was when his dad moved out and the second when football definitely wasn't coming home. But he'd never seen him so upset. Staring at nothing in particular, Alfie seemed unable to focus on George's words. On anything around him, actually.

'Alf? You okay, mate? Were you there?' His eyes scanned over Alfie for any signs of injury, but thankfully, there was none. He was dressed in jersey shorts and a baggy vest and George guessed that he'd likely jumped out of bed and threw them on to get there.

'No.' He mumbled. 'She was all alone.'

Remorse swelled in George's chest and he needed a distraction before he drowned in it. 'Do you know what happened? Was another car involved? Where did they find her?'

'I just fucking told you.' Alfie growled. The redness in his face now matched his eyes. 'I wasn't there.'

Stepping back, George cleared his throat and gave his friend an understanding nod. Alfie obviously needed space and he wasn't going to deny him that.

Moments later, the horrific silence was broken when the door to the ward opened with a buzzing sound and Aimee's mother, Tammy, came out sobbing. She was obviously distraught and wiped her eyes with a scrunched up tissue that looked just as wet as her tears.

'Georgie.' She muttered, squeezing his arm. 'She'll be so happy you're here.'

'Tammy, is Aimee o-'

'Is she awake?' Alfie interrupted. His eyes widened.

Tammy shook her head. Tears still ran down her cheeks but she smiled. 'No, sweets. Not yet. They're doing tests now. She'll be all right though. I know she will.' Her grin was forced, probably for her own benefit more than anything. George didn't believe it for a second, however, he silently prayed that Alfie did.

Gently pulling Tammy to one side, George gave her the same sympathetic smirk he'd given the others just moments before. 'What happened to her, Tammy? Is she going to be okay?'

'Oh Georgie. I just don't know. She wasn't herself this morning. My dad, her grandad, passed last night and she hadn't slept a wink.'

George gasped. Guilt tightened like a vice on his rib cage.

'I told her we could wait for food shopping but she wouldn't rest. She had to get her mind off of it. Then all I know is the police are knocking on my door telling that my baby has been found. Her car was on its side in the lanes.'

Heat soared through him whilst he tried to process her words. The image of Aimee in that car made him want to vomit. 'I am so…. so sorry.' He muttered, not sure who he was saying that to. 'About your dad. And Aimee. She'll be okay, though, Tammy. Aimee is stronger than all of us put together.'

'Thank you, Georgie. It's so lovely to know that Aimee has good friends like you three.' She choked then pressed the damp tissue to her eyes. 'She loves you all so much. She talks about you every day.'

He was winded, like someone had kicked the shit out of him. He'd been the worst friend to her and she still loved him. 'Erm.' He swallowed hard, stumbling over what to say. 'Do the police know what happened?'

She shook her head again. Tears streamed down her face and one of the family members jumped up and urged her to sit.

Wiping the beads of sweat from his top lip, George glimpsed back at the door he'd come through. So much gloom in such a confined space was unbearable and it filled the corridor like fog. He needed fresh air to gather his thoughts. Actually, he needed to be outside before he threw up.

He stepped over to Alfie again and sucking in lungful's of sterile-scented oxygen, he gently put his arm around his friend. The fella's back was rigid. Anguish radiated from him 'Do you want a drink, mate? A coffee or something?' He glanced at the exit again. 'I better ask Tammy if she wants one too.'

'*She's* getting 'em.'

'Who?' He asked, irritated that he couldn't escape for a couple of minutes. But just then, George saw her walk through the door at the end of the corridor holding three paper coffee cups. It was Ellie. *His* Ellie.

Her face was washed of all make-up and her eyes were dull. She'd obviously been crying. Still, George's heart fell into his gut.

'When did she-?' George stopped himself. He didn't want to be pissing Alfie off. And it certainly wasn't time to mention how a girl who lived over an hour away had gotten there way before him.

He tried not to watch her advance. He wanted to play it cool. To not make a big deal of seeing her again. He'd waited months for her gaze to meet his and there she was. Twenty feet away. But he hated himself for even thinking about it. He was meant to be there for Aimee for fuck sakes, not bringing up all that shit with Ellie again. Had he always been so fucking selfish? Truthfully, he knew the answer.

She handed the drinks to Alfie and two family members then, without warning, she flung her arms around him and squeezed him close to her. It was an embrace he'd received many times from her over the years, one that silently told him she needed consoling. And he knew how to do that. He rested his chin on her head as she nestled in his collarbone and held her tightly. It was something they'd do whenever the other had been upset. And it's impact hadn't faded for him.

Being apart for so many months, it would've been the perfect way to meet again. Most likely both would cry a little and say goodbye to their relationship for good. But the solid lump growing in George's throat wasn't for the imaginary and lost reunion he'd always dreamt of; it was for Aimee. For the terrible situation they were all in together.

'Georgie.' Her voice trembled as much as her body did. 'I just can't believe this has happened to her.'

He squeezed her, breathing her in – the scent of her skin brought back so many memories they'd shared. It was what he'd needed before. What he'd wanted so badly that he'd emptied countless bottles to replace it. 'I know....I feel sick.' He could barely speak with rising tears burning his eyelids. 'I just don't....when did it-?

'Three hours ago.' Alfie grumbled. 'You're late as usual. *Everyone* tried to call you.'

'Not now, Alf. We're here for Aims.' Ellie pulled away with a smile. It was one he'd studied so hard that he could've drawn it from memory. Yet it had somehow lost power over him.

Scowling, Alfie turned to George with hate in his eyes. 'I rang you like fifty times.'

'I'm really sorry, mate.' George sniffed. His attempt to console Alfie with another hug was immediately shrugged off. 'I don't have a mobile. I lost it. Actually, I threw it in the river the other night after the pub. Like an idiot.'

Ellie raised her brow. It was apparent she knew why he'd lobbed his phone. 'Alf, he didn't know something like this was going to happen, did he? No one did, babes.'

'He doesn't know fuck all. Because he's been ghosting us for ages. He doesn't give a fuck about any of us anymore. Only himself. I don't even know why he's here. It was killing Aimee that he was ignoring her. She was so upset. He's a selfish prick!' Disgruntled moans came from the family members and George felt even smaller than he already did.

Swallowing hard, George nearly chocked on his guilt.

'Alf!' Ellie reprimanded and for a second, George saw Aimee in her. The looks the girls used to give him and Alfie when they'd embarrassed them by doing something stupid.

Blowing through rounded lips, George nervously edged closer to whisper. He was certain that was all he was actually capable of doing anyway. Like his voice had been stolen for penance. 'You're right, mate. I'm a selfish prick. I've been acting like a knobhead for so long. I'm so, so fucking sorry. I love you and Aimee so much.'

Taking a swig of coffee, Alfie then turned his head away. His shoulders hunched and jaw jutted. He was triggered and George knew it could go one of two ways. Either Alfie would lash out, usually with his fists, or he'd shut down. George hoped it'd be the latter.

'I don't want to talk about it now. This ain't about you. Or me. We're here for Aims.' He grumbled.

With relief washing over him, George lowered his gaze onto the floor. 'I know.'

The three of them stood in silence, this time it wasn't so horrific. More like a mutual vigil for their friend. George was silently calling for Aimee to wake up and he knew that Alfie and Ellie were doing the same.

He prayed to any deity he could think of; promising a lifetime of good deeds in exchange for help. Swearing that he'd never abandon another friend ever again. Yet the longer his wishes went unanswered, the more he realised that his track record for doing just that was too solid. Just hours before, he'd left Jack alone without a word. And fuck, he was sorry he had. He promised the universe, that as soon as Aimee woke up and he knew she was going to be okay, he'd go to Jack's and beg the fella to forgive him.

The morning seemed endless, as though time had stopped in that white-walled corridor. Maybe it had. Without a watch or a phone, he had no fucking clue what the time was. He couldn't ask either. It just felt too rude. Doctors came and went from the ward, sometimes calling for Tammy and other relatives to enter. Each time, George's stomach dropped. The desperation clearly grew worse for everyone and communication simmered down to nothing other than nods and raised eyebrows.

'Tams!'

George peered up to see his mother rush through the door. Marching straight to Tammy, she flung her arms around her and the pair burst into tears. Their sobs ricocheted around them all. Strangely, the sound of loud, unrestrained crying made everything more comfortable. More human. If his Mum brought anything, it was usually noise. And for once, he was grateful.

'Her leg is smashed to bits.' Tammy's words were almost drowned out by her tears. George could barely make them out. 'And…..internal bleeding. They don't know if she'll pull through.'

Gasping for air, George pulled at the collar of his T-shirt. Maybe he preferred the silence after all. He was suddenly desperate for fresh air again.

Moments later, Aimee's mum was called back into the ward, and watching her let go of Maxine's hand was an image that almost broke his heart. It was as though Tammy was walking into the unknown alone. Broken.

George needed out. Away from the trauma for just a moment. He needed to speak to someone that wasn't distraught. Someone that could talk without crying. He needed Jack.

Walking over to his mother, he asked quietly to borrow her phone. Of course, she was already sitting down and in a four-way conversation with Aimee's family but he couldn't let that stop him.

'Mum, I need your phone.' She ignored him – the type of deaf ear that mother's excel at when not wanting to be interrupted by their children. 'Mum!'

'Whats wrong, Georgie?' She finally looked up at him and pretended to not know he'd been there.

'I need your phone.'

'Where's yours?' She fished into her handbag. With the amount of crap she usually kept in it, he had no idea how long he'd have to wait.

'I'll tell you another time.' He glanced back at Ellie, remembering how her words had hurt him so much that he'd threw his phone. And for some reason, he smiled. 'It's not important, anymore.'

Once he had her mobile, he lied to Alfie about going for a piss and wandered in the corridors searching for signal. The place was like a fucking nuclear bunker and finding a bar of reception was like finding a happy thought. Admitting defeat, he followed the signs to the exit and punched in Jack's phone number. He hadn't realised he'd even memorised it until it started to ring.

As the afternoon sun hit his face, a phone melody played somewhere outside the hospital's entrance and the smell of cigarette smoke wafted to his nostrils. He recognised the ringtone and the aroma immediately and almost burst into tears.

'Jack? What are you doing here?' He beamed at him. For a moment, it didn't seem real. But there he was. Puffing on a cigarette under a "No Smoking" sign, with one foot resting on the wall.

Jack's lips curled and all things George dreaded that morning when he fled his flat were nowhere to be seen. No embarrassment. No regret. Just him. And seeing the man's face – those beautiful hazel eyes – bought burning tears to his own.

Jack opened his arms and George immediately fell into them. The touch of his body made everything instantly better. He didn't want to let go, to lose that feeling. Never. But he knew he had to. He couldn't ignore reality. Not anymore.

'I hope you don't mind me being here. Your mum brought me. I knocked for you a while ago to see if you was all right about-'

'Mate, I'm sorry for this morning.'

Jack shrugged it off. 'I know why you did it.' His words were soft and caring. 'How's Aimee?'

All George could do was shake his head.

'Are *you* okay?' Jack asked.

George leant into him once more and pulled him in tight. 'Jack, I need to say this....I have to tell you....now....before anything happens to you. I'm so sorry about this morning. I really am. I will never do anything like that to you ever again. I want to be with you. If you want to be with me.'

'George, it's okay, man.' He rubbed George's shoulder. 'Let's talk later.'

'But you have to know that....that....I lo-'

'I don't need words.' Jack squeezed his arms around his back. 'This is all I need. Just you.'

Months of pain lifted from George. All right, the words hadn't actually been said, but he didn't give a shit. He loved Jack and Jack loved him for fucks sake.

'You have me.' He whispered, clinging on for just a moment more.

Letting Jack finish his cigarette – so much for the fresh air, George soaked in the sunlight for a minute or two. 'I need to go back in.'

Jack nodded. 'I'll be right here, man.'

Snorting, George grabbed the fella's wrist. 'Come with me, please. I need you.'

There wasn't another word between the pair as they walked along the halls in silence, following the signs for the ward. Each other's company was enough.

Taking a deep breath, George pushed open the door to ICU and the chaos in front of him momentarily paralysed him. Alfie was biting his fist, whilst Ellie, Maxine and Tammy were crying. The other family members were a mixture of blank expressions and sobs.

His heart dropped into his belly with a thud.

'Mum? Whats happened?' George called out. Panic scratched his vocal chords.

'Oh, darlin.' She bit her lip. 'Poor Aimee….she's… she's….they're trying to resuscitate her.'

Chapter Thirty Four

A whole three months had passed since that nightmarish day at the hospital. The sight of doctors and nurses running toward the bed of his best friend had been emblazoned into his memory every time he'd closed his eyes. And the sound of Aimee's mother screaming for her daughter and Ellie's frantic sobs echoed around his brain every time life went quiet. Still, October had come around and the world kept on spinning. Green leaves had turned to yellow and the heatwaves of summer had given way to chilly nights.

Everything seemed different since that day. As though every trivial thing no longer mattered. Through tragedy came an epiphany. An enlightenment that he wished he'd found without the trauma that had upturned so many lives.

Pulling the door open to Dave's Café, George scanned his empty booth before looking for the person he had come to see. His boyfriend. Jack was behind the counter - a white apron covering his blue jeans and his go-to black t-shirt. Okay, so maybe not everything had changed. The fella had worked there as much as he could. Mainly to help Dave out until he hired a new apprentice cook but the extra cash really helped him with his supplies. "Jack of Hearts" Tattoo Parlour had gone from strength to strength over the last couple of months, making him the most desired man in Coggletree. Not least by George. Obviously.

Dave's café had proved just as popular in town, bringing back the hordes of teenagers into the seats. The place where George had so many wonderful memories had been updated with twenty-first century appliances and a well needed lick of paint. The old classics had returned too, mainly the milkshake and slush machines, along with Dave's own take on gastro cooking. The "pulled pork double whammy" being a firm favourite. It was proof that change could be good.

Jack greeted George with a smile, a gorgeous feature that George had come to treasure as much as rely on.

Scooting into the booth, George winked in return then lifted the laminated menu from its wooden rack. He didn't need to read it, he'd been there so many times since it'd opened that he knew it from memory. But he needed the distraction from staring at Jack's perfect mouth. Perfect everything.

'Hey, man.' Jack slid into the seat opposite. His smile had been replaced with a curious gaze. George was ready for the next words to come from his lips. 'So? How did it go today?'

His year-long apprenticeship had finally come to an end. Passing with flying colours, Perrygate Farm had seemingly appreciated all the hard work he put in and offered to interview him for a permanent role. Pay rise too. Of course, George jumped at the chance. Even if it did mean putting up with Knobert and those fucking sunglasses.

George nodded. 'I got it. I got the job.'

He didn't know why he couldn't text Jack the news earlier. He was ecstatic about it. He was. Really. He just hated to flaunt his good fortune at such a bad time.

'Never doubted it for a second, man.' Jack wrapped his hand around George's. 'Fucking made up for you. We need to celebrate. Drinks? Bed?'

George bit his lip. 'Definitely both. But it feels a bit wrong to celebrate though.'

'George, you're allowed to be happy.' His eyes didn't move from George's gaze. 'You can't feel guilty anymore.' He stopped there and George knew the invisible cogs in Jack's brain were thinking of how to mention Aimee's accident without actually saying those words.

'I just feel like shit for even smiling sometimes.'

'Jesus, man. You have to stop beating yourself up about it. You weren't driving the car. You didn't cause the accident.'

'I know. I know. But if I hadn't been such a cock to her then it wouldn't have happened. She wouldn't have been on her own.'

Jack's hand tightened around George's knuckles. The warmth filled him with love. 'Have you spoken to Alfie? He coming for lunch?'

'He said he'd meet me down here.'

The brass bell rang as the door opened behind him and George tensed. His guts turned before he could. Taking a deep breath, he shifted in the seat and peered behind.

There was Alfie, sweat beading his furrowed brow. The perfect example of a downtrodden man. And there was Aimee, moaning at him as he pulled her wheelchair through the door. She was still a little bit bruised, mainly from the follow up surgeries. But she was beautiful as ever.

'All right, babes?' She called out to him. 'Come and help me, please. Alf can't steer this thing for shit. He's literally got T-rex arms or something.'

As Jack went to fetch four milkshakes for them, George sprang from his seat and rushed to his besties. Aimee still had the huge cage of steel around her leg – the thick pins piercing through her shin and calf. 'I didn't know you were coming, Aims.' He leant down and planted a kiss on her cheek. 'If I'd known, I would have picked you up.'

'I spent two months in hospital, babes. I pretty much missed the whole summer. I need the last bit of sun before winter.'

'It's October, Aims.' He rolled his eyes then turned to Alfie. 'About time you passed your driving test isn't it, mate. Whats it been? Five times now?'

'Four, actually.' Alfie slammed his fist into George's shoulder. 'I didn't fail the last one. They wouldn't let me take it because I was too ill.'

'Hungover.' George coughed. Shoving Alfie out of the way, he grabbed the handles of the wheelchair and steered Aimee backwards through the aisle and stopped her at the booth. *Their* booth.

'Hey, Aims.' Jack placed a tray of shakes onto the table. 'How you doing? You look great.'

'Don't lie.' Alfie laughed. 'At this rate, she won't need to dress up for Halloween.' He bellowed.

Aimee clamped her eyes shut. 'Alf, I swear down, if you say that *shit* joke one more time, I'm going to rip this leg off and beat you to death with it.'

With George's help, Aimee lifted herself from the chair and slid into the booth. He could tell she was hiding the pain but would never question her on it. She was too proud to be seen as weak and he fucking loved her for it.

'How did it go with hospital today?' He asked.

'O M G, Georgie. The nurse was totally hitting on me. He was so hot. Total vitamin. Honestly, I wish he was my gynaecologist.'

'You're gross.' Alfie moaned. 'Besides, your gynaecologist would need a Search and Rescue team to go in after him.'

'Alf,' she rolled her eyes. 'Go buy a red convertible like every guy with a small dick does. Oh wait, you can't drive.'

George laughed to himself. Their love/hate bullshit was still as strong as ever. Even after a near death experience.

'So, Aims. The hospital? How did it go?' George asked again.

'The doctor was horrible. I knew she was going to be when she called me in. She's got eyebrows that need scaffolding. Know what I mean?'

He didn't. 'I meant about your leg, Aims.'

'Oh, that's fine. She said I've got a couple more weeks with this cock blocker on.' She nodded to her cage. 'Then she's going to put a cast on me instead.'

'That's amazing, man.' Jack beamed at her whilst squeezing George's shoulder.

'Aims, I'm so happy for you.' George leant in and kissed her again and savoured the scent of her skin. She hadn't used fake tan since the accident, well not so much, and he actually missed the scent of biscuits on her.

'Me and all, babes. I'm bloody dying to have a bath. And my "you-know-what" is screaming for a good seeing to. If you know what I mean.'

George and Jack howled in unison. They knew what she meant that time, all right. Predictably, Alfie huffed.

'Anyways. Enough about me, babes. I'm sick of talking about this bloody thing. How did your interview go?' She clapped her hands together in anticipation. 'That's why I'm here.'

'Don't worry about that.'

'You kidding me?' She scowled. 'I've just been pushed around the streets with a leg hairier than Alfie's unibrow. How did it go? Please tell me you got the job.'

He sank his teeth into his bottom lip. The thought of being proud made him feel slightly nauseous given the circumstances. 'I, erm. It went-'

'He got the job.' Jack interrupted. 'He's just being stupid because he feels bad for you.'

'Oh babes. Don't be silly. I'm fine. I get to sit down all day.' Her smile was electric. 'I'm so proud of you. I knew you'd get it.'

'Fuck yeah.' Alfie slammed his fist hard into George's shoulder again. 'Get in there, mate. You get a pay rise and shit?'

George nodded. 'Yep. Not that I'm buying you lunch though.'

'Ah, come on mate. My dad hasn't had any jobs for me for ages. And what with Aimee making me buy her pizzas all the time, I'm skint.'

Aimee's eyes widened in shock but after a second, she just nodded. 'Sounds about right, actually.'

'You looking for a job, man?' Jack sipped his milkshake. 'My uncle is still after that apprentice. Want me to have a word? I know he's definitely looking to train someone up.'

'Fuck!' Alfie boomed, the contents of his mouth splattering the table. 'You'd do that for me?'

'Course, man.'

Seeing the two fellas get on so well made George's body tingle. The pair of them had got on like a house on fire ever since Aimee's accident. Alfie didn't seem to give a fuck about him and Jack being together either.

'That would be sweet, mate. I'll come with you and meet him if you want. Just say when.' Alfie gulped more milkshake.

'Well, no time like the present.' Jack slid from the booth. 'Come on, bring your drink too.'

Alfie followed him toward the counter where Dave was serving, clearly run off his feet by the orders. Still, the man took the time to offer a smile, wipe his hand on his apron and shake Alfie's. By Dave's happy face, the job was pretty much his.

'He is such a keeper, babes.' Aimee beamed whilst pointing a painted nail their way.

'I'm so glad you two finally got it on.' George smirked.

'Me and Alf?' She sighed. 'Please, that's never going to happen.'

George watched her for a moment as she simpered at Alfie. Whatever the pair of them said, they were mad about each other. George had no doubt that she was completely, one-hundred percent in love with Alfie and it was obvious the fella was in love with her too. That had been made undeniably clear at the hospital when he'd thought she'd died. Still, George would let them keep their charade up until they realised it too. Just for the bants, mainly.

'I was talking about Jack.' Aimee grinned at George. 'He's, like, the loveliest man I know. Apart from you obvs. And sometimes Alf.'

George looked over to his boyfriend. The man that had changed his life for the better. Aimee was absolutely right. 'He is.'

Aimee wrapped her manicured hand around his. 'You look so happy, Georgie.'

'I really am.'

'And your mum and dad are all right about it all? You know.' She nodded over to Jack.

'To be honest, my dad didn't care. He was so okay with it that it's brought us a lot closer. We're like how we used to be. Turned out that he didn't want me to be an estate agent like I thought. He just wanted me to be happy.' He snorted.' It's my mum that's the fucking problem.'

'No way, Maxine is lovely. I'd never thought she'd have an issue with you being with a guy.'

He laughed. 'She doesn't. It's the opposite, Aims. She now thinks I'm interested in going shopping and picking out new fucking cushions to go with the new fucking rug. She even bought me a "Live. Laugh. Love." sign for my bedroom.'

The pair erupted into laughter. Unstoppable happiness erupted from his mouth and it felt amazing.

'What's so funny?' Jack slid back into the booth, his arm brushing George's neck as his hand fell onto his shoulder.

'Nothing. Just my mum.'

Jack grimaced. 'Not more cushions, man?'

Alfie returned moments later. A smile stamped on his face and the remaining half a cheeseburger in his hand. 'He's taking me on. I have a trial next week. Fuck, I'm gonna be a fucking a chef.'

'That's one way to kill the business.' George scoffed.

'And the people of Coggletree.' Aimee shook her head in disbelief.

Alfie grumbled in mock disdain then squished the burger to her mouth. Aimee slapped his arm and pouted. Her eyes sparkled. Clearly for him.

The afternoon flew by and George knew that their lazy days would soon end. They were all adults. Proper ones. Alfie would start the apprenticeship, Aimee would hopefully be able to get back in the salon, Jack was busier than ever and George was now full-time and permanent. Adulting sucked.

Whilst George wheeled Aimee to the door, Alfie dragged his feet behind, clearly dreading the verbal abuse that was awaiting him as soon as he took over. George had offered to drive them back but the last rays of sun were still to be had. Apparently.

'Oh, Georgie, before I go. Ells is coming back next week. She wants to meet up for drinks if you're about. You too, Jack.'

The pair of them nodded to each other. 'Sounds good to me. Be good to go for a drink, eh, George?' Jack said.

It had been weeks since George *needed* a drink. He'd had many, of course. But he no longer depended on alcohol. He found solace in the network of people around him. His friends, his family. Jack. The people he loved were all he needed in life.

'Yeah. It'll be great to meet up.' He wasn't lying either. He had no hard feeling towards Ellie. Not anymore. She was a massive part of his life, and before they ever dreamed of getting together, they were buddies. Still were. And he'd never turn down an occasion to spend time with Alfie and Aimee. 'That's what friends are for.'

At the rear of the café, George climbed the metal steps to the flat with Jack, their fingers intertwined.

'I have a leg piece to do in forty-five minutes. Want to come in for a bit?' Jack pressed his lips onto George's. His groans told him exactly what he wanted.

George's stomach flipped. The temptation to follow him into the flat and drag that gorgeous body upstairs was nigh on killing him. 'No can do, Jackie boy.' He huffed. 'I promised my Nan I'd go "dogging" with her and little Pam.'

'That's pretty messed up, man. You know that?'

George leant in for another kiss before letting go of his hand. 'I know.' He nodded. 'But that's why you love me.'

Jack stroked his hand along George's back. Electricity tingled up his spine. 'It's one of the reasons. So, tonight then?'

'I've got a few bits to do before work tomorrow. I'm permanent now. Can't be late anymore.'

Truth was, by sorting his shit out, making amends with his friends and falling in head over heels in love with Jack, George was content to spend time by himself. Actually, he loved those spare hours where it was just him and his thoughts. Being alone no longer meant being lonely. Sure, his mum would want to celebrate him getting the job, promise to make a slap up meal and then order a takeaway instead, but all George wanted to do was lay on his bed, play some songs then have an early night.

'You ready for your first day as a real farmer?'

'Nope.' George's fingers curled in the dip of Jack's lower back. 'That's why I need to get a proper night's sleep tonight.'

Jack twisted the key in the door then pulled George closer, pressing against him. 'You saying you don't sleep well next to me?' His lips touched the bridge of George's nose.

'You never let me sleep.' George kissed his neck and squeezed his arms around him before letting him go.

'Okay, I see your point.' Jack lingered at the doorway. His perfect lips curled. 'But there's something I need to show you, man.'

George raised an eyebrow. 'Oh yeah? You're trying that one again?'

Jack's face lit up with a smile. 'No, really.' He pulled the collar of his black T-shirt down and revealed a brand new tattoo on his chest. The bare patch had gone, and in its place was an image of a black and white bird; it's wings spread in flight.

'A magpie?'

'I've been waiting years for something important to ink there. I needed something to fill that place.' Jack skimmed his thumb over the new tattoo over his heart. 'What do you think?'

George swallowed hard. He loved it. So much. 'Why a magpie, though?'

'For you. For us, really. It's not "one for sorrow" anymore.'

George leant forward and kissed him. The taste of Jack drove him wild. He was everything. 'I love you.'

Jack hummed, squeezing him again. 'I love you.' He eventually pulled away, his hazel eyes stared lovingly at him. 'So much.'

George's phone buzzed in his pocket and he knew it was Pam calling him because he was late. About twenty minutes late, actually. 'I got to go.' He jutted out his bottom lip then smiled.

'See you tomorrow?' Jack licked his lips.

George allowed himself one more look at Jack before reaching the top of the stairs. He couldn't believe that man was his. Beaming, he didn't hide his happiness. 'Definitely.'

Acknowledgements

A massive thanks to all of my friends for the laughs over the years - this book was made from them. Thanks to Sarah for showing me the ropes so many times and to Donna for her artistic talents. And thanks to Barry for putting up with me and the constant earache.

Printed by Amazon Italia Logistica S.r.l.
Torrazza Piemonte (TO), Italy

12689674R00182